UNFINISHED JUSTICE
Historical suspense thriller

by

Janis Hutchinson

CROSS AND PEN MINISTRIES
1318 37th St. Unit 1506
Everett, WA 98201 (425)783-0476
www.JanisHutchinsonBooks.com
janishutchinson@comcast.net

Unfinished Justice

This is a work of fiction. Names, characters, places and events are either products of the author's imagination or are used fictionally. Any resemblance to actual persons, living or dead, or events is entirely coincidental.

Text copyright © 2015 Janis Hutchinson
All rights reserved.
Published by Cross and Pen Ministries, Everett, WA
Text arranged by Digital Book Designs.
Cover and book design: Digital Book Designs
ISBN: 978-0-578-18021-2

Library of Congress Control Number: 2016938492

REVIEWS

"Riveting...suspenseful...with compelling characters and tension that pull you into a powerful story of loss, redemption and faith. A gripping page-turner...courtroom action, unexpected treachery, betrayal, and one man's fight for justice against all odds. A fantastic read!"

—Robert Dugoni, New York Times and #1 Amazon Best Selling author of *My Sister's Grave*

"In this tense fiction debut from Hutchinson...a falsely accused reporter sentenced to a chain gang vows revenge on the man who really committed the crime...Gunther Buford.

"While Bowman is suffering on a chain gang, Buford, under the fake name of Gus Mooreland, rises in the ranks of the Western Pacific Railroad, unaware that the reporter he sought to kill remains alive and intent on revenge.

"Hutchinson's dual narrative of the experiences of these men is expertly contrived...the fast-paced core story is served up with a good deal of dramatic energy, and the novel's concluding scenes are genuinely gripping as Bowman slowly and uncertainly orchestrates his revenge on the man who ruined his life.

"An effective page-turner about a killer's new identity and a prisoner's long-simmering plot."

— *Kirkus Reviews*

About the Book

~~~

Unfinished Justice was inspired by an event that occurred in the small desert town of Wendover, Utah. There, the author became acquainted with the main character of this book, Ed Bowman (*not his real name*), who was a member of the adult Sunday school class she taught during her former thirty-five-year membership in the Mormon Church. He was later exposed as an escapee from a Virginia chain gang who had been convicted for murder.

Devastated by the church's dealings with him and impressed with his poignant story, she vowed she would someday write about it. However, a great deal of literary license was necessary in order to incorporate the elements required for historical suspense, including the addition of fictional characters and events, all of which necessitates the book being classified as fiction. The time period is also set in an earlier time than actually occurred.

Other books by Janis Hutchinson

Out of the Cults and Into the Church: Understanding and encouraging ex-cultists

The Mormon Missionaries: An inside look at their real message and methods

Available on Amazon, Barnes & Noble, Nook and iTunes.
http://www.amazon.com/Janis-Hutchinson/e/B001KHWDM0

Dedicated to my beloved granddaughter, Kimberly Clark, in heartfelt appreciation for her invaluable input.

ACKNOWLEDGEMENTS

~~~~~~

My task was made considerably lighter by many who furnished historical facts about the early town of Wendover, Utah and the Bonneville Salt Flats: The late Dr. Bruce B. Lamus of Everett, Washington and former resident of Wendover; William E. Pitt, Justice Court Judge, Tooele, Utah, also former resident of Wendover, who supplied information about the old jail house at Tooele, Utah; the late Robert Scobie, former Western Pacific Railroad employee at Wendover, Utah; and Ronald R. Bateman, author of *Wendover Winds of Change.*

For legal insight, I am indebted to Royce A. Ferguson, Attorney at Law, Everett, Washington, who contributed his expertise by critiquing those parts of my book concerning judicial procedure for criminal cases and rules of extradition. Also, to Brian K. Hammer, Attorney, for supplying other pertinent information.

For historical information on the Virginia State Penitentiary, I greatly benefited from the work of the late Paul W. Keve, author of *The History of Corrections in Virginia.* He had a passion for historical details and I acquired delightful tidbits about the Penitentiary and "Penitentiary Bottom" in a telephone conversation with him shortly before he died.

Special and deserving thanks goes to Steven Squire, Librarian at the *Department of Criminal Justice Services* at Richmond, Virginia, who aided me in researching Virginia's early prison and legal system, its chain gangs and the early town of Richmond. Also Larry Trailer, Director of Communications at the *Department of Corrections* in Virginia; the *Virginia Department of Historic Resources* at Richmond, Virginia, and the *Virginia Parole Board*

I am indebted to Thom Anderson, Administrator at the *Western Pacific Railroad Historical Society,* for his extensive research and personal knowledge, not only for the Western Pacific Railroad in general, but for the specific stations at Wendover, Utah and Keddie, California; also for technical information on steam engines, boilers, crown sheets, foaming, and dangers of explosion.

Additional thanks to my son, Blake Hutchinson of Susanville, California, who provided me with train history videos, and to Joe Keller of Everett, Washington, retired switchman for the *Great Northern/Burlington Northern Railroad*, who supplied technical information on boxcars.

Appreciation for track maps and information on cross country railroad lines during the book's time period, goes to Richard W. Hogan, Community Relations Director at *Old Dominion Railway Museum*, at Richmond, Virginia; *Old Dominion Chapter of National Railway Historical Society* at Richmond; *Old Dominion Steamship Company* at Richmond; and the offices of the *Chesapeake & Ohio Railroad*.

Invaluable material was provided by the following libraries: The Richmond *Museum of the Confederacy* at Richmond, the *California State Railroad Museum Library*; Gregg Kimball at the *Library of Virginia*; the *Virginia Historical Society*, the *United Daughters of the Confederacy, Caroline Meriweather Goodlett Library*, the *Richmond Times-Dispatch*, and the *North Carolina State Library*.

Providing technical and helpful data on the Model T Ford and other older cars were William Fletcher, of Stanwood, Washington, Bernard Van Aalst, Jr., of Mira Loma, California, and the late James Royer of Norwalk, California.

A debt of gratitude to my granddaughter, Kimberly Clark, for her astute observations and suggestions in critiquing the final stages of my manuscript; also, the following individuals who untiringly reviewed the manuscript in its beginning stages: Sharon Mikkelson of Everett, Washington; my daughter, Debra Fazio Estes of Red Oak, Texas; and Pat Williams of Ogden, Utah.

CHAPTER 1

August 5, 1938 - Richmond, Virginia

~~,~~,~~

Ed Bowman was running out of time. Forced to park blocks away from the courthouse, he raced through downtown Richmond despite the 102-degree heat, desperately praying he wouldn't drop dead before he got there.

He leaped off the curb and sprinted across the traffic-congested boulevard amid discordant sounds of drivers pounding horns and late afternoon cars rushing through intersections.

This was no turtle run. He had sped the forty miles from Hannigan's serene, wrap-around porches and magnolia gardens to the city's monolithic buildings and noisome crowds, his chest exploding with excitement. Reporting on this murder trial would change his life.

After ten years as a typesetter at the *Casey Clarion* and pleading to be given a chance to prove himself as a full-time reporter, he was delighted when Mr. Casey threw up his hands and said, "Okay, Ed, you've got the assignment—but only as a test."

Ed had covered a few minor trials before, but this one was the determining factor. If he did well, his world would be transformed. No more mind-numbing obituaries, fillers and small-town news for him.

His dream was to work his way up to Investigative Journalist at the prestigious *Richmond Times-Dispatch*. He knew that would take time, but for now, if he proved himself on this assignment and Mr. Casey promoted him to a full-fledged reporter, he was on his way. It would also contribute to solving at least one of his problems— his cantankerous mother-in-law Josephine who insisted he would never amount to anything. If a miracle happened and she changed, fine, but his main motivation wasn't about her.

Something deeper inside drove him. Whether it would materialize after all these years or not remained to be seen. But now, he had to focus on the prospect of covering a murder trial of this magnitude.

Gunther Buford, a thirty-five-year-old prison guard, faced the chair for the rape and murder of "Richmond's sweetheart," as the *Richmond Times-Dispatch* called twenty-six-year-old Sue Davis. The presses dubbed it the "trial of the century" giving the story huge coverage with all the gruesome details, and extending sympathy for the warden's loss of his daughter.

Riddled with anxiety, he tore past Loew's Movie Palace and Woolworth's Five and Dime. Although the trial was tomorrow, a lot rode on what he accomplished today. He didn't dare botch something this big considering the massive, elbow-to-elbow turnout expected in the morning. He glanced at his watch.

The Henrico County courthouse would be closing soon and he needed enough time to familiarize himself with the interior and locate Superior Court. Knowledge of the building's layout a day ahead of time would tell him exactly where he needed to go the next morning. He needed to appear like a pro when he walked in, instead of a green reporter on his first trial-assignment. He'd be sitting with reporters from Richmond's prominent newspapers.

He thought of his sweet Sarah. He wasn't sure she understood how important this was to him.

"Promise me, hon," he said before pulling out of the driveway, "don't tell anyone where I'm going." He gazed at her with a determined, I-have-to-do-it look.

"It's just that—" he felt the wash of red rise from his neck and into his cheeks, "Some might laugh about me driving all the way to Richmond a day early for a practice run. But honey, this is huge and—"

She leaned in and stopped his words with a kiss. "I do think you worry too much, sweetie." She gave him one of her smiles that always melted his heart. "Love you," she called as he backed out of the driveway.

He had managed to leave work early at 3:30, hoping to arrive well before five, but despite speeding most of the way he arrived in Richmond later than planned and hadn't anticipated the heavy traffic.

He hurtled airborne down the sidewalk, his legs pounding the pavement. Whipping around the corner he squinted through the blinding sun and heat waves that radiated from the sidewalk.

There—the Old Dominion's famous, red-bricked structure. He glanced at his watch again. Four-forty. Close. Twenty minutes to spare.

He bolted up the famous steps and onto the arched portico where the Declaration of Independence had been read publicly for the first time, then pushed the massive doors open and stepped inside.

A funereal quiet met him. He emitted a tremulous, almost reverent breath, like he had stepped into sacred space.

The historical glory of the Victorian structure oozed from its burnished floors and vintage furnishings to the shiny marbled walls where ornate-framed pictures of Virginia's governors and civil war heroes hung. The sepulchral silence stretched down a long palatial corridor with cushioned feet and then did a lazy soft-shoe up a gray and white marbled staircase. Ed gawked at the elegant two-story landing above him. Could Superior Court be up there?

"Can I help you?" A paunchy man sat at a desk wearing a size-too-small blue shirt with buttons on the verge of popping open.

Ed angled over in the man's direction, aware of the conspicuous squeak of his leather shoes echoing in the stillness.

"Where can I find Superior court?"

The man pointed. "Take the staircase up to the second floor. Bear in mind, we're closing in twenty minutes."

"Thanks," Ed nodded. "I won't be long." He headed for the stairs, glancing around as he did. The place was pretty empty. He wouldn't run into anyone from Hannigan. He shouldn't care, but they'd sure think him stupid making the trip a day early.

He slid his hand along the dark, oak railing and climbed the marbled staircase to the second floor, where the lemony smell of polish and cleaning solvent smarted his nostrils. At the landing, he ambled down a long corridor of memorabilia—Confederate flags, the Bonnie Blue Flag flown at the attack on Fort Sumter, the Stars and Bars, and old civil war caps.

He spied two sets of double doors over which hung a large wooden plaque. *Superior Court. The very court Aaron Burr was tried in.* He poked his head through the doorway. Stepping inside,

11

he sat on one of the rear benches and looked around.

This was big...really big. Here, his new career would begin. He'd become something—not only for himself but also for Sarah, the love of his life, not to mention impressing his crabby mother-in-law, the bane of his existence. He could still hear Josephine's caustic words to Sarah. *"You should have married someone with a better job!"*

The mere thought of the woman made him nauseous. But everything would change now, including overcoming a longer-standing problem that rode him constantly.

He studied the judge's elevated oak-paneled bench behind which hung a yellowed portrait of Jefferson Davis, then shifted his gaze first to the jury box, then to the counsel tables for the defendant and attorneys. He imagined the room jammed with spectators. He looked up. The balcony above him would be packed with coloreds. He, of course, would be sitting in the reserved seats down at the front with seasoned reporters from the major newspapers.

"We're closing up, sir." A lady stepped from one of the side rooms carrying a stack of yellow binders in her arms.

"Yes, ma'am." Ed stood. "Headed out right now. Thanks."

He exited the courtroom with a confident strut. Piece of cake. He now knew the floor plan and where to go in the morning.

He strode down the corridor toward the staircase, anticipating tomorrow's excitement. He didn't know much about the court system or attorneys other than there was always a prosecuting attorney for the State, a defense attorney for the defendant, and a jury. He'd soon get educated. Thank goodness he didn't run into anyone from Hannigan.

He barely turned the corner to the next hallway when he sucked in a quick breath. He never expected to run into *them*— Michael Payne and Barry Triving, defense attorneys for Gunther Buford. He recognized them from pictures in the *Richmond Times-Dispatch.*

The two men, dressed in expensively cut, three-piece suits, crisp white shirts and silk neckties, stood talking in the empty corridor ahead of him. Triving was young, about thirty and short, about five feet four. According to the *Dispatch,* he recently joined the firm of *Payne, Baxter, Hoyle, and Hammer.* Michael Payne, a much older man with graying sideburns and supervising counsel for the trial, had a long-standing reputation in Richmond.

Ed stifled a gasp. It was like having a bonus check drop into his lap. He needed to hear what they were saying. He'd print an exclusive no other reporter could match. He skulked closer and hid behind a marble column, his pulse hammering in his head.

Michael Payne's agitated voice echoed down the hallway, reverberating from the marbled walls like growls of thunder.

"You know the firm's financial dilemma, Barry, if we don't win this one. *Starcrest Pharmaceuticals* represents big money, and with the mess they're in with their CEO, might not sign on with us if we don't get Buford off. You've got to yank out all the stops on this one." He leaned over, reached into his briefcase and pulled out a document. "C'mon, I've got to stop by the Recorder's office on our way out.

Triving nodded, and pointed down the hall toward the men's lavatory. They moved in that direction.

Ed, his heart in his throat, followed behind at a discreet distance and watched them enter the men's room. Now what?

He could nonchalantly amble in, go into one of the stalls and listen, but they wouldn't say anything revealing if someone else was in there. Or would they? Indecision glued him to the spot.

After a few seconds he pressed his lips together and marched toward the restroom. He thrust out his hand to push the door open when Payne and Triving exited. He had waited too long.

"Scuse me," Ed said.

They passed, giving him no more than a fleeting eye-glance. Ed had no choice. He went in.

Once the door swung shut, he glanced about, leaned over and took a quick look-see under the stall doors. All empty.

He heard the attorneys' muffled voices outside. Tiptoeing to the door, he opened it a sliver, wide enough to peer out with one eye. *Say something...talk!* Stress squeezed his brow. He didn't have to wait long.

"Now, listen," Payne said, wagging an emphatic finger in Triving's face and glancing down the hallway both ways to make sure they were alone, "You already know Buford is probably guilty as sin. You can't let that deter you."

Ed's eyes widened. Guilty? They were his defense attorneys! He couldn't believe what he heard. Was this normal? He obviously had a lot to learn.

"Everything," Payne continued, "hangs on your cross-examination of the prosecution's key witness, the sales clerk who claims she sold a one-of-a-kind set of earrings to Buford that matches the single earring left on the body. You know what that means. It could result in a guilty verdict. You've got to go all out on this. The firm is counting on you."

"No problem," Triving responded, flashing a broad smile. "You know it's the area where I shine, and—"

"You *better* shine! Payne snapped, giving him a steady stare. The county prosecutor is one tough bulldog. You need your cross-examination of the clerk down pat, and be relentless. Can she swear beyond a doubt Buford purchased them? Moreover, what makes her so sure since she only saw him once? Is she positive the earrings were one-of-a-kind? If she says yes, challenge her to prove it."

"Yes…Michael. I've got everything all covered."

"Double check again with Gordon to see if he's found similar earrings in other jewelry shops yet, to prove her wrong." He issued forth a throaty tobacco-cough, cleared his throat of rumbling phlegm, and continued.

"Try to discredit her as a credible witness. Have you dug up her morals? Everyone has skeletons in their closet. Since she came forward and volunteered her information to the prosecution, come up with a possible motive. Put the fear of God into her. She's a woman. She'll scare easily. The firm," he said through his teeth, "can't afford to lose." He gave a meaningful cock of his head. "Got that?"

"Sure. Of course, Michael." Triving pushed his chin forward in thought. "Here's what concerns me. Even though the judge has already initiated a sequestration of the jury, the newspapers are having a field day. Who knows what those reporters will dig up next. Something could possibly trickle to the jurors."

"Nah," he shook his head. "No chance. We're okay on that." He scrunched his brow "All we have to be concerned about is getting this guy off—at least hope for a hung jury and have the judge

14

declare a mistrial." He turned and started down the hall. Triving stuffed the file folder into his briefcase and followed him into the Recorder's office.

Ed waited until their footsteps receded down the corridor then hurried out of the restroom and rushed down the staircase. This was more than he hoped for.

Exiting the building, he raced back to his car, jumped in his old '31 Ford Coupe and sped the forty miles back to Hannigan, eager to write his explosive story.

Along the way, one burning question plagued him. He needed to run it by Mr. Casey first.

His answer could quash his whole story.

Chapter 2

~∿∿~

Ed burst through the front door of the *Casey Clarion* and into the pungent smell of ink and newsprint. He charged down the back hall into Mr. Casey's office.

"Mr. Casey, I've got to know something quick!"

The man with graying hair and a large belly, twenty years Ed's senior, sat in a leather-upholstered chair behind a dark mahogany desk going over a stack of papers. He looked up and pressed his lips together. "I've gotta lot of work to do here, Ed."

"It'll only take a minute."

"Okay, okay. Take a seat and get your breath." Mr. Casey pushed the green visor from his forehead, leaned back in his chair and waited a few seconds. One eyebrow formed a skeptical arch. "Go ahead, spit it out."

Ed slid into a straight-backed chair, and using his arms in dramatic, sweeping gestures, repeated everything that had taken place. "And the sales clerk claims the single earring left near the victim's body matches the set she sold to Buford. And Buford's own attorneys admitted his guilt!"

Mr. Casey sat forward, his eyes wide with surprise. He gave an approving look. "Hmmm. Great work, Ed. Yes, a real exclusive."

Ed felt a hot flush of excitement. "But is there anything unethical about writing what I overheard?" Ed scooted forward on his chair, fixed his gaze on Mr. Casey's face and held his breath.

"None at all, Ed. The paper had two similar situations and both times I checked with our attorney. Technically, it's not unethical for a reporter to write what he hears because he's not part of the legal system. Nevertheless, there is a kind of ethic involved here." He stared in thought over Ed's head, tapping his chin with the end of his pencil.

Ed leaned forward and waited.

"Here's what you do. Say the story is from a first-hand, reliable source but don't reveal yourself as the person. You can mention the defense's concern over the sales clerk's upcoming testimony, but when it comes to Buford's attorneys admitting their client's guilt, generalize that part of the conversation and don't use any quote marks around what they said.

"The prosecution obviously intends to introduce the sales clerk's testimony about the earrings after opening statements tomorrow. You'll have to work late. We'll do an early morning special," he said. "The only thing you'll be doing is providing the information about the earrings hours before the trial starts—plus, of course, pulling the plug on the defense. Papers will really sell." Grinning, he slapped both his palms down on the desktop.

"Get going...we'll scoop the *Richmond Times-Dispatch* for sure. I'll tell Richard to ready the type. Get the copy to him as soon as you can, and bring me the original as usual."

"Yes, sir!" Ed sprang from the chair, bolted out of the office and back down the hall to his desk. Dropping into his chair, he grabbed a pencil and a sheet of paper and began.

First, he made sure he included his five Ws, then cut redundant words, labored over space limitations, double-checked his spelling, and wrote draft after draft. He slaved for nearly two hours, toiling over the perfection of every word as if his very life depended on it. Mr. Casey had drummed into him, in his German vernacular, that it wasn't brilliance or intelligence that made a good reporter but *Sitzfleisch*, or chair glue, the ability to persist in a task without giving up. Well, he was definitely glued to his seat for this.

Rolling two sheets of clean paper and a carbon into the platen of his typewriter, he began pecking at the keys. First, the headline: *Defense Nervous in Buford Trial.* Yep, sounded good. He tore into typing the rest of the article. *According to a reliable source...* When finished, he yanked the set of papers out of the carriage and hustled toward the print room. Would the reporters he'd be sitting with tomorrow ask him how he managed such an exclusive? Imagine those prestigious journalists asking *him*. He hoisted his chin high. No doubt they would be envious.

Richard sat waiting at the Linotype in the room that always smelled of metallic shavings and caustic chemicals. Gray-haired with a complex set of deep wrinkles, he had been a long-time friend of Ed's father and due to retire soon. Ed thrust the article into his hands.

"I hear this is a pretty big scoop," Richard said, looking it over. "The boss just alerted me. Sounds like you're on your way up."

Ed's spirit soared at his words. "Let's hope so," he said. "It's sure a lot better than writing obituaries and fillers. Of course, before I can call myself a full-fledged reporter I have to be on a trial basis first and then wait for Mr. Casey to tell me. Don't know how long that will take—for sure, not until after the trial. Got to prove myself over the long haul."

"Well, don't let Mr. Casey scare you. If you do a good job and produce more exclusives like this, I don't think you have anything to worry about." Richard smiled, his lined face crimping into corrugated creases. "I'll start readying things and wait for Mr. Casey to give me the final go-ahead." He set the article on his easel.

Ed grinned. "Thanks for the encouraging words, Richard." He took a few steps toward the doorway, then turned and looked back over his shoulder. "Say, are you still planning on having dinner with us on Saturday?"

"Sure Ed. Wouldn't miss it. I plan on bringing some cracklins."

"Great. Mama says she'll make her famous Appalachian chowchow. I think Sarah plans on ham, red-eye gravy, grits, and a mess of fried mustard greens. If the weather holds good we can sit out on the veranda and enjoy some possum toddies."

"Sounds good to me, Ed."

"Well, I gotta get. Looking forward to your coming." Wheeling about, Ed sprinted down the hall to Mr. Casey's office.

"Here's the original." He slapped the paper into the in-box on the corner of his desk.

"Good work, Ed." He reached for it. "Richard got his copy?"

"Yep. Just handed it to him." Mr. Casey lowered his head signaling the end of any conversation, and began reading.

Ed sauntered back to his desk, apprehension needling him. Mr. Casey had to reword a few sentences of a previous article. Would this one measure up? He wiped his sweaty palms on his pants. It had to.

He flopped into his swivel chair, leaned back and rolled his neck from side to side to relieve the tension. If all went well, his career as reporter was definitely in the bag. His sweet Sarah, of course, would be proud of him whether he got the promotion or not, but he wanted to make her even more proud. Josephine, of course, was another matter. He sucked in his lower lip.

Sarah insisted her mother would come around and he shouldn't try so hard to prove his worth to her. He chewed on that for a few seconds. Nope. Knowing Josephine, he still needed to do something spectacular. His new position, if he passed the test, would finally make him somebody in her eyes.

But even if it didn't, there was more to his motivation than his problem with her—that of overcoming his poor start in life that included a shameful brush with the law when he was twelve after his dad died. Small-time stuff, nothing major, but his sullied reputation stuck with the townspeople for years.

He recalled the neighborhood gossip at the time, typical of a small burg of only two thousand. *"Poor Widow Bowman who has no husband to help raise that incorrigible boy."*

Unfortunately, eleven years later people in town still remembered. *No wonder he's low man on the totem pole at the Clarion,* they persisted, which only added to his lack of self-worth.

Well, he'd show them. He knew how to resolve that. His dad once told him the key. "A bad reputation is like a flat tire. You can't go anywhere until you fix it."

Well, he was on the road to doing just that. Advancement in his career would swing everyone in his favor. Soon he'd be viewed with respect.

He leaned back and laced his fingers behind his head. Just imagine Ed Bowman, only twenty-three and your long-held dream is close to materializing. From typesetter to reporter, then on to Investigative Reporter at the *Richmond Times-Dispatch.* His coveted goal was about to pay off.

"Yep," he murmured, tipping his head back and closing his eyes, "I'm headed for the big-time." Nothing can stop me now.

Early the next morning the telephone rang. Dawn barely peeked beneath the half-drawn window shade of their bedroom. Scarcely awake, Ed squinted his eyes, turned on the bedside lamp and looked at the clock.

Sarah lifted her head from the pillow. "Who could be calling at this hour, hon?"

"No idea. Nearly time for me to get up anyway. Opening day of the trial, you know."

Leaning on one elbow, he reached for the phone. He looked back at her and grinned. "Probably Mr. Casey wanting to tell me the morning edition sold out and to compliment me." He cleared the grogginess from his voice.

"Hello?"

"This is Barry Triving!" the voice shrieked.

Ed bolted straight up. The man's malignant tone was a clenched fist ready to strike. He swallowed hard.

"I just saw this morning's *Clarion!*" Triving yelled. "What right do you have to reveal a private conversation?"

"But Mr. Triving..." He remembered what Mr. Casey told him. "I have no connection with the legal system, to the trial or—"

"Buford is innocent!" he volleyed back. "Your story will ruin any chance for our client. It'll influence everyone, and an innocent man may go to the chair...all because of you. What kind of a reporter are you anyway," he snarled, "claiming we think our client guilty? You haven't even heard the evidence yet. You should be barred from the courtroom."

"Mr. Triving, if—"

Triving ranted and raged for another full minute expelling a whirlwind of expletives, and then hung up with a loud, ear-splitting click. Ed yanked the receiver away from his ear and with trembling fingers replaced it on the hook.

He slumped back on the bed. The thought of running into Triving at the trial this morning sent needle-like barbs shimmying down his spine.

Sarah, now alert, sat up and placed her hand on his shoulder. "What is it, dear?"

"Oh Sarah." His eyes shifted to hers. "What have I got myself into?"

CHAPTER 3

Tuesday, August 6

~·~·~

Ed, his insides fairly bursting in anticipation of opening arguments, especially the key witness's testimony, heard the fevered commotion before he even rounded the corner. What if he ran into Barry Triving? He couldn't forget the man's vitriolic telephone call. One side of him wished he were back in Hannigan, safe from any confrontation, but that wasn't an option. He had to be right here, right now. Too much was hanging on this.

The frenzied crowd, electrified by the sensationalism of the trial, filled the sidewalks with ear-deafening voices and swarmed the steps like flies anxious to feast on a cadaver. They wanted to see Buford convicted.

Ed stopped for a second to catch his breath. He fastened the front three buttons of his new tweed jacket despite the perspiration that glued his shirt to his chest. The heat was unbearable. He should have worn his seersucker instead. But no matter how hot, he wasn't about to take it off. He needed to look professional. He'd be sitting with reporters from the *Richmond Times-Dispatch* and other prominent newspapers.

Straightening his tie, he pushed a few loose strands of hair back into place. He squinted through the heat waves sizzling up from the pavement, searching for an opening in the stream of people who shoved their way up the steps of the red-bricked courthouse.

Pressing into the throng, Ed wedged his lanky frame from side to side and in-between bodies, flashing his *Casey Clarion* press card hoping it would give him preference. He flourished it with pride—his graduation diploma into the upper echelon of the newspaper world.

"Excuse me... Excuse me," he muttered, weaving between the sweaty mass.

"Quit shoving!" yelled a man with flabby jowls, his face red from the sweltering heat and with breath so bad it could pickle herring. The man pushed Ed into a blubberous lady with a talcum-powdered face framed by a tangle of orange hair the color of spaghetti sauce. She bulldozed her way ahead of him.

Once inside the doorway, Ed elbowed his way through the spectators who jammed the corridors. He squeezed between sweat-soaked hucksters from the Franklin Street Open-Air Market, cannery workers reeking of fish from the Old Dutch Market, and businessmen in suits and wilted starched shirts.

Shoving his way forward with sweat trickling from beneath his armpits, he envisioned his next article. He felt confident Mr. Casey would promote him in spite of the uneasy feeling something was going to go wrong. Strange. He felt it in his gut—like something unsuspecting was waiting to leap out of nowhere and attack him with some distressing situation. What?

A confrontation with Barry Triving? But the man didn't know what he looked like. A run-in could only happen if someone pointed him out. Besides, what could Triving really do in this crowd other than throw him a mean look?

He shook the portent away. Stupid to give those kinds of feelings credence. He was just nervous at having a murder trial of such importance thrust upon him. He needn't be concerned. After all, he reasoned, all he had to do was take notes. He firmed his body and steeled himself against anything unforeseen happening, bolstered further by Sarah's confident words to him that morning, "Go get 'em tiger!"

Ed angled his way upstairs through the wild scramble of spectators who pushed up the marbled staircase like determined salmon swimming upstream.

Pressing down the hallway, he shoved through the ill-shaped bodies wedged in the courtroom doorway, all trying to cram through at the same time.

Managing his way inside, he was immediately smacked in the face with the odor of sweat-soaked bodies, cheap cologne, and cigar smoke. The whole place smelled like one huge sweat gland. Wrinkling his nose, he gave a resigned shrug. All part of the job.

He panned the main floor. Spectators, their faces the color of over-ripe strawberries, stood across the rear in the standing-room-only section and along the two sides of the room whipping makeshift paper fans. Now and then they gazed up at the four whirling fans hanging from the ceiling as if staring at them would bring more relief.

"Hi there!" A voice came from his left. Ed turned his head. The greeting came from a slightly older, broad-chested man.

"Bob Wilkinson, *Virginian Pilot*. Saw your badge."

"Ed Bowman, *Casey Clarion*. Ed thrust out his hand.

Jostled by the crowd, the man shook it as best he could. "Good to know you"

"Follow me," Ed said crooking his finger, starting down the main aisle and pushing through the cluster of wriggling spectators vying for seats. "Our benches are down at the middle front section." Bob followed.

"*Virginian Pilot?*" You're all the way from Norfolk. Right?"

"Yep." The man's sun-bronzed face beamed, pleased at the recognition.

"Spent a few summers down there when I was a kid," Ed said, "shucking oysters with my dad."

"How do you think the trial will go?" Bob asked. "Guilty or not guilty?"

"Well," Ed replied, raising one eyebrow, "I think everyone is assuming he's guilty unless proven innocent, so it looks like thumbs down for the guy. I'm trying to reserve my opinion until everything is presented." Ed saw no need to tell him about overhearing Buford's attorneys.

"Fair enough," came the reply.

Ed gave a quick glance over the sea of heads, then down front to the counsel table looking for Triving. No one inside the bar enclosure yet. Relief washed over him. Could the man really ban him from the courtroom?

Well, come what may, no one, especially Triving, was going to intimidate him. He'd stay for the whole trial and complete his assignment. One thing his mama drilled into him as a child was determination. "*A dependable person,* she told him, *plows a straight furrow and goes to the end of the row.*"

Struggling through the packed aisle, Bob close behind, he zigzagged his way in stop-and-go steps amidst shouts bombarding his ears by individuals squabbling over seats.

"You can't save them! I got here first. Squeeze together tighter!"

Ed glanced up at the coloreds' balcony that ran around the three walls like a second-story veranda. He signaled Bob with a slight inclination of his head.

"See? Packed to capacity."

"Yeah, this is the worse crowd I've ever experienced," Bob said, shaking his head.

"Well, miserable as conditions are," Ed said, "everyone will stay even if standing room only."

"Guess they want their pound of flesh," came Bob's passive response. "The warden's daughter was quite prominent in the community."

Ed reached the two roped-off pews near the bar enclosure. He had hoped for an aisle seat so he could see the defendant's face better when he was brought in. The picture in the Richmond newspapers wasn't very good. A more current one hadn't come over the *Clarion's* Teletype yet.

"Gotta show your pass." A man in a khaki-colored uniform with official-looking badge on his shirt held out his hand.

Ed showed it to him, and looked back for Bob. He was caught in a tangle of people.

"Say," the man said, checking Ed's name and looking back up, "I read your article in the *Casey Clarion*. Pretty explosive stuff."

"Thanks." Ed beamed. The man's words were music to his ears.

The uniformed man pulled the rope aside while Ed slid onto the mahogany bench. Seconds later, Bob scooted in beside him. Ed undid the buttons on his jacket, pulled out a handkerchief and wiped the sweat from his face.

"Boy, I could sure use an ice-cold glass of my Sarah's mouth puckering lemonade."

"Your wife?"

"Yeah. Married three years and still madly in love." Ed grinned.

Bob let out a hearty laugh, then shot him an omniscient smile. "Give yourself time."

Ed resented the joke. Some marriages were made in heaven. His and Sarah's love would last forever.

"To the contrary," he said, nonchalantly waving Bob's remark off with his hand and flashing back a controlled smile, "don't think that will ever change. Lucky to have married such a wonderful and beautiful gal. Don't know what she saw in me. I'm tall as a flagpole, with freckles to boot." He followed his statement with a sheepish grin and chuckle.

Bob rendered a good-humored chortle as an apology for his previous remark. Ed accepted it. Nevertheless, just thinking about Sarah sent him into a love trance. He recalled her oft-repeated words to him.

"Honey, know why I love you? It's your broad chest and because you're so doggone handsome. And those smokey-blue, bedroom eyes of yours? When you touch me I shimmer in velvety pinks and magentas and melt like golden butterscotch." She'd dramatically whip one hand to her forehead and feign a swoon. He smiled at how she enjoyed waxing poetic over their lovemaking. He guessed he didn't have to worry about his freckles.

"Well, Bob," Ed leaned back into the bench, "I want Sarah to be proud of me for covering this trial. I'm also hoping to win my mother-in-law over. She thinks her daughter should have married someone with a high-rise corporate job instead of working for a newspaper."

"Good luck with *that*." Bob emitted a vigorous laugh. "I take it this is your first assignment?"

"At least one this big." Ed gave a proud smile.

"Pretty heavy-duty, but I'm sure you'll do fine. If I can help, let me know. I've been at it for some years now." He reached for the brief case down by his feet. "By the way," he said looking back up, "I'm hoping to get transferred here to Richmond. Got family here."

"That's great, Bob. We'll probably run into each other now and then." Bob returned to shuffling through his brief case.

Ed looked toward the front. The defense and prosecutor's chairs still stood vacant. He twisted around and looked at the double doors to see if more reporters were arriving. Two entered and headed down the opposite aisle. Flourishing their badges with casual gestures, they walked with the confident swagger of pros. Ed did a quick study at what they wore. No tweed.

The men showed their pass to the uniformed man at the opposite end of Ed's bench and slid in. They immediately turned to face each other and continued conversing.

"Excuse me a minute, Bob. Just going to scoot down and say something to the reporters at the end." Ed stood, took in a nervous inhale, and edged his way down the bench. No doubt they had read his article.

"How are you? Ed Bowman here. *Casey Clarion*. Quite a trial, isn't it?"

The man with his back to Ed swiveled around, mumbled a hello and shook his hand.

"Yeah, *Times-Dispatch* here." The other man leaned forward. "*Richmond News Leader*." They immediately resumed their private conversation, leaving Ed to feel like a bump on a log.

Shuffling back to his seat, his insides twisted like a knotted rubber band. Strange they hadn't shown any interest in him when he mentioned the *Clarion*. If Triving and the uniformed man in the aisle read his article, surely they must have. They should at least be purring a little over him, asking how he got his information. He let out a slow exhale. Maybe they didn't see it. The *Clarion* was a pretty small paper. He sat down and watched Bob pull a yellow legal pad from his briefcase.

Within minutes, five more reporters arrived on Ed's side of the aisle.

"Excuse us." Slipping past them, they moved down to the far end with the other two reporters where they were heartily greeted. More came down the aisle and joined them.

Feeling slighted but too intimidated to try again, Ed guessed they were justified in ignoring him. Why should they pay him any special attention? Many of them were well seasoned and he was new to the game. They probably had journalism degrees and he had only a seventh grade education. Plus, he worked for a small-town newspaper these big-timers wouldn't look at twice. Determination smoldered. He wouldn't let it get to him.

"Look. They're coming in," Bob said. The noise in the courtroom lowered.

Ed turned his focus to the three fancy-suited attorneys who entered and crossed the space in front of the judge's elevated bench. The prosecutor, Lee Smalding, came first, followed by Michael Payne and Barry Triving.

Ed stiffened and his stomach did a couple of flip-flops, but common sense came to the rescue. The man was too occupied now to be thinking about him. Ed sagged his body back to normal.

The three attorneys ambled to their counsel tables and began pulling papers and binders from their trial bags.

Someone behind Ed whispered. "Look, here he comes!" Ed turned. Everyone's gaze was glued to an open door on the far side of the room. Deputies were escorting the defendant in.

Buford wore a tan suit, white shirt and tie, all of which seemed out of place on him. To Ed, he looked more like the plaid shirt type. He also noticed his unique way of walking—a side-to-side waddle typical of the obese.

He stared and wondered. What kind of a man would commit such a terrible crime? He looked just like any other guy. Well, sort of. He looked tough, but what single step had he taken that caused him to go down the wrong road? No doubt they had the right man because Payne admitted to Triving he was probably guilty. Even so, would they get him off? He thought of *The Case of the Sulky Girl*, the new novel out by Erle Stanley Gardner he had finished reading. Buford's attorneys would have to exhibit the skills of a Perry Mason to get him off.

Buford kept his head down and eyes focused on the floor. That bothered Ed. He could hardly see details of his face except to note his jowls hung forward giving him a haggard look.

Ed nudged Bob with his elbow and pointed. Bob lifted his head from his paperwork and studied Buford with interest.

"Looks older," Ed whispered, "than the picture in the papers."

Bob shrugged. "They probably took it from his employment file when he first hired on at the pen. Could have been years ago."

The deputies seated the defendant at the counsel table next to Payne and Triving. Ed could only see the man's back now, although once in a while he glimpsed a side-view if Buford happened to turn his head to talk. He also noticed a distinctive strip of white in his coal-black hair that ran from his right sideburn over his ear and down to his neckline.

A hush immediately settled over the courtroom. The jurors, seven men and five women, walked in, their entrance galvanizing. Their poker faces portrayed the gravity of the case. They looked neither to the right or left, only stared at the place on the bench where they were to sit. Ed grew pensive at their solemn demeanor. How did they feel knowing a man's fate rested with them? How would he feel in their place?

The bailiff stepped to the front. Ed flipped open his tablet, reached into his pocket and grabbed a pencil. Gripping it with sweaty fingers, he was ready to go with his own inventive shorthand of abbreviated words and symbols. Bob was ready too, but more relaxed. Ed guessed that came with time.

"All rise. Superior Court of Henrico County is now in session, the Honorable Judge Rufus Jackson presiding." The judge entered from a door to the left of the elevated bench.

Ed found him rather fascinating, mainly because he looked so old. He mentally classified him as a white-haired old geezer, probably near seventy. Sitting down in his high and lordly chair, he banged his gavel exhibiting not a shred of emotion.

"Good morning ladies and gentlemen. You may all be seated. Bailiff, please call the first case."

The Bailiff stepped forward and issued forth his announcement in a strong, strombolian voice.

"The court will now hear criminal case No. 50-080-E, the State of Virginia versus Gunther Buford."

Ed noticed the prosecutor twist around in his chair, his face pinched with concern, scanning the courtroom looking for someone. Who was he expecting? The sales clerk was, no doubt, already here. She'd be sitting near the front row, unless the attorneys had invoked the rule allowing her to wait outside the courtroom. No way to tell since Ed didn't know what she looked like. Smalding had to be looking for someone else pertinent to the case.

The clerk swore the jury in. Judge Jackson pushed his glasses down on his nose and stared at Lee Smalding. "Is the State prepared to present its opening statement?"

"Ready for the People, Your Honor."

"Is the Defense?" he asked, directing his question to Barry Triving.

"Ready for the Defense, Your Honor."

Ed wondered. Would Triving "shine" as promised? And did Gordon, the guy Michael Payne mentioned, find enough evidence for similar earrings at other jewelry stores to diminish the sales clerk's damaging claim?

Smalding, on the other hand, was known as "the bulldog." Would he live up to his reputation? Would he pack a powerful enough wallop to convince everyone of Buford's guilt, or would he save his bulldogging for cross-examinations? A huge pulse of expectancy beat through his body.

The spectators sat riveted to their seats. Even the air seemed to hold its breath. The only sound heard was the whirring drone of the overhead fans.

Ed inched to the edge of the hardwood bench, his body tight with tension and electricity zigzagging up his spine. He gripped the note pad with one hand, his pencil in the other, geared and ready to go. This was a hair-raising moment. Which attorney's opening statement would prove more convincing?

He barely breathed.

CHAPTER 4

~~~~~

Judge Rufus Jackson drew a handkerchief from his robe and wiped the sweat from his forehead, then looked down from the bench at the prosecutor.

"The State may proceed with its opening statement."

Lee Smalding, a large, butterball of a man about fifty with wire-framed glasses and graying sideburns, buttoned the jacket of his blue-and-white-striped seersucker and stepped from behind the counsel table. With a photograph in hand, he walked with a casual gait to the front of the oak-paneled jury box and laid it on the lectern.

"Good morning, ladies and gentlemen." His deep resonant voice was heavy with Southern inflection. "My name is Lee Smalding and I represent the State.

"I don't need to tell you that you are on the jury of the most important murder trial Henrico County has tried for a long time—the brutal rape and cold-blooded murder of an innocent young woman, twenty-five-year-old Sue Davis, daughter of Warden Davis who serves as administrator at the State Penitentiary." He paused, locking his eyes on the jurors' faces.

"Many of you are familiar with the victim's prominence in Richmond, notably her efforts to raise school standards and her volunteer work for the Governor and the Harry Byrd Organization." He stepped over to the lectern.

"This is her photograph," he said, holding it up to the jurors. "She was raped and stabbed to death fourteen times by the defendant and a red bandana shoved into her mouth to silence her screams. She fought for her life before she died." Two lady jurors reached for hankies and dabbed the corners of their eyes.

Smalding began pacing. The jurors turned their heads and followed him with their eyes.

"The State will provide three witnesses who will tell you it was common knowledge among prison personnel that the victim considered her relationship with the defendant strictly platonic but the defendant did not. You will hear from four other witnesses who will testify the defendant has an uncontrollable temper. That temper, coupled with unreciprocated love, triggered Sue Davis' murder." He swept his gaze from one end of the box to the other, looking each juror in the face.

Ed took frantic notes, trying to keep up with Smalding's list of details why the defense had no case. When he mentioned the sales clerk's name he jotted down, *Agnes Rochester...sales clerk at Windham's Jewelry store...saw earring in photograph of crime scene leaked to newspaper...supplied photo of store's earrings, supposedly one of a kind and sold to defendant.* He instinctively looked up and stared at the witness stand imagining the sales clerk victoriously clinching the case against Buford. That is, unless Barry Triving indeed proved to shine.

"I'm convinced," Smalding concluded, "once you hear the State's witnesses and evaluate the evidence presented, you will be compelled to find the defendant guilty as charged."

Smalding turned and with a walk meant to relay confidence in Buford's guilt, returned to his table and sat down but not before anxiously looking around the courtroom again. Ed glanced back at the double doors. Someone from his office? Last minute evidence?

Bob leaned over to Ed and whispered. "Pretty impressive guy."

"Yeah, he's good," Ed replied. "Sure makes Buford sound guilty." Bob nodded, and went back to his notes. Ed turned to a clean sheet, anxious to hear the defense's opening statement.

The judge looked down at Triving.

"The Defense may proceed."

"Thank you, Your Honor."

Barry Triving scooted his chair out from the table and stood. Like most small-statured men his Napoleon complex was obvious, and he overcompensated for his size by standing straight as a board. And no seersucker suit for him. He wore a loud, gray and white chalk-striped suit with black and white spectator shoes. With deliberate, business-like steps, his bearing aggressive and cocky, he took the largest strides his short legs could manage and marched up to the jury box. His pompous strut reminded Ed of a Banty rooster.

Triving's first baritone words boomed out like an explosion of dynamite. His microphone voice echoed off the walls, startling the jurors and evoking Ed's traumatic encounter with the voice that chewed him out on the phone. He knew right then he wanted no further run-ins with the guy.

"Ladies and gentlemen of the jury, my name is Barry Triving and I represent the defense. My client is not guilty of the crime he is accused of. He is an innocent man. Like all the personnel at the prison, he cared for Sue Davis and grieves over her untimely death.

"Once you hear the defense's witnesses and evaluate the evidence..." he stepped closer to the jurors, trapping them in a gaze of electric intensity "...there will be no hesitation on your part to render a verdict of 'not guilty.'"

Bob leaned over. "This is where he'll give a sympathetic bio of the defendant."

Ed was all ears to hear that. What kind of a bio would a murderer have? He leaned forward, one elbow propped on his knee, his fist tucked under his chin.

"Gunther Buford," Triving continued, "is an upstanding citizen who has a strong dedication toward the cause of justice. Why? Because when he was sixteen a burglar brutally murdered his parents. This left him with a resolute sense that criminals should pay for what they do. As his contribution to society, he determined to work in a capacity where justice is meted out to offenders. Mr. Buford took a job as guard at the penitentiary and has been a conscientious employee of the State for fifteen years. He is a respected member of the community and it is a pleasure to represent him.

"The State, however, would have you believe he had an infatuation for the victim which, when not returned, triggered the murder. Ladies and gentlemen, the defendant had no romantic thoughts about her and would never have caused her harm."

Ed listened to him explain away the prosecutor's statement of evidence, including the earrings. Evidently Gordon did a good job. *Similar earrings,* he wrote in his shorthand, *found at other high-classed jewelry stores in Richmond.*

"Further," Triving said, his baritone voice increasing in volume, "we will provide evidence the sales clerk had an ambitious motive. It will explain why she volunteered to be a witness for the prosecution. What was that motive?" He narrowed his eyes. "To place herself in the limelight of public attention to promote her side career—a model."

A low hum sounding like a swarm of bees came from the spectators and swept through the courtroom. Triving appeared pleased and paused long enough to allow time for the jurors to be affected by the response. He continued.

"I submit to you, ladies and gentlemen, at the conclusion of this trial the State will not have proved its case beyond a reasonable doubt and you will be compelled to find him 'not guilty.'" Thank you."

Ed watched him swagger back to the counsel table, head high, chest out. At the same time he noticed a young man scurry down the aisle from the back door to the counsel table and whisper in Smalding's ear. The prosecutor's face remained stoic. Ed couldn't tell if it was good or bad news.

"Does the Prosecution wish to call its first witness?" Judge Jackson looked at him.

"One moment, please, Your Honor." Smalding spoke to the young man who then turned, went back up the aisle and out the back door. Smalding stood and faced the judge. His voice, a solemn monotone, carried throughout the courtroom.

"Unfortunately, Your Honor, our subpoenaed witness, the sales clerk, is not here and she is crucial to our case. Two weeks ago, she voluntarily approached our office with vital information and was deposed. I spoke to her yesterday. She said she would definitely be here. She is a responsible person of high character, so it is unlikely she is deliberately avoiding a court appearance. A message from her family has just been relayed to me. They cannot locate her. They are concerned and are checking the hospitals. Since this is an unforeseeable event I would like to request an adjournment."

Ed couldn't see Buford's face, but noticed his body contentedly relax into the back of his chair. Did he have anything to do with her disappearance? He chided himself. He'd read too many Perry Mason novels. How could he from a jail cell?

"Mr. Smalding." The judge pushed his glasses down to the tip of his nose and peered over them. "You are aware you may go ahead without the witness and read her deposed statement?"

"I am aware of that Your Honor, but would prefer she be here. This is the State's key witness and her presence and verbal testimony are critical."

The judge looked at Barry Triving. "Does the Defense have any objection to an adjournment?

Triving glanced at Michael Payne and smiled. "No, Your honor."

More time for them, Ed thought, to plan more defense strategies.

The judge leaned over the side of the bench and spoke to the deputy clerk who sat at a desk below.

"When's the next available date?"

The clerk thumbed through the docket. "Thursday, Your Honor, the day after tomorrow. Ten o'clock."

"Mr. Smalding," the judge said with a granitized edge in his voice, his unblinking eyes boring into the prosecutor. "I naturally expect you, or the sheriff, will see to it your witness is here on the scheduled date." He reached for his gavel.

"Since the Defense has no objection, this court stands adjourned until Thursday, August 8th at 10 a.m." He brought the wooden hammer down, provoking a kaleidoscope of emotion-filled groans from disappointed spectators who immediately began shuffling toward the aisles and exits.

"Today was all for nothing," one man griped. Others nearby echoed the sentiment. Ed was also disappointed, but couldn't shake wondering what happened to the clerk.

He thrust his pencil and tablet into his jacket pocket. He had envisioned his article for the evening edition detailing explosive revelations from the witnesses, especially the sales clerk, hoping to impress Mr. Casey. Now he had to wait until Thursday. He let out a long exhale. At least he didn't have a run-in with Triving—also, his premonition of something unforeseen happening to him turned out to be his imagination. He turned to Bob.

"Good meeting you."

"Same here," came his reply. "Probably see you Thursday."

Ed nodded. "Hope everything works out for your transfer to Richmond."

"Thanks. So do I."

Ed inched his bone-weary body through the sea of smelly spectators, looking forward to unwinding at home and giving Sarah a blow-by-blow description. After lunch, he'd go to the office and write his article covering the opening statements, the unexpected adjournment, and speculate on what happened to the State's key witness. Ah, yes. He could make that exciting. A missing witness always adds mystery. He'd get that written and then spend the rest of the day relaxing at home.

Nothing much was going to happen between now and Thursday.

Henrico County Jail
That same night—10 p.m.

The guard shuffled down the stone corridor and stopped in front of the last cell. He shoved a rolled-up newspaper through the bars.

"Couldn't get the *Times-Dispatch*, Gunther. All sold out. But here's yesterday's *Clarion*."

The prisoner sprang off the cot and with one quick swoop grabbed it up before it hit the concrete floor.

Hurrying back to the edge of his cot, he plopped down and angled the front page under the dim light bulb hanging from the ceiling. He gaped at the headline, fixing his eyes in an incredulous stare. *Defense Nervous in Buford Trial.*

Grim-lipped, he read the rest of the article unable to believe what he was reading. His own attorneys admitted his guilt? Billows of infuriation fumed across his face. He could hardly stifle the harsh choking sound erupting from his throat.

He threw the paper aside and clamped his eyes shut. Even with the sales clerk out of the way, admission of his guilt by his attorneys would influence jurors. Even if sequestered, somehow they'd probably hear about it.

He stood and paced the cell floor, his thoughts in a convulsive frenzy. He clamped his jaw tight, pressing his lips together until his mouth was a thin horizontal slit in his face. He'd never get a hung jury now.

He snatched up the newspaper, looked at the byline, and spat out. "Ed Bowman! He's gonna pay dearly."

Storming over to the bars, his voice reverberated down the stone lined corridor.

"Guard! I need to get a message to someone."

CHAPTER 5

Midnight - August 7

~~~~~

Darkness descended on Richmond. A figure crept through the deepening shadows of the wooded residential area, the humidity and unbearable heat forcing the man to breathe hard through an open mouth. Thousands of screeching cicadas intensified his anxiety.

He hunkered down for a few seconds to quiet his jitters. Swiping the sweat dripping from his forehead, he tugged a black knit ski mask down over his face, then dropped down on all fours and crabbed through the tangle of underbrush. He had to hurry. No resting. He took a nervous inhale.

It wasn't like he'd never done something like this before—but the timing was wrong. If caught violating his parole to spring Gunther, he'd be sent back to the pen for sure. He'd never survive another stint in that brutal place. Nevertheless, any con who had received favors from Gunther in the pen, knew his reputation. You didn't cross him. If you owed, you'd better pay. His ungovernable temper evoked fear even in his closest friends, if one could call them that. He also hadn't forgotten Gunther's ominous warning when Gunther had summoned him to the jail.

"You gotta get me out of here, Billy Bob. Do that and get rid of the sales clerk so she won't testify, and you won't owe me no more—and you know what that means if you don't come through!"

There was no question. He wasn't about to cross *him*. He had to square his tab with the man. He had a long arm—even from a jail cell. He ran his tongue over dry lips.

Peering through the tangle of Virginia Creepers, he swept his gaze across the houses and yards visible under the streetlights. Every shadow was scrutinized. He saw no movement. He heard nothing. Only the ear-splitting whine of the cicadas. He moved out from behind the trees with decisive strides, and soon left the residential area.

Within twenty minutes he entered the commercial district and stood across the street from the county offices. He zeroed in on the jail, a small, white stuccoed building at the far end. He glanced at his watch. Yes, he timed it just right. Gunther said at 1:00 a.m. the second guard would leave. He hunkered down, waited and watched. Sure enough, right on time he saw the guard leave. He had one hour with only one guard on duty before two others came to relieve him at 2:00.

He bolted across the barely-lit street into some tall shrubberies, and then bee-lined to the end of the block. He crept forward with cushioned steps on the walkway of crushed gravel leading to the door of the jail and eased inside the stone entranceway. With only one guard his blackjack should do the job, if he could catch him by surprise. He hoped he wouldn't have to kill the guy. After doing in the sales clerk, he didn't want another murder on his head.

He pulled out a pick-and-tension wrench from his pocket and manipulated the lock until he heard the metallic click. Inching the door open, he slipped inside, closing it behind him.

The hallway was dim, lit by a single light bulb that cast a sickly yellow on the rock walls. He tiptoed forward and saw the jailer dozing on a chair with his back to him. Beyond, was the arched entranceway leading to the cells. He withdrew the blackjack from his hip pocket and slunk forward.

Barely had he raised his arm when the jailer, his eyes wide with surprise, turned and leaped to his feet. Billy gave him a slashing kick in the groin before the man could reach for his holstered revolver. The man sagged and fell backwards but quickly regained his balance and lunged forward. He shot a fist deep into Billy's belly.

Dropping his blackjack, Billy's lungs gave a violent exhale, his knees buckled and he crumpled to the cement floor—but only for a second. He heard the click of the safety lock. He scrambled back to his feet and sprang forward as the jailer grabbed for his holster and pulled out his Colt .38 Police Positive. A short left hook to the man's jaw made him stagger backward and drop the revolver. One more punch and the man went down. Before the man could get to his feet, Billy grabbed up his blackjack and brought it down on his head with a loud crack. The man's body thudded to the floor. A second hit in the head with full force immobilized him. The man lay silent.

Yanking the key ring from the man's belt, he leapt over the motionless figure and sprinted through the archway.

Racing down the shadowy corridor, he whipped his head from side to side searching each cubicle of sleeping prisoners and calling out in low tones.

"Gunther?"

"That you, Billy?" A figure in the last cell leaped off a cot.

"Yeah," he whispered back, thrusting the key into the lock and pulling the door open. "The guard's out cold. Hurry!"

The figure in the cell bolted forward. Together they charged down the hall toward the rear of the building. Heaving their bodies against the door it swung open. They ducked down by a nearby Model-T pickup.

Gunther's eyes smoldered. "You took your time gettin' here. It'll be morning soon and the next shift will be coming on. Did you take care of the sales clerk?"

"Yeah. She won't testify. You know my reputation." His voice cracked slightly.

"Did you get to my place," Gunther pressed, "and find the package?"

Billy reached into his jacket pocket, withdrew a large manila envelope and handed it to him.

"Got it. Just like ya asked. Had a dickens of a time getting that floorboard loose." His facial muscles twitched while he studied Buford's expression. He hoped the man would say he planned to leave the state. He needed to be free of the guy.

Gunther said nothing and opened the flap of the envelope to check the contents. He pulled out a bundle of cash and began counting. He glanced up, giving Billy a withering stare. "Better not come up short."

After assuring all the money was there, Gunther fingered through some personal papers, and then stretched his fingers to the bottom of the envelope. He pulled out a single earring and breathed a sigh of relief. The blood-encrusted mounting held a round emerald surrounded by eight rubies, the rim encircled with iridescent mother-of-pearl.

He shoved everything back, reached into his shirt pocket and pulled out the clipping of the *Clarion* article he had torn from the newspaper. Placing it inside, he folded the envelope over twice and crammed it into his pants pocket.

"Now...the gun."

Billy nodded, reached into his jacket and pulled it out.

"Got you a thirty-eight Detective Special—short barrel—six-shot...everything you asked for. Serial number's been filed off..." He took a deep breath.

"Gunther, don't you think...well, maybe you oughta...high-tail it out of the state? I mean, after killing the warden's dau—"

"Shut up!" he snarled. "Yeah, I'm going, but I've got a score to settle first with that reporter. Blast him and his newspaper article." He ground out the words between clenched teeth. "With the sales clerk out of the way the jury couldn't have considered the earrings and my attorneys could have gotten me off. The reporter sure threw a wrench into that. If I stay in jail now, I'm as good as fried. Bowman's got a one-way ticket to hell comin'."

"Gimme your mask!" he snapped. Billy yanked it off and dutifully handed it over, and watched him tug it down over his head. Gunther gave the parking lot a quick once-over.

"So..." Billy hesitated, "are we...square?" He suspended his breathing.

"Yeah," Gunther muttered. "Ya sprung me, so don't owe me no more."

"Thanks," Billy mumbled, relaxing in relief. He leaned back against the car waiting for the man's next move.

Gunther jumped to his feet, sprinted across the yard, and disappeared into the shadows.

Chapter 6

~~~~~~

Ed hotfooted across the traffic-laden intersection heading for the courthouse barely beating an electric signal's red semaphore arm in the process of pivoting to "stop." The heat, hot as the hinges of hell, blasted the concrete and burned through the soles of his shoes nearly cremating his feet. This time, he wore his tan and white seersucker jacket. No more tweed for him.

He looked forward to the sales clerk's testimony today and hoped Mr. Casey would be completely bowled over with his coverage. He leaped up on the opposite curb and hurried past century-old granite buildings, men in business suits pushing through glass doors, and restaurant aromas mixed with the noxious exhaust fumes belching from vehicles. He strode forward with wide, confident steps.

His career was definitely on the rise, and he'd allow nothing to stand in his way—not even Barry Triving. Stopping for a second, he used the jacket of his sleeve to wipe the sweat dripping down from his forehead into his eyes.

"Extra! Extra! Read all about it! Buford trial continues today!"

The tousle-haired newsboy stood on the corner wearing patched knickerbockers and a gray cloth cap, waving the *Richmond-Times Dispatch* high in the air.

Ed paid particular attention. The boy wasn't hawking the headline that came across the Teletype that morning—Howard Hughes' 91-hour airplane flight around the world. In a way, it didn't surprise him. The trial hung heavy on everyone's mind today, especially one question. Would the sales clerk show up? His face flickered confidence. She'd be there. If Smalding couldn't find her, sheriffs were good at it—especially those subpoenaed.

Before he rounded the corner he heard the hullabaloo. One single eye-gulp took it all in.

Crowds jam-packed the front sidewalk and lawns. Cars double-parked cattywampus letting passengers off. Car doors slammed.

Brakes screeched in the street. Neighborhood dogs yowled. People pushed, shoved, and charged like a herd of angry rhinoceroses, eager to get inside and find a seat. "Quit your shovin'!" they squallered. "Get out of the way! Move faster!"

Ed beavered his way forward, brandishing his pass, and jostled through swarms of ladies in floral print dresses smelling like a potpourri of Mum deodorant, Rose water, and perspiration. Next, he collided with farmers dressed in blue striped bib overalls exuding the malodorous smell of sweaty work boots and socks. They looked like they had just hopped off their tractors long enough to come to the trial. He pushed ahead, all the while thinking about the clerk. He visualized her taking the stand and securing the case for Buford's guilt.

He raised up on his toes to see what was slowing the line, at the same time wondering if he would see Bob Wilkinson again.

"Hey, Ed!"

"Well, speak of the devil," Ed called back laughingly. "I was hoping we'd run into each other."

"Well," Bob asked, shoving in closer, dodging the jab of a bony elbow, "do you think the clerk will show up?"

"If not," Ed said, "the prosecutor, so I'm told, will have to read her deposed statement. Either way, Triving will have his work cut out for him. But whether the guy is guilty or not, justice will definitely prevail."

"Aw, come on now, Ed, how can you be sure of that?" Bob raised an eyebrow.

"Oh, I'm confident of that. My mama drummed it into me often enough. *"Son, God always sees justice is meted out and everything works for good."*

"You believe her?" He looked Ed straight in the eye.

"Yep. Her insights come from the Good Book."

Bob said nothing, but stared contemplatively at him.

Fifteen minutes later they made it up the steps to the portico and through the door where the corridor floor shook with the heavy tromping of feet. Ed squiggled forward, the press of the crowd pinning his arms so close to his torso he felt he was in a straight jacket.

"Wow, Bob. This is worse than the first day of the trial." He looked to one side. Bob was gone. He twisted around and saw him

46

caught in the wild scramble behind him.

Ed reached the staircase, propelled along by frenzied spectators who stampeded up to the second landing, charged down the marbled hallway, and wormed their way through the courtroom's two sets of double doors. Finally, he was inside.

The ceiling fans above him spun at full speed. Portable ones stood at the front of the room and on windowsills, wherever they could be placed. All were oscillating and humming in varying speeds and pitches sounding like a disharmonic grammar school orchestra. They helped some, but the oppressive humidity and body odor remained entrapped in the smutchy haze of brownish-yellow cigarette smoke spreading across the courtroom.

Ed maneuvered his way down the packed aisle toward the roped-off section, noticing both benches in front were already full with only a few places left. He looked around for Bob, and then showed his pass to a security guard. He glanced at the clock on the wall. Twenty minutes to go. The guard pulled aside the rope and Ed shuffled in front of the already-seated reporters and squeezed his frame into an empty space.

Twisting around, he saw Bob elbowing his way down the opposite aisle to a seat. Ed waved. Bob raised his opened hands in a helpless gesture. Ed crimped his mouth. He had hoped they could sit together. He'd like to know him better.

He settled back, his attention called to the three reporters on the bench in front of him. They spoke in low tones, their heads huddled together as if privy to information he didn't have. Ed leaned forward. He only heard bits and pieces.

"What about the jailer? The police...?" Ed raised his eyebrows. What had happened that he hadn't heard about?

The hands of the brass-rimmed clock on the wall clicked to nine fifty-five. Finally, ten o'clock. A hush settled over the room.

Ed gripped his pencil, ready to go, but after a few seconds questioningly cocked his head. He stared at the picket-fenced bar enclosure, narrowing his eyes in puzzlement. It was time to start. Where were the fancy-suited lawyers pulling papers from briefcases? Clerks scurrying back and forth with files? Neither were the court transcriber and Deputy Clerk in their spots. They hadn't even brought in Buford. Spectators began whispering. Something was not right.

The door next to the judge's bench opened. All eyes fixed on the bailiff as he walked to the front.

"Ladies and gentlemen—" He paused and cleared his throat. "Gunther Buford has escaped and has not yet been apprehended. The trial is continued to an indefinite date."

Incredulous gasps rippled throughout the courtroom. Even with the growing suspicion something was amiss no one, not even Ed, was prepared for the bone-jangling announcement.

"Well, guys," one of the reporters in front of him exclaimed, "that confirms it. He's still on the loose." Leaping to their feet, they bolted up the aisle and out the rear doors before the shocked spectators had even moved out of their seats. Other reporters followed suit.

Ed jammed his tablet and pencil back into his jacket pocket and did the same. Shoving through the now-moving bodies, his flesh quivering with goose bumps, he pushed up the aisle and squeezed his way through the double doors and into the commotion-filled hallway. Reaching the front door, he bolted down the steps two at a time, and raced two blocks to where his car was parked.

Riveted by the bailiff's electrifying announcement, a thought hit him as he ran. His premonition about something going wrong actually came true, only it wasn't about him. It foreshadowed Buford's escape.

He unlocked the car door and jumped in, thrust the key into the ignition and started the engine. Well, maybe the premonition *was* about him. Until they caught the guy, there'd be no more trial for him to cover. That could delay his promotion.

He processed that while he spun the steering wheel around and maneuvered his car away from the curb. There was only one solution. He had to write today's article better than any of the others he'd done so far—enough to tip the scales of Mr. Casey's pending decision. Pulling out into the street, he sped the forty miles back to Hannigan.

Forty-five minutes later, he dashed through the door of the *Clarion* and skidded to his desk. Grabbing a piece of paper from the drawer, he rolled a sheet of paper into the platen of his typewriter and began typing, throwing draft after draft away, then beginning all over.

Like his first two articles it didn't come easy. He shouldn't be surprised considering his lack of schooling. His dad's death left him no choice but to quit school and help his mama. In view of such a poor start he was ecstatic over the promise of a new career. This article had to nail it with Mr. Casey despite the delay in trial. Surely, the police would catch Buford in a couple of days—at least within the week.

For two tedious hours he bled over every word and sentence, making them as perfect as he could. Elated, he yanked the paper out of the carriage with time to spare for the two o'clock run. He glanced at the clock. Mr. Casey would be arriving soon.

He sauntered down the hall toward Mr. Casey's office, apprehension needling him. Would his article measure up? Certainly, his coverage of Buford's sensational escape should clinch his promotion. If not, he'd have to wait until the trial resumed.

Entering Mr. Casey's office, he laid the article in the in-box and returned to his desk, wiping his sweaty palms on his pants. Flopping down in his swivel chair, he pushed against the floor with one foot and propelled the chair into a couple of relaxing twirls while he focused on what he had left to do.

He needed to finish writing the interview with the owner of the butcher shop, Slim Hackett, who wanted to be sure everyone knew about his new meat slicer, and also check with the coroner for obituaries. He sighed. Pretty boring stuff after covering a murder trial.

He leaned back, folded his arms behind his head, and stared up at the ceiling as the chair continued to circle. His whole insides exulted. Just imagine. His first role as a trial reporter and he was covering one of Richmond's biggest murder trials. A shiver of joy rippled through him.

Proud of his article and confident about his future, he felt justified in feeling a little boastful, regardless of one of his mother's clucking admonitions, "*Pride goeth before a fall, son.*" He gave a good-humored smile, stretching it into a cheeky grin.

Yep, nothing short of the world coming to an end could stop him now.

Chapter 7

~~~~

Mr. Casey shouted over the racket of the press. "Hey, Ed!" He hustled from the printing room and strode across the wood-planked floor, newspaper in hand, his large belly leading the way.

His face, flushed from working, sported a three-inch goatee he once said would lengthen the look of his round face. Beneath his ink-smudged bib apron he wore a blue, Big Yank work shirt and navy corduroy trousers.

The jimmy-jams hit hard. Ed clenched the handle of his coffee mug and watched him head his way. The newspaper had already gone to print and Mr. Casey had said nothing to him about his article beforehand. And Mr. Casey, whose real name nobody could pronounce, followed his German temperament of needing everything precise and exact. Was it a good sign?

He sipped his coffee, raising his eyes over the rim attempting to read Mr. Casey's expression as he approached. What if he had to rewrite the article? Maybe he was about to tell him he couldn't make it as a reporter. How could he tell Sarah? Worse yet, Josephine. The knot in his stomach intensified.

"Here's the run for the evening edition," Mr. Casey said in his thick German brogue.

Ed tensed all the way to his feet. He set his coffee cup down on the desk and said nothing. He felt like a comma waiting for the rest of a sentence that wouldn't come.

Mr. Casey shoved his duckbill cap back from his forehead and grinned. "Great job, Ed. *Ist vunderbar!*"

Ed stared up in surprise. Electric tingles shot down his spine. "Really?"

"Ya, I only had to change a couple of words." He smiled, slapped the paper down on the desk and folded his arms across the front of his ink-stained apron.

Ed's heart rate climbed. He grabbed up the paper and stared at the headline *Accused Murderer Escapes*. He dropped his gaze to three words, *by Ed Bowman.*

His insides swelled, and he glanced farther down the column. With the exception of Mr. Casey's possible word changes—wherever they were—he recognized his five Ws and all the sentences he had bled over. He glanced up and flashed a radiant smile.

"I couldn't have done this without your faith in me, Mr. Casey. Although," he added in a somber tone, "Gunther Buford's escape means I won't have any more trial to cover, unless, of course, he's captured. What if he isn't? He's probably in Timbuktu by now."

Mr. Casey smiled and patted him on the back. "Don't worry, Ed, they always get their man. Remember," he chortled, rolling his eyes, "according to your mama, justice always wins out. She's right, you know. Besides, you'll have other assignments. You've proven yourself. You got *sitzfleisch*, and that's what pays off, Ed—" His sentence broke off. "I mean, *Reporter Bowman.*"

Reporter! Ed's heart leapt.

"Thank you so much, Mr. Casey!" Euphoria swept through him as he gripped the newspaper in both hands and stared at it again. He made it!

"My sweet Sarah's going to be so proud."

"What about Josephine?" Mr. Casey tilted his head.

Ed let out a despondent sigh. "No idea. I've all but bent over backwards trying to be the perfect son-in-law, but in her eyes I'll never be good enough for her 'baby'. She still calls her that."

Mr. Casey arched a questioning brow. "Didn't her attitude change at all when she found out you were covering the trial?"

"Somewhat, but I still haven't won her over. When I told her I hoped to become a reporter, her last snorting words were, 'I'll believe *that* when I see it!' She can really make life hell at times. Plus, she won't quit her snide remarks about my troubled days as a youth." He let out a long exhalation but forced a brave smile. "Hopefully, that will change when she learns about my promotion."

"Well, as far as I'm concerned, Ed, you've really excelled." He grinned, giving him a pat on the shoulder. "And you made your mama a lot happier."

Ed snickered. "Well, guess I had to do something. Mama cried too much and I couldn't stand to hear her loud prayers coming from the bedroom pleading with God to save my soul."

Mr. Casey threw his head back and let out a hearty laugh. He turned to go back to the printing room, then stopped mid-stride and looked back.

"By the way Ed, in all your excitement about the trial and your promotion, don't forget you've got a deadline with the upset at the grocery store caused by old lady Blackwell."

"Yep, I'm on it."

It took Ed twenty minutes to finish the Blackwell article, but he couldn't get Gunther Buford out of his head. He strode into Richard's office, dropped it on his desk, then returned to his desk and sank into his chair.

Swiveling around, he stared out the picture window that stretched full-length across the front of the building and studied the distant sweet potato fields. He recalled his premonition-like feeling of disaster he had before the trial. A quick smile curved on his face. Even if it meant Buford, everything for Ed Bowman was turning out fine. And his mama will be pleased.

He let out a light chuckle, thinking of her Bible-spouting words. She insisted the whole universe ran on the scriptures and everything always worked out for good—especially for her son—because Romans 8:28 said so. He smiled and waved away a fly with a swish of his hand. Maybe everything does. Who knows?

Crossing his arms behind his head, he leaned back and listened to the scrunching sound of the chair's metal-coiled hinge. Yes, a promising career with position and prestige lay ahead, bringing respect and a limitless future. He saw his next byline.

"*Gunther Buford Captured! Gives Exclusive To Reporter.*"

His fantasy went even further, "*Ed Bowman Wins Pulitzer Prize.*"

His face flushed with excitement. Reaching over, he yanked the top-drawer open and pulled out a clipping. He looked at the picture of the ten-story, steel and concrete building of the *Richmond Times-Dispatch*. A few more years under his belt as reporter and he felt sure he'd qualify for a job with them. Now, that would be big time. He swung the chair around and plopped both feet on top of his desk imagining Josephine eating crow.

Mr. Casey's voice jolted him out of his daydream. Ed yanked his feet from the desktop.

"I'm leaving for an appointment," he called, hustling across the hardwood floor toward the front door. The leathery scent of Lifebuoy swirled about him from a shower in his office's private stall. He wore his appointment-going, blue and white striped Oxford shirt, tan slacks and shiny patent leather shoes.

"Won't be back. The truck's already left with the distribution. Richard will be here in a couple of hours to set tomorrow's type. Lock up if you have to leave before then."

"Sure will. I'll also call the Richmond police for any updates on Buford, and check if they can send a more current picture of him to us on the teletypewriter. I'll also check with the AP's Wire photo. Anyway, I'll be here for a while. I'm waiting for Sarah and her mom. I'm taking them to dinner."

Mr. Casey paused, threw him a sympathetic look. He whipped out a thumbs-up.

"Viel Glück!"

"Thanks," Ed responded with a shrug. "I'll need all the luck I can get."

"Got your strategy all planned out?" Mr. Casey grinned good-naturedly while resting his hand on the doorknob.

"Yep," Ed said, propping his elbows on the desk, "I've rehearsed everything in my mind—relaxed conversation during dinner casually interjecting details about the bailiff's announcement of Buford's escape, and how I got the exclusive about the defense attorneys. Got to prime the pump by only giving a little at a time."

He stretched his mouth into a playful grin. "First a little during the salad, next the main course. During dessert I'll lower the boom and announce my new position. Hopefully," he said, stretching his arms over his head, "I won't sound like I'm bragging too much but its all the ammunition I've got left." He snickered. "She just might be rendered speechless for the first time in her life."

"Sounds good." Mr. Casey pulled the door open, shutting it behind him.

Ed got up from his chair and sauntered down the long, narrow hallway leading to the rear of the building. He flipped the lights out, leaving the back of the building in shadows. On his way back to his desk he glanced at the clock.

Sarah and her mom would arrive in forty-five minutes.

Josephine would naturally start in on him with some critical dig, or pitch a hissy fit over something with that spitfire tongue of hers. He grimaced. Well, he could put up with it until they got to the restaurant.

He sauntered over to the water cooler, pondering the magnitude of police work in tracking a criminal down. Buford was guilty or he never would have run. He mused on that for a moment. He grabbed the paper cup, held it beneath the faucet, and pushed the button. He pictured himself as a lawman encountering the problems and danger required to chase a crook. Nobody could ever pay him to do that.

He raised the cup to his lips, drained it, then filled it a second time and strolled back to his desk. For now, until the guy was captured, he'd have to settle for other reporting breaks. He'd luck into another exclusive scoop, especially if his mama was right that God and the universe were busy working everything together for his good.

He tossed the empty paper cup into the wastebasket, and then dropped into his chair and sank back. Raising his right leg, he pressed the tip of his shoe against the top edge of the desk and gave a shove. The chair commenced to rotate in a circle. Leaning his head back, he watched the ceiling slowly spin above him and imagined being interviewed by the *Times-Dispatch*.

An hour passed. The large, antique clock on the wall clicked to six forty-five. Ed grew twitchy. Sarah was usually prompt and the sun was already smoldering over the horizon. He continued watching out the window.

The phone rang. Twirling his chair around, he grabbed up the receiver.

"Honey," came her voice. "Don't worry. I'm on my way. Just leaving the house now."

"Great, I was beginning to worry."

"No need. Just sit tight."

He relaxed into his chair. She'd be here soon but wished she'd hurry. He always worried for fear she might get in a wreck. If anything ever happened to her? He couldn't stand the thought and quickly dismissed it.

The roar of Sarah's '31 Deluxe Model-A Roadster, bequeathed from her late father, jolted him out of his concern and he sucked in a breath of relief.

The vehicle came to a stop in front of the building, one tire running up over the curb. He smiled at her usual attempt to parallel-park. He noticed she was alone. Strange. While it would be nice to have dinner without Josephine, it was crucial to have her go tonight.

He rose from the chair and headed for the door, his pulse racing at the thought of Sarah's willowy body gliding into the room. She always smelled good, like the fragrance of blossoms drenching the air after a rain—and her radiant face captivated him every time, especially the way she looked at him with those blue-green eyes of hers. His face flushed just thinking about her.

Sarah breezed in, her burnished mahogany hair fluttering about her shoulders. She wore the powder-blue blouse he loved, a silky, hip-clinging tan skirt and navy high-heels that lengthened her legs.

"Hi, sweetheart," she cooed, putting her arms around his neck and giving him a big kiss. He breathed in her perfume and grinned. She smelled like the yellow tea roses in her garden, the ones with the apricot-tinged petals.

"Where's Josephine?" He gave her a bear hug.

"Oh, Mom had one more errand to run. You know her." She rolled her eyes. "On the go every minute. She said she'd meet us here. Now, honey, don't you worry about this evening. Everything will be fine. Give her time. She'll come around."

"Well, let's hope so. C'mon over to the chair and you can sit on my lap. Nobody here but us."

She giggled. "You're such a romantic, Ed." She sashayed across the room and sank into his lap, putting one arm around the back of his shoulders and looking at him with an angelic smile that set his heart pounding.

"Mmm," she whispered in his ear, "this is nice."

He let out a chuckle. "Can't get too chummy," he teased. "Your mom will be here any minute. So will Richard." He swung the chair around toward the window. "Hope your mom isn't late. I made reservations. I also have some good news to tell both—"

A noise sounded in the back hallway. Ed swiveled the chair back around.

"That you, Richard?" Strange. He never used the back way. He gently nudged Sarah off his lap. She shifted over and perched her hips on the edge of the desk.

In the shadows of the corridor, the figure of a man moved. Ed felt spiders crawling up his back.

He instinctively knew it wasn't Richard.

CHAPTER 8

$\sim\!,\!\sim\!,\!\sim$

Ed squinted, trying to identify the man who stood concealed in the shadowy back corridor. It definitely wasn't Richard. Ed felt a curious dread. Behind him, he heard Sarah's labored breathing.

"We're closed. If you're looking for Mr. Casey, you'll have to return tomor..."

The man took a few more steps. His demeanor was *not* friendly, and something about his walk seemed familiar. Then Ed saw the black ski mask pulled over his face. He immediately leaped out of his chair and stepped in front of Sarah.

"Are you Ed Bowman, the reporter who covered the Buford trial?" The man's stare fixed on him.

A cold fist closed over Ed's heart. "Yes...and you are?"

"Shut up!" The man's eyes blazed. He stepped from the hall into the dimly lit room. Ed saw the gun in his gloved hand and stood mute in shock, his eyes wide. Sarah's breath caught in short spurts.

"This," the man shouted, raising the gun, "is for ruining my life! I could have gotten off."

Ed gave a start. Gunther Buford!

"Honey...under the desk!" He gave her a shove just as a shot rang out. The bullet missed Ed as he lunged forward, slid across the smooth hardwood floor, and wrapped his arms around the man's legs.

Gunther fell to the floor, shoved one foot into Ed's stomach, then wrested himself free and scrambled back to his feet. Ed leapt back up. Gunther swung with the butt of his gun, giving a side-blow to the head. Ed reeled for a second but remained on his feet. Gunther poised his gun for another shot.

Grabbing his wrist with one hand, Ed pried Buford's thumb from the gun handle, forcing it backwards. Gunther let out a shriek and shot his other hand into the side of Ed's temple and pulled the trigger. The gun discharged, then slipped out of his hand and clamored to the floor.

Ed, stunned from the head blow and startled by the gun's report in his ear, lost balance and fell backwards. His full weight dropped with a thud to the floor, his head taking a second blow. Partly conscious, he lay there, unable to move.

Gunther looked down at Ed's motionless body. "Gotcha! You're dead now, Ed Bowman. You won't be writing any more stories." He took a few quick steps over to where the gun lay to retrieve it. Just as he leaned over to grab it, gyroscopic flashes of headlights shot through the front window and circled the walls. A car honked a signal of arrival. Gunther jerked back up, spun around, and fled down the back hallway.

Ed lay for a minute, still dazed. He rose up on one elbow, sat up and shook his head, then maneuvered weakly onto his knees. He remembered the clatter of the revolver hitting the floor and immediately looked for it. He spied the metallic glint, crawled forward and snatched it up.

Balancing on his haunches, he gripped the weapon in both hands and pivoted on his heels toward the hallway. He listened. No sounds. He crept forward, inching his way down the darkened corridor to the back door. Relief swept through him. Buford was gone.

Hurrying back, he looked for Sarah. In the dim light he saw her crumpled on the floor under the desk where he had shoved her. He scooted forward. She had to be scared out of her wits.

"Hon? You can come out now." She wasn't moving. Had she fainted?

He knelt, placed the gun on the floor beside him and leaned over. Her perfume, mingled with the smell of sweat, rushed upward into his nostrils. She moved slightly.

"Thank goodness, you're okay," he gasped. Grabbing hold of her hand, he gave it a reassuring squeeze. "We're safe now. He's gone. Got to call the police right away. Maybe they can catch him."

Still holding Sarah's hand, he reached up with his other hand, felt across the top of the desk and flipped on the lamp. When he looked back down, his breath stalled in his throat. Her face was the pallor of cement. A cold chill washed over him. Her blood-matted mahogany hair draped one cheek. Blood soaked the front of her powder-blue blouse and a pool of red spread on the floor beneath her. Ed's words gushed forth in a loud exhalation.

"Sarah...no...no!" He slid both arms beneath her shoulders and lifted her.

"Sarah, honey... " His throat constricted.

She opened her eyes.

"Ed... Sorry, darling. So glad it wasn't you. Love yo..." She went limp in his arms. Her head fell to one side, her eyes fixed in a vacant stare. Ed blinked in shock. A numb sensation formed in the pit of his stomach. Tears shimmered his vision. He let out a strangling cry.

"Sarah, you can't die!"

He shook her gently. With one hand he pushed her bloodied hair away from her face, then clutched her to his chest as tidal waves of shock and grief swept him into a churning whirlpool of anguish and convulsive sobs. He lowered her from his chest and looked at her through his tears.

"It should have been me, hon...it should have been me. Oh, my sweet, sweet Sarah."

How long he held and rocked her he didn't know, but then anger suddenly took over his grief. Spasms of fury rippled through him. The rising torrent filled his body, swelling up into his throat.

"Gunther Buford!" he ground out between clenched teeth. Grim-lipped, he looked at the gun lying on the floor. Reaching out with one foot, he gave it an angry kick and sent it sliding across the hardwood floor.

At the same moment, the front door opened and the light flipped on. Josephine walked in with Richard close behind.

"Why are the lights..." Her words trailed off. She froze. Both stared at Ed holding Sarah's bloody body and the gun sliding across the hardwood floor.

Josephine's face went pale. She let out a shriek. "Sarah...baby!" Her legs buckled, and she collapsed onto her knees.

Ed looked up at Richard. "Call an ambulance...the police!"

Richard instantly rushed over to the desk, grabbed the phone and began dialing.

Josephine inched her way across the floor on her knees toward Ed, gasping between sobs. "Oh Lord, Ed! What have you done?"

Ed jerked his head with surprise. "Josephine, this is not what you think. There was an intruder..."

Richard hung up the phone and looked down at Sarah's body, his face reflecting shock. "They...said a patrol car was already close by."

The wail of a police siren closed in. Ed rose up, looked over the edge of the desktop and saw the patrol car pull up to the curb. Within seconds, four uniformed men leaped out of the car and burst into the building, guns poised.

Josephine, still sobbing hysterically, stopped long enough to turn and look at them.

"He shot my daughter," she screamed, swiveling back around and pointing at Ed. "He's killed her!" The police focused their guns on him.

Waves of desperation surged through Ed. He looked at Richard. "Tell them! There was an intruder."

Richard looked around and gave a two-shoulder shrug, his face wincing in perplexity.

Two of the policemen rushed forward, wrenched Ed away from Sarah, and yanked him to his feet.

"No. Let me stay," he pleaded. "She's my wife. I didn't do this! It was Gunth—"

One of the cops gave him a hard smack on the side of the head. "Save it," he growled.

Ed struggled against their grasp while they handcuffed his wrists behind his back and dragged him across the floor to the door. Fear palpitated through his body. He twisted around to take a final look at Sarah, and then shot a pleading look at Josephine who now cradled her daughter in her arms.

"Josephine. Tell them...you know I loved her. I couldn't have done this!" She looked up and glowered.

Panic ricocheted through him. Every nerve leaped and shuddered. The officers rushed him through the door, shoved him into the patrol car, and whisked him away.

A day later, in the gray, windowless cell of Hannigan's jail, Ed sat slumped over on the edge of his cot, consumed with the thought he had failed to protect Sarah. Hot tears fell heavy from his eyes. For hours he listened to the pounding of his heart, amazed it could still beat in such anguish.

All of it seemed unreal. He could barely process what had happened. All of it seemed unreal. His long-time dream of becoming a reporter had finally come true and then had turned into a nightmare with his dear, sweet Sarah's murder.

"Don't worry son," his mama had tearfully assured him in an earlier visit. "That man will be caught. Remember, justice always wins out and God..." She broke down. Ed already knew what her next remark would have been—the one about God working everything out for his good.

He hoped she was right, but things didn't look good from his perspective. He failed to convince Hannigan's police captain who the shooter was.

Ed replayed the captain's caustic and derisive words over and over, recalling how he proudly strutted back and forth with the stance of an almighty God who sees all, knows all, and ready to pronounce guilt and execute punishment on the spot.

His fervent declaration of innocence, trying to explain why Buford had it in for him and how the wild shot meant for him killed Sarah instead, fell on deaf ears—the ears of a man pushing for advancement to police chief who needed a big arrest.

"After escaping from jail," the captain barked, "Buford sure wouldn't stick around just to kill one reporter. He'd be running for his life. Plus," he pointed, "your prints are the only ones on the gun. And there's no way to trace a weapon with a defaced serial number."

Heaving waves of despair crashed over Ed. "If you'd only listen—"

"Save it all for the trial." The captain walked out on him.

Ed groaned and held his head in his hands. If only he hadn't written what he'd overheard. If only he hadn't been so absorbed in pursuing a career to impress Josephine. All of it ended up costing Sarah her life.

He would have to live with that forever.

His trial was quick. Josephine never came forward to help— Sarah's death only fueled her negative opinion of him. Richard saw no intruder, so could only testify to what he saw when he walked in. Although Mr. Casey vouched splendidly for his character, there were no witnesses to the shooting to corroborate his innocence.

His court-appointed attorney didn't do much except tell him it wasn't a good idea for him to take the stand. "It will go better for you," he said. Ed believed him.

The jury rendered their decision based on Josephine's declaration, circumstantial evidence, and the police captain's politically ambitious testimony.

The judge's ominous words forced a startled gasp from Ed.

"*Ed Bowman, you have been found guilty by a jury of your peers and are hereby sentenced to the Richmond State Penitentiary for the rest of your natural life.*"

CHAPTER 9

~~~

Three thousand miles away, Gunther Buford hunched over a mustard-colored, four-drawer dresser. A large splintered mirror sat on top, leaning against a wall of faded wallpaper. His breath came hard in the sweltering desert heat, intensified by the muggy air swooshing through the swamp cooler in the window. Mornings were always hot.

He stared at his slightly distorted image in the cracked glass, wiped the moisture from his forehead and studied his face, now bronzed by the desert sun. Sliding both hands over his dyed black hair, he slicked it back and reached for a hand mirror while glancing at his watch. He had forty minutes before reporting to work.

Turning around, he scrutinized the back of his head in the hand mirror and nodded approval. He twisted his lips into a curl of satisfaction. The narrow strip of white hair running from his sideburn to his neckline was no longer visible. He swiveled back to the dresser. Picking up a small gray comb, he leaned into the mirror and meticulously smoothed a few hairs of his new pencil-line mustache.

With his new look and name—Gus Mooreland—plus losing forty pounds, no one would ever recognize him. He hardly recognized himself. Fortunately, cops would be combing the larger cities. They'd never suspect him hiding on the salt flats in this chawbacon town of unsuspecting Mormons who only focused on homemade bread and going to church.

Grabbing his keys from the top of the dresser he crammed them into his pocket. Yes, providence had definitely smiled on him by letting him know about Wendover. Other escaped cons had fled here in the past as well. That didn't mean he liked Wendover. He detested it, but at least he wasn't in a cell waiting to be strapped to ol' Sparky. He scooped up his comb and wallet and stuffed it into his other pocket. Unquestionably, the salt flats and his job on the Western Pacific railroad were perfect to implement his long-range plan.

The ring of the telephone made him turn. He sauntered over to the bedside table and picked up the receiver.

"Yeah?"

"J. J. Dugan here."

"Oh, Mr. Dugan. What's up?"

"Supervisor Hutch asked me to call. Need to change your shift today. Hope you don't mind. Can you take the three o'clock shift in the afternoon instead of this morning? We've got some sun kinks and pull-aparts needing joint bars, also some drilling done about two miles out on the track. Need you to supervise a different crew for that."

"Sure. No problem."

"Thanks, Gus."

He placed the receiver back on the cradle. Not working this morning was fine, but he still intended to go to the depot in time for his on-purpose, ten-minute get-together at the beanery with Kevin. So far, he'd made good headway with the local sheriff. Getting chummy with him was crucial to his plan.

He took a last glance in the mirror and tucked in his khaki work shirt. He drew his lips into a smug smile.

In one more year, he'd have his plan worked out. With a recommendation from Supervisor Hutch, along with his established work record and impressive resumè authenticating his new identity as Gus Mooreland, he could transfer out of Utah to a Western Pacific location in populous California. No one would ever find him after that. He'd be home free with no worries about ever being caught. Since working his way up to Track Foreman the last year, who knew how high he'd go by the time he was transferred? In due course, he'd have a position of authority and respect. He nearly had it at the pen. Come heck or high water, he'd regain it.

He moved quickly over to the bed and plunked down on the edge. Leaning forward, he had barely pulled on his work boots, laced them up and yanked the cuffs of his pants down over the tops, when the bed gave a sudden jolt and the linoleum under his feet vibrated. He glanced at the clock. Right on time.

Within seconds, the predictable screech of the whistle signaled the arrival of the morning train that thundered in from Nevada and passed by on the tracks fifty yards behind his section house.

The whole bedroom shook as the steam engine whooshed past, belching and wheezing with its brakes screaming, preparing its approach to the depot down the road a quarter of a mile. It happened every morning at five, alerting him he had thirty minutes to get to work.

He sat on the bed and wearily pivoted his head in a circle to work the burning tension from his shoulder blades. Even though reassured with the way things were going, he felt like he'd been chewed up, spit out, and then run over by a freight train.

So much had happened in Richmond. His arrest...escape... barely getting out of Virginia after he killed the reporter...dodging the cops in his cross-country flight. Worse yet, he couldn't quit thinking about the warden's daughter. He lowered his head and groaned.

"Sue, if only..." His thoughts thickened with emotion. He should have controlled himself better. All he wanted was love. Her love. Rejection had always been hard for him to handle.

He pushed himself up from the bed and angled back to the dresser. Tugging open the top drawer, he rummaged under his underwear and grasped a large manila envelope. Pulling it out, he shoved his hand inside and touched the object at the bottom. He felt a rush of satisfaction as he slid the blood-encrusted emerald and ruby earring out and fondly held it in his palm. The police had the other one. His big mistake was not taking the time to find it after it fell to the floor during his struggle with Sue. He gently ran his finger over it.

"Your blood." He smiled, stroking the blackened layer embedded around the mother-of-pearl edge. "Part of you is still with me, Sue." Old ripples of longing rose within him. "Definitely, hot," he whispered. If only she had cooperated. He knew she felt the same for him. His stomach knotted. Why did she play so hard to get? He dropped the earring back into the envelope. Why couldn't he seem to let go? She certainly wasn't the first person he'd killed. That list stretched far into his past, starting with his uncaring parents.

Anger tightened his face. Her fault she was dead. She had no right to lead him on with her flirty ways and then not follow through.

"Well, what's done is done," he mumbled, shaking his head. Can't cry over spilt milk. He inhaled deeply. At least he got to have her once. Better than nothing.

He carefully placed the envelope toward the back of the drawer, arranging his underwear and work-stained socks over it.

He glanced at his watch. He needed to hurry. He couldn't miss coffee with Kevin.

The phone rang. He raised a questioning eyebrow and trotted over to the phone. It was Dugan again.

"Gus, sorry to throw a monkey wrench into things, but could you also work three hours this morning with your regular track gang, in addition to this afternoon? Joe just called in sick. With such a long day for you, you can take tomorrow off."

"Sure. Okay with me." He dropped the receiver back on the hook and plodded down the hall.

Lumbering into the kitchen, he swooped up his lunch bucket from the counter, reached for his duckbill hat hanging on a nail, and headed out the front door.

Crossing the tiny yard of baked ground, he started down the dirt road, his lips curling in disgust as he assessed his surroundings. Nothing grew in this alkaline landscape but scrub trees and cottonwoods. Not even grass. The worlds jumping off place if there ever was one.

He pictured Richmond's lush vegetation and cypress trees, sweet gums, azaleas, rhododendrons—especially all the department stores, the Farmers' Market on Franklin, the greasy spoons where he ate, and his usual places of entertainment. Resentment boiled.

"Blast that reporter!" he muttered. "If he hadn't spilled that story, he wouldn't be on the lam. He felt the vein at his neck pulsate. His attorneys could have easily gotten a hung jury, especially after Billy took care of the prosecution's key witness. He heaved a sigh of resignation and then stretched his lips into an icy smile. At least he finished Bowman off.

Approaching the WP Yard, he wrinkled his nose at the oily fumes of diesel fuel. He detested all of it, including the sounds of switch engines, boxcars coupling, the roundhouse's metal saws buzzing, and machinists banging on metal. It was all a horrible racket. Well, he had to get used to it. His future California job would consist of the same.

He strode across the yard and around to the front of the station, angling his steps toward the Beanery. He still had time before reporting for work. He saw Kevin's patrol car and felt he had made headway already with continued opportunities to inveigle him over coffee. Stepping up on the boardwalk that stretched across the front of the building, he pulled the weather-stained, screened door open and stepped inside.

Kevin, tall and angular, sat at the counter in his usual brown uniform, proudly sporting his sheriff's badge of authority on his shirt. Gunther guessed him about thirty-five.

"Hi there, Kevin." Gunther sauntered up to the counter and slid on to the leather-cushioned stool.

Kevin lazily raised an open palm and waved a greeting. "How you doin', Gus?"

"Oh, can't complain. That is, except for having to put up with them pesky cockroaches. First year I was here, spent the whole night trying to squash every one of 'em."

Kevin threw his head back and let out a peal of laughter. "Gus, They're not picking on you, ya know. They infest everyone's homes.

"You likin' your job? You've been here some time now." He blew across the top of his cup and sipped his coffee.

"Sure do." Gunther threw him a convincing grin. "Glad they took me on so quick. Barely landed here when I got hired on."

"Well," Kevin replied, grabbing a napkin and wiping away the frosting on his mouth from a cream-filled doughnut, "anyone willing to work in this desert territory is always grabbed up with open arms. One good thing about you coming…" he gave a teasing grin scrunching up his crows-feet, "…we all enjoy listening to that southern drawl of yours."

Gunther forced a smile, but upset he hadn't managed to rid himself of it yet.

"Well," Gunther said, "aside from the cockroaches, ya know something else? The salt flats are growing on me." At the same he tried to catch the eye of the waitress.

Kevin rendered a jovial chortle. "Good. It happens."

"Hey, Queenie!" Gus called. The waitress, her back to him, stood at the opposite end of the counter. She turned.

"I'll have a cup of that great java of yours."

"Sure, hon. Comin' up."

Gunther eyed her low-cut blouse and ogled her backside when she bent underneath the counter to grab a coffee mug.

"Great gal, huh?" Kevin drawled. "Personality, too."

"Yep," Gus replied. "Sure better'n the one before her. Those butter-bean teeth of that gal could have eaten an ear of corn through a picket fence."

Kevin slapped his hand down on the counter and let out a roar of delight.

"Here's your coffee, hon." Queenie set the ceramic mug on the counter.

Gus planked a dollar bill on the counter. She swept it up with one hand, lowering her crescent-shaped eyelashes long enough to give him a seductive, come-hither look, then turned and sashayed back to the other end of the counter.

"Well, gotta get to work now, Kevin." Gus twirled the stool around and slid off.

"Yeah. Me too, Gus. Good chattin' with you." Kevin stood and dug in his pocket for change to place on the counter.

Gunther sauntered out the front door and headed for the tracks where he knew his crew would be waiting. They hated his guts. He knew that, but he'd had enough bad encounters throughout his childhood to steel him against what people thought of him— even his parents. Sometimes the men complained to Supervisor Hutch but he didn't have to worry about being fired. Getting the job done by being tough is what counted in this no-man's-land. The supervisor was definitely on his side.

He saw the men by the tracks at the rail car waiting for him, then heard his name being called.

"Hey, Gus!"

Gunther turned back. Kevin stood outside the Beanery on the boardwalk.

"Me and the wife are going to Blue Lake Saturday. Why don't you come along? If you've got a girlfriend, bring her too."

"Great, Kevin!" he yelled back. He thought of Queenie. "Thanks for the invite."

"I'll let you know what time, later." Kevin turned, gave a final wave and headed for his patrol car.

Gunther grinned.

He was in.

Chapter 10

Richmond Outskirts - July 15, 1941

~ᵕ~ᵕ~

Spasms of pain screamed down Ed's spine. Scrunched and shackled between fourteen inmates, his bony rear-end bounced against the hard, wood-splintered floor of the swaying cage attached to the back of the moving prison truck. A flashflood of pain like 10,000 volts of electricity shot diagonally across his hips, then into his tailbone and up his back. He gripped one of the cage bars to lessen the impact, stifling a teeth-clenched cry. His breath came in gasping spurts. *No outburst...endure the pain...can't blow this.*

The vehicle rattled down the bumpy, pot-holed road through the blistering, hot Virginia countryside, whipping by sagging fences and locust-buzzing fields. Smothering dust clouds spewed from behind causing hacking coughs to tear through Ed's chest. It ended with a desperate gulp of air that sucked in the putrid stench of the inmates' unbathed bodies. He nearly puked.

He shot a furtive glance up at the guard who sat atop the cage staring down between his opened legs. He held an electric cattle prod, ready to shove the shaft through the bars and zap any troublesome inmate.

Ed scowled. Gunther Buford should be the one enduring all this. The monster murdered his sweet Sarah, the love of his life, and destroyed his career at the *Clarion* along with a promising future with the *Richmond Times-Dispatch.* And his reputation? He hard-knuckled his fists. He could only imagine what people in Hannigan thought of him now. Josephine was probably on cloud nine, telling everyone how right she was.

Four wretched years with no hope of parole or pardon. Neither God nor the principles of the universe had enacted any justice for him. Nothing had worked out for good like his mama promised.

Well, he could no longer wait for God. He would take matters into his own hands—track down Sarah's killer and bring him to justice. Make him pay. Get his life back. Was there any possibility he could escape from where he was being taken? That question, like a cankerworm, lay coiled in his brain eating away.

He painfully pulled out one bent leg from beneath him and shifted to his other. Barely had he done so when a sudden shout came from one of the prisoners, startling all the inmates.

"Can't stand it anymore!" the man yelped. In loud exhalations and heaving chest, one of the prisoners struggled to his feet, straightening his body as tall as he could.

The long cattle prod shot down through the metal bars thwacking the man on the shoulder with the dreaded sound of the electric spark and sizzle. Ed instinctively hunkered back out of range, recalling the one time he connected with a prod.

Zaaap-clack-clack-clack.

The inmate let out a piteous shriek and fell to the floor, arms flaying, muscles contracting, his fingers turning claw-like.

"Ain't no way you got any liberties!" the guard yelled down. "Now sit, and stay that way!"

The inmate, his breathing labored, lay still for a few minutes on the wooden floor, and then rolled over on his back. His stomach began to rise and fall in waves.

Ed recoiled. He knew what that meant. So did the other prisoners. They scooted back as fast as they could, shackles clanking, chains scraping against the wooden floor. Ed followed suit, shoving up against the men's bodies where they huddled in the farthest corner of the cage.

And just in time.

Greenish vomit shot like a projectile from the man's mouth splattering all over the floor and landing on a few prisoners' pant legs. Ed wrinkled his nose. It smelled like a mix of a dead polecat and feces. He stared at the nauseating scene and the flies swarming toward the greenish mess. His stomach rolled, but he managed to quell his gag reflex.

Prison life was worse than he imagined. The guards' penchant for brutality and inhumane treatment was unbelievable. He straightened his aching back to take more air into his lungs but slumped back into a hunched position. Too many beatings had taken their toll on his now thin frame. How he stayed alive this long was a puzzle. Now, he was headed for something worse.

Men sent to where he was going could expect an early death—so he was told. He shuddered. Would he survive long enough to plan a successful escape? Did he have the strength? He had lost 40 pounds since his incarceration and was in lousy condition physically to try anything. Moreover, did he have the guts? A cold chill traced his spine.

He lowered his head and stared at the number 405 printed on the tattered, sweat-soaked uniform hanging on his emaciated body.

Gone was the physique Sarah so admired. He wiped away the sweat dripping from his shaved head and imagined her fingers running through his once thick hair, then slid his hand down over the small, rope-like scar at his eyebrow running down his cheek. The injustice of his situation welled up like bile.

He leaned forward, elbows on his folded legs, and curled both fists beneath his chin. Pulling off an escape would take hard-hitting, fearless follow-through. He could be shot in the attempt. Did he have the daring to chance that?

Normally, he wasn't an aggressive guy, mostly passive, doing what others told him, and never ruffling the waters. In his opinion, timid and unassertive. The bravest thing he ever did was getting up the gumption to hound Mr. Casey for his advancement. Even at the trial, talking to the other reporters took a lot of courage. Yet, in his mind, especially in daydreams, he was the complete opposite—confident, self-possessed, assertive. Which man was he? Did any of the inmates wonder the same about themselves? He looked at their hardened faces, sullen eyes and set jaws soured by years of imprisonment, trying to decipher their expressions.

He pondered the option of not escaping. He knew what would happen. The insidious environment, like a carnivorous monster, eventually swallowed each inmate one slow gulp at a time. What followed was dissolution of body, mind and spirit until nothing remained but the mangled and decayed remains of what was once a man. He visualized his life plunging downward into worthlessness, nonbeing, a cipher—zilch. He'd turn into something worse than being timid and unassertive. What if he already had? Wave-spumes of desperation crashed over him. He couldn't let that happen. He pushed his shoulders back and flexed his chest. He would escape, or die trying.

First, he needed to find an ally—someone willing to help in case he needed last minute help. Preferably a prisoner with only a short time left of his sentence who wouldn't want to blow it by tagging along.

He twisted his neck around, sweeping his gaze over the inmates and zeroed in on one sitting by the bars. His shirt identified him as 602.

Like most prisoners, the man's thin shoulders were hunched. His mutilated ear, whiskey nose with flared nostrils, and large, bulging eyes gave him a ghoulish look. That was one more consequence of prison. A man's looks simply changed.

Wearily rolling his head around his shoulders to work the strain from his neck, he then wriggled between the men's slimy, foul-smelling bodies and shoved his way through an open space by the bars where 602 and others knelt, their bedraggled faces pressed against the cage bars. Scrawny arms and stick-like fingers groped through the openings as much as their wrist chains allowed, hoping to touch a hanging tree branch whizzing by, a roadside bush, anything to help them connect to the world they once belonged.

Ed took a moment and did the same, reaching out his arm and gawking with wonder as the truck shot past sun-parched tobacco plantations and sweet potato farms. He breathed in the heady fragrance of spearmint, chicory, the musky odor of freshly plowed soil, and his heart leapt at the sight of a vendor's truck sitting in a field crammed with watermelons. Cardinals on fence posts, startled by the speeding vehicle, took off in a flurry of red and gray, their bodies silhouetted against the brilliant sparkle of the James River. Every sight and intoxicating smell throbbed with life at its best, a life he felt desperate to reclaim.

He deliberately cleared his throat to get 602's attention.

"I've never been on a chain gang before," he ventured. "What's it like where we're headed?" Six-o-two gave him a cold, unblinking stare before responding in a flat monotone.

"Pretty grisly." He briefly fingered his mutilated ear.

Ed cocked an inquisitive brow, fighting to sound casual. "So, it's as bad as they say?"

"Well," 602 responded with a wave of his hand and rattle of wrist chains, "probably better if you stay ignorant. No sense agonizing over what's gonna happen. Nothin' you can do about it anyway."

Not agonize? Ed's jaw clamped down hard. What else was there to do?

"The grapevine says it's worse than the pen," Ed pushed.

"Remains to be seen," 602 responded. He turned away, signaling the end of their conversation. The hope for more exchange gnawed at Ed, but some inmates were like that.

He nodded an acknowledgement.

At least, he broke through.

The truck veered a sharp right onto a dirt road lined with scrub trees. Ed grabbed one of the bars, grimacing as his tailbone hit the wood floor. The truck rumbled two hundred more yards then came to a stop in a wide-open clearing.

The door of the cab flew open and a stocky man in a rumpled, brown uniform jumped out. He strode to the rear of the vehicle. Fumbling in his pocket, he pulled out a key and unlocked the cage padlock. Yanking the door open, he reached inside, grabbed a four-step stool and placed it on the ground.

"Okay, get out," he ordered.

Ed didn't know whether to feel relief or fear. What awaited him?

The fourteen inmates, their emaciated faces tense and drawn, stood and hobbled forward one by one, dragging their duffel bags. Climbing down into the crushing heat with the white-hot sun hammering down on their baldheads, they lined up a few yards from the truck.

Ed shuffled to the doorway behind 602 and stepped onto the rear of the truck bed. Steadying his shackled feet on the edge he climbed down, at the same time giving a quick scan of the place.

He felt the blood drain from his face.

Through the shimmering waves undulating from the baked terrain, he saw it—one hundred yards down the dirt road surrounded by a fence—the place prisoners whispered about.

The place no one expected to survive.

CHAPTER 11

~·~·~

The abrupt stop of the prison truck stirred up cumulous billows of gritty, strangling dust. Ed stifled a cough as he shuffled across the turfless ground to where the rest of the shackled prisoners stood in line. The sun hovered like a red-hot ball of glowing metal over them and the heat radiated from the ground like a blast furnace.

Ed shaded his eyes with his hand, squinting against the blinding glare. He knew it would be bad, but not this bad. The desolate landscape walloped him like he'd been thrown into a body slam. They were in the middle of nowhere on a parched stretch of sun-cracked land consisting only of a few tufts of weeds and rock.

He stared at the baked, colorless ground. Idyllic pictures of Hannigan rushed in with all its kaleidoscopic colors and smells—Sarah's flowers, the fresh scent of cut grass, wet smell of water, and the click-click-click of the lawn sprinkler. He dug his teeth into his lower lip. Nothing like that here. Only the rank of sweat-soaked men, his own body's stink, and the putrid odor of throw-up wafting from the cage.

Six-o-two, observing Ed's expression, moved in closer. "What'd ya expect?"

Ed crimped his mouth. "Just thinking. Sure a far cry from the lush surroundings I enjoyed in Hannigan. To come from that," he gestured with a sweep of his hand, "to this. It's as if God forgot this place."

"God?" Six-o-two gave Ed a long, cursorily look and rubbed the back of his neck. "He don't have nothin' to do with nothin'. How long ya been in?"

"Four years, six months."

"You'll get used to it," came the listless response. "Give it a little more time."

Ed let out a slow breath. No amount of time would ever make him get used to it.

He took in the rest of the sun-scorched area stretching 200 feet square around him. If he did make it over the fence, there were no trees or bushes for hiding except around the far edge of the perimeter. There, thin clumps of scrub trees and a few scrawny Box Elders and Yellowwoods stood like stem pipes, too skinny to even throw a shadow let alone hide behind. Nothing appeared in his favor.

Checking to see if the guard was looking, he shot a more studied look down the worn pathway that led to the compound. He didn't like what he saw.

Through the compound's fence, three run-down buildings and a few drab, gray tents sat on the sun-blistered ground. All of it exuded an ominous air. He unconsciously wrinkled his nose. A far cry from his green-carpeted yard full of Sarah's fragrant flowers. Any smell from that place would be the rotten odor of sweaty men and the stench of death.

"You'll never get outta that place," came 602's wry comment. "And don't expect any help from me if you try."

Ed minced his lips, surprised 602 picked up on his intentions. The guy just didn't understand. This place was his last chance. All the same, 602's discouraging comment affected him. Was he right? If he managed to escape, could he move fast enough across this clearing, get to the spindly trees and the highway, without being seen? More importantly, how could he hitchhike to Richmond's train yards 30 miles away without being identified by his stripped suit? He felt like a racehorse tethered at the starting gate, hearing the bugle but unable to run.

"Go *get'em tiger. You can do it!*" Sarah's words from the morning of the trial elbowed their way inside his head sparking his determination.

Yes. He could do it. Maybe God and the universe had simply delayed for some good reason and would help him at some point. By taking things into his own hands he would only be giving God a helpful shove in the right direction.

"Stop lookin' around so much," 602 muttered, his voice edged with annoyance. "You're givin' yourself away. The juice ain't worth the squeeze."

Six-o-two's words twisted through his soul like a corkscrew. He couldn't ignore his feelings. Rumbling deep in every fiber of his being was his obsession to escape and track Buford—make him pay for Sarah's murder and get his life back. It pounded like a jackhammer in his bones, throbbed through his veins and wrenched his gut until he could hardly stand it. It's all that kept him going.

What did his mama always say? *Plan your work and then work your plan.* If he had any hope for a future that's what he needed to do—quit paying attention to all the negatives, and strategize a foolproof plan—but one step at a time. In the meantime, 602 might drop some useful information.

"Probably won't be much different here than at the pen," Ed said, hoping for any tidbit.

Six-o-two cautiously checked the whereabouts of the driver and guard before responding. They were looking under the truck's hood.

"No difference, except for," he said in hushed response, "Boss Jeb."

For a split second Ed suspended his breathing. He'd almost forgotten.

"Yeah, heard about him," he whispered back. "Maybe the rumors are exaggerated. I mean, how could anyone be worse than the bosses at the pen?"

The hood of the truck slammed shut. Ed drew in a quick breath as a guard eyed him.

"Straighten up yur line, 405!"

Ed gave a reluctant tug on his duffel bag and shuffled in closer to the inmate on his left.

The guard strode to the head of the line and knelt down. Up and down, up and down he went like he was genuflecting, checking each prisoner's shackles.

"Face it," 602 grunted, picking at a snaggletooth with his fingernail, "we ain't gettin' out of here alive."

"Think so?" Ed took a deep breath. "Well, I have no intention of dying in this God-forsaken place or letting my life deteriorate like the rest of these poor souls." He gave a toss of his head down the line toward the hardened faces of the other inmates. Old or young, felon or misdemeanant, it made no difference. Anger creased their deeply etched, leathery faces. Sunken, expressionless eyes displayed bitter despair.

"Maybe it's too late for them," Ed insisted in a low tone, "but not for me. I'm going to get my humanity and self-respect back, make a decent life for myself, hold down a steady job again—"

Six-o-two shook his head. "Quit dreamin'."

Why, Ed wondered, did he pick this guy?

The driver looked up from where he knelt. "Shut up! Didn't I tell ya? No talkin'!"

Ed clamped his mouth shut but turned slightly, staring in an unblinking gaze at the compound again, trying to guesstimate the size and height of the fence. He pictured himself in a full run.

"Nothing," Ed said, turning to 602, "is going to stop me fr—"

Six-o-two cleared his throat. "Shhh…"

The guard, checking each man's fetters, moved closer until he knelt in front of Ed. Examining his shackles, he gave a vicious wrench on his ankle fetters. Ed clamped his jaw tight against the pain. The raw ulcers on his ankles were now bleeding.

The guard stood with a grunt like a potbelly pig, and waddled back to the truck. Yanking the cab door open, he groped behind the front seat, pulled out a heavy squad chain and let it drop to the ground with a thud. Picking up one end, he dragged it over to the string of men, and threaded it through the iron rings of their wrist shackles.

"Okay, get moving!" the driver snarled, motioning them down the pathway toward the compound.

Linked together, dragging their duffel bags, the bony men hunched over in the incinerator-like heat and lumbered forward, their bodies sagging, heads drooping like diseased plants suffering root damage. All shackles jangled in rhythm to the men's shuffling feet, their walk resembling the burdened tread of men on their way to the gallows.

"How you doing, 602?" Ed's tongue felt like one huge cotton ball. He could hardly pry his inside cheeks and gums apart with his tongue.

Six-o-two didn't respond. His eyes were focused on the gated entrance to the compound.

Ed looked up at the gray, weather-beaten sign hanging over the entranceway. *State of Virginia Division of Corrections—Road Camp*

Nine. His lips went tight. *Death Camp Nine*, he silently corrected.

Three guards stood to one side of the entrance, legs astride, rifles poised. Their callous, power-hungry expressions foretold what Ed could expect. Same as at the pen—brutality. Another guard gripped leashes that held back two bloodhounds straining against their collars, their loose jowls dripping saliva.

Ed hobbled through the gate with a suffocating weight of dread. Could he really escape from a place everyone called Hell?

Chapter 12

~~~

Ed trudged through the gate of the chain gang camp, his legs aching from the weight of the chains and the shackles rubbing the bleeding sores on his ankles. He studied the fence encircling the perimeter, topped with five rows of sharp, barbed wire. His heart sank. No chance of climbing over that. No chance at all.

He examined the elevated gun platform to his left, a rectangular structure on stilts rising six feet higher than the fence. A guard, his rifle cradled in one arm, looked down from the window and grinned.

Ed pushed in close to 602.

"Look at him," he said in guarded tones. "Sure tells us a lot about what we can ex—"

"Okay, you slime balls," the truck driver barked, cutting Ed off. "Stop here."

Upon cue a guard exited a tent and swaggered forth like he was king of the hill. Clutching a rifle in one hand he handed it to a trustee, and then planted both feet firmly on the ground, legs apart, both hands behind his back, and peered down his nose.

"Take a good look, men," he snarled. He turned and pointed to a rickety shed a few yards away.

A half-naked prisoner lay sprawled on the ground, his clothes in shreds. Blood, the color of aged Burgundy, pooled on the hard ground around him. His backside, arms and legs were raw where chunks of flesh had been torn away. The man's mouth hung open, his vacuous face frozen in muted agony.

"That's a prisoner who tried to escape this morning. Hounds got him."

Ed stood transfixed, his face glazed with shock. Torture, he understood. After four years it was a way of life, but he never had his flesh ripped off by dogs.

"So," the guard continued, his eyes narrowing, "I shouldn't have to say nothin' to you worthless scum bags about escaping.

There ain't no way you're gonna get outta here."

Ed's heart shriveled. "Is he dead?" he choked out in a bare whisper.

"If he is," 602 muttered back, "consider him lucky."

A pulse of sickness swept through Ed. If he escaped like this poor guy tried, the dogs would get him for sure. That left only one solution—a plan he'd been mulling over.

If he managed things right, barring any unforeseen problems from the notorious Boss Jeb, he could work up to the position of trustee. At the pen they drove trucks outside the confines to get supplies. Could he manage that here? With a vehicle there would be no smells for the hounds to track, giving him lead-time. He would not have to wear a striped uniform, and his hair would have grown back. With no chains or shaved head to betray him, he'd have a fighting chance.

The guard walked over to the body and gave it a hard kick. The man let out a cry followed by a deep, gurgling moan.

"Still alive." He turned to two trustees. "You know where to take him."

The trustees shared an uneasy look with each other. One grabbed the man's arms, the other his feet, and they carried the quivering body toward the rear of the compound and disappeared behind some tents.

Ed widened his eyes in curiosity. What's back there? He needed to find out.

"All right you creeps, move forward."

The rattle and clank started up again. Three escort-guards with shotguns moved in and positioned themselves at strategic points.

Ed limped along, making sure he didn't miss a thing. He riveted his dust-swollen eyes on the stocks, commonly called the Jack, a five-foot square wooden board standing upright in the center of the yard with vertical side-braces fixed into the ground. The huge plank contained two holes in the upper half for a prisoner's arms, two on the bottom for the feet, placed high enough so one's body hung rather than braced by the ground. A hinge with a padlock at the side allowed the top half of the board to be lifted from the bottom half.

"Take a look," 602 mumbled.

"Yeah," Ed returned under his breath. "Spent six horrible hours in the Jack. A day I sure don't want to remember."

"Know what you mean," 602 nervously swallowed. "But that ain't all." He motioned with his head.

Near the fence stood a perpendicular coffin-like structure, narrow in width and six feet high. The sweatbox. With no room to lie or sit down and exposed to the fierce rays of the sun and freezing cold at night, a man could die if left in for too long.

"Yep, I see it. No one has to tell us what *that* is."

"Nope." Six-o-two's face changed to a dark mask. "Sure don't. Only been in the infernal contraption once."

"Once is enough for any man." Ed said

He continued his visual sweep of the yard and took in six prison cages called pie-wagons. He had seen others like them at the pen. Made of wood and mounted on wheels they were eighteen feet long, seven feet wide and high, with steel bars crisscrossing the front. A wrinkled tarp lay on the roof to drop down in case of bad weather. Used to transport prisoners to work sites, they also served as living quarters. Each cage contained three or four cots.

"Probably where we'll be sleeping." Ed groaned, shifting his grip on the squad chain to stretch his swollen fingers. "The few I've seen," he said, wrinkling his nose, "always smelled like rotting garbage and looked like wild animal cages."

"Well," Six-o-two retorted, "Ain't that what we're supposed to be?"

Ed bridled. His mama always told him he was the apple of God's eye. Was he or wasn't he? No evidence of that so far.

They lumbered farther into the compound. Their destination, judging from the direction they were being led, was a dilapidated, clapboard barrack.

"Okay, stop here!"

The men came to a halt. The familiar smell of fried pig fat and aromatic fragrance of coffee wafted through the open doorway, immediately identifying it as the mess hall.

An unkempt, gorilla-like figure slowly emerged from inside the building. Sharp talons closed around Ed's gut. He then got his first glimpse of the man he had heard so much about—Boss Jeb.

Three hundred pounds of blubber moved into the harsh

sunlight. An open shirt and missing buttons exposed the man's bare chest and stomach. In his fifties, his fat-sagging belly spilled into folds over the top of his belt and down to a gun holster strapped around his hips.

Ed stared into the bloated face and the man's watery eyes that resembled two raw, blood-streaked eggs. Above the venomous smile, his nose immediately caught Ed's attention. Large and hooked like an eagle's beak, it prefigured a man determined to conquer.

An ominous foreboding swept through Ed. His stomach pitched and went rock hard, recalling the many warnings he heard back at the pen.

"Of all the guards, watch out for Boss Jeb."

"A real monster," others said.

The grim reality of their words hit hard as Ed took in the grotesque figure.

He held his breath and waited for the monster to speak.

CHAPTER 13

~⁀~⁀~

Boss Jeb's gargantuan body filled the doorway of the mess hall. He spat a quid of tobacco that landed in a brown splat on the bottom step, then moved a few paces across the threshold and onto the landing. His bloodshot eyes narrowed in disdain.

"You're a miserable lot," he sneered, his voice brimming with distaste. "If you think you're gonna have it easy on this here chain gang, you ain't—and it don't make no difference whether you're from the county jail or the pen.

"Welcome to hell. I'm the devil in charge." He moved one hand down to his holster and slowly ran his fingers over the handle of his revolver.

Ed's breath caught short. It didn't take any brains to see Jeb would be his most formidable obstacle. He had underestimated everyone's warnings.

"My best trait as chief guard and boss over this here road gang," Jeb snorted, strutting to the edge of the porch landing and peering down his beaked nose, "is enforcing punishments. So, here's the rules."

Just what Ed was waiting to hear. Monster or not, if he kept all the rules perfectly he could avoid any run-ins with the guy and make trustee. Everything counted on that. If he failed, he might as well kiss the rest of his life goodbye.

"You say, 'Yes boss' and 'No boss' to all guards and me," Jeb continued, breathing hard through his open-mouth, "except..." he motioned with a twist of his head toward a wood-framed house, "...to the Captain, who ain't here right now."

Ed glanced over at the neatly painted white house with yellow trim standing in contrast to the rest of the unsightly tents and buildings. Would the captain be like Jeb?

"To him," Jeb said, his beefy chest laboriously heaving with every word, "you remove your cap and say, 'Yes, Captain' or 'No, Captain,' and only when spoken to. Remember," he hissed, "you don't sass a free man. If any of you get belligerent, you get the leather...or worse. And," he added, "if you got any rabbit in your blood and are thinkin' of hangin' it on the limb, forget it, you won't make it—especially you guys from the pen. You'll be recognized right off with your shaved heads—and I don't need to tell you about the dogs."

Ed's toes curled in his shoes. He gave a furtive side-glance at 602 to check his reaction, but his expressionless eyes were set like chinks in his face.

Jeb slowly descended the three remaining steps, each thump of his massive legs threatening the rickety structure. Stepping out in front of the line of men, he paraded back and forth in a cocky strut, sweat sliding down his bare chest in rivulets.

Ed smelled the man's body odor as he passed, a stench between a chicken coop and a dead cat.

Jeb strode back and forth, slow and confident, insinuating himself with purposeful intent like the gliding of a boa constrictor sizing up its prey. He paused just long enough to give a few inmates scathing stares. His glance proved withering and each man's head tick-tocked down like the hands of a clock. Ed saw their looks of despair and sensed the pulse-revving beat of their hearts.

Resuming his grandiose speech, Jeb's blubberous belly pulsated with every word.

"Every day except weekends you'll be taken out on the road. You'll labor from dawn to sundown, fourteen hours a day, two smoke breaks and dinner on the road.

"I'll be your 'walking boss, so..." he leaned forward, his cobra-like eyes riveting on the men, "...you better learn how to keep the lick. And there'll be no eye-ballin'. That means no staring at cars or people in the free world. Anyone caught doing that spends a night in the box."

Tucking both thumbs inside his belt he gave his trousers an upward yank, spewed out another tobacco wad, then motioned with his hand to the truck driver.

"Undo 'em, Bubba."

The driver fumbled through his pants pocket and pulled out a key. Stepping to the end of the line, he picked up the end of the squad chain, shoved the key into the iron padlock, and gave the hinge a hard twist. The inmates knew what to do. They hefted the huge weight, sliding it through their iron rings until the full length lay coiled on the ground like a monstrous dead snake.

Jeb turned and gestured to someone inside the mess hall. "Get out here, Jim!"

A lanky trustee with bulging eyes too large for his face appeared in the doorway. Hunched over, looking like a scarecrow with no pole to hold him up, he gripped a large galvanized pail of water in one hand. He sidled down the steps and hustled forward, waddling from side to side like a duck with frozen feet. One leg appeared lame.

"You think he's a snitch?" Ed asked 602 in low tones while he studied Jim as he walked by. "Some trustees are squealers."

"A lot are," 602 whispered. "Ya never know. But you gotta watch 'em. Out on the road if anyone looks like he's trying to escape, even if he ain't, trustees will be the first to shout, 'Man gone.' The escapee will be shot, and as long as he's dead and can't protest his innocence, the snitch will be granted an immediate parole as reward."

Ed recoiled. He understood. Prison was no picnic. Who wouldn't want to get out? He studied Jim with mixed feelings. As much as he hated to admit it, if as trustee he had the prospect of reducing his sentence or going free, he might do something like that. He caught himself and let out a muted groan. The inmate mentality was already seeping in. He had to get out before it completely took over.

Trusty Jim scurried over to a wide tree stump and tossed a couple of potato sacks as towels onto the ground. Picking up two dented tin basins from the ground, he hit the bottom a couple of times with the heel of his hand and tapped the dust out, and then placed them on top of the stump and poured the bucket of water into them.

"Okay." Jeb grumbled, giving the men one last contemptuous look. "Line up and wash, then go get your feed." Swiveling around, he thumped back up the rickety stairs. An old hound ambled out of the mess hall and stretched its body full length out on the landing. Jeb stopped long enough to lean over and give the animal an affectionate scratch behind the ears before disappearing inside the building.

The guy cares for dogs? Ed was unable to picture Jeb capable of loving anything.

Looking forward to the basin of water, he followed the men to the stump where each man in turn splashed water on his face, and then lined up near the mess hall where Jim knelt to check their shackles before they could enter.

Ed, after washing, angled his way over to stand in the mess line with 602. He peered around the corner of the mess hall into the rear of the compound, hoping to see something that might fit into his escape plan.

The acreage stretched some sixty yards to the back fence to a guard tower rising high in the air. Next to it was a chicken-wired kennel where four bloodhounds were heaving themselves against the pen, baying at the scent of the newcomers. Ed could almost smell their sweaty bodies and pondered the likelihood of outrunning a dog. His stomach went queasy remembering the inmate the dogs chewed up.

He swept his gaze to a small tool shed sitting amidst clumps of brown weeds. Parked next to it was a road scraper, an old Model-T flat-bodied truck, and four prison vehicles with cages on the back for hauling prisoners. He also spied a small, two-windowed whitewashed building. His eyebrows climbed. No indication what it was for. He turned to 602.

"You think that building near the kennel is another tool shed?" he asked, motioning with his head.

"Dunno," 602 said, looking over Ed's shoulder. "Don't look like it. Too large. Could be where the guards took that guy they caught escaping. They headed that way."

Shuffling up to the head of the line, Jim gave a tug on his ankle chains. "Okay," came his low, monotone voice, "file in for chow."

Ed maneuvered up the steps with his chains, dragging his duffel bag, hoping once inside he might connect with another inmate—a possible ally more congenial than 602.

Entering the hall, the sickening odor of sweat-caked bodies rushed into his nostrils, and sunken, hollow-eyed faces glanced up from the tables giving the new inmates the once-over.

The oblong-shaped hall with its drab, rough-hewn floors and walls were filled with wooden tables and benches separated by an aisle down the middle. Whites sat on one side, Blacks and Mexicans on the other. Like the pen, it was an arrangement imposed by both guards and prisoners. Ed estimated about fifty men.

He studied the sullen faces, searching for a half way friendly one, but like all cons their expressions were set in concrete. Any one of them looked like they would easily shove a shiv into a man's back for something as minor as a sneeze.

Two burly guards, their eyes narrowed to squints and six-shooters on their hips, stood on a raised platform at the front of the hall, watching. Stepping down from the platform, they began pacing the aisles constantly turning their heads back and forth, their steel-cold eyes making malevolent sweeps from table to table.

"Looks like they're hoping for a reason to shoot someone," Ed said.

"Ain't you got that figured out by now?" 602 grumbled. Ed said nothing and continued his survey.

To the right, an open door led into the kitchen. The robust smell of coffee quickly turned Ed's thoughts to food. He gave 602 a shove.

"Let's chow down." They scooted toward a table and slid onto a splintery bench, shoving their duffel bags underneath.

The meal, much like at the pen, consisted of a square of dry corn pone, three slices of fried pig fat and a dose of sorghum.

"Whatever happened to Hoover's promise of a chicken in every pot?" Ed said humorously, hoping to lighten 602's mood.

Six-o-two rolled his eyes in disgust and kept on eating.

Ed remembered the scene near the gate. "Guess the escapee is dead," he said between mouthfuls.

"Yeah," 602 spluttered, stuffing a piece of corn pone into his mouth. "And don't figure it won't happen to you."

Ed ignored his remark and then nudged him in the ribs with his elbow. He cocked his head in the direction of a prisoner who sat at the next table. "Look. Over there." Young, maybe twenty, the youth's blonde hair fell into thick bangs over his forehead.

"Must be a Fish," Ed speculated. "Doesn't look like he's been in jail before."

"Yep." 602 glanced up. "His head ain't shaved neither, so he's not from the pen. Must be a county bird."

"Sorta feel sorry for him," Ed said, shoving a piece of pork fat into his mouth and washing it down with coffee. "He doesn't have the hard face of a criminal. Looks rather innocent. Wonder if he got a bum rap, like I did?"

"Yeah, right," 602 mumbled.

Ed bristled, wondering how much more he could take of 602. He kept his eyes on the Fish. His hope rose a little. He looked like a good prospect to win over.

"Meal's over!" a trustee barked.

Ed felt a nervous flutter in his belly. What next? More from Boss Jeb? He mentally sifted through the rumors about the man.

All the warnings had to mean something.

Chapter 14

～～～

"Chow's over! File outside and get in line!" Benches scooted and shackles scraped across the worn, wood floor of the mess hall. Ed dragged his duffel bag to the door and stepped outside into the sweltering Virginia heat. The late afternoon sun bounced off the ground with a vengeance. Six-o-two followed. Jeb stood nearby overseeing everything with an eagle eye.

Ed counted the number of trustees. He noticed no lack. What if they didn't need any more? A worm of panic slithered through his stomach.

"You're doing it again," 602 warned. Ed didn't respond. He focused on the trustees herding the men into two lines, regulars in one, new arrivals in the other. The regulars were immediately led off to cages near the captain's house.

The process continued, leaving Ed, 602 and five other men with Jim. Three trustees carried sheets, gunnysacks and brown denim uniforms in their arms indicating no more prison stripes. A guard with a shot gun stood ready to follow.

Ed did his math. With four to five men per cage being the max, the six of them would be split up. He scrutinized the six inmates' grim faces. Which ones would he end up with? Making trustee and escaping depended on as much information he could glean from whomever he caged with. None of them looked very promising.

"Start movin.'"

"Trusty Jim," his nickname from what Ed surmised during table talk in the mess hall, motioned for them to follow. His voice was timid and faint—mumbly, Ed decided, like men at the pen whose spirits had been broken. He leaned over to 602.

"Listen to the way he sounds. He's lost it already. That's not going to happen to me. I'm still Ed Bowman—"

"Yeah? Well, don't be so sure. My name's Duff, and that don't make no difference at all. You ain't a name anymore, just a number. Best you get that into your head."

Ed bristled. "Well, maybe that's how it is for you, but not for me."

Duff shrugged the comment off.

They headed for the other two pie-wagons, each placed end-to-end with a chicken-wired guard booth wedged in-between.

"Okay, stop here!" Jim shouted, his voice now decisive and commanding.

Ed raised his eyebrows. What a difference now Jim was out of Boss Jeb's earshot. He even stood up straighter like a pole had been shoved up his spine. Maybe being in charge of inmates was the way a man got some degree of respect and self-worth back. He could use some of that.

The three trustees handed out the denim uniforms, two bed sheets, and a tin spoon.

"Now, listen up!" Jim said in his new voice

Ed anticipated more rules. Right now, learning them was his priority. His second priority was befriending inmates in his cage so he could pump them for information about the camp and Jeb. Even though they were also new arrivals, rumors flew and were passed on. He might pick up something.

"Here's the rules," Jim began. "When you get inside your cage you'll start off with the two clean sheets you just got handed. Shove the dirty ones through the bars of your cage where they will be picked up. On laundry day you'll get one clean sheet. Toss out the bottom one through the bars. Put your top sheet on the bottom and the clean one on top. Don't throw out the wrong sheet or you'll spend a night in the box. Bring your spoon with you on the job. If you forget it or lose it, you don't eat."

Simple enough, Ed thought with confidence.

After placing four inmates in one cage, he came to the last one. Ed and two other men were left. That meant he was stuck with 602 or, he corrected himself, Duff. He didn't know the other inmate. Would he get anything out of him?

Jim moved up the creaky steps of the cage and thrust his key into the padlock. Giving it a hard twist, he tugged the door open. The rusty hinge screeched like a prisoner in agony. Ed and the other two climbed up the wobbly steps.

"Pick your bunks," Jim ordered.

Moving through the doorway, a putrid smell assaulted Ed's nostrils. It was worse than a stinky outhouse. He glanced at the floor. It was crusted over with greenish-yellow crud. He guessed it a conglomeration of vomit, urine and excrement. He felt like puking.

The four cots were lined against the back wall, the ends facing out toward the bars. Ed dragged his feet down the narrow, two-foot aisle and stared at the filthy, straw-filled mattresses. Small holes guaranteed the presence of mice. Who knew what else? A thunder bucket sat on the floor beside each cot, along with a galvanized pail of drinking water and a dipper.

Ed chose the cot at the far end. Duff plopped down in the next bed. The other inmate took the one near the door leaving one empty cot between them indicating he didn't want to talk with anyone. Not a good sign, Ed thought.

Leaning over, Ed pulled back the edge of the blanket. The sheets, glazed with dirt, felt slimy to the touch. He cringed as two cockroaches scurried from beneath the blanket.

He immediately yanked the filthy sheets off from the cot, then reached over to the bars and stuffed them through the narrow opening onto the ground. He smoothed the clean sheets onto his bed hoping they'd smother the stench of the mattress. Good thing his mama didn't live long enough to see the squalor he had to live in.

"Get on your cot, your feet toward the end."

Jim bent over and grabbed the end of a heavy chain lying coiled in one corner. Marching down the aisle, he threaded the night chain into the rings at the bottom of each cot, through the men's ankle shackles, and then padlocked the end of the long chain to a u-shaped contrivance protruding from the floor.

Ed blinked at the heavy chain. No way to break those. He glanced through the bars. The guard, ready with the shotgun, stood outside, his finger on the trigger.

"I'll be the night watchman in that coop." Jim pointed to the wire-covered enclosure between the cages. "I'm responsible for keeping order just like the BT's at the pen. At second bell, it's lights out. If you have to get up to use the bucket, you ask, 'Getting up here?' Then you wait for me to call back and tell you it's okay.

Wake-up time is three thirty a.m. When you exit the cage in the morning, bring your thunder buckets with you and empty them into the pit outside."

He lit the kerosene lamp swinging from a bent nail on the ceiling, and then sauntered out the door locking it behind him with a loud snap. Ed shuddered at the ominous sound. It reverberated through the cage like the jaws of a steel trap clamping shut.

Sitting on the edge of his cot, he scrutinized the inmate near the door.

Nearly as repulsive looking as Duff, black stubble covered his face except for bare spots of pockmark scars. His mottled teeth were yellowed from years of smoking, and a nervous tic caused his baldhead to shake.

Might be fifty, Ed speculated. He may know something about the camp.

"Name's Ed," he offered hesitantly.

"Moose," came the terse reply.

"According to the grapevine," Ed said, "it's going to be tough under Boss Jeb, maybe worse than at the pen. I just hope they don't do the same punishments here like shoving needles under fingernails. Fortunately," he added, emitting a nervous laugh, "Never had that done to me."

"Me neither," Duff chimed in.

"Well," Moose said, "don't count your chickens too soon. You never know what's gonna happen on a chain gang—especially like this here one."

"Of course," Ed went on, "that doesn't mean I've had it easy. I've been put in solitary, endured the stocks, and taken some pretty rough beatings. Pled innocent when my wife was killed, but it didn't do any good. Guess it's beyond debate at this point."

"We all got bum raps," Moose retorted acidly.

"Yeah," Duff added. "You ain't no different than the rest of us."

"What do either of you know about Jeb?" Ed pushed. Their sarcasm aggravated him.

"Like I told you earlier," Duff offered, "only his reputation. He's someone you don't never want to cross. Don't know much more about him than that."

"What about you, Moose?" The man didn't respond and Ed

98

felt his insides sag. The guy's silence probably meant he knew something. Maybe a few days of rubbing shoulders would open him up. He didn't want to turn the guy off by prodding too much on the first day.

Ed said no more and spent the next twenty minutes going through the contents of his duffel bag shuffling through yellowed papers. He pulled out an old newspaper clipping dated May 5, 1932, the announcement of his new job at the *Casey Clarion*. He remembered feeling like a puffed up toad-frog that day. For a brief moment, he felt proud again.

Fingering through more papers, he came to his 1938 article about Gunther Buford's short-lived trial. His gut twisted tighter than a wrung washrag recalling Mr. Casey's words.

"Son, you're doing great. Take my word for it, you have a bright future ahead of you."

He thought he had one too.

Shoving the clippings aside, he rummaged through old letters. Curiously, he came across one he received in the pen from Bob Wilkinson, the reporter from the *Virginian Pilot* he met at the trial. Bob's letter was kind, saying he found it hard to believe Ed was guilty, and if he needed anything to let him know.

At least one person in the outside world besides Mr. Casey believed in him. He stared at the return address he'd made a point of memorizing back at the pen, then tucked it back into his bag. Who knew but what contact with him at some point might prove providential.

He pulled out two faded photographs. One of his mama, the other of Sarah. As always, he gently placed them on his knee, pressed out the creases with his fingers and smoothed the bent corners.

Deep blues and purples seeped through him as he stared at his mama's care-worn face, remembering her oft-repeated remark at the beginning of the trial. *"Dear, the good book says everything is going to work together for your good."* Best she died, Ed thought, so she couldn't see how the scripture hadn't worked.

"Whacha lookin' at?" Duff asked, swiveling his body around to face Ed.

"Oh, just a picture of my mama." He turned it around and held it up. "Don't think I appreciated her as much as I should have." He turned it back and wistfully looked at it.

"She was sure proud of me when I landed my job at the *Clarion*. I was a reporter, you know."

"Yeah?" Moose sat forward on the edge of his cot. "I read a lot." He pulled a thick book from his duffel bag and proudly waved it in the air. Ed felt encouraged. The guy was opening up.

"Mama always bragged about me to the neighbors," Ed continued, eager to take advantage of Moose's change. "I heard her tell them, '*I was afraid he'd never amount to anything, but look at him now.*'"

"Does your mom visit you?" Moose asked.

"No. She died shortly after my trial. Heart attack. Guess the stress proved too much." He clamped his lips. One more portion of guilt he had to carry.

"Got a wife?"

Ed held up her picture.

"Whoa! Some knock-out," Duff exclaimed.

"Yeah, she was the love of my life." He opened his mouth to say more, but the lump in his throat prevented him. Uncomfortable seconds of silence followed while the memory tore his insides to pieces.

"Maybe another time I'll tell you more about her." His words quavered. Duff and Moose were silent.

"Life was good back then," Ed eventually resumed, clearing his throat and shifting the conversation away from Sarah. "Yep, I was coming up the ladder at the *Clarion* with real potential. Now all I have are memories and regret for a life I could have had. One day, I'm going to get it all back."

Duff grunted and Moose remained quiet. Ed bristled, their thoughts apparent. Neither of them understood. Escaping was more than just detesting prison. He had to track Buford down and get his life back. He also had to salvage what was left of his humanity—save Ed Bowman, the man, before 405, the inmate, totally took over and he became like other prisoners who existed as near-corpses in a gray, dead world.

He carefully placed the photos and clippings back into his duffel bag and lay back on his cot, no longer in the mood to talk.

Too many unhappy feelings ate at him.

The yard, now growing dim in the deepening dusk was quiet and peaceful except for the whirring screech of the cicadas. Ed wondered how they kept going without quitting from sheer exhaustion. He wondered the same about himself.

Scooting his back up against the cage wall, he propped his arms behind his head. Staring through the bars, he studied the barbed-wire fence and the gun tower silhouetted against the lavender sky. He analyzed the distance between his cage and the fence, and visualized creeping in the purple shadows, making it through the gate, bolting down the dirt road to reach the highway, and returning to Hannigan to see all his old haunts. Would he ever see that day? Only if he made trustee and escaped.

He'd then manage his way to Richmond and gain information about Buford's whereabouts from snitches and parolees who had access to the prison grapevine. He knew the lower end of town where they hung out. He might even contact Bob Wilkinson, but would have to give that more thought. One way or the other, he'd find some kind of lead to start his search for Buford.

The next three hours dragged by in small increments. The metallic clang of the "lights out" bell sounded across the yard by a trustee banging a metal bar around the inner perimeter of a barrel-ring hanging from a tree branch. Moose put out his cigarette. Duff rolled onto his side and closed his eyes.

Down the line of cages the inmates' chatter subsided. Soon, all was still except for the continuous whine of the cicadas.

An hour later, Ed heard the counts being called out, each trustee's voice carrying in the night air.

"Eight in two cages here, boss."

"Eleven in three cages...one in the box."

"Fifteen chained and secure."

Jeb swaggered into sight, checking off the numbers on his clipboard and riveting his eyes on the occupants as if they were cockroaches needing to be stepped on.

"Four in one, three in the other," Jim called."

Ed scrupulously studied Jeb as he strode by. He looked like a man who relished having prisoners make mistakes. To out-fox him he'd keep all the rules and conscientiously mind all his "yes sirs" and "no sirs." Being a model prisoner was the key to his making trustee.

Scooting down from the back wall, he lay down and curled up in fetal position. Three thirty would come soon. His first day on the gang, he'd get on Boss Jeb's good list. He closed his eyes.

No sooner had he entered the dozy stage when he raised his head with a start and cocked his head.

"You hear that, Duff?" he whispered. He rolled over, reached out his arm and gave him a shove on the shoulder. "Sounds like screams." He pictured the chewed-up escapee. Surely, there was no way *he* could still be alive.

Duff raised his head, his voice edged with annoyance. "Probably the cry of a Whippoorwill," came his groggy response. "Don't wake me up again." He dropped his head back down and began to snore.

Ed tightened his face. He couldn't be concerned. Nothing he could do to help the poor wretch. He drifted off to sleep again, visualizing his first day on the gang and keeping the rules to perfection. Jeb might even use him as an example to the others.

Ed jolted awake again, not from screams but from a nightmare. The hydra-headed monster he so often dreamed of was thwarting his escape. The portent was so vivid he couldn't dismiss it as fantasy. It was a warning dream. Did the monster represent Jeb? If not, who? Duff? Moose? Both? The young blonde man in the mess hall?

He thought back on the childhood, storybook pictures of hydra-headed monsters in the book on Greek mythology his mama read to him. Greek monsters always had more than one head. How could he have forgotten?

The dream wasn't warning him about a single individual. It was forewarning him there was more than one monster he needed to watch out for.

If any of them ratted on him to get a reduction in their sentences, his chance for escape was over. He'd never find Buford, never avenge Sarah's death, and never get his life back. Never.

He clenched his eyes shut. Besides Jeb, he now had to be on guard for others.

Who?

CHAPTER 15

~~~

The noon sun was hot as hell-fire. Gunther sat straddled across a stack of ties at the Shafter, Nevada railroad siding, munching on a tuna sandwich.

He glanced over at his crew who didn't seem to mind doing maintenance work at desolate places like this. They sat thirty feet away from him near a tool shed eating their lunch—but not with him. He knew they couldn't stand him. He didn't care. In another year, he'd be out of here and wouldn't have to put up with them or the desert.

He shifted his gaze and studied the sun-baked flats. The hard alkali ground was a blinding white under the garish sun, and shimmering waves of purgatorial heat distorted the landscape. His lips curled with loathing. This job was like working in a crematorium. Using the back of his shirtsleeve, he wiped the salty sweat dripping from his forehead before it could sting his eyes.

Reaching for his lunch bucket, he pulled out his thermos and an apple while scrutinizing the red and black, tar-papered roofs in the small town in the near-distance. He let out a troublesome grunt. Hardly thirty people lived in this woebegone town with its post office and broken down schoolhouse. Every town within a ninety-mile radius of Wendover was practically the same. It was revolting to think of anyone living forever in a place like this.

Nevertheless, he was lucky to land in Wendover. At least it had a nightclub for gambling. Wendover was also larger—300 residents according to the last survey. He opened his thermos and placed it between his legs. Pouring coffee into the lid, he took a swig, nostalgically thinking of Richmond's population of 200,000.

Wendover had its drawbacks, but he guessed he had it pretty good considering he'd managed to escape the electric chair, make it all the way to Utah, and land a job to boot. As desolate as this Godforsaken place was, at least he was free. Only a year to go until his plan materialized. He took out his pocketknife and flipped the blade out. Grabbing up his apple, he sliced it in half, took a bite, and glanced at his watch. He looked over at his crew.

"Ya got ten minutes left!"

Looking at his crew, he narrowed his eyes. One man on his crew made him nervous. Very nervous.

Jake was asking too many questions. The guy seemed intent on finding out his background. Of course, the men already knew he was from the South because of his accent, but someone in the clerk's office leaked information from his personnel file that he hailed from Richmond—a fact he felt necessary to include on his application in case quizzed about the city he came from. Jake always asked him questions when others were around to prevent him from weaseling out of answering. *"Hey, boss. Tell us about all those pretty Southern Belles. Did you live in Richmond long? How many years did it take to get that accent of yours?"*

So far, he was able to provide answers. The questions were happening so often now he no longer thought it was because the guy was naturally nosey. His last prying question was about the job he had prior to coming to Wendover. On his application he had put a vague, "law enforcement," but managed to say he worked as night security guard at the Old Dutch Market on Seventh and Franklin.

If Jake persisted with any more questions, he'd just come out and tell him it was none of his dang business. He couldn't afford to have anyone throw a monkey wrench into his plans. Not now. He had made friends with important people in Wendover, like Sheriff Kevin Thompson. Chumming with him carried huge weight in the community. Further, he was making headway with Queenie, the waitress at the Beanery. Having a long-time resident as his girlfriend could prove an asset and cement the town's acceptance of him.

Thinking of Queenie, he grinned. She was just his kind of gal. Not too nice, but nice enough and amply endowed. Her husky voice, sensuous eyes with their come-hither looks, and the way her blouse fell open when she leaned over the counter, really got his juices turned on. She definitely made Wendover tolerable.

Pouring more coffee into his thermos cap, he took a few sips and stared into space over the cup's rim thinking about her. As much as he was attracted to her, she didn't hold a candle to Sue.

Sue was different...sweet, actually. Maybe that's what drew him to her in the first place. Most all the girlfriends he ever had were the one-night, roll-in-the-hay, kind. For the first time in his life he believed he'd fallen in love—or at least what he thought love was supposed to feel like. He wasn't sure since his parents never gave him any.

All he knew was the way Sue made him feel. When he chatted with her in the warden's office, red-hot magma coursed through his body leaving his insides smoldering in molten lava. At night when he imagined having her, eruptions of raging, fire-like oranges and yellows swept over him in tidal waves. The afternoon he tried sex with her, she fought him. Why? He was sure she was just as hot for his body as he was for hers. He shrugged. No man could be blamed for being rankled. The teeth of his mind clenched. Now she was dead. All her fault.

He took a last bite from his apple and chewed slowly. Tonight, he'd be seeing Queenie. He doubted she would reject him. He knew her type. Loose, but would lead him on for a while. That was the way the game played. Until then, he'd handle it the best he could. He had to. He needed to stay in Wendover long enough for Gus Mooreland to earn his transfer to California.

He slurped down the last bit of his coffee, clamped his thermos into his lunch bucket and snapped the latch shut. Swinging his leg over the railroad tie, he stood and squinted against the sun.

"Okay, you men. Grab your tools, and let's hit them rails!"

Chapter 16

~~~~~

"**P**ile out!" Trusty Jim's voice sliced through the muggy air suffusing the cage, cutting into the sinews of Ed's sleep-dazed mind. He snapped awake and bolted upright from his mattress. He had only managed two hours sleep due to the shroud of waterlogged humidity that saturated the pie-wagon.

He peered with filmy eyes through the bars of the cage. Kerosene torches serpentined across the darkened yard, filling the sticky air with the smell of burning coal oil. Next down the line of pie-wagons came the banging of cage doors followed by jangling chains, guttural groans, and the slow swishing steps of sleepy inmates shuffling across the compound.

Within minutes the flares appeared in front of Ed's cage. Strong fumes whooshed inside, smarting his eyes. He squeezed his eyelids shut.

Trusty Jim swung the door open and strode down the aisle. Unlocking the night chain, he slid it out of the men's ankle rings with a jangling clatter, and coiled it up in a pile on the floor.

Ed grabbed his thunder bucket with anticipation, and stepped into the narrow aisle. Even though sleep-deprived he felt a nervous excitement. His first day on the gang. He planned to be a model prisoner, keep all the rules perfectly, and be one day closer to his goal of trustee. After that he'd be out of this hellhole.

He lumbered towards the door. All he needed to remember was not to eyeball, and grit his teeth if he didn't like something. He also had another objective. Find out more about Jeb from one of the other inmates. To get in his good graces, the more information he had, the better. He'd do that during lunch break. Hopefully, he wouldn't zero in on a stoolie.

Duff and Moose grabbed their buckets and staggered down the steps. Recalling the warning of the hydra heads in his dream, Ed searched their faces. He detected nothing amiss. Of course, Duff already knew he wanted to escape, but so far Moose didn't—unless

Duff decides to tell him. He flinched. Would either of them squeal? Which one?

The air quivered with heat as he climbed down the darkened cage steps and dumped the contents of his thunder bucket into the open pit. The splash of the men's night collection broke the greenish brown slime crusting the surface. The putrid stench wafted upward making Ed contort his face.

"Smells worse than a fly-buzzing outhouse on a summer afternoon," he mumbled to Duff.

"What'd you expect?" came the sleepy retort. "Life on a chain gang stinks."

Jim and two torch-carrying guards herded them toward the mess hall in a brume of fiery sulfur. As they neared, Ed sniffed in the pungent aroma of coffee and looked forward to a steaming, hot cup.

Inside, breakfast consisted of sorghum, a fried piece of tasteless hoecake and three small pieces of greasy pork middlings. What he wouldn't give for Sarah's grits, redeye gravy, and flaky, butter-dripping biscuits. Just thinking of her made his heart tighten. He recalled the day she lovingly touched his hand during breakfast and without a word they left the table, went into the bedroom and made love.

He imagined having her again, and his mind tugged toward the erotic memory of being wrapped in that golden butterscotch of lovemaking she loved to describe. His face flushed as he swallowed down the last bite of hoecake. He scrunched his brows together. Gunther Buford would pay.

"Meal's over," came the call. Ed slurped down the last drop of coffee from his tin cup, then moved to the door where Jeb stood outside on the steps.

"Come by me, come by me," he hollered, making sure every inmate made eye-to-eye contact with him as they exited.

Ed felt an intuitive shudder. He set his jaw and moved past him.

"Okay, git to the gate and the trucks!" Jim barked.

The men trudged past the captain's house to the gate where each inmate called out a number and turned his head so the one behind him could hear which one to use next. Ed followed suit. Jailbirds from the county jail learned fast enough—even the blonde Fish Ed noticed at dinner the night before.

Guards stood by the vehicles with torches. Ed climbed up the rear steps of one and entered the dark cage. Nine others piled in after him. The inside was so dark Ed couldn't make out any faces.

The guard slammed the door and locked it. The metallic bang made Ed jump. It felt like the door of life itself had slammed shut, locking him in the dismal darkness of death.

He peered through the shadowy bars and watched the last minute riggings and hitching of guard trailers to the rear of each truck. Eight guards with pistols and shotguns scrambled into their trucks. A guard strolled by the cages, took the count and called it over to the guard at the gate, Al. He wrote it down. Then, with a wave of his hand he gave the go-ahead signal.

The lead vehicle jostled down the darkened washboard road, the sliding and rattling chains sounding from each truck.

Slivers of headlights from the one following Ed's danced erratically through the bars allowing him to see the face of the man next to him. It was Moose.

The black whiskers on his face were thick, and his baldhead sported short stubble of new hair. Red pimples dotted his swarthy complexion, especially around the nose. His eyes surprised Ed. They were dark brown with a soulful look he hadn't noticed before. Maybe the man wasn't as tough as he envisioned.

"Guess Duff ended up in another truck," Ed ventured.

"Suppose so." Moose responded

"Never worked on a chain gang before."

Moose eyed him, his head-tic keeping time with the jouncing of the truck.

"Well," he said, "I been on one before, long enough to know the ropes. Got transferred here from a camp in Powhatan County. Just learn to follow the rules and be sure to sweat."

Ed raised a questioning eyebrow. Moose didn't explain, so he let the remark pass.

"Anyone ever try to...escape?" he asked haltingly, knowing he was giving himself away. Despite his warning dream, he had a gut feeling he could trust Moose.

"There's only four ways to get out of here," came the matter-of-fact reply. "*Work out*, meaning you serve your time but die before it's up. *Pay out,* meaning after serving a year you can pay two thousand dollars to the parole board and buy a pardon. *Die out* by deliberately planning a poor escape and hoping you get a bullet in the back. Last one, hangin' it on the limb and being lucky enough to escape without gettin' shot or chewed up by the hounds.

"Of course," he grumbled, anger glistening in his eyes, "even if your time for release or parole arrives, your chance will be deliberately screwed up by some guard. They enjoy doing that."

A sickening sensation slugged Ed in the stomach. He only had two options. Either die out, or hang it on the limb. As far as some guard messing him up, that simply wouldn't occur if he minded his Ps and Qs.

The trucks arrived at the site and pulled off onto the shoulder. Guard trailers were unhitched and cage doors unlocked. It was still dark but now light enough to detect the horizon line.

"Everybody pile out!" Jeb shouted.

Ed climbed down from the truck. At noon, he'd wheedle Moose for information about Jeb—work it in naturally into the conversation like it was just something to chat about.

"Line up on the shoulder," Jeb growled, "and sit down until the sun comes up."

The men plopped down on the ground chatting in low tones while guards ambled up and down the road with dogs and flashlights. In the faint light, Ed studied what little of the countryside he could make out.

No silhouettes jutted up against the dusky horizon except an occasional tree. He assumed the fields stretched for miles. Probably sweet potatoes. A train whistle sounded in the distance. He took note. He'd probably need to hop one.

The sun peeped over the horizon like a luminous egg yolk, and the warble of a meadowlark cut through the morning silence.

"Git your tools!" a guard called. The men reluctantly rose to their feet. The heat would soon be pulling at their skins.

Ed followed everyone to the tool truck and lined up for his implement. His resolve pounded inside his head. Don't eyeball... bite your tongue...do everything perfect.

Grabbing a shovel from the back end of the truck—a banjo, the guard called it—he dropped it into his wheelbarrow. Gripping the handles, he pushed it forward and followed the men down the road where two waiting guards explained each man's duties.

On the shoulders, men were swinging bush axes and picks with forehand and backhand strokes, slashing through palmettos and briars. Moose, he noticed, had a yo-yo, a long, rake-like handle with a triangular A-shaped blade at the bottom.

Ed's job was in the barrow ditch. His job was to shovel up loosened rocks and soil, scoop the debris into the wheelbarrow, push it up to the road and dump it into piles. Rocks went in one, soil in another which would be scattered on the road. Later, an asphalt truck would spray tar.

He eased himself down into the trench and began shoveling. So far, so good, he thought.

Guards with rifles and hounds stood at the far end of the work area. Others paced in-between shouting curses at the men in the ditches as if they'd already done something wrong. Jeb wasn't idle either. He marched back and forth along the road inspecting the work and using a walking stick with a sharp prong on the end to point out whatever was overlooked or done wrong. Ed winced. Would he use that on prisoners?

Ed soon found out what keeping the lick meant.

All movement occurred with military precision. Picks, shovels and yo-yos rose in the air at the same time and came down together. When dirt was thrown into the wheelbarrows, every shovel clicked simultaneously on the metal edges. Everyone's movements acted like the pendulum of a clock ticking away the backbreaking hours while the singing of a black inmate set the tempo.

Unable to identify most of the chants, Ed recognized one from when the pen leased him out on a short railroad stint.

"A long steel rail!" came the moan.

"Ump!" the rest responded in chorus as pickaxes and shovels rose in the air.

"An' a short cross-tie," he crooned.

"Ump!" the chorus repeated as pickaxes and shovels hit the ground.

"It rings lak' sil-vah..." Up they came again.

111

"And shines lak gold..." Picks and shovels fell.[1]

Up, down...up down... They all moved together, Ed keeping time.

"One," he whispered under his breath, "gonna keep the rules... two, gonna make trustee...three, gonna get out of here..."

Over and over the rhythmic chant continued, sixteen shovelfuls a minute, nine hundred and sixty an hour, while the sun beat down on the men's weary backs sucking energy from every pore.

Ed's body throbbed and stung like hell-fire. He felt like he'd been thrown into an incinerator. His chest heaved and his knees shook, but he kept a tight lip. So far, he was doing great. He had the monster at bay.

He took a quick glance over at Boss Jeb who, at the same moment, turned and caught him looking. Ed's mind rolled into panic.

He quickly ducked his head. An odd fear, like a spectral forewarning, shuddered through him. Would Jeb call that eyeballing?

Despite his determination to observe the rules, the day wasn't over yet.

---

1. Chant from, *I Am a Fugitive From a Georgia Chain Gang!* Robert E. Burns (Vanguard   Press, New York, 1932), 142-143)

CHAPTER 17

～～～

"**A**lright, water 'em up!" Jeb shouted over the clatter of tools and metallic clang of shovels hitting edges of wheelbarrows. The chanting and swishing of implements stopped.

Ed groaned with relief, plunked his shovel into the wheelbarrow, and dragged his bone-weary body up the embankment to the top of the ditch where prisoners lay on their backs anxiously awaiting the waterman.

Ed crumpled to the ground in exhaustion. The digging and climbing up and down the sides of the barrow pit opened wide the sluices for pain everywhere in his body. Hammers banged inside his head and against his temples.

So far, Jeb had made no move since he caught him staring at him earlier. Maybe the premonition-like feeling he had wasn't a warning at all, just fear. Nevertheless, he'd watch for the least little thing that could possibly be construed as an infraction. His whole plan rested on it.

"Water 'em down!" came the call.

The waterman with watery blue eyes moved in a slow shuffle with his bucket. Plunging the dipper into the bucket and handing it to each man, he made a point of looking each one in the face and giving him a smile before he moved on.

Ed stared at the man, amazed at his age. His frame was hunched and his skin deeply creased. He looked at least a hundred. Ed took the dipper, swished the water around in his mouth to loosen the gritty dust stuck in his teeth, swallowed, and then looked around for Moose. He saw him leaning against a tree stump. He moseyed over and plopped down on the ground next to him. Moose grunted a hello of sorts.

After a few unimportant comments to get him talking, Ed explained how he and Duff had ridden from the pen to the camp in the same prison cage.

"What do you know about him, Moose? He's sort of a quiet guy."

"Knew him in Powhatan," Moose replied, a cigarette dangling from the corner of his mouth. "Been in and out of prison most of his life, mainly for assault and burglary."

"What about the waterman?" Ed really didn't need information on him but it helped the conversation.

"A lifer. He's one of five trustees. Everyone likes him and calls him Ol' Pap. A few treat him like he was their own daddy.

"There's four others," Moose continued. "The Boiler. Good cook. Goes by the name of Scratch. Got the nickname because he was a forger on the outside. Had a big reputation in the pen for doing bogus documents for inmates and ex-cons on parole.

"Then there's Numbers." He blew out three brownish smoke rings. "He works in the captain's office and keeps the books. Convicted for embezzling."

"Figures." Ed grinned. "Guess Trusty Jim got his name from being a con man, or is it short for trustee?"

"Yep, to the last one. Don't know what he's in for. Some trustees, of course, aren't too bad. Jim's one of them. But the one you gotta watch out for is Squeaky. We call him that because of his high-pitched, twangy voice. He'll do anything to earn points with Jeb.

"Then," he went on, his lips curling in disgust and motioning his head toward the truck, "there's Jeb himself. You don't want to mess with him *at all*."

"Yeah?" Ed raised an eyebrow. Now, he was getting somewhere. "Why?"

"Cause he's obsessed with impressing the State. He used to be a guard at the pen but was indicted for murdering one of the cons. Since brutality is a necessary part of a guard's job he was pardoned but demoted to working chain gangs. Hopes to get his old job back. Thinks he can prove himself by being extra tough on inmates and making sure no prisoner escapes. He's a man possessed when it comes to huntin' down an escaped prisoner." Ed felt a cold tremor.

Moose took one last drag from his cigarette butt before grinding it into the dirt. "Worse yet, Jeb also—"

"Pick 'em up!" came the shout.

Ed got to his feet, disappointed at the interruption.

Doddering back to his work in the ditch, the torrid sun burned like a heated opal in the sky. Over and over Ed shoveled, loading

114

his wheelbarrow, and climbed up the side of the ditch with the heat scorching his lungs with every breath he drew. His baldhead, despite his cap, felt cooked to a crisp. He persevered with tenacity, daring not to slow down, furtively keeping an eye on Jeb

On one of his trips up the incline he spotted the Fish, the young man he saw in the mess hall, working the other side of the road along the edge of the shoulder and keeping good time with the lick.

Ed decided to give him the nickname of Benny. His blonde hair reminded him of his yellow dog. Why he had to name him he didn't know, except he had to put his mind on something other than how much his body hurt—or maybe it was because the youth looked innocent of any crime and felt an affinity with him. Two innocent men in prison. Maybe Benny could prove an ally.

Ed turned to start back down into the ditch when a sudden clatter of shackles and a loud yelp made him turn back. He looked across the road. Benny had tripped and fallen, but sat there making no attempt to get up.

Squeaky immediately ran over shouting obscenities in his twangy voice. "Get up you worthless pile of manure!"

Benny flashed him a look of defiance. It stopped Squeaky short. Jeb didn't miss it either and marched over.

"You got a problem?" Jeb roared, leaning over the embankment, his face red with rage.

"Yeah, I got a problem!" Benny retorted, sticking out a defiant chin and shooting Jeb a confrontational look.

Ed shuddered. At the pen, men got the water torture if they spoke out of turn.

The chant and the lick slowed while the men worked and watched. Ed did the same, picking haphazardly at the piles of rock and soil with his shovel.

"All I ever done was steal a cow," Benny shouted, the veins in his neck standing in ridges. "But it was my ma's cow someone stole from her!"

Jeb motioned to Squeaky and Trusty Jim. The two men scrambled to where Benny sat on the ground and dragged him to the water truck. Benny fought, struggled, and dug his heels into the dirt. Jeb paid no attention to the men. Ed figured he wanted them to watch.

Squeaky forced Benny down on his back, pinning his right arm with one knee. Jim did the same to his left. Squirming and kicking, Benny refused to give up. It was like watching a chicken that knows it's going to have its head chopped off.

Quick-stepping over to one of the trucks, Jeb grabbed two empty pitchers and plunged them into a large galvanized kettle of drinking water. Filling each one to the brim, he returned to where Benny lay. Holding one pitcher high in the air, he nodded to Jim.

Jim repositioned himself above Benny's head and pried Benny's jaws open while he held his head secure between his knees. From high in the air Jeb began pouring water into his opened mouth.

Benny struggled and gasped for air, but none was to be had. Jeb kept pouring the water full force into his throat while Benny choked, gagged and threw up. When one pitcher emptied, Squeaky handed him another. There was no break in the torture. It was a near-drowning experience. Each time Benny started to fade away Jeb would stop, wait for a sign he was reviving, and then begin again.

Ed counted four times Benny lapsed into unconsciousness, wondering which time would prove fatal. The same question reflected from the other inmates' faces.

The fifth time Benny came to, his skin was a grayish blue. He looked nearly dead.

"I'll...be good...boss," Benny spluttered in a bare whisper. "I'll be...good. Please boss...no more," he wheezed. "No more... "

Jeb nodded. Squeaky and Jim picked Benny up and dragged him back to the road where he was kicked in the groin at the edge of the ditch and sent rolling down the incline. Barely alive, he was expected to climb back up to the shoulder and keep the lick. Jeb threw a stare at the men and the work chant immediately picked up.

Ed trudged down the embankment and thrust his shovel into the hard soil. Why should a son who was simply getting his ma's cow back be sent to prison, let alone tortured?

Gotta do everything right, he told himself, or he'd find himself in Benny's shoes.

At noon, Jeb's voice boomed out. "Lay 'em down. Let's eat dem beans!"

Ed collapsed onto the ground beside Moose. He motioned with his head at Benny lying on the ground looking barely alive.

"Sure feel sorry for the fish."

Moose shook his head. "The guy should have kept his mouth shut." He nonchalantly blew out a smoke ring. "Ya never know which day will be your last."

"Well, that may be, but—"

Ed jerked his head up at the sound of the mess truck bouncing up the road. The vehicle pulled to a stop, the door flew open, and the driver hopped out.

"That's Scratch, the cook," Moose remarked.

Ed thought him rather strange looking. Although young, about thirty-five, his hair was a shocking white. More unusual were his heavy, black eyebrows that met together at the bridge of his nose, the ends slanting up to points near his temples.

"Those pointy eyebrows," Ed joked, "make him look like the devil." Moose issued an indifferent shrug when the awaited call came...

"Come and get it!"

Ed lined up and looked forward to eating the boiled cowpeas and corn pone. Once on his plate, he discovered the peas were gritty with sand and full of tiny worms. Grim-lipped, he tried picking them out but eventually gave up. He gagged twice but eventually became pacified knowing at least the tiny critters were dead. The cornbread wasn't any better.

"This bread is so dry, a maggot could choke on it."

Moose shook his head, gave a half smile and continued eating his with relish. "You'll get used to it."

"Pick 'em up!" drawled Jeb, grabbing his rifle from the hood of his truck.

The men resumed work, swishing their yo-yos through the dry weeds, whacking at bushes with axes and tearing out roots. Ed felt he was doing great. He glanced across the road. Benny looked like he was on the verge of collapsing.

Two more hours of shoveling and the afternoon heat grew more intense. Ed drove himself by sheer will power. Thud...thud. His head pounded to the rhythm of the lick. He grew nauseous, and wondered if it was the worms. At the edge of the road near

117

where Moose worked, he paused for a brief second to flex his back and wipe the sweat from his face.

Something heavy suddenly struck him full force in the back. Pain riddled through his bones and the sky began to spin. Falling forward he slammed into the dirt face first. Turning slightly on his side, he saw Jeb towering over him, raising his rifle butt a second time. Down it came, smashing across his lower back. Ed gasped for breath, nearly vomiting up his beans.

"No one takes the liberty of wiping it off," Jeb growled, "unless he gets permission. You ask, 'Wiping it off, boss?' Then, you wait for an okay. Understand?"

"Yes," Ed managed to gasp.

"What did you say?" Jeb yelled, leaning over.

"I said, yes," Ed groaned.

"Yes what?" Boss Jeb shouted. He lowered another hard slam of his rifle into Ed's bony back.

"Yes...*boss*," Ed croaked in a faint whisper. He was sure something was broken.

"Back to work then!"

Ed tried to rise but could only get to his knees, each time pain ricocheting through his body and pulling him back to the ground. He was certain he'd never stand, let alone work.

"Do it, man," Moose said under his breath.

Mustering all his strength despite spasms of searing agony coursing down his spine, he managed to stand and stumble over to where he had laid his shovel. Dizzy and sick, he pushed his wheelbarrow down the ditch and started the rhythmic lick.

Oof...umph...oof...umph. Over and over he thrust his shovel into the hard dirt, then moved back up the embankment with hot pokers of pain stabbing through his frame. Jeb stood up on the road looking down, watching.

Hour after hour Ed managed to keep the lick in mute agony. Jeb still watched.

Discouragement riddled his insides. His first day, he groaned, and a run-in with Jeb already. How could he make trustee, now?

The sun touched the horizon and the long-awaited call came. "Lay 'em down!"

Ed staggered toward the tool truck, his back in misery, his knees trembling and threatening to give out any second, barely able to push his wheelbarrow. He dropped his shovel and the one-wheeler by the tool truck. Red-hot coals sizzled through his frame as he limped toward the truck's cage. No way could he manage those steps.

"C'mon," Moose said, moving up alongside. He took his arm and gave him a lift up. Ed's face twisted in pain as he stumbled through the opening and collapsed onto the hard floor. The other nine men piled in, stepping over him. The cage door slammed shut. Truck engines coughed, sputtered, and pulled off the shoulder onto the highway.

Ed managed to lift himself to one of the seats. He pressed his face against the narrow opening between the bars letting the hot breeze blow on his face.

"Something's broken," he moaned.

"Naw," Moose replied, "you wouldn't have been able to stand."

"Well, then," Ed gasped, "maybe cracked."

The trucks turned onto the camp road and pulled up to the gate. Cage doors were unlocked and the sweat-covered men climbed out. Exhausted, they passed through the gate calling out their count with dry, strangled croaks.

Ed walked in hunched position, unable to hold his body erect, and eased forward through the gate. His breath came in shallow spurts. Deeper ones caused too much pain. Moose followed close behind.

Staggering across the yard, Ed reached the washing stump. He splashed the muddied water on his arms and face, then tottered over and stood in the mess hall line. Jeb stood at the door calling out his usual rhetoric.

"Come by me. Come by me. I want to smell you!"

"So, that's what you meant by sweating," Ed turned and whispered to Moose. "Well, I certainly did that."

"Pipe down!" Moose warned.

Straightening his back as best he could, Ed moved up the steps.

Suddenly Jeb's arm shot out in front of him, his hand landing with a locking thud on the opposite side of the doorjamb. Ed looked up.

"Whoa there, Number 405," Jeb snorted. "I don't smell you." His eyes narrowed to slits. "I don't smell any sweat."

Ed's stomach pitched.

"Whatcha been doing on the road all day?" Jeb growled. He didn't wait for an answer.

"Slackin' off, that's what. The state expects you to pull your share of the work just like the rest. I don't think you worked hard enough, 405. No sweat—no work."

Ed's heart sank. His goal of trustee dissolved into the ether.

Jeb smirked and motioned to two guards. "The leather will teach ya."

Two sets of strong hands pulled Ed into the building, Jeb following behind, and dragged him down the center aisle and threw him against the front platform. The men seated at the tables watched quietly.

"So, you won't work, huh?" Jeb snapped.

"But I did...boss." Ed's voice was hoarse, his mouth dry as cotton.

"Remember what you was told? You don't sass a free man! Get your pants down."

Ed took a quick look at the men at the tables. Some watched while others looked away. Humiliated, he slowly pulled them down and bared his buttocks.

The two guards grabbed his arms and forced him face down onto the front edge of the platform.

In his peripheral vision Ed saw Jim meekly hand Jeb a long, leather strap. It was no different than the ones at the pen, six feet long, three inches wide and a quarter inch thick.

Jeb stepped back from the platform. "Blast you, I'll learn you to work on this here chain gang. Ten licks oughta do it."

With a loud crash the heavy strap came down on his back and buttocks. Ed felt his body go limp. He tensed for the next blow. Down it came with a sickening whack, then another and another. Then came a slight pause. Ed knew exactly what *that* meant.

Jeb turned the strap so the whip would strike on its edge and snorted a scornful laugh. Ed braced himself.

Down it came, slicing through his flesh one blow after another. Ed's face twisted in pain. Blood ran down his backside. After the eighth time he could take no more.

"Please, boss...stop," he whispered. "Please...boss."

"So, it's please is it?" Jeb's lips twisted into a sadistic sneer. "I guess we know who's boss now." He turned to the men at the tables. "We know," he shouted, "we're here to work and rules gotta be followed!" Don't we?"

"Yes, boss," the inmates mumbled in unison.

"Well, Number 405," Jeb said, turning back to Ed, "you're no different than the rest of these worthless good-for-nothin's. You ain't no one special. You're a number. You got no rights excepting what the State and I give you. Understand?"

At that moment Ed would have said anything.

"Yes...boss," he weakly whispered, "I... I understand."

Jeb nodded to the two guards. They jerked Ed's limp body to standing position and pulled up his pants, urine and blood running down his legs. Nausea overwhelmed him and the room began to sway.

His stomach heaved and up came beans and corn pone all over the floor. Then, in a dream-like state Jeb's angry shouts faded.

It was the last thing Ed remembered before passing out.

CHAPTER 18

~~~

Explosions of pain jolted Ed back to consciousness. Fire crackled down his spine, tearing through his hips and legs. He let out a teeth-clenched groan. It was dark and the smell of his sweat-sopped body, putrid stink of the mattress, and the thunder buckets told him he was back in his cage.

He opened his eyes expecting to see Jeb, whip in hand, standing over him. Instead, Moose and Duff hovered above his cot.

"How ya doin'?" they asked in hushed tones.

"Not so...good," Ed managed. "Jeb just about did me in."

"We gotta take your shirt off and pull your pants down," Moose said. "They'll stick to your wounds and infection can set in. It'll be more misery than you're having now. I seen it before."

Ed nodded. "I don't think I can move," he gasped, "the devil is twisting the sharp prongs of his pitchfork through every bone and muscle of my body."

"I'll do it," Moose said. He undid Ed's belt, glancing toward the guard's cage. Trusty Jim had his back turned.

A rush of pain forced a yelp from Ed's mouth.

"Bite down on your pillow so you don't make no noise."

He did, grimacing as Moose rolled him onto his side and proceeded to pry his blood-soaked pants loose from the drying scabs. Sharp quills of pain staccatoed down Ed's back despite their gentle tilting of him, one way then the other, until they worked his pants over his hips and down to the ankles. At the same time, Duff carefully pulled the bloodied strips of his shirt away, trying not to pull skin with them.

Ed studied them, wondering how either one could possibly be two of the hydra monster's heads in his recurring dream. They were treating him pretty decently.

"Now you gotta turn over on your stomach so the air can get to your backside," Duff said, dropping the last piece of his shirt into the thunder bucket.

Ed tried. Waves of molten lava surged through every nerve

ending until, inch by inch, he managed to roll over, all the while emitting torturous sounds into his pillow.

"Can't decide...which hurts more...my back or buttocks." His tremulous words came in painful quivers. "At the pen, I had more flesh. Now, nothing but skin and bones. How," he moaned, "am I going to work on the road tomorrow?"

"Don't know," Duff whispered, "but you gotta try."

"Yeah, do everything you can to keep in Jeb's favor," Moose interjected. "He's one mean critter and don't allow for nothin'."

How would he manage it? The thought of Jeb brought up every ounce of his loathing. Was making trustee even possible at this point?

"Forget about any ideas of getting even," Moose added perceptively, "or thinking you got to show everyone you're still a man. On a chain gang you ain't a person no more and never will be. You're just a number. The sooner you learn that, the better off you'll be." With those words, he and Duff crept back to their cots.

Not a person anymore? Ed fiercely resisted that. He was most definitely somebody. He was Ed Bowman, reporter for the *Casey Clarion*, with a promising future ahead of him—not a number.

The rest of the night was sheer agony. The temperature lowered into the 90s but did nothing to quell the chills ravaging his body. Shivering one minute and burning up the next, the throbbing of his muscles rose and fell in shattering spasms. Even the slightest movement of a leg or arm sent coal-sizzling tremors through his frame. Occasionally an agonized moan escaped. No one seemed to be disturbed by it, not even Trusty Jim who sat on his cot in the chicken-wire enclosure.

Ed lay awake all night. Sleep was out of the question.

Three-thirty came too soon. Ed heard the familiar rattle of chains across the compound. He opened his eyes and saw the flicker of red and yellow torches heading his way.

"You doin' okay?" Moose called from his cot.

"As well as can be expected," Ed responded. "Guess I should consider myself fortunate. I've seen men at the pen die within a few hours after a beating."

"You're right," Duff replied. "Count yourself lucky."

Ed rolled over on his side. His breath came in short spurts as the scabs on his back broke open. He raised himself gingerly, and slowly twisted around until he sat upright on the edge of the cot. Working his blood-stiffened pants up to his waist, he buckled his belt. He had no shirt. It was in his thunder bucket. Nevertheless, he'd be ready for work if it killed him.

The procession of torches stopped in front of the cage. The door flung open, and Jim marched down the aisle to the far end of the cage. Stooping over, he undid the padlock on the night chain and pulled it free from the men's ankle rings. On his way out, with hardly a break in stride, he dropped a clean shirt on Ed's cot.

Ed put it on, assessing a somewhat kinder view of Jim. He leaned over and grabbed the handle of the thunder bucket. His backside stung like fire as he stood, and a low guttural sound escaped from between his lips. Moose threw him a sympathetic look before heading out the door.

Ed carefully moved into the narrow aisle, one hesitant step at a time. More wounds on his buttocks ripped open. The bloody fluid dribbled down the back of his legs.

Moving stiffly through the doorway and down the steps, he dumped his thunder bucket with the pieces of his blood-soaked shirt into the pit. He placed the pail on the ground near the steps, and then turned in the direction of the mess hall.

"Whoa, there!" Jim stepped forward and took hold of Ed's arm. "Follow me."

A stranglehold of despair clutched Ed's heart. He hobbled behind Jim across the compound toward the gate. Where was he taking him? Maybe a short lecture from Jeb or the captain? Would his first offense be forgiven?

They passed the painted house. Ed saw the captain step out from the screen door and mosey across the front porch puffing on a cigar. He paused beneath the porch light and briefly looked at them. His expressionless eyes stared over the rims of his glasses that hung on his cucumber-shaped nose. He looked away, took a deep drag on his stogie and exhaled a puff of white smoke. Carefully pressing the cigar against the railing, he rolled the remaining ash off. Swiveling around, he went back inside.

Jim led Ed past the gun tower. It was then Ed saw where he was going. His spirit sank.

Jeb stood at the sweatbox, a tall, upright box on a wooden platform barely high enough for a man to stand up in and narrower than an outside, one-holer privy.

"Well, 405," Jeb drawled, "seems like I've got to get that mind of yours right."

Ed's pulse pounded like a piston. He was in no condition to be put into the sweatbox. He quickly spoke.

"Oh, that beating yesterday got my mind right for sure, boss."

Jeb slowly drew himself up to full height. "Nope. The beating wasn't for everything you done. Your whippin' was for taking the liberty of not asking to wipe it off. But you was also eyeballin'. Did you think I didn't see you? You need to get your mind straight about that."

He spread his lips into a cynical smile, drawing his tongue slowly across his lower lip like a man anticipating a good meal.

"I'm afraid you need a little time in the box."

Panic slithered through Ed's insides. He had to play it cool. Take his punishment like a man. Maybe that might impress the monster. Somehow, he had to make it with this man.

"Let's see..." Jeb stroked his chin. "Which should I use? Should it be double shackles? Hmmm. Or...."

Obviously, he had already decided, for Jim walked straight to the four steps leading up to the door of the box, leaned over and picked up two iron instruments with sharp points.

"I think the spikes ought to do it, don't you think, 405?"

Ed took a deep breath. Spikes in addition to his beating—plus also in the sweatbox? He said nothing as Jim picked up the dreaded spikes, took off each of Ed's ankle irons, and affixed the instruments.

Spikes consisted of two sharp, ten-inch long nail-like projections. They extended outward from each ankle band, one on the front and one on the back, and then curved back inward a few inches. If the legs were bent even slightly the spikes dug into the shin, the other one into the back of the calf. The instrument also made it impossible to lie down, sit or crouch without the legs being lacerated. He would have to sleep standing up, or just not sleep at all.

"You got something to say?" Jeb barked.

126

"No, boss."

"Get him in there, Jim," Jeb growled, waving an arm. Turning, he trudged off across the yard toward the mess hall.

Jim motioned Ed over to the box. Ed already knew the drill from the pen. After Jim undid his ankle shackles, he removed all his clothes, slipped on a nightshirt that hung on a nearby nail, and placed his shirt and pants near the bottom of the steps.

Jim clomped up the steps and yanked the door open.

"Get on in," he motioned with his head. Jim reached up and pulled the string to the light bulb hanging from the edge of the roof, a signal to the rest of the men a prisoner was getting his just dues, and then stepped back. He waited, his face expressionless.

Ed tottered forward trying not to bend his legs. Even with his best effort, the sharp points of the skewer-like spikes pierced the front and back of his legs.

Slowly maneuvering side to side like a stiff mechanical toy, he moved up the four wooden steps and entered the booth. It smelled of men's sweat, urine and defecation.

Leaning against the back wall, he stared into Jim's face as he closed the door. He heard the padlock snap on the outside, the two-by-four drop down into the u-shaped brace, and Jim's gravel-crunching footsteps fade away.

Standing in the darkened box, Ed convinced himself he could certainly endure a single day in the box. At least he hoped it was only for that long.

Hours passed. The sun beat down with a vengeance and the suffocating heat in the box made breathing difficult. Sweat rolled off his body, soaking his nightshirt. He grew weaker by the minute, making it difficult to keep standing.

He didn't dare let his legs buckle.

At the end of the day Ed heard the trucks pull up and the road gang shuffle through the gate and cross the yard to the mess hall. Later, after supper, he heard the clamor of the men's shackles as they headed to the cages, and then the jangling of the heavy night chain being strung through their ankle rings. Cage doors slammed shut.

The full black of night descended. Weak, exhausted, perspiration drenching his body, he had to sleep somehow. He leaned forward, stretching both arms out in front of him, and pressed the palms of his hands against the door. Keeping his legs straight he drooped his head onto his arms and closed his eyes. No sooner did he doze off then his legs buckled and the spike's sharp points jolted him awake.

He tried other positions. Nothing worked. His back and hips screamed with pain. His toes were losing feeling.

He heard the eight-thirty bell for "lights out," and the BT's voices pierce the night air with their cage counts. Then all was still, except for the shrilling screech of the cicadas. He figured if those red-eyed, shrimp sized bugs could keep going, so could he.

Then Ed heard another sound and his heart sank. He knew exactly what it was—Palmetto roaches scurrying across the floorboards. Soon, they'd be crawling all over him. He hated the ugly things. They'd be sucking up his blood and sweat and chewing on his scabs. But more than his fear of them was his pressing need to lie down, sit down, anything to relieve the pain and sleep.

Taking a deep breath he bent his knees, gradually sliding his buttocks down the back wall toward the floor. He clenched his eyelids as the dried-over scabs on his back scraped open and the spikes dug deep into his shins and calves. Blood trickled down his buttocks and legs. "More food for the roaches." He grimaced, hoping he wouldn't sit on any of them.

Taking another deep breath, he continued sliding down until his knees pressed up against his chest. Soon his bare rear-end was sitting on the rough floorboards. Thank goodness, on nothing else. His movement had scattered the roaches back into their holes and cracks—but they would be back.

Now settled into the small space, he braced both legs against the bottom of the door and slowly inched his toes up. With his legs finally straightened out above his head, he dozed off in jackknife position while the blood from the spike-wounds dribbled down his legs.

How long he slept, he didn't know, but lack of circulation awoke him—also something else. He felt the prickle of whisper-like feet crawling all over him, especially around his buttocks and hips where most of the blood had settled.

Panicking, he blindly hit at them, flipping them in every

direction trying to get them off. He heard their hard-shelled bodies hit the walls and fall to the wood floor. He scrambled to an upright position, ignoring the spikes digging into his legs. In the process he squished a couple of roaches under his feet. He cringed. It was bad enough when he had shoes on.

He experimented with other positions. Tired and miserable, none of them relieved his distress or allowed sleep.

He stood in the muggy darkness thinking of his good intentions to keep the rules. A hard knot twisted in his chest. Moose was right. No matter how good a prisoner might be, a guard or some chain gang boss will foul it up. Resentment radiated off him like heat waves. Hate consumed him...hatred for the guards, hatred for Jeb, and hatred toward the unfairness of life.

"No one in the world," he gasped, "cares whether I live or die—not even God."

He dropped his chin onto his chest, feeling embittered and abandoned. His mind filled with jumbles of thoughts...Sarah dying in his arms...Buford getting away...years of mistreatment and humiliation at the pen. It all took its toll. Tears, long pent-up, burst forth in an onrush of hopelessness.

"I'll never make trustee," he moaned. "I'll never get out of here, never find Buford, and I'll probably die in this Godforsaken place."

Chapter 19

~~~

Hammers banged and thudded against Ed's temples. He survived the night, but now the broiling sun beat down on the sweatbox and the suffocating shroud threatened to crush the very breath out of him. Each time he strained to draw in what little oxygen he could, an asphyxiating tourniquet squeezed the breath back out. His chest heaved. He gulped for air. His legs, shaking from the tension of standing continually, buckled, driving the picks deeper into his flesh.

Keep it together...stay conscious. Got to make trustee...owe it to Sarah...

Then he heard it, or did he? Footsteps?

He wrenched himself from his vapor-like stupor and hung on. His body trembled like a withering leaf clinging its last desperate hold onto a branch before plummeting to its death.

Heavy boots clomped up the wooden steps. He heard the key in the padlock snap open and the heavy two-by-four lifted out of its brace. It dropped with a clunk. Every nerve in Ed's body quivered. The door swung open.

Ed instinctively raised his arms to shield his eyes from the blinding glare. Jim backed down the steps and stood off to one side.

"Come on out, 405," came Jeb's voice. He stood a few feet away swinging his blackjack in a half circle with one hand and letting it smack onto the palm of the other. Ed hesitated. He knew he wouldn't survive more.

Blinking, he took a few staggering steps and slowly inched his way toward the door. Hanging on to the frame, he took a few tremulous steps out of the box and managed the four steps down to the ground. At the same time he glanced at his wobbly legs covered with bloodied punctures.

"How'd your night go, 405?" Jeb grinned.

"Okay...boss," Ed croaked, his swollen tongue as moistureless as the baked ground he stood on.

"Speak up," Jeb bellowed.

"Yes, boss!"

"Glad to hear that."

Ed strained to speak, his nerves stretched to its limit. "You don't have to worry any, boss, cause my mind's right for sure." He felt on the verge of throwing up.

"Well, it's about time, 405. You know it's for your own good."

"Yes, boss."

"Cause if you can't follow rules and get your mind right, you ain't no use to anyone."

"Yes...I know that boss." Ed studied Jeb's face. Was he planning something else?

Jeb stopped slinging his blackjack and stuffed it into his hip pocket. Tucking his thumbs down inside his belt, he gave his trousers an upward yank. With a cocky look he nodded to Jim, and then strutted off toward the mess hall. Ed sagged his body in relief. He was off the hook. At least for now.

Jim knelt down, removed the spikes, and then picked up Ed's clothes from the foot of the stairs and handed them to him. Ed pulled his blood-soaked nightshirt off, slid on his shirt and pants and stood quietly while Jim reaffixed his ankle chains.

"Go get something to eat," Jim mumbled, "and for heaven sakes get that mind of yours right." Ed didn't' respond.

Stumbling across the compound, his legs a mass of misery. He hated himself for kowtowing to Jeb. *Yes, boss, no, boss, I got my mind right, boss.* The man was a bitter taste in his mouth. He felt less than human. Worse yet, he was no closer to his goal of trustee—in fact, further from it.

He dizzily staggered over to the washing stump and sat down, grimacing as he did. Lumps of squashed roach shells were stuck to his buttocks. *Think. Think of some way to work into that monster's favor.* But before he could do that, he was more frantic for water.

A tin basin filled with dirty water from the men's wash the night before sat on the ground near the stump. In desperation, he reached over and grabbed it. Lifting it to his lips he swished the water around in his mouth and then guzzled it down. He didn't care how filthy. It was wet. He poured the rest over his head to relieve the swooning sensation, and then over his legs to relieve the burning punctures.

He needed sleep. He got up from the stump, steadied himself for a second, and hobbled off in the direction of the cages.

If Jeb said getting his mind right made him useful to others, what abilities did he have that he could offer? At the pen he worked in the factory, machine-milling parts for cabinets and furniture. Although proud of his skills, he saw no use for them at the camp. The grapevine said new barracks would be built soon to replace the cages, but the WPA would probably build them. He wracked his brain. Nothing came.

Struggling up the steps to his cage, he felt grateful it was Saturday—everyone's free day—if it could be called that. He pulled the door open and limped down the narrow aisle past Moose and Duff who were playing cards. In their hands they held a few coins, their draw on their weekly road wage.

Weaving and bumping against the ends of the cots, Ed collapsed onto his bed his body feeling like poured concrete. His pants, stiff with road grime, blood and urine, stunk worse than the bedding. The two men looked up.

"See you survived," Moose said quietly. "Rough night?"

"Yeah, Moose, real bad...got to get some sleep."

"Too bad when a guy is put in the box," Moose murmured to Duff. "Some men might try to hang it on the limb." Ed flinched. He knew where Moose was headed.

"Of course," Moose added, momentarily looking sideways at Ed while laying his cards down, "if he's smart he won't expect any help. Anyone caught being an aider gets the same punishment as the one taking it on the lam." He reached into his shirt pocket, drew out a tobacco pouch and sprinkled some onto a thin tissue, then continued.

"He'd probably try it when he's out on the road. Then he'd only have about thirty or forty minutes before the manhunt gets going full swing." He rolled the tissue and licked the edges shut.

"With police patrols swarming the roads, posses organized in every direction, not to mention the hounds, it'd be a miracle if he made it."

"Yep, you're right about that," Duff drawled, studying the cards in his hand. "I'd hate to think what Jeb would do to him if he were caught."

Ed stared at the ceiling. Moose and Duff' meant well but nothing was going to stop him from trying. After all, what did he have to lose? Die from being tortured, or take the risk of escaping and maybe make it?

Tired, his eyelids sagged. Moose and Duff's voices drifted into the distance as inky blackness closed in on him.

"Two bits going in!"

"I'll match that..."

Gripped in a drug-like sleep, Ed spiraled down into a bottomless pit of relief, free from pain and misery. Or, so he thought. Sarah was there, extending both arms to him with tears coursing down her face. Every time he reached for her she would recede a few steps back. He fell on his knees begging forgiveness for not protecting her and promising to bring Buford to justice.

It was the last scene he remembered before sinking into total oblivion.

Ed slept until jarred awake by a loud noise. Startled, he raised his head. Moose stood outside the cage banging a stick against the bars.

"Wake up, Ed! You're wasting Saturday. Have ya forgot? It's our free day."

Ed groggily sat up, balancing himself on one elbow. "Don't care, Moose. Would rather sleep."

"Well, if you don't get out here, Jeb might accuse you of not having your mind right. Get out and play some quoits." He turned and took off.

"I'm coming," Ed groaned. Moose was right. He sat up, took a few swigs of water from the dipper in his bucket, and then sluggishly got to his feet.

Moving into the aisle, Ed limped out the cage door and down the steps feeling like a dead man. Only sheer will power got him across the yard.

Inmates wandered about. A few, in private conversations, sought shade under the few willow trees. Some went into the commissary to draw on their meager pay of pennies to play craps.

Ed ambled to where they were playing quoits, a game similar

to horseshoes. He joined in, hoping the exercise would relieve his sore legs and back. It was too much. He quit.

He glanced about to see if Jeb was around, and saw Trusty Jim leading an inmate from one of the tents. The man's fingers were bleeding, pain evident on his face.

"That's Rufus. He got the needles," Moose said, quietly moving alongside. Ed shuddered, unable to tear his eyes away from Rufus' agonized expression. "Poor guy."

"Quit worrying about him," Moose retorted. "Rufus probably did something to deserve it."

"Yeah? Maybe he didn't." Ed thought of Benny.

"Well, that may be so," Moose said with a scowl, "but this here's a chain gang." He turned and headed for the commissary.

Desperation etched its way across Ed's face. Tomorrow or next week that could be him. He had to come up with a plan...fast. Think of some way to get in Jeb's good graces before the monster found another excuse to punish him.

He sauntered over to a small hickory tree. Sinking onto the ground, he looked up through the tree branches trying to get the gears in his head churning. He listened to nearby inmates' conversations—speculation on whether the new barracks would materialize, endless chatter about ex-wives, and then a passing comment of significance. Jeb and the captain were in Richmond for their monthly meeting with the warden. It was then, an idea formed.

Jim had some degree of pull with Jeb. How much, he wasn't sure. He knew inmates at the pen often tried what he was now thinking, so Jim might say yes or no depending on his mood. He spied him sitting on the mess hall steps. He'd dare it. He stood and nonchalantly shuffled over, his stomach twisting in knots.

"Yeah?" Jim asked, looking up surprised.

"Just thinking," Ed began timidly, "Since I'm not up to playing any of the games and don't feel like just sitting around, you got anything that needs to be done? It'll give me a little something to do...help my body to flex and work out the pain."

Jim studied him and pulled his eyebrows toward the center of his nose. Ed squirmed.

"Yeah, c'mon." He got up, motioning with his head to follow.

Ed let out a quiet exhale. Work was the last thing he wanted to do but it was an important move. He glanced toward the quoits court. Some of the men were watching. He didn't care.

For the next three hours Ed unloaded food cartons and arranged them on shelves, focusing on doing the best job he could considering the pain in his legs. He also organized tools, filled up the grease buckets for the dump truck mechanisms, and made sure each bucket had a paddle spreader. Although he ached all over, he felt good inside. He had put his plan into motion and maybe made some kind of inroad with Jim. He hoped it would earn him some brownie points. He reported back.

"That's all," Jim mumbled, dismissing Ed with a wave of his hand and displaying no expression one way or the other.

Perturbed, Ed expected a more positive reaction. He walked off not knowing whether to feel victorious or not. He wouldn't give up. He'd watch for more opportunities. Something had to work.

The rest of the day went smoothly. Periodically Ed returned to his cage and began his ritual. He examined his blistered palms, flexed his arms, twisted his body to the right and left, and made a scrutiny of the pick-sores on his legs to check for infection.

Moose walked in and sat on his cot. Lighting up a cigarette, he stared at Ed.

"Feeling better?"

"Yeah, somewhat. Sores from the spikes are still painful, but most of the whipping cuts on my back are on the mend. Only a few make me wince.

Moose paused for a second and exhaled smoke from his nose. "You want to talk about what you were doing this afternoon?" His eyes stared right through Ed.

"Not really. And you know why."

"Yeah." He shrugged, looking away. "What I don't know won't hurt me. Guess I gotta appreciate that." He leaned over and extinguished the end of his cigarette butt in the water bucket and carefully withdrew it to save for later.

Ed listened to its momentary sizzle, and then stretched out on his cot to take a nap. He quickly sank into the welcome escape of sleep.

When Ed awoke it was dark. Moose and Duff were snoring. How late at night, he wasn't sure. What awakened him were screams. This time there was no doubt they came from the direction of the building out by the kennels. Someone was being tortured. Benny? But Jeb had already nearly killed him with the water treatment. He rolled over, shifting his body into a different position.

Mustn't think about the guy. Gotta focus on my own survival and how to make it through Monday on the road with no run-ins with Jeb. Also, come up with more ideas to earn points with Jim. Tomorrow, Sunday, he'd figure it out.

He drifted off anticipating a sound sleep, but instead had a nightmare of Jeb forcing needles under his fingernails, then being thrown into a box of giant roaches that crawled in and out of his body's orifices. He awoke in panic.

Was the dream foretelling another run-in with Jeb? If so, his goal of trustee was over. Well, at least tomorrow was Sunday. He breathed a sigh of relief. All inmates were locked in their cages.

He had nothing to worry about from the monster.

CHAPTER 20

~~~~~

"It's only six-thirty a.m.," Moose remarked, looking through the bars. "Today's going to be a scorcher—yep, hotter than horseradish." He judged the time by the length of the fence-pole shadows.

"Yeah, another sweltering one," Ed responded glumly.

Weather, however, wasn't on his mind. He was worn out from lying awake most of the night wondering if he made any headway with Jim. Also, if Jeb still had it in for him. At least it was Sunday. Locked in his cage, Jeb couldn't get at him. He'd spend the time thinking up more strategies to make trustee. If he didn't come up with something soon, he could kiss his escape goodbye.

"Sweat box light is on," Moose drolled.

Ed got up from his cot and joined Moose at the bars.

"Yeah, some poor guy is still in there. Wonder if it's Ben... I mean, the Fish?"

"For Pete's sake," Duff snorted. He sat on the edge of his cot rolling a smoke. "Each guy's got to look out for himself. Can't you get that through your head? If it is him, he simply needs to wise up, follow the rules, and learn how to keep that mouth of his shut."

"Yeah, I suppose so," Ed replied. Ambling back to his cot, he sat down cross-legged, shoulders hunched, and resumed his thinking. If a miracle happened and he made trustee, he could sure use help from someone on the outside. Who did he know?

Bob Wilkinson? He recalled the letter he received at the pen saying he found it hard to believe Ed guilty. Nah. Too risky. He scrunched his eyes into narrow slits. He'd also be asking Bob to jeopardize his job at the newspaper. He couldn't do that to him.

He stretched out on the cot, crossed his arms behind his head, and stared at the ceiling. Who could he get to help? His mouth dropped open. *Of course. Avery!*

"What ya thinkin' about?" Moose cocked his head. "You sure got a funny look on your face."

"Oh, just thinking about family," Ed said, covering up. "Got no

139

siblings. Closest immediate relative I have is my cousin, Avery. We had good times together as kids. After becoming adults we lost touch. Unfortunately, my mama didn't much approve of him."

"Yeah? Why's that?"

"I was bragging to her about my coverage of the first day of a murder trial and how I got to sit in the special section for reporters. She said she was proud of me, but I shouldn't get too puffed up. She told me, 'Remember, the Good Book says pride goeth before a fall.'" Ed grinned. "I had, you know, one of those scripture-spoutin' mamas."

Moose laughed. "You know, sometimes you almost make me believe you're innocent." Ed ignored the remark and continued.

"I told her there shouldn't be anything prideful about being excited over the opportunity of a lifetime. Well, that's when she said, 'You don't want to end up like your wayward cousin, Avery.'"

Moose's eyebrows jutted up, eager to hear a good story. "How bad was he?"

"Oh, not that bad. As a teenager, Avery spent a couple of nights in jail for burglarizing a car shop. Boy, did he love cars. Tried to convince my mama he straightened up afterwards, but didn't do any good. Last I heard he worked at some county job in Richmond. Lost track after that."

"Well," Moose said, "at least he did better with his life than we did."

Ed didn't tell Moose the whole story. Nor did he ever tell his mama. Avery would have faced a long sentence in prison if he hadn't provided an alibi for him—a false one at that. Reluctant at first, Avery's repentant attitude and the vow he'd never do anything like that again influenced him. The alibi was something Ed felt guilty over for years. But Avery kept his word, stayed clean and got a decent job. He also told him, *"I owe you one, good buddy. One day, I'll make it right with you."* Yep, Avery owed him.

He eyed the paper and pencils for letter writing placed under the bars by Jim. He'd write, using their secret code. He hoped Avery would remember.

He pictured their youth, and how they used the codes in cryptic messages to each other when playing cops and robbers with the neighborhood gang. His mouth curved slightly at the memories.

He and Avery played the robbers, always planning daring escapes.

"You'll never catch us!" Avery would bark to those taking the role of the cops. Then he'd roll his eyes at Ed. "We're too slick for that, aren't we, Ed?"

"Yeah. Me and Avery, we've got a system."

They were given a five-minute head start and both took off lickity-split.

"Sixteen," Avery hollered, as he ran one direction and Ed the other. That meant they needed to make a fast getaway.

"Five," Ed yelled back, running like mad down the hillside, meaning they were to meet at a designated spot where they had hidden their beat-up bicycles.

"Twelve," Avery screamed as he barreled through bushes and out of sight, indicating it was a life or death situation. Two meant spies were watching, eight meant to cancel plans, and three was a cry for help. Ed could still hear their excited calls echoing down the wooded hillsides.

He'd take the chance he still lived in Richmond and send it to the last address he remembered.

Picking up the piece of paper, he wet the tip of the pencil with his tongue. He needed to use three, five and twelve. Trustees censored all letters.

Dear Avery,

I'm hoping you still live in the same place and receive this letter. You'll know by where this is coming from what's happened to me. I used to be at the pen but now doing roadwork at Prison Camp Number 9. I hope you can come and see me. Call the prison to get directions.

Guess you know by now ma's been gone nearly *four* years. I sure do miss her. If she were here I know she'd be visiting me all the time. My wife was murdered *three* years ago. Yes, *three* years is a long time to be without her.

We had some fun times when we were kids. Remember that big family we used to play with, the one with the *twelve* kids? I believe *twelve* is right. And those *two* crazy ones, Jake and Fred? Well, enough about the past. It would be nice if you could visit me. Hope you get this.

Your cousin, Ed.

He read and reread it, proud of how he disguised the codes. Now, if only Avery remembers. More importantly, would he come? If he still worked for the county, maybe with his connections he could nose around and find something useful about Buford. Also, provide him with a car once he escaped camp and could get to Richmond. It was a long shot.

Folding the letter, he placed it in the envelope and addressed it. Leaving it unsealed according to rules, he placed it on the floor next to the bars for pick-up.

Just then the cage door opened. Squeaky poked his head in and motioned to Duff. "You got a visitor," he said in his twangy, nasal voice. Duff, maintaining his usual poker face, exited the cage and lumbered across the yard.

Ed watched him and heaved a big sigh. "If my mama were alive," he said in a thin whisper, "she'd visit me."

Yeah, I know," Moose returned in a slow monotone. "Mamas are like that."

"Of course," Ed said wistfully, "If she were, I know how it would go. She'd struggle not to cry—and of course she would. Then, she'd try to encourage me with one of her stand-by scriptures, 'Everything's going to work together for your good.'"

Moose shrugged his shoulders. "Well, at least it sounds good."

The heat wore on and horse flies, drawn by the foul odor, buzzed in and out of the thunder buckets. With lightning speed they attacked wherever bare skin was exposed.

Ed picked up a magazine and shooed the flies about his head. Moose stood at the bars apparently not bothered by them. Ed joined him while still furiously fanning away the flies.

He followed Moose's stare down to the fence at the gathering of Sunday visitors where mothers fussed over children's appearance, adults paced nervously like it was their first time, and a few women clad in navy blue dresses, their hair up in buns, carried black Bibles under their arms. With only a skeleton crew on Sundays, Ed didn't see how the guards could monitor conversations—which would work out great when and if Avery came.

Ten minutes later they watched Duff wave goodbye to his

visitor, then exchange words with Al at the gate before starting his trek back to the cage. Squeaky followed behind.

"Al's worth talking to," Moose said, slapping at a fly. "He's not quite as mean as the rest. You can talk to him as long as no other guards are looking. He passes on camp gossip."

Duff acted strangely when he entered the cage, and sat down on his cot without saying a word. After Squeaky locked the door, Duff spoke in low tones.

"Word has it Trusty Jim is leaving. His parole finally went through."

Excitement surged through Ed. But it was short-lived. If Jim left, his source for getting in good with Jeb was gone. He'd have to start all over with a different trustee, and who knew what kind of guy he'd be? He swung at more flies while he and Moose both turned and faced Duff, eager to hear more.

"That ain't all," Duff remarked. "The Fish done went and heel-strung himself."

"Heel-strung!" Ed let out a short gasp, familiar with inmates' practice of cutting the Achilles tendon up the calf.

"But the Doc doesn't come out to this camp," he said. "Without medical attention it'll become permanent. I saw a con back at the pen do it. They never sent him to the infirmary and from then on his foot flopped like a limp rag."

"Well," Moose said, stretching his arms over his head, "he got a razor from somewhere."

"I bet he thinks that'll get him off the hook," Duff said. "Is he ever dead wrong. Even if he can't work on the road no more, or even if sent back to the county jail, Jeb's gonna get his pound of flesh first." Ed winced.

"Can't feel sorry for him none." Moose reached into his shirt pocket, rolled a cigarette paper and licked its edges shut. "This is a mean stir. Every man has to look out for himself. And you," he raised his voice slightly, looking directly at Ed, "I'm surprised you ain't learned that yet. You act like the Fish is your brother or something."

Ed didn't respond. He had to admit he felt a strange sympathy for Benny. Poor guy, only trying to get his ma's cow back. But Moose was right, he simply couldn't spend his energies thinking about the Fish's predicament.

Four o'clock came, or so Moose claimed. The ball of white fire beat down on the top of the roof making the cage hotter than the devil's kitchen. More biting flies swarmed in and swooped about Ed's bare ankles and scabs.

Dropping onto his bed, he curled up in a ball and draped the blanket over his head, but quickly decided the rank smell of the bedding would kill him before the flies did. He threw the cover off and leapt into the aisle.

Cursing and waving his arms, Ed grabbed up the magazine again, trying to shoo them out of the cage. Moose and Duff rolled their eyes and half-grinned at each other.

The magazine slipped from Ed's hand, shot past Moose, and landed on the floor. It slid to a precarious stop beneath the bars where it dropped over the edge onto the ground.

"Hey you, Number 405!" roared a familiar voice. "Whatcha think you're doin'?"

Ed froze. He slowly turned. Jeb appeared around the corner of the cage twirling his pointed walking stick between two fingers like a propeller. Jim dutifully followed behind.

"Just exercising, boss...swishin' flies."

Sauntering up to the bars, Jeb scrutinized the crumpled magazine on the ground.

"Well," he said, "it looks to me like state property is being destroyed. The State gives it to you scumbags as a favor. Now, yur just making me think you still got an attitude problem, 405."

Ed glanced at Moose and Duff who ducked their heads and focused on rolling cigarettes. Two huge horse flies buzzed about Ed's neck. They landed with stabbing bites. He didn't move.

Jeb gave him a long, contemptuous look, smirked and motioned for Jim to unlock the cage door.

"Get out here, 405."

With insides shaking, Ed climbed down the steps and stood in the oven-like heat.

Jeb pushed his wide-brimmed hat back from his forehead, then folded his arms across his sweaty chest, pushing folds of greasy-looking flab down onto his stomach.

144

"Well, Number 405, I can see we still got to get that mind of yours right." He crooked his finger at him. "C'mon."

Ed traipsed behind, his heart hammering. What would it be this time? A whipping? Needles, like Rufus? He'd never survive another twenty-four hours in the sweatbox with spikes. Not in this heat. He might as well forget about escaping, or God trying to work anything out for his good. As far as his letter to Avery—probably a lost cause. He felt like a dead man walking his last mile.

They marched by the painted house where the captain sat on the front porch leisurely balancing his chair back on two legs. He casually looked up from the pile of papers in his lap. Unconcerned, he looked back down.

The small procession trudged to the front of the compound near the gun platform, turned right, and headed toward the sweatbox. Ed noted the light bulb still on. Whoever was inside would be released to make room for him. Everything was over.

Jeb brought the small group to a halt and began to pace. He stroked his chin as if deep in thought.

"Well, Jim, we got us a problem with 405. He still don't have his mind right. Now when a man's mind ain't right he can't be trusted."

Jim nodded.

Ed raised his head. "Boss, you don't have to worry at all about me because—"

"Now, you take Jim here," Jeb interrupted, "he's had his mind right for some time. He's done so well, he's gone and shook his time. Gonna be paroled."

Why's he telling me this?

"So I asked Jim the other day, got any ideas for your replacement? Know what he said? 'How about Number 405?'"

Ed's stomach lurched.

"Well, I said back to him, I don't think Number 405's got his mind right yet. Didn't I say that, Jim?"

"Sure did, boss."

"So, I told him we'd just have to see. I especially like a man who has already tasted the consequences of breaking the rules. Now, 405, you think you could be a trustee and do what you're told?"

Ed could hardly believe what he was hearing. Finally, his ticket out! Ed managed to cover his elation with a stoic expression.

"Yes sir, boss. I finally got my mind right, sir, and you'd find I'd be a hard worker."

"Well, 405, I'm not sure I approve, but the captain took Jim's word for it. You'd follow orders?"

"Yes, sir."

It wouldn't be easy kowtowing to Jeb, but if he didn't, he'd end up dead before he could escape.

"Open 'er up, then," Jeb said, motioning Ed toward the sweatbox.

Ed advanced up the wood steps feeling the exhilaration of his new position...also its downside. In the eyes of the inmates he'd be viewed differently—a defector to the enemy, a potential squealer. Nobody would trust him. What about Moose and Duff? Would they treat him the same?

He lifted the two-by-four out of its brace and swung the door open. The suffocating heat of the box gushed out smacking him in the face, along with the foul stink of sweat, body odor, urine and feces. It was enough to make him gag.

Huddled on the floor in a heap was an emaciated figure.

Ed gasped.

It was Benny, or what was left of him.

CHAPTER 21

~~~

Benny lay in a heap on the floor of the sweatbox. Ed barely recognized him. His face was purple and swollen with bruises and gashes, his blonde hair matted with blood, and his mouth hanging open like a dying man's last petrified gasp for air. Was he dead? Ed immediately thought of his yellow dog, the day it lay crushed on the highway.

Much to his relief, Benny moved ever so slowly. He raised one trembling hand and shielded his eyes from the glaring sunlight that poured through the open doorway.

"Get him out here!" Jeb yelled.

"C'mon," Ed said softly. "You've got to get up."

"I ain't gonna make it," came the feeble response.

Ed leaned over and slipped his hands beneath Benny's shoulders. The fetid stink of urine, defecation and sweat, rushed up into his nostrils.

"Sure you are," he said, easing him to standing position. He glanced down at Benny's heel-strung foot caked with blackened blood. Would he ever reach a point where he'd do something like that?

Benny, now standing, leaned against the back wall and looked past Ed's shoulder to where Jeb stood in the yard. His eyes widened.

"He's going to kill me for sure," he whispered. "I been prayin' all night to die, but then I think about Ma. I'm all she's got and—

"Leave him be, 405!" Jeb shrieked. "Get yourself out here."

Ed inched away and stepped back through the doorway. Turning, he walked down the steps and stood by Jim.

Benny staggered to the door dragging his strung foot. Grasping both edges of the frame for support he slowly hobbled onto the first step, teetered, and then tumbled down the rest. He lay on the ground, a crumpled mass of trembling flesh.

"Lost a little of your spunk, eh, 415?" Jeb skittered over to where Benny lay. Swinging his foot back, he kicked him hard in

147

the groin. Benny let out a gasp. Ed's heart felt a vicarious pain. It was all he could do to keep from rushing over and helping him. Is this what being a trustee was going to involve? Stand by and watch someone tortured?

Benny struggled to rise. Jeb whipped out his revolver and hit him on the side of the head with the butt. Blood spurted down the side of Benny's face. Raising his arm higher, Jeb swiftly brought two more hard whacks down on his head and shoulders.

Ed panicked. He shot a quick glance at Jim who stood like a tin soldier but flashed him a warning expression. Ed took the cue. He stood and watched.

Benny fell forward on his knees from the pistol's impact, his face slamming into the dirt. Rolling over, he curled into a ball and wrapped his arms around his head for protection.

"Get up you foul-smelling beast!" Jeb screamed. "Stand up like you oughta!" Benny, his body quivering like jelly, did his best to comply. Ed braced for whatever was to come next.

Jeb raised his arm to strike again but then stopped mid-air. He turned and faced Ed.

Prickles plunged down Ed's spine.

"Now, 405, you see I'm just trying to teach this here fish a lesson. He's gotta get his mind right or he's going to have a bad time while he's here. Ain't that right?"

Ed nodded.

"All of us got to assume our responsibility and do what it takes to teach prisoners for their own good. Take him out back."

Ed raised his eyebrows. What was out back? He knew only of the small tool shed, the unidentified clapboard building, and the dog kennel. He pictured the chewed-up escapee. Surely, Jeb wouldn't sick the hounds on Benny. Chills tore through every nerve ending.

Get goin', 405."

Ed moved forward with uneasy, heavy steps. Benny stood hunched over with one hand holding his stomach, balancing on one leg to favor his strung foot. Ed hooked an arm beneath Benny's armpit. Supporting most of Benny's weight, he gently prodded him.

Benny staggered, keeping his eyes downward, focusing on picking up his flopping foot high enough to clear the ground. With every step he gasped with pain. Lifting his head, he looked at Ed.

"Promise me," he said in low, halting tones, "if something happens...you'll let my ma know?"

Ed swallowed hard. "What's her name?"

"Madge...Madge Yates. Lives in Richmond, near the Franklin Street Open Air Market...531 South Eighteenth Street."

Ed knew the section of town. As kids, he and Avery often went to the public market to listen to the darkies sing and watch the hucksters bring produce in on their canvas-covered carts.

"Promise...me?"

"Yes," Ed whispered. What else could he say? No telling if he'd ever have the opportunity.

"Thanks," Benny whispered. He lowered his head back down and concentrated on his foot. They moved unsteadily toward the mess hall with Jeb and Jim following behind.

Ed's mind raced. Whatever was about to happen to Benny, he wouldn't be able to help him. What if they put needles under his fingernails? His stomach twisted. He'd have to stand there and watch.

"Keep going!" Jeb bellowed, "to the white building."

Ed steered Benny around the corner of the mess hall and into the wide expanse of yard extending some three hundred feet to the kennel and the clapboard building.

"Move it, 405!" Jeb impatiently called out.

Approaching the building, the four hounds immediately sprang from the shade of an overhanging scrub tree and began baying.

It was then Benny raised his head. No sooner did he see where they were headed when he instinctively pulled back. Ed saw his eyes fill with fear. The screams he heard in the night—they must have been Benny's. And the building? Was it there where the tortures were performed?

Rounding the back of the building they entered a circular clearing devoid of weeds except for a vertical iron pipe nearly as tall as a man that stood perpendicularly from the ground. A sickening sensation twisted Ed's insides—a hitching post! He saw the handcuffs dangling from the horizontal bar attached to the top.

Standard procedure was to handcuff a prisoner to the horizontal bar at mid-chest level. If a guard was out of sorts he might decide to raise the bar so the prisoner's hands were higher than his head. This forced the inmate to stand for hours in that position. Other times, the bar was lowered to prevent him from standing up straight and to keep his back bent.

Ed recalled his own nine agonizing hours on it—the excruciating pain in his spine, urinating in his pants, the sunburn, dehydration, weakness, and guards taunting him with water. He took in Benny's pathetic figure. He was in no condition to survive *that*. How could he save him?

Stupid question. He couldn't—not without jeopardizing his position as trustee and giving up all hope of escape. Maybe Jeb's intent was to leave Benny on for only a few hours. He could possibly survive that.

Ed squinted into the copper-colored sky. The afternoon sun, still a massive ball of fire, shone down with a vengeance. With no breeze, the bar and handcuffs would be generating heat of at least one hundred degrees. Maybe hotter. Ed thought back to his own blistered wrists. He still bore the scars.

"Okay, 405," Jeb snapped, "take off his shirt and hitch him up."

Ed's face pinched tight as he undid Benny's shirt and removed it. Placing it over his shoulder, he nudged him toward the post. Surprisingly, he met with no resistance. Benny's face said it all. He had given up.

Ed took hold of the handcuffs which were nearly too hot to handle, and quickly snapped the cuffs around the limp wrists. Benny sucked in a couple of quick breaths. Lowering the horizontal bar a few inches to make sure it was even with Benny's chest, Ed leaned in next to his ear.

"I'm sorry," he whispered. "Don't know what I can do to help." Benny nodded weakly. "Remember what you promised about my ma..."

"Don't worry—"

"Raise it higher, 405," Jeb ordered, "above his head."

Ed reluctantly complied, then walked back and stood by Jim, Benny's shirt still hanging across his shoulder. His pulse whooshed so loud, he was sure Jim could hear.

Jeb ambled over to a large wooden box sitting against the back of the clapboard building. Flipping the lid open he fumbled inside

150

and dragged out a few whips, debating which one to use.

Ed gawked. Benny was also to be whipped?

Jeb withdrew one, and clomped back toward the clearing.

Ed studied the whip. Instead of a single length of smooth finished leather, it consisted of six lengths of dried, hardened thongs of rough rawhide. Interwoven and protruding from each cord were sharp wires with hooked ends designed to tear the flesh. Ed's mind rolled into a panic. No way would Benny live through that! How far was Jeb going to go?

Jeb ambled up to him. "Here, 405." He held out the whip. "You said you could follow orders."

Ed blinked with incredulity. *He* had to whip Benny? He took the handle with tremulous fingers. This was his test. If he refused he'd be demoted back to working on the road, probably tortured first. Once back in chains, he'd never escape. He slid Benny's shirt off his shoulder and placed it on the ground.

Inching his way toward Benny, he stared at the pitiable scene before him. With Benny's back to him and his raised arms handcuffed to either side of the horizontal bar, it reminded him of the picture in his mother's bedroom of Jesus on the cross. Only Benny was hanging backwards.

Jeb impatiently cleared his throat.

Ed slowly adjusted the whip in his hand, making stalling gestures. Could he do this? There was only one way. Forget about the man he used to be. Ed Bowman wouldn't do it but perhaps 405 could. He wiped the sweaty palms of his hands down the sides of his pants, each time transferring the whip into his opposite hand. Benny could survive a couple of hits if he went easy. Jeb certainly wouldn't demand more than that.

With a twist of his wrist, he flipped the wire-tipped thongs behind him into a pile on the ground, poised to strike. He wouldn't swing hard.

Raising his arm, he pulled the heavy cords up from the ground and swung them forward as easily and lightly as he could, high and rounded up into the air so the thongs would lose their force when landing.

The sharp wires thudded into Benny's back, ripping flesh. He let out a shrill, desolate cry that shot through Ed like an electric cattle prod. He stood wide-eyed, stunned at the amount of blood from only one light strike.

Ed glanced back and raised his eyebrows in silent appeal at Jeb who stood watching with his arms nonchalantly folded across his belly. He only smirked and motioned with his head for him to continue.

Turning back to face Benny, his emotions felt like a huge python writhing inside slowly crushing the life out of him. Maybe he could bring the whip down slightly off aim so some of the thongs would miss. He drew the whip back, aimed a little to the right and hurled it forward. Three of them landed on Benny's right shoulder and slid down his side. Even those few did their job, drawing more blood than before.

Ed's thoughts ping-ponged back and forth, torn between the right thing to do and his desire to survive and escape. He should stand up and defy Jeb regardless of the consequences. But, admittedly, he was afraid to oppose him.

Something else hit him harder than that. The claw-like truth scraped through his insides. He wasn't only agonizing over what was happening to Benny, but to himself. He wasn't Ed Bowman anymore—just a pitiless, empty shell of a man with no guts.

Maybe if he pretended it wasn't Benny hanging on the post. Instead, Gunther Buford. That might work. A couple more easy hits and surely Jeb will say it's enough.

He brought the whip back ready to hurl the wire-tipped thongs forward on his image of Buford but his mind-game didn't work. It was really Benny hanging on that bar. This was a nightmare beyond anything he'd ever encountered.

He stood statue still, the whip hanging loosely in his hand. He could do no more. He would suffer Jeb's wrath. Maybe he'd still manage to escape…somehow.

Turning, he stared at Jeb helplessly. Instead of the expected onslaught of infuriation, Jeb's voice was slick and smooth like oil.

"You got no spirit, 405. Here, let me show you how it's done."

He marched forward, grabbed the whip from Ed's hand and shoved him to one side. Ed shuffled over to stand by Jim, picking up Benny's shirt from the ground as he did.

Swirling the bloodied, wire-tipped thongs in a circle on the ground to coat them with dirt, Jeb raised the deadly instrument over his head. He threw it forward, cracking it down square onto the middle of Benny's back. Ed glanced over at Jim who gazed straight ahead, expressionless.

Jeb continued hurling the whip. Sweat poured down his reddened face and his chest heaved like a man possessed. Ed trembled, growing more alarmed by the minute as the thongs slammed into Benny's now motionless body.

After six more vicious hits, Benny's flesh hung in strips. He was no longer moaning. In fact, Benny no longer moved. He just hung there. Blood was everywhere and horse flies were swarming in for their feast.

Jeb raised the whip again. Ed looked at Jim with an expression of desperate appeal. "Jim?" he whispered. "This is murder. You gotta do something."

To his relief, Jim responded by slowly walking up to Jeb. Without a word, he laid one hand on his shoulder. Jeb turned with a jerk, his face a livid purple. Jim calmly motioned with his head toward Benny, whereupon Jeb stared at the lifeless form. He slowly lowered his arm letting the treacherous thongs pile up at his feet.

Jim strode toward the bloodied body. Ed quickly joined him. One look said it all. Benny was dead.

Calmly and methodically Jim undid the handcuffs. Benny's body crumpled to the ground. Ed reached down, gently took hold of one shoulder and rolled him over face up. The smell of urine and blood drifted up into his face.

He could think of only one thing. Benny had been jailed and senselessly killed all because he tried to get his mama's cow back. As far as Jeb was concerned, Ed knew no one would ever find out. No reason it would be any different here from the pen. Now Benny's mama had no one, and she'd never know what happened to her son. He thought of his promise. *Madge Yates...531 South Eighteenth Street.*

After a long silence, Jeb muttered, "You know what to do, Jim."

Jim motioned for Ed to follow him to the building. Reaching into the box where the whips were, he withdrew two shovels and handed one to Ed.

Returning to where Benny lay, Jim placed his shovel across the

153

body indicating Ed do the same. Jim picked up Benny's feet. Ed lifted his shoulders.

With the two shovels crisscrossed on top of Benny's body, Ed helped carry him toward the back fence by the kennel. Jim apparently knew where to go. The hounds lay in the shade watching, their heads resting on their out-stretched front legs.

At the designated spot Jim dropped Benny's feet. Ed lowered his end, wondering how they were going to dig in such hard ground.

Jim thrust his shovel into the dirt. Ed did too, amazed at the earth's softness once the crust broke through. How many others were buried here?

He took a guarded side-glance at Jeb who was now leaning against the corner of the building in the shade of the overhanging eaves. With his arms folded across his stomach, he watched with smug satisfaction. The curl of his upper lip said it all.

He and Jim continued digging as hordes of flies darted about on the body. With every shovelful Ed couldn't tear his eyes away from Benny's yellow hair all matted, his vacant eyes staring up into the sky. What could he tell his mama? That he stood by holding Benny's shirt while her son was killed and did nothing?

They lifted him, dropped him into the hole, and then proceeded to fill it in.

Jim said nothing. Neither did Ed.

The only sound filling the muggy air was the scraping of their shovels, buzzing of horseflies, and the piercing screech of the cicadas.

CHAPTER 22

~~~

Saturday morning, heat waves from the early sun bounced from the ground as Ed hustled across the compound, his shoes scuffing against a few dirt clods. Trusty Jim's parole was set for today. Part of him said it might not happen, the other part said it would. His whole future rested on whether it did or didn't. He had to make sure.

Reaching the gate, he looked around. He saw Jim standing on the captain's porch shaking hands, then sling his duffel bag over his shoulder and move down the steps. Ed could only imagine how happy the guy must feel, but no more than he did. This meant his new role as trustee was in the bag and he'd achieved the first leg of his goal. The second leg of course, contained a new set of dilemmas for him to wrestle with.

It's not like he didn't know about them. They'd bugged him night and day, but there was no way to address them prior to being made trustee. Now, he had to solve them or escape would be out of the picture.

Jim approached the gate and gave a surprised glance at seeing him.

Ed raised a hand. "Thanks for everything, Jim. Good luck."

Jim acknowledged the gesture with the semblance of a half-smile. Shifting his duffel bag to his other shoulder, he turned and took one last look about the compound, then moved through the gate.

A blue Ford coupe waited a few yards away. Jim climbed in. The engine coughed, expelled a burst of backfire and took off down the dirt road. Turning left at the junction, it disappeared from sight.

Ed took a euphoric breath and moseyed back across the compound, turning his thoughts to his new set of problems.

He needed someone to falsify ID papers for use on the outside. Moose once commented that Scratch had run a business at the pen faking documents for prisoners. Ed had already made considerable headway with him, but even if he were willing to forge them he'd still have to cozy up to Numbers for the paper and ink from the office. He grimaced. Numbers, pretty much a loner, was far from easy to approach.

Last, he had to figure out how to leave camp without causing suspicion in order to give him enough time to get ahead of the hounds. He also had to sketch an escape route using side roads to bypass roadblocks. He plodded toward the commissary engrossed in thought. Although not as major, there was another problem. His new job.

It would have its perks but also its downside. For starters, the men would distance themselves from him. That hurt. He saw Moose heading his direction. He hoped he and Duff would continue their friendship with him.

Ed studied him. Would he prove to be one of the hydra heads? He had asked that question so many times over but always shook it away. Somehow he trusted the guy. Even if Moose sensed he was planning an escape, he didn't dare share that with him. Moose already made it plain he wouldn't be an aider. He nodded a greeting as he approached.

"Guess I should congratulate you on making trustee," Moose remarked, rubbing his chin whiskers. "Course, you know," he looked down and shuffled one foot in the dirt, "what the men think."

"Yeah, I'll turn stoolie." Ed forced an uncomfortable smile. "Comes with the territory."

"I don't know you're any better off," Moose said, reaching into his shirt pocket and pulling out a pouch of tobacco. "Not much different working under Jeb on the gang, or as trustee. You still gotta tow a tight line. One wrong move—"

"Except," Ed cut in, "I've got no chains, and my hair's growing back. Plus, no more back-breaking work on the road."

"Guess it has a few plusses." Moose dug into the pouch and stuffed a wad of tobacco inside his cheek. "But don't assume you got it made. You're still on dangerous ground." He turned in the direction of the quoit court, hesitated, and then looked back over his shoulder.

"Don't let your guard down," he cautioned, "even for a second."

He walked away.

Moose was right. There was no way he dared think he was safe. Squeaky watched him like a hawk. One slip-up and Jeb could consign him back to chains—worse yet, beat him to a pulp and bury him out by Benny. He angled toward the commissary.

For now, however, he saw no immediate problem. He would perform his new duties perfectly, which consisted of monitoring bed sheets going to and from the laundry, seeing washbasins were ready for the road gang at the end of the day, handing out supplies to new arrivals, and managing the commissary. The commissary was his favorite job. Jim taught him well in the few days prior to his leaving. On Saturday he would see all the men from the gang, although he had to be realistic—they might not speak to him.

Climbing the steps, he pulled a key from his shirt pocket, unlocked the clasp to the door and ambled inside. So much to figure out.

Another thing—could he count on Avery's help? He hadn't heard from him. All he would need would be for Avery to hide a car, money and some clothes somewhere in Richmond. He also worried about their conversation on visitor's day due to a new development. With the new barracks now built, visiting would no longer be at the front fence. Guards would more closely monitor all talking. He would have to formulate sentences he could use with hidden meanings so Avery would understand, but not the guards.

Dawdling over to the wooden desk by the counter, he grabbed up the inventory notebook and reached for a pencil intending to tally the stock. Instead, he laid it back down and let out a troubled sigh.

The only real ace he had in his deck was Avery. He just had to come through.

One month later, he received Avery's letter. Ed exulted with joy as he sat alone in the trustees' barrack on the edge of his cot. As expected, the envelope had been opened for censoring but he saw nothing blacked out. He grew more excited with each line.

Dear Ed,

I would have written sooner, but I moved and your letter was forwarded. I didn't know you were in prison. I called and got directions, so I'll come to see you.

Yes, five years has been a long time. You say your wife was killed four years ago. I understand. Really sorry for that. And yes, I remember the twelve kids we played with and the ones who weren't right in the head.

It's about ten miles for me to drive. The county told me the next day for visiting is August 11. I'll come because I owe you. Things will work out.

Your cousin, Avery

Great! Avery understood and had repeated the code numbers. His mind raced. The eleventh was next Sunday. This was really pushing things tight. Would they be able to relay everything to each other?

He also had to get Scratch to forge ID papers as soon as possible and sketch out his escape route, but without a truck how would he get to Avery's car before the hounds caught up with him? Could he outfox Jeb and the captain some way?

He barely folded the letter when an image came to mind— Uncle Remus' story of Brer Rabbit's encounter with Brer Fox and how he always outwitted him. It was one of the many bedtime stories his mother used to read. He could picture every detail of the scene as mama sat on the edge of his bed while pine knots crackled in the kitchen stove.

Brer Fox caught Brer Rabbit by using a tar baby. When Brer Rabbit tried to talk to it and didn't get an answer, he struck it on the side of the head. With his hands stuck fast, a victorious Brer Fox jumped out and laughed. "I'm going to barbecue you today, for sure!"

Ed nodded. Yep, that's sure what Jeb would like to do to me.

His favorite part was Brer Rabbit's cleverness in making Brer Fox think he didn't want to be thrown into the briar patch, when that was what he wanted all the time. When his mother came to that part, he would cry out on cue, *"Skin me, snatch out my eyeballs, tear out my hair and ears by de roots and cut off my legs. But please, Brer Fox, don't fling me in dat brier patch!"* Born and bred there, it's what he wanted the fox to do.

Could he somehow trick ol' Brer-fox-Jeb, like Brer Rabbit did?

158

If so, what did he need he could pretend he didn't want? It took only a split second. A vehicle! Of course. How? His answer came sooner than he thought.

Monday morning, he turned the corner of the mess hall and spied the captain and Jeb talking. Ed avoided both of them whenever he could, so made a hand gesture to his head as if he'd forgotten something and whirled about on his heel to head back in the opposite direction. He wasn't fast enough.

The captain glanced up and called. "Come over here, 405."

Ed turned back, noting Jeb was mumbling something to the captain and shaking his head in disagreement. Ed took off his cap as he approached.

"Have you ever driven a clutch truck, 405," the captain asked, "one that doesn't need cranking?"

Noticing the disapproval on Jeb's face, Ed's mind shot into high gear.

"Well, yes sir. Drove one inside the pen when I worked in the woodworking factory, but I don't want to drive any more if I can help it. I was, uh, in an accident once. Getting behind a wheel makes me awful nervous."

"You heard him, Captain," Jeb interjected. "Besides, he ain't been a trustee long enough to leave the camp."

The captain, ignoring Jeb, continued. "I have to use Squeaky for something else, so we need someone to drive the supply truck to the pen for a while."

Twisting and wringing his cap, Ed played it up as big as he could, including a depressing sigh.

"With all respect, sir, there must be one of the other trustees who can do it. I might get into a wreck."

Jeb's facial expression gradually changed, and Ed sensed the sadistic gears turning. He could almost hear Jeb's maniacal Brer-fox-chuckle. If Jeb thought there was a chance he might foul up, maybe even run the truck off the road, he'd demote him back to the gang or else torture him to death.

"Well, Captain," Jeb quickly spoke up, "perhaps I was wrong. Maybe he can be trusted." He turned to Ed.

"You think you'd get rabbit fever, 405?"

159

"No sir, boss. I'm not thinking about anything like that. I just want to keep my nose clean and make the best of my time. I don't want the law one step behind me for the rest of my life. No siree."

"But," Ed added, facing the captain directly, "if it's all the same to you, sir, I'd prefer not doing it."

The captain turned to Jeb. "He can probably do it if he has to." His tone made it plain he'd already decided.

"Well," Jeb drawled, "you know best, Captain. I'm always willing to give an inmate a chance to prove himself. Yeah, why not? I can keep close tabs on him." Jeb looked like he was already anticipating what kind of punishment to mete out.

"Okay, have him take over the drive indefinitely until I decide differently." He nodded to Ed.

"It's settled then, 405. Tomorrow after breakfast, report to Jeb."

Ed groaned, trying to look as miserable as he could while responding with an obedient, "Yes sir."

The captain and Jeb walked away. Ed mentally patted himself on the back, and inside he was jubilant. "Good thinking," he whispered.

Yet, driving the truck didn't mean it was time for him to escape. He had to build Jeb and the captain's confidence with his trustworthiness. Tomorrow's run to Richmond would simply prove his dependability for future drives. During that time he would fine-tune the details so nothing could go wrong. He also had to connect with Avery.

The next morning couldn't arrive fast enough.

After breakfast he reported to Jeb who ushered him across the yard to the car shed. Handing him a map and ID papers to show at the prison, he pointed to a gray, 1937 half-ton paneled truck parked inside.

"This is the one you'll use. The other truck," he said, pointing to a '31 Model-A pickup, "is for Squeaky's use for other things.

"You sure you know how to drive this, 405? Don't need no crankin'. All you gotta do is turn the key and push the starter button."

"Uh...yeah," Ed said hesitantly.

"Anything happens to this truck, you're dead. Understand?"

Ed winced and twisted his face into a beseeching look.

"You have exactly until two o'clock this afternoon to get the truck back, ya hear? You gotta be pullin' in at the gate then. Not five minutes after...not even one minute after. Got that?"

Ed nodded. "I won't have to do this every week, will I boss?"

"You'll do exactly what yur told," Jeb snapped. "Here's the key. If you're not back on time you'll find out soon enough what that means. I'll be checking with the pen to see when you arrive. If not there, one call to the Richmond police and they'll have you nailed."

Taking the key, Ed climbed into the truck making sure he stumbled over the running board. He placed the map and ID papers on the seat beside him. Fidgeting with the key for a few seconds, he shoved it into the slot on the steering column. Unlocking the wheel, he pulled the chrome-plated ignition stem to "on" and pushed the starter button. The engine coughed, sputtered, and caught. Gripping the steering wheel until his knuckles turned white, he hesitated long enough to convince Jeb this was no easy task.

"Get going," Jeb ordered.

Ed shoved the gearshift into position and pressed on the accelerator. The truck lurched forward across the yard in uneven jerks. Ed made sure it did.

At the gate, Al moved up alongside the cab before waving him through.

"Don't screw up. Jeb's real touchy about a driver gettin' back on time, even by one minute."

"I'll try not to," Ed returned.

He took off down the dirt road, reached the highway and shot the truck onto the open road. Once out of sight from the gate, he relaxed and grinned. He could hardly believe he was on his own without chains or guards.

He passed people in cars coming and going, free as a bird. After he escaped he'd be just like them. The excitement was intoxicating.

"We did it—me and Brer Rabbit." He howled with laughter, reveling in the sound of his voice.

His jubilance proved short-lived as he drove past the road gang. The sight of the men hunched over slashing weeds with their yo-yos in the hot sun, the monotonous chant and guards shouting curses at the men, wrenched him back to reality.

One slip-up today and he'd be back out there with them. Worse yet, dead…buried next to Benny.

CHAPTER 23

~~~

Once past the chain gang and away from the stench of tar and grit, Ed's spirits lifted. He expanded his nostrils wide and breathed in the sun-dazzling smells that drenched the air—the nose-tingling fragrance of cerulean trees, honeysuckle, and freshly plowed pungent fields. He gawked at yellow cornstalks, blue cornflowers, and purple flora until he was giddy with joy. He shouted through the open window into the blast of breeze whooshing into his face.

"Thank you again, Brer Rabbit!"

He couldn't believe how masterfully he finagled Jeb and the captain into letting him drive the supply truck to Richmond. He chuckled and jutted his chin out. *"I won't have to do this every week, will I? I might get in a wreck..."*

This wasn't, however, a joy trip. With only once-a-week trips for supplies, today was his only day to plan his escape route. Next week would be too late. Avery was coming next Sunday.

The James River glittered near the distant horizon line. The junction would be coming up soon. Jeb made sure to point it out on the map at least three times.

"You can't miss it, 405. At the junction you turn left on the main highway. Got that? It'll take you straight into Richmond. Remember, be back no later than two o'clock sharp. Not five minutes after...not one minute after..."

He glanced at the rolled-up map lying on the passenger seat and slowed the truck. Pulling off onto the shoulder, he grabbed up the map and jumped out of the truck. Hurrying around to the front, he unrolled the map and spread it on top of the hood. He leaned in close.

"Hmmm." There had to be a shortcut bypassing the main highway—one he could use today to give him extra minutes to pick up a railroad timetable. At some point he might have to hop a boxcar after using Avery's car to drive into lower Richmond to see what he could find out from former cons. Previous assignments for the *Clarion* told him exactly where to find them.

Scrutinizing the map, he ran his finger along a small squiggly line. "Aha!" His discovery triggered a shot of adrenaline. There— just before the junction.

He traced a side road that wound east. Instead of going through Richmond proper it would take him the back way through the Riverview, Mt. Calvary and Hollywood cemeteries, and bring him in behind the prison instead of the front. The road looked short enough to save him twenty minutes. Surely there would be a general store along the way to pick up a timetable.

Leaping back into the truck, he threw it into gear and took off. For the next three miles he peered through the windshield with intensity, watching for the road. A hundred yards before the junction he spied the small, dirt turnoff.

Twisting the steering wheel a sharp left, he veered off the black top, grimacing as the truck hit one pothole after another. For another mile he dipped up and down over the rutted road, his stomach bunched into a rock-hard knot. Maybe this route wasn't a good idea. His thought quickly boomeranged to a positive. The police would assume that too. His spirits lifted.

He passed a small community of squatter shacks and then entered a town square. On his right, he saw a two-pump gas station with a red and white Flying A Gilmore sign above it. Across the street sat a general store. Further down, scattered farmhouses sat back from the road. He pulled into the service station.

A black man with a straw hat pulled over his face sat dozing on a wooden chair by the pumps. At the sound of Ed's truck he shoved the brim of his hat back with one finger and glanced up.

"I'm looking for a train timetable," Ed said, leaning out the window. "Got one?"

"No, suh," he drawled. "But ah'm sure dey's got one over there." He pointed across the street to the store.

Ed pulled out and crossed the street. Parking, he sat for a few seconds to compose his nerves before climbing out of the truck, then stepped onto the wood-planked sidewalk. Approaching the storefront he heard the metallic twang of a banjo coming from inside, accompanied by singing.

"Way down South where I cum from is where ah got my learn'n,

I fell in love with a pretty lil' girl and her name is Barbey Ellen."

He smiled at the old mountain song and pushed the door open, triggering a tinkling bell that announced his entry.

Strong whiffs of leather rushed into his nostrils. He surveyed the floor-to-ceiling shelves lining the high walls, and then the display tables. They contained the usual commodities of feed and harnesses, yardage, toiletries and coal oil lamps. He looked to see where the music was coming from and saw two white men at the rear of the store sitting on wooden apple crates singing, accompanied by a Darkie who plucked away on a banjo.

Sauntering across the hardwood floor toward the counter, he shifted his gaze upward. A thin, balding man of about sixty curiously eyed him from atop a stepladder.

"Looking for a railroad timetable," Ed said. "Got one?"

"Yep, think I do," the man said with a slow drawl. He climbed down, moseyed to the counter and reached behind a jar of green jellybeans. He shoved a small pile of brochures forward.

"Sort of old, but guess trains don't change much." Ed took one.

"Where you headed?" the man asked, scrutinizing Ed's clothes. "From the camp ain't you?"

"Nothing to worry about," Ed replied in a matter of fact tone. "I'm a trustee. Just goin' into Richmond to pick up supplies. One of the bosses wanted me to pick up a schedule."

Stuffing the timetable into his shirt pocket, he purposely made a point of walking nonchalantly through the rest of the store to examine other items before heading out the door. As long as he played it cool, the storekeeper had no reason to become suspicious.

"Thanks," he called back over his shoulder, glancing as he did at the large clock on the wall. He was still ahead time-wise. The bell tinkled as he exited.

He took his time climbing into the truck, just in case the clerk was watching. Pressing the starter button, he backed out and headed down the street at a purposefully slow speed. He heaved a sigh of relief when he reached the limits of the town and sped up.

Whizzing the truck down the washboard road, he passed a few scattered farmhouses and waterlogged fields, and soon spotted the sign. *Richmond - 10 miles.* His heart rate climbed.

Fifteen minutes later, he gunned the car to the top of a hill, giving him a bird's eye view of the James River. Flour mills dotted the shorelines and boats were docked at river piers. Beyond that lay Richmond proper. In the distance he made out the prison, also the honor farm where he was beaten for not picking enough cukes. He'd have no problem finding his way at this point.

At the city's fringe he took the road that meandered through the three cemeteries. Reaching the back of the prison, he entered the deep ravine called "Penitentiary Bottom." Atop the three elevated hillsides that half-circled around the back of the pen like an amphitheatre, were broken-down shanties and lean-tos where the Darkies lived. He remembered the place well. He and Avery used to scramble up to one of the three hilltops and watch inmates below shovel up coal left by railroad cars, and lug it back inside the prison.

Driving through the ravine he pulled around to the front of the prison. At the gate, he grabbed his ID papers off the seat and thrust them through the open window.

"Just got a call from the camp," the guard remarked, scrutinizing the papers. "Seems they're checking on you. I'll call back and tell them you're here. What's wrong with Squeaky?"

"Oh, the captain needed him for something else," Ed replied.

He shifted gears, eased through the gate and headed down the long driveway. Memories edged his teeth as he passed by the gray, u-shaped cellblocks and the section behind where the stocks and hitching posts were. Soon, he sighted the loading docks.

Ed noted boxes already stacked on the edge of the platform. An inmate wearing a white bib apron stood waiting. Ed didn't recognize him. Good. He needed to get loaded up as fast as he could with no conversation.

"Where's Squeaky?" the man drawled.

"Not coming this time," Ed said, climbing out. The man said no more, and proceeded to help load the boxes.

After twenty minutes, Ed signed the receipt and hopped into the truck. Easing out the clutch, he started back around the curve and down the main drive to the gate. He casually nodded to the guard.

"Got the time?"

"About one fifteen," the man said, after glancing in the back of the truck.

One fifteen? Ed panicked. He had exactly forty-five minutes to get back to camp. He'd take the back-road shortcut and hit the metal hard. The guard waved him through.

He took off, retracing his route through the three cemeteries and to the outskirts of town. Gunning the engine, he raced toward the hills, passed through the town square with the Gilmore gas station, and onto the shortcut road. He hadn't gone far when he let out a frustrated breath and had to slow. He hadn't figured his new load into the time equation of going over the potholes and ruts.

He could hear Jeb's warning. "*Anything happens and you're late—you're dead.*" He kicked himself for not returning on the main highway. What if he didn't make it on time? Sweat dribbled down his temples. Sometimes, old Brer Fox did catch Brer Rabbit. He gripped the steering wheel. Fear and panic flitted about in his head like bees trapped in a mason jar.

By the time he reached the end of the shortcut and maneuvered the truck onto the paved highway he felt too much time had elapsed. He still had a thirty-minute drive ahead of him. His breath came in staccatos.

Floor boarding the accelerator, he visualized what Jeb might do. He could consign him to a night in the box with spikes, whip him, crop one of his ears, worse yet, his toes so he couldn't run. He stomped harder on the pedal, remembering Benny's bloodied body and the shallow grave.

Fifteen minutes later he smelled the tar, passed the chain gang, and swerved onto the dirt road leading into camp. He sped up to the gate in a cloud of dust.

Uh oh. Jeb was there, glaring down at his watch. Al was jotting the time down in the log.

He had no idea if he was late or not—certainly, not by more than a minute or two at the most. But Jeb warned, *"Even if one minute..."*

Double-checking the flap on his shirt pocket to hide the timetable, he managed a calm expression on his face.

Jeb marched up to the window, his face hard as concrete.

"Well, you got about three minutes in your favor," he snapped. "That's cutting it close. You should have been here fifteen minutes ago. What took ya so long?"

Ed took a slow breath. "Well, boss, I found the James junction but turned the wrong way and went right instead of left. I told you driving makes me nervous. It was my first trip and if there has to be a next time..." he purposely rolled his eyes, "I'll make better time for sure."

Jeb's disappointment was apparent, but at least Ed knew he made it by two o'clock. Al was his witness.

Pulling the truck through the gate, he drove to the mess hall and around to the kitchen door. In the side-view mirror he saw Jeb following on foot.

What if Jeb claims by turning the wrong way he used up too much gas? His throat constricted. He slid out of the seat and hustled to the back of the truck imagining other excuses Jeb might use to punish him. The worse punishment would be Jeb prohibiting his use of the truck. He'd never escape.

He opened the back door of the truck and with trembling hands began hefting boxes out. Jeb halted and stood some twenty yards away, glowering.

All thumbs, Ed dropped one of the boxes. Out of the corner of his eye he saw Jeb scowl and walk away.

"Blast it," Ed muttered as he picked up the box. He's thinking up something. What?

He didn't have to think long.

Jeb knew Sunday was visiting day. Would he deliberately foul that up? Cold claws closed around his gut. Avery's visit was his one and only opportunity to set up escape plans.

He trudged back to the barracks, holding his composure by a mere thread.

All he could think about was the prospect of finding Buford. Where was he?

CHAPTER 24

~~~

Gunther sped his car down the main drag of Wendover, upset he had to work a late shift. The evening was unusually hot—so muggy, he could smell his own stinky B.O. He had no time for a shower. It paled into insignificance to what he needed to accomplish tonight.

He whipped past the State Line Hotel's restaurant and service station hardly paying attention to the mishmash of food aromas mixed with the diesel fumes of huge, cross-country trucks that were refueling.

He gunned the accelerator and crested the top of the small hill dividing Utah from Nevada. His goal tonight was to clinch his friendship with Cowboy and get him on his payroll. From the gossip on the track gang, he learned the man had no scruples and was willing to do any job if his palm was greased well enough. Definitely, his kind of guy...someone who would follow orders and do whatever had to be done should a messy situation arise to threaten his new identity. Who knew what might crop up? He had to be prepared.

He had invested the last two months in his strategy to bring Cowboy onboard, taking a week at a time to build camaraderie. Tonight, he had to play his cards just right. If he failed, he'd have to look for someone else. So far, he knew of no one else in town who qualified.

He slowed and turned in to the *A-1 Star Café and Casino,* the only restaurant and gambling place on the Nevada side. Beyond it spread the sage-brush-covered desert and a 110-mile long stretch of highway leading to Elko.

Pulling up to the front of the café, he turned off the engine and slid out of the seat. With long strides he moved toward the front door, hoping all would go down as planned.

Shoving the door open, he stepped inside to the clatter of utensils and plates accompanied by a blur of delicious aromas— coffee, steaks, hamburgers and onions sizzling on the grill.

He swept his gaze about the room. Not too many customers tonight. Six or seven men sat at the counter eating. A few were playing the only three, one-armed bandits, in the far corner. Not much to do in Wendover after one got off work except that. He chose Wednesdays because they were slow nights. A minimum of customers around would allow Cowboy to take a break from his gaming table.

"Hey there, Nora." He gave the cashier a wave as he moseyed by. A wiry lady in her fifties, with a face dry and wrinkled as a smoked herring, looked up and grinned.

"Good to see ya, Gus. Ready for a juicy T-bone?

"Nah. Not tonight. Probably later this week. I'm headed for the back room where the action is."

"Good luck." She threw him a toothy smile.

He moseyed toward the rear of the café and pushed a set of maroon drapes aside. Shoving through a swinging door, he entered a smoke-filled room of noisy slots and coins clanking into metal trays. Gunther immediately assessed the situation.

Cowboy was the only dealer standing at the Black Jack table. Everyone had indeed described him well—a tough-looking hombre. He had no idea what the guy's real name was. Nobody did. He acquired the nickname from being the only man in town who wore a ten-gallon hat. His distant manner gave the impression he didn't want to make friends, so Gunther figured the guy might have spent some time in the hoosegow. All the more reason he had zeroed in on him.

His purpose tonight would be the same as all other weeks—resume friendly contact, but this time accelerate his plan to an even more chummy level. He strolled as nonchalantly as he could over to the green-felted table where Cowboy was stacking chips.

"Hi there, Cowboy. How's your night goin'?" Gunther flashed him a casual but skillful smile. Cowboy looked up, his droopy eyelids looking as heavy as manhole covers. He parted his lips slightly, revealing a nicotine-stained set of crooked teeth.

"Evening Gus," came the return. "Same as usual. Can't complain."

"Don't look like you're too busy this evening. When you get a break, c'mon over to the bar and I'll buy ya a drink." He'd never seen Cowboy drink with anyone before. His response would tell what inroads he had made so far.

Cowboy paused, raised an eyebrow, and then slowly nodded. "Sure, Gus. Won't pass that up. Be there in a minute."

Gunther gave a thumbs-up acknowledgement and sauntered back over to the bar congratulating himself, pleased his new alias in Wendover was working so well. He scooted onto a stool.

The bartender, his back to him, was drying jug glasses with a towel and placing them on a shelf beneath a long mirror that stretched the length of the bar. Looking in the mirror, he spied Gunther and turned.

"What'll it be?"

"Couple of beers."

The bartender nodded, grabbed two mugs and shuffled over to the beer dispenser and pulled the handle. The deep frothy sound whetted Gunther's thirst—not only for the drink but also for his time with Cowboy.

Gunther used the mirror to take a quick glance behind him at the Black Jack table. Cowboy was turning it over to someone else.

He took a swig of his beer. Yep, he had a feeling tonight would work out. It would be like the good old days at the pen when inmates and ex-cons on parole agreed to work on the sly for him. Money always talked.

Cowboy left his table, sauntered over and slid onto the stool next to Gunther, his face relaxed. Gunther shoved the mug of beer in front of him.

"Thanks, Gus," he said, offering a lop-sided smile. "A cold beer will really hit the spot."

"Things going good for you?" Gunther asked.

Cowboy withdrew a pack of matches and a cigarette from his shirt pocket. Lighting it, he inhaled deeply and blew out a gray plume of smoke.

"Well, Gus…" he waved one hand casually as if what he was to say wasn't really that important, "to answer your question, I guess I could have had a better week."

Gunther smiled and gave him a friendly pat on the back. His previous overtures were about to pay off.

"Drink up, friend. Tell me about it."

CHAPTER 25

~~~

Sunday afternoon the sky was a cerulean blue with a few puffs of white clouds. The warm sun felt good on Ed's back as he hurried across the yard toward the visitors barrack. He could hardly wait to see Avery. He rehearsed the coded numbers to use. Would they communicate well enough to plan his escape? He entered the barrack and sat down. Trustees were the first to get seats.

Fifteen minutes later, the inmates, ankle chains clanking across the wood floor, were herded in. Four lines of tables extended the length of the room. Each line consisted of a double set of tables pushed up against each other width-wise. This maintained a two-table distance between inmate and visitor so nothing could be passed between them.

Five guards, their hands resting on their six-shooters, strategically positioned themselves—one at the door and at the far end of each line of tables. A guard looked in Ed's direction. He tensed all the way to his feet. Did Jeb tell them to keep a special eye on him?

Glancing around to assess how the guards planned to monitor conversations, he gathered they would walk up and down the aisles between the lines of tables, listening. He would have to use those few spaced opportunities to relay his coded plan to Avery.

The room grew silent as the clock on the wall ticked to one fifty-five. The knot in his stomach tightened

Ed was dying to see his old boyhood chum. He momentarily forgot about the guards to reminisce over his and Avery's youthful adventures when they roamed the woods pretending to be members of Stonewall Jackson's army. Dark-haired Gladys Benton, their only female playmate, played the part of Belle Boyd, the South's secret agent. She was pretty for a kid. Ed smiled, wondering what became of her.

At two o'clock, relatives, friends, and teary-eyed wives pushing hesitant children, piled through the door. Ed searched every face coming through. Yes. There he was! His six-foot frame filled the entrance. His throat tightened with emotion.

He would have known him anywhere. He'd lost a little hair and put on a few more pounds, but his face and steel blue eyes with the crinkles at the corners always hinting of some secret no one else knew, were still the same.

Avery glanced up and down the line of tables and looked right past Ed. Realizing how emaciated he must look, Ed raised his arm and waved.

Avery paused, stared for a second at Ed, and then hesitantly headed toward the table as if still unsure. Then his mouth widened into a big grin.

"Ed, ol' buddy! After all these years it's great to see you." Ed felt like leaping over the tables and hugging him.

He glanced warily over his shoulder to see where the guard was. One started down his aisle. A cold sweat broke out across his forehead. He wasted no time.

"Avery, glad you could come. Sure wish our visit could be longer but we only have thirty minutes. I hear you have *eight* children now. I always wished Sarah and I could have had at least *two*." He shot his eyes toward the guard in his aisle. "Never made it." His voice quavered. "Probably a good thing." He tried grinning, but his nerves were so tense it was a wonder he didn't throw up all over the table.

Avery nodded, acknowledging the cloaked exchange. "Yep," he replied, "our kids would've had great fun playing together—just like we did. Remember? *Sixteen* of us used to play together."

Ed picked up the number and breathed a sigh of relief. Avery knew there had only been four. Sixteen meant a get-away vehicle would be left in a designated spot. But where? A growing avalanche of anxiety mounted. Then Avery shot him a clandestine look.

"Say, do you remember Buster, the yard man we had for so many years?"

"Yeah," Ed responded, knowing there was no such person. He turned his head slightly. The guard was closing in. He flexed tight as a drum.

"Well, poor ol' guy," Avery continued, shaking his head, "died of a heart attack. Only fifty. They buried him in the Negro Burial

Ground at Barton Heights. Remember that place where we watched the county hangings when we were kids?" He studied Ed's face for a sign he was picking up his clues. Ed smiled an acknowledgment.

"Deserted now," he continued, "but a lot of Darkies still go down there to bury their kin. Actually, I refuse to spend any time there. Too spooky." He laughed.

Ed nodded. Avery planned to leave a car there but wouldn't wait around. Good thinking. If the escape ended up unsuccessful he wouldn't be implicated. If questioned by police because of his visit today, Avery would tell them his cousin knew where he lived, that he collected cars, and evidently stole it.

A guard strolled directly behind Ed, paused and stared down his nose.

Palpitations of fear shifted up Ed's jugular. He leaned forward as casually as he could. Placing his elbows on the table, he propped his chin on the heel of both hands, feigning interest in what Avery was saying. The guard moved on.

"Yep, Ed, sure do enjoy my kids. We live near the capitol now, a block away on Grace Street. Just took my oldest boy down to the waterfront to see the trains pull out. He loves that place. We have a great time together. I park my car near the Mayos Bridge," he said with emphasis, "in the vacant lot on Dock Street. You know where. Not far from the train yard."

Ed grasped Avery's meaning. After he picked up the car at the burial ground and finished using it to find any leads on Buford, he was to leave it at the Dock Street vacant lot. From there, he could catch a freight if that was in the order of things.

Say, did you know, Ed? I have two cars now."

Ed widened his eyes. *This is it.*

"Really? You're sure coming up in the world, Avery. Your job must be paying well." He held his breath and hung on to Avery's next words.

"Cars are my pride and joy. Got a 1928 Arabian sand, Model-A Roadster. Four cylinders, clutch and gearshift, with a top speed of 65 miles per hours—best of all, an electric starter. You don't have to do any cranking unless the battery goes dead. Did a great job getting me here from Richmond without any problems."

Ed listened, his nerves growing more taut. Avery went on.

"Paid two hundred fifty dollars, second hand," he continued. "The guy I bought it from kept it up real good. Nobody touches it, not even my wife."

Ed's face etched in desperation. He wasn't going to leave that one for him? *Get to it, Avery.*

"Guess you can tell I'm a nut for old cars," he chortled. "I also have another one, a '24 Model-T. Real proud of that one—176.7 cubic-inch engine, twenty horsepower, four cylinders, a ten-gallon gas tank and magneto headlights. It's souped up to run almost as fast as my roadster. As much as I love it," he continued, "I do loan it out to friends now and then."

Ed glanced at the clock. Ten minutes left. The guard reached the far end of the aisle, turned and strutted back toward them.

He felt as if all the air were being sucked out of the room. How were they to relay which day for him to leave the car? Goose flesh rippled up the back of his neck.

He didn't have to wait long to find out. Everyone's chatter stopped as a commotion broke out on the other side of the room.

All five guards responded like lightning. Descending upon a burly inmate, they pounded him with clubs and heavy-fisted blows. The inmate fell to the floor, guards on top of him.

Ed took advantage of the moment, hoping he had long enough. He leaned in across the table, his heart galloping like a racehorse toward the finish line.

"I'm a trustee now, Avery. Don't have to work on the gang anymore, and every Monday I get to drive into Richmond for supplies."

Avery was quiet, gnawed on the corner of his lip, looked down at the table and traced a finger around a knothole. After a moment, he looked up.

"Sounds good. I drive into South Richmond for my job. I work in the courthouse as Night Security Guard."

Ed's blood pounded in his throat. He gave a quick look at the guards who were still busy with the inmate.

"Avery, listen. With your job connections, will you see what you can find out about Gunther Buford? He's the one who shot Sarah and then escaped. Once I'm out of here, I've got to find him."

A yelp sounded from the rear of the room as the guards pulled the inmate back on his feet, handcuffed his hands behind his back and shoved him toward the door. The other guards returned to strolling the aisles. Ed felt his chest tighten.

Avery nodded, speaking quickly. "Don't worry, Ed. After getting your letter, I already began nosing around. I owe you one, remember? And working at the courthouse I have important connections with the police department."

Ed's hopes soared. Did he find something already? He might even hear of an ex-con who could reveal some crucial tidbit.

Avery quickly changed the subject, flashing a big grin for the sake of the guard who approached.

"Yep, the job's good, but the wife hasn't been feeling well. Been down sick with a bad throat, so I have to miss work to take care of her. I probably won't be able to return to work *this* Monday—probably a week from then."

Ed swallowed hard. Could he manage everything in that short of time? He had to. This would be their only meeting until next month and who knew what Jeb might do to him during the interim? He had to respond fast. The guard strode closer.

"Yeah, Avery. Sore throat's a bad thing—can always turn into something worse. But I agree. It ought to be better by a week from Monday. Maybe during that time you'll be able to see what you can find out about our old friend I just mentioned."

The guard ambled past them. Ed's breath stalled in his throat. All he could do was throw a helpless, questioning look at Avery.

"Yeah, I'll do my best."

It was settled. Ed expelled a deep breath.

"Visiting time's up," shouted a guard at the back of the room. They both stood. Ed's knees felt weak.

"Sure would like to shake your hand for coming," Ed said. "Can't, of course." The guard stood a couple of feet away.

"Been real good to see you, ol' buddy." Avery turned and started for the door.

"By the way," Ed called after him, "who did you marry?" The guard eyed him.

"Remember our little secret agent, Gladys Benton?" Avery grinned. "Never could resist her."

Moving along with the other visitors, Avery twisted around

one more time and gave Ed a final wave, adding a special thumbs-up before disappearing through the doorway.

Ed couldn't believe they'd communicated so well. His plan was coming together. Soon he'd be out of here and free. The thought was almost more than he could handle. Was it too good to be true? It took only a few minutes before the inevitable negatives charged in.

He envisioned Jeb catching him before he could escape, then torturing him to death and burying him out by the kennels. Needle-like barbs shimmied down his spine. He crimped his mouth in determination. Nope. That's not going to happen.

Firming his body, he stood and followed the line of men filing through the back door. Exiting the building, he stumbled across the yard toward the commissary, his body a cauldron of swirling emotions.

Unlocking the door, he lurched over to the counter and collapsed on a stool to wait for his breathing to settle back to normal so he could organize his scattered thoughts.

Drumming his fingers against the countertop, he rehearsed the plan. From Avery's clues, he'd pick up the car at the burial grounds, ditch the camp's truck among the trees, use Avery's get-away car, and then wing it from there.

If Avery couldn't find information about Buford's whereabouts, he'd have to go down into the raunchy part of Richmond and look up the place where the ex-cons hung out and try not to be spotted by the cops. Richmond would be crawling with them.

If no luck, the only thing left would be to hop a fast freight out of town. Even that wouldn't be easy. He'd have to evade the Bulls, the railroad detectives. He bet anything that's what Buford did. Why would he hang around Richmond? But where did he go? He sighed. All of it could end up a wild goose chase. He prayed Avery would find out something. In the meantime, he had work to do.

On his next trip to Richmond, he'd do a dry run to the Darkies' cemetery to check things out. It could look different after all these years. Then he'd take the shortcut through the three cemeteries to Penitentiary Bottom, skirt around the ravine, bypass the prison entrance, and shoot out onto Adams. Heading north he'd catch Fritz Street, which would be a straight drive to the burial ground.

178

"So much to do yet," he moaned. He needed Scratch to forge a fake ID and letter of recommendation from a business so he could get a job wherever he landed. He was pretty sure he'd do it, but what would he demand as payment? What if he squeals and Jeb finds out?

Ed slumped over the counter and buried his face in his hands.

Two weeks.

By then, he'd either be free...or dead.

CHAPTER 26

~~~

Ed tossed and turned all night with a vortex of maddening anxieties spinning in his head. *Two weeks...two weeks.* Could he work everything out by then? His face flushed hotter than the heat suffusing the sweaty darkness of the barrack. Questions besieged him.

How easy would it be to approach Scratch for the bogus papers? Would he snitch on him? Would his and Avery's plan work? Everything had to be ready by next Monday—the car would be at the cemetery waiting for him. What if the captain stopped him from leaving in the truck? His body felt like it was being squeezed through the wringer of his mama's old Maytag.

Weariness eventually took over. In a half-dream state Ed thrashed about on the mattress like a wriggling worm trying to escape a hook. Jeb had impaled him into the ground with the sharp end of his walking stick.

He jolted awake and flung the sheet off. Leaping out of bed, he tiptoed over to the window, glancing cautiously at the sleeping trustees. He pressed his bare chest against the screen. He imagined a cool wind blowing in from Hannigan, bringing with it the honeyed, leathery scent of Sarah's yellow-ruffled roses, tangy smell of her daisies, and the cerulean-green fragrance of the two weeping willows in their front yard. He pulled away from the screen. What little muggy breeze there was brought no relief, only the stench of the nearby waste pits.

Shuffling back to his cot, he sat on the edge and held his head in his hands. What kind of payoff will Scratch demand for the bogus documents? Tobacco? Liquor?

Liquor was certainly out of the question. He could easily confiscate tobacco from the commissary, but money? He only had two dollars in his pocket. His four-year earnings, which he barely drew on, probably added up to a hefty sum. Nevertheless, whatever his account held he couldn't take out a large sum without causing suspicion. He glanced back at the screened window. He thought of the ID papers.

It would be dawn in a few hours. Scratch would already have left for the mess hall to prepare breakfast. The best time to approach him would be now. What if he refused? The hammers in his head pounded harder. He had to face that reality.

He stood and quickly dressed. Tiptoeing to the doorway, he crept down the steps and skulked across the darkened yard, looking warily about. The only lights in the inky blackness were flickers of fireflies, the lamp at the guard booth at the gate, and the one hanging over the mess hall door.

Reaching the hall, he quietly opened the door and stepped into the dark, deep-as-death, silence. Fear, like an icy wind shivered him into a million pieces. He looked up front to the platform. Off to the right a light came from the half-opened kitchen door. Moving on cushioned feet through the dimly lit hall, he reached the kitchen door and peered in.

Scratch, his strange looking white hair disheveled, stood hunched over a metal table kneading a large hunk of lard into a ball of dough. He was alone.

"Morning," Ed said, pushing the door open.

Startled, Scratch looked up. "How come you're here so early?"

"Need to ask a favor. Got a minute?"

Scratch's eyes narrowed. "Ask away."

"This is...uh, private."

"Nobody else around," Scratch returned.

Ed hesitated.

"Hurry up with it, man. I got breakfast to fix."

"Okay," Ed blurted. "I need a letter of recommendation from a company in Newport News saying I was employed there for the last four years and was a good worker. I also need an alias." He held his breath until his lungs burned.

Scratch continued his kneading making no comment. Ed waited, his stomach pitching and plunging like a tidal wave.

"A fake ID will cost."

"I know," Ed replied. "Don't have any money except two dollars, and you know I can't draw a large amount from my account. I can get whatever you want from the commissary if Numbers can overlook the inventory not being right." He bunched the skin around his eyes giving Scratch a pained stare, and watched his face for a hopeful sign.

"Well," Scratch pursed his lower lip, "Numbers just might indeed be a problem. Got to use the office, you know. Paper, typewriter, pen and ink. Big job. No telling if Numbers will be willing."

Ed forced a slow inhalation. He knew better. Scratch and Numbers were buddies.

"But I think I can handle him," Scratch drawled. "Of course, he'll want something out of this too. It'll cost you extra."

"Name it," Ed said, relieved he didn't have to deal with Numbers. "If there's anything in the commissary, you know I've got access—"

"I'll get back to you." Scratch's abrupt response signaled the end of their conversation.

Ed swallowed hard. He turned to leave and looked back over his shoulder. "Need it done this week. Can you let me know today, before I leave for Richmond?"

"Said I'd get back to you," came the sharp retort.

Ed returned to the commissary and spent the rest of the morning going over the weekly inventory and routinely prepared a requisition of general items needed from Richmond to turn in to Numbers. At the same time, he tried to imagine what kind of payoff Scratch would demand. He visualized the consequences if Scratch double-crossed him. It would be more than just back to the road gang—he'd be joining Benny out by the kennels. He exhaled a series of short breaths.

Thirty minutes later, he pocketed the requisition. Locking up, he headed toward Number's one-room office, a small, wood-planked building with tarpaper roofing that sat behind the captain's house and filled with musty stacks of flyspecked paper.

Numbers, a green visor pulled low over his forehead, sat at his desk studiously poring over files.

Ed cleared his throat. "Here's the list of supplies to call in to the pen for today's run."

Numbers glanced up from beneath his slanty, caterpillar eyebrows. Without speaking, he motioned with his hand toward the in-basket, and then resumed what he was doing.

Sauntering back across the yard to the commissary, Ed rubbed the back of his neck and thought about Moose. He wanted to say good-bye to him. He already decided Moose couldn't be one of the monster's heads. Aside from Avery, he was the only friend he had. He'd do it on Saturday, when he came into the commissary. The last two times Moose and Duff came in they lingered to chat in spite of his becoming a trustee. He felt good about that. He unlocked the door and trudged inside.

The hours dragged. Ed kept busy with minor tasks expecting Scratch to walk through the door any time. What if he didn't come? Growing more antsy by the minute, he moseyed outside and sat on the steps to wait.

Thirty minutes passed when Ed saw him meandering across the compound toward him. Scratch threw him a look and motioned with his head. Ed jumped to his feet, scrambled up the steps and hurried inside. Scratch entered, and Ed nervously dead-bolted the door behind him.

"If you want the things you asked for," Scratch said gruffly, "you got to be willing to take the consequences if caught."

Ed hesitated. "Caught?"

"That means," he replied, handing him a piece of paper, "between Numbers and me we want everything on this list—and you got to get it today on your drive to the pen. If the captain, Jeb, or the police in Richmond catch you, Numbers and me will deny everything. You take all the heat. On the other hand, if everything goes smoothly you'll have everything you want by Saturday. Got it?"

Ed meekly nodded, glanced at the paper and then did a double take. Porno magazines, whiskey, hypodermic needles, bamboo pipes, rubber tubing, opium, gongers. His heart pounded. Everything was contraband.

"This is only the second time I've done this run," Ed spluttered. "I don't have these kinds of connections."

"No problem," Scratch said. "We've got a man there—has access to the doc's office—and he already knows you're coming. He'll have the stuff ready when you pull up to the dock.

"When you help him load the truck, all you got to do is watch for him to signal which boxes need to be hid. The hooch and dope go in the compartment beneath the front seat. The rest of the boxes

184

fit underneath the truck—braces are already in place. Twenty minutes after you leave camp pull over and examine the hiding places so you won't waste any loading time. Got that? When you get back, park the truck by the small building near the kennels. Leave the key in the ignition. I'll take care of the rest."

"You're sure Jeb doesn't know about this?" Ed noticed Scratch pause before responding. He didn't like that.

"Yeah. This is just between you, Numbers and me. Of course Squeaky knows, since he used to do the run."

Whisking the list out of Ed's hand, Scratch undid the deadbolt on the door and exited.

Ed staggered over behind the counter and dropped down on the stool.

He was in a catch 22. Whether the captain and Jeb knew or not, if he refused to get the stuff on his run Scratch could report him to Jeb and frame him some way just to get even. He had to play along. If he refused he wouldn't get his papers, maybe lose his status as trustee and no longer have access to the truck. He glanced at the clock. Time to leave. He grabbed up the commissary keys.

Locking up, he strode across the yard to the carport. He checked the gas and oil level in the truck and climbed in. Getting past Al at the gate went smoothly.

Twenty minutes on the road, he pulled the truck over and hopped out. Hustling to the passenger side he opened the door, leaned inside and yanked the seat up. Beneath it was the empty compartment for hiding the dope and hooch. He let the lid fall back, then squatted down on the ground and looked beneath the truck. Sure enough, the angle-braces were all in place, just high enough to miss the road. Once loaded, he'd have to watch the bumps.

Climbing back into the truck, he drove another ten minutes before turning onto the short-cut road. With the extra twenty minutes it would save, he would also zip out to the burial ground for his dry run and see if everything was as he remembered—get an idea where Avery might leave the car. He said near the gallows. His mouth went bone-dry.

The whole scenario radiated danger.

CHAPTER 27

~~~

Ed took the shortcut, reached the outskirts of Richmond, and sped through the three cemeteries until he entered Penitentiary Bottom. Keeping out of sight of the front prison gate he took off for the burial grounds in Barton Heights. He arrived in less than fifteen minutes.

It wasn't the way he remembered. The entranceway to the cemetery was obscured by pigweeds, bramble bushes, and scattered pieces of broken fencing. Gunning the engine, he drove over the debris with the truck tilting side-to-side, and rumbled down a shadowy, potholed road lined with dark, massive gum trees. They had grown taller and fuller from what he remembered as a kid.

Passing the Negro Burial Grounds, he found the clearing with the broken-down remains of the old gallows. He didn't expect to see the wooden beam from which prisoners hung. Each town's sheriff always transported their own beams. The platform, the only permanent part, lay on the ground rotted from disuse.

He stayed just long enough to get a feel for the place and surmise where Avery would leave the car. There was a good open space to the left of the gallows. He hoped Avery might also surprise him with a lead on Buford, although admittedly a slim chance.

Revving the motor, he swung the truck around, drove back to the entrance and sped back to the prison.

The same guard stood at the gate.

"They're waitin' for you," he said. "I'll call ahead to the dock." Waving Ed through, he stepped inside the booth and reached for the phone.

All went without a hitch. At the loading dock an inmate slid beneath the truck and placed some of the contraband in the angle bars while Ed hid bottles and other packages in the hidden compartment beneath the passenger seat. Another inmate loaded the back of his truck with the normal supplies.

Signing the packing slip, he nodded an acknowledgment and

casually strolled back around to the driver's side and climbed in. Turning the key, the truck roared to life. He pulled down the long driveway to the gate, his pulse pounding in his ears and anxiety stabbing his gut.

He forced a smile to the guard who opened the back doors of the truck, scrutinized the load of boxes, and then waved him through.

Feeling like a crazed bat trying to fly out of hell, Ed resisted the impulse to step on the gas. He drove slowly until he reached the main thoroughfare. He glanced in the rearview mirror. The guard was leaning against the booth. Everything appeared normal. He relaxed, turned the corner out of sight, and then stomped on the accelerator and headed for the main highway. With his load, he couldn't take the shortcut's road back.

The only remaining hurdle was to check in at camp on time and be scrutinized by Jeb. His big concern, however, was if Scratch decided to tell Jeb about his request for the bogus documents. Jeb could stop him from driving to Richmond next Monday—forever, for that matter. He couldn't let that happen.

He reached the camp junction in record time, turned onto the dirt road and putted up to the gate. Luck was with him. Jeb was nowhere in sight—probably out with the gang. Al waved him through.

The next day, Ed replayed his escape plan over with resolved tenacity. After finding Avery's car, getting rid of his uniform and changing into the clothes Avery would leave in the car, he'd take off and drive directly to the seamy part of Richmond and see what he could find out about Buford from ex-cons—one man in particular. He once contacted him when doing a story. He'd know about any rumors floating around.

After that, he'd hightail it as fast as he could to the Fulton freight yards in the lower canal basin on Orleans Street before roadblocks were set up. Sheriffs' posses and bloodhounds would already be hot on his trail. Bus stations and highways leading out of Richmond, including trains, would also be watched. His best chance to get everything done was a good head start. He analyzed the railroad timetables and narrowed his choice down to the Chesapeake & Ohio.

His plan sounded good, but he worried as an old line from a poem occupied his thoughts—*the best laid plans of mice and men often go awry.*

Why was that rumbling around in his head?

A warning?

CHAPTER 28

~~~

Saturday, inmates strolled about the yard. Ed looked forward to seeing Moose in the commissary. What could he say to him without revealing too much?

By late afternoon Moose ambled in. Two other inmates meandered about the store. Ed spoke in low tones, his head down while he debited his account for tobacco.

"Moose, you've been good to me, and I'll never forget how you helped me when I was whipped. You've always been there for me."

It was all he could manage. He wanted to blurt out more—how he'd been his only friend and how much it meant to him, but knew better. He figured Moose would catch on he was going to hang it on the limb but couldn't put him in the dangerous position of knowing too much.

Ed looked into his face. For an intense moment their eyes locked.

Moose, without dropping his gaze, whispered, "That's what friends are for." Stuffing the tobacco in his shirt pocket he headed for the door. He glanced back with a smile tinged with concern, then exited.

He knew.

Sunday, Ed's anxiety worsened. Scratch promised the papers by Saturday and he hadn't heard from him. Today had to be it. Tomorrow was pushing it too close. What if he had to leave without the papers? He felt like an overstressed balloon ready to explode.

He sat on the commissary steps after supper staring intently across the compound, his line of sight focused on the back door of the mess hall. No sight of Scratch yet. He scrutinized every tent and barrack door.

How long should he wait? He would see him in the barrack later, but other trustees would be there. What was holding things up? After all, he got the contraband for him. Ed slumped back against the railing.

What if Scratch snitched? Jeb may have told him to go ahead, forge the papers, and let him drive to Richmond tomorrow then secretly notify the authorities. The cops would be waiting for him. They'd have a right to gun him down.

He'd give Scratch one more hour. If he had the papers, he'd soon be off to find Gunther Buford.

All the possibilities of something going wrong drove him crazy, and the irritating screech of the cicadas didn't help. Nothing ever seemed to disturb their perpetual buzzing. It was as if today were like any other day.

It wasn't.

CHAPTER 29

~~~

Gunther shoved the sun-blistered door of the trainmaster's office open and stepped inside. A blister of hot air swept into the office from the salt flats deflecting the breeze of three rotating fans that whirred at high speed.

"Shut that door!" a clerk yelled in annoyance as a swirl of withering heat swooshed over his desk.

"Yeah, yeah." Gunther closed the door behind him. Today's sweltry heat promised ground hot enough to fry spit on, but the weather wasn't what worried him. His jaw went rigid.

He had no idea why Supervisor Hutch was calling him in. If it was bad, it could ruin everything. He headed down the long hallway toward the man's office, running nervous fingers around the top edge of his pants to make sure his shirt was tucked in. How could his performance possibly be at fault? He worked the men hard and got the work done on time.

Well, whatever it was, it had better not jeopardize his plans—not after investing a year in this God-forsaken place. He scowled. If it did, he'd have to start over and find another place to establish a new identity. His anxiety mushroomed as he approached.

Peering in, he knocked lightly on the doorjamb. Supervisor, Bob Hutchinson, sat at his desk and motioned him in. Gus stepped across the threshold.

"Mr. Moreland." The supervisor got up from his desk, smiled, and extended his hand. "Okay to call you Gus? Please sit down."

Gunther wasn't sure about the supervisor's nice tone. Maybe because he was preparing to lower the boom.

"Sure thing, Mr. Hutchinson."

"Call me Hutch, Gus, everyone does." He circled back around his desk and sat down.

"I called you in to tell you we're promoting you to Foreman over the track gang that works on the Burmester line. I have to hand it to you Gus. Most newcomers who hire on never stick around long enough to make a go of it."

A quick exhale wisped from Gunther's lips. He let his body sag back to normal. A promotion not only meant more money but more respect and less suspicion.

"Thanks, Hutch." He flashed his best smile. "Really enjoy my job."

After another ten minutes of outlining his new duties, they shook hands and parted.

Gunther headed for the beanery to tell Queenie, feeling quite smug over his new position. She, of course, would spread the word to the men who came in. Good. Soon, everyone in town would accept him with no reservations.

Queenie would also tell Sheriff, Kevin Thompson. He came to the depot every morning and end of the day, both times for coffee and jawing. Gunther always planned to be there when he came in to do more schmoozing. Nothing too buddy-buddy at first, just good-humored chitchat. Kevin's invitation to go fishing at Blue Lake together was a first step.

Soon, he'd be in solid. He had no doubt he'd win him over completely.

After that, California—he'd be home free!

CHAPTER 30

~~~

Ed stomped in a huff toward the mess hall across the darkening compound. Irritation rippled across his face. He had waited an hour and a half at the commissary, the sun was nearly setting, and Scratch hadn't brought the ID papers yet. Without them he'd have no cover while he searched for Buford.

He climbed the mess hall steps, his nerves taut and ready to snap like a stretched rubber band. What if he rubbed Scratch the wrong way by asking again? What if he changed his mind? Panic clung to him like thick syrup.

Inching the door open, he peered cautiously around the corner of the doorjamb. Dread pressed in on him as his probing gaze swept back and forth, table-by-table, scrutinizing every inch of the room. Small muscles twitched at the back of his throat. He saw no one. He stepped inside.

Up front, a narrow shaft of light spilled from beneath the half-opened door of the kitchen. The rattle and clank of utensils sounded. Ed crept down the dimly lit aisle.

Reaching the door, he peered through the narrow opening and saw Scratch place a kettle in the cupboard and then undo his apron. Ed took a deep breath and pushed the door open.

Scratch looked up in surprise. "Oh, it's you."

"Yeah," Ed replied. "Thought it might be easier if I came here." His throat went dry.

Scratch shot Ed an impatient look. "They're not ready yet."

Ed's heart sank. "But," he spluttered, "you said you would. After all, I got the stuff for you."

"Yeah, yeah. I'll get them to you tomorrow morning."

"I got to have them for sure by then...before I leave for the pen." Desperation edged his voice. "No later."

"Just got one thing to do yet," Scratch retorted, looking him squarely in the eye. "You don't have to worry. You'll have 'em."

"When and where?" Ed pressed.

195

"In the commissary. Meet you there at ten. I'll bring the notebook with the weekly inventory sheets. They'll be inside the back cover."

Ed nodded, turned and stumbled out of the kitchen fearful he'd totally lose it. He barreled down the dimly lit aisle. Scratch had better keep his word. But why the delay?

Did he plan to double-cross him by reporting him to Jeb? Inmates normally never squealed on each other but a few ignored the honor code in return for special favors. He felt his face lock with tension as he absorbed the impact it would have on his plans.

Anxious to get back before Jeb or the captain saw him, he hurried out the door. At the same time, he heard the back door of the mess hall slam shut. He and Scratch arrived at the trustees' barrack at the same time. Neither one of them spoke.

Ed went directly to bed. He closed his eyes, his heart thumping so hard in his chest he was sure the others would notice his bed shaking. He had to face one reality. Scratch just might not come through. A piercing anxiety fell over him and he felt as if he were plummeting to his death down a mineshaft. He groaned. His whole plan was doomed for failure.

"*No, it isn't,*" his mother's voice broke in.

"Yes, it is. I'll get caught for sure."

"*Sarah's death was not your fault,*" came the response. "*You don't belong here. Just believe everything is going to work out for your good.*"

"But, how?"

She didn't answer.

Monday morning, Ed scurried across the yard with a better attitude. His four-year dream of escaping was close to becoming an actuality. Scratch promised he would come through today at ten o'clock. His chest felt like it would burst. He entered the commissary hardly able to contain himself.

Whiling away an hour in the stock room, he watched the clock. It was near ten. His heart rate climbed. The old fears rushed in. He was taking a huge risk trusting Scratch wouldn't rat on him.

He pictured the scenario...Jeb marching in and pointing his finger. "Thought you could get away with this, didn't you?" Ed visualized being dragged off to the building by the kennels...needles

196

under his fingernails...a deadly whipping at the hitching post...the sound of dirt being shoveled on top of his body. He looked at the clock again.

Eleven-thirty...twelve-thirty.

His insides shriveled. Scratch said ten o'clock. A sinking sensation fell on him like a heavy chunk of concrete. Where was he? He had to leave for Richmond by two.

At one thirty, Scratch pushed the door open. He nonchalantly shoved a binder across the counter. "Here's the new inventory sheets." With no other words he pivoted on his heel in a u-turn and left. The door slammed shut.

Ed stared at the notebook holding his breath until the pressure in his chest forced him to exhale. What if everything he asked for wasn't here? He reached for the notebook, bracing himself for disappointment.

With hands trembling, he opened the cover and flipped through the pages. There were the usual things. Outline of commissary duties, list of required stock, and lastly, blank requisitions. He turned the last page. A surge of elation shot through him.

"They're here!" He widened his mouth into a grin.

Fumbling with the two sheets of paper tucked inside the back pocket of the binder, he slipped them out. The first, his letter of recommendation:

Mason Furniture

Fine Virginia Craftsmanship

Cabinets, Tables, Chairs • Antique Refinishing

527 Browning Street

Newport News, VA

To whom it may concern:

Edward Riley, an outstanding employee, has been in our service for the last ten years, first at our Richmond branch for eight years, then later at our office for two years. It is with regret we are closing our doors after twenty-five years of business and must let our valued employee go.

This will assure the recipient of this letter that there should be no hesitation in hiring Mr. Riley as a skilled, able, and honest worker.

Respectfully,

John Squires, Manager.

Ed's heart leapt. There was no way anyone could check out a defunct company. Now to his ID.

He carefully unfolded a birth certificate displaying the official State of Virginia seal in the left-hand corner. He marveled at its look of authenticity, also its artistry. In the center, a fancy scroll-like banner read, *Remember thy creator in the days of thy youth.* "Nice touch." He proceeded to read the text.

This is to certify Edward Riley, a male, was born on May 7, 1910 in the city of Richmond, County of Henrico, State of Virginia, to Albert Riley and Marie Riley, husband and wife.

Below were their signatures with their births, marriage date, and the attending physician's handwritten scrawl. Ed nearly cried with joy. Scratch really came through.

Folding the documents, he unbuttoned his shirt, taped them to his chest, and then left the building. It was two-fifteen. He should have been in that truck and out the gate before now. If he arrived at the Negro Burial Ground too close to dark he might not find Avery's car.

He meandered across the compound in a slow, purposeful amble toward the car shed. He would simply be casual, climb into his truck and drive through the gate. When he got to Richmond, he'd take extra precautions by using different streets just in case Scratch did blow the whistle on him and police were waiting. Next, he would—

The roar of a car engine made him whip his head around. A Model-A pickup sped in from the highway. With brakes screeching, it skidded up to the gate in a cloud of dust. He saw Squeaky lean out the car window in a lather and exchange agitated words with Al. Then, gunning the motor, he zoomed into the compound and drove straight for the captain's house, bringing the car to an abrupt stop in front. Squeaky jumped out, bounded up the porch steps and pounded on the door. The captain immediately appeared.

After a few hurried words, the captain, his upset apparent, blurted something to Scratch and waved his arms in the direction of the kennels. Squeaky sprang from the porch, leaped back into the truck and took off, roaring the car into the back of the compound. Ed watched him head for the small building where the contraband was stored. He looked back. The captain, rushing down the steps two at a time, hustled toward the mess hall.

Ed felt a weightless chill. Something serious was up. Whatever it was, the trustees' barrack would be the first place to hear about it.

Bolting across the compound, he hurried inside the building. Three other trustees were already there. Ed sat on his cot and waited. It didn't take long. Squeaky stuck his head through the doorway.

"Shakedown!" came his frenzied, high-pitched reedy voice. "Officials are coming from the warden's office. Due in an hour. Get out there and search the cages and barracks. You know what to look for. Don't let them find anything."

Ed, his mind a mass of muddled confusion, sat on the edge of his cot frozen to the spot. How was he to leave now? Was this just a routine check? Or did someone at the pen tip the warden about his getting the contraband? He'd be the patsy if the stuff were found. The captain had directed Squeaky behind the mess hall, and the contraband he got was in the building by the kennels. Maybe Squeaky took care of it.

He slumped over and held his head in his hands. Things couldn't be worse. *Think, Ed, think.* The warden's men would be here any minute. Judging by the fence-pole shadows it was far after two o'clock. He had to leave for Richmond now!

He had to move fast.

CHAPTER 31

~~~

Ed, not knowing how to handle the situation, locked his face in desperation as he exited the trustees' barrack. Could he drive through the gate before the warden and his men pulled in? He might only have minutes, perhaps seconds. What if Jeb gave Al instructions to stop anyone from leaving? Should he chance it? Indecision glued his feet to the ground. Panic swirled in his brain. He closed his eyes.

God, if you're working everything together for my good, like mama said, then get to working. I'm in a crisis here.

He had barely opened his eyes when something unusual caught his attention. A seagull, not seen too often this far inland, soared into the compound. Its snow-white body descended upon the roof of the mess hall, poised motionless for a few seconds, then spread its long, pointed wings and glided across the yard. Orbiting a couple more times, it swooped down close to the gate, circled, and then soared away in the direction of the James River.

It's a sign to leave!

Bolting across the yard toward the mess hall, he paused at one end of the building and cautiously peered about. Guards and trustees were rushing about banging barrack and cage doors, checking for hidden contraband.

Ed shifted his gaze to the gate, the captain's house, back to the trustees' barrack, and then scanned the whole yard. Jeb was nowhere in sight. Neither was the captain. It was now or never.

With long strides, he hustled toward the car shed, matching the same hurried pace of the other trustees who scurried about the compound. Instinctively, he pressed his hand against his chest and double-checked the ID papers he had taped to his skin.

Entering the three-sided stall, he ducked into the shadows at the front of the truck and peeked over the car's hood. Down at the gate Al, instead of relaxing in his booth as usual, was impressively strutting back and forth in preparation for the dignitaries.

Should he go this very second? What if he met the warden's car on his way out? Should he wait until after they drive into the compound and then risk it? A piercing anxiety fell on him.

Uh oh...too late.

Two vehicles raced up the dirt road and pulled up to the gate. Ed recognized Warden Jackson in the lead car. Four men were with him. The second vehicle behind him, a paneled truck, probably carried search guards. What was he to do?

He heard Al's curt, "Yes, sir" and "No sir," then saw him point in the direction of the mess hall. Good. Jeb and the captain were in there.

With one eye on the warden's car he crept around and opened the cab door of the truck. Fumbling under the mat he grabbed the key, then slid into the seat and crouched low just as the official procession passed by.

Through a broken slat in the rear of the shed wall, he watched. The two vehicles pulled up to the mess hall. The sound of their motors brought the captain and Jeb to the door. Ed's insides tightened. Would they go inside the hall or back to the captain's house? Please, let them go inside. They did. He let out a couple of quick breaths.

Tight-throated, he turned the key, backed out and drove toward the gate. Would Al stop him? He fingers turned sweaty on the steering wheel. *Remain calm, Ed.*

"Still going?" Al's face expressed surprise.

"Yeah, too bad," Ed responded matter-of-factly. "I was sort of hoping I wouldn't have to go today, but it's business as usual. Jeb and the captain figure routine ought to be kept as much as possible. Show we're not nervous about anything. If I clip right along I should make it back before dark. You might want to call the pen and let them know I'm starting out late." Ed immediately felt a spasm of irritation. Why did he tell him to do that?

"Sure." Al waved him through and turned to the booth to make the call.

Driving down the dirt road, Ed kept his eye on the mess hall door in the side view mirror. They were still inside. He reached the highway and turned left onto the blacktop.

Stomping on the accelerator, he reached the James River

junction in record time. Heading east, he watched for the dirt cutoff. "Ah!" He gave the wheel a sharp left.

Speeding down the rutted road he passed the squatter shacks, and then slowed as he entered the small town with the general mercantile store. The same black man in the straw hat sat snoozing at the Flying A Gilmore pump. When he reached the end of the street, he sped up. Fifteen minutes later he saw the Henrico County sign.

"Only ten more miles," he whispered. The anticipation was electrifying.

Fifteen minutes later, he crested the hill above Richmond. He turned onto Colorado Street and skirted the edges of the three cemeteries. From Spring Street he turned on Belvedere and circled around the back of Penitentiary Bottom to Byrd Street. He now had a clear shot at Adams. It would take him straight to Barton Heights and the burial ground. If Scratch double-crossed him and Jeb alerted the cops, they'd never think of taking this route—but it would be a different story after he left the burial grounds.

The sky was already turning cobalt blue. He felt the heebie-jeebies coming on. It would be darker on the cemetery road because of the trees—so dark, he might have difficulty finding Avery's car. He pushed the accelerator harder and watched for Fritz Street.

"There!" Veering a sharp right, he headed for St. James Street, turned left on Wellford and entered the road to the burial ground. The dark, twisting road looked nothing like on his first run. He flicked on the headlights. The beams shot into the shadowy honeysuckle thickets and Sweet Gums.

Proceeding down the washboard road, he peered into the inky blackness. Where are the graves? The clearing with the gallows? He felt his features go slack. He should have reached them by now. What if Avery hadn't left the car yet? His breath came faster. If delayed, would he still come? How long should he wait around? His heart thumped harder.

Rounding a sharp angle in the road, his eyes widened. In the headlights he saw the dilapidated burial markers with their crudely etched names. Another fifty yards he entered the familiar clearing and spotted the foundation of the old gallows.

Staring into the blue-black darkness, he saw something shiny reflecting from the far side of the area. It had to be Avery's Model-T. He stretched his mouth into a jubilant grin and gunned the engine.

Maneuvering the truck around to the opposite side of the gallows, he set the brake, jumped out and scrambled across the clearing to the car. Reaching for the door handle, he yanked it open. He made out a large cardboard box on the floor of the passenger side. Balancing one foot on the running board, he leaned across and dragged the box up onto the seat. On top was a note.

Grabbing the piece of paper, he ran around to the front of the prison truck and held it in the glare of the headlights nearly bursting with expectancy.

Ed,

You know where the keys are—same place we hid them in the old days. I checked with a guy I know in the police department and discovered a friend of Buford's, an ex-con named Billy Farnsworth, had been brought in for violating his parole. I found out he had no bail money or attorney, so visited him at the county jail and told him I would put up his bail and pay a retainer to an attorney to get his defense started if he could tell me where Buford went.

He jumped at the chance but claimed he didn't know Buford. I think he was lying. But he said he could possibly have headed for the salt flats of Wendover, Utah. The prison grapevine vouches for it as a safe haven for escapees.

You and I are even, now, Ed. Tomorrow, I'll be reporting my car stolen to keep myself in the clear. Be sure and destroy this note.

Good luck!

Avery

Good ol' Avery. The information was far more than Ed expected. Now, he didn't need to go into Richmond to question ex-cons. He had a destination—Utah. He scuttled back to the Model-T, stuffing the note in his mouth.

While he chewed and swallowed it, he checked the rest of the box's contents. An overcoat lay on top. He quickly thrust his hands into both pockets and produced three packs of cigarettes and some matches. Next, a pair of blue trousers and a plaid wool shirt, even some underwear, socks and shoes. He felt euphoric.

Beneath those, lay a small gunnysack containing bread, cheese, and a supply of red apples. He took a huge bite out of the cheese. His salivary glands fairly overflowed.

At the bottom of the carton was a small, five-inch square box. Ed could only hope. He lifted the lid and widened his eyes. "Cash!"

Hurrying back to the headlights, he carefully unfolded the bills and counted them. He could hardly believe it—five hundred dollars! Tears came to his eyes. Avery was certainly paying him back for the alibi he provided years ago, plus some. Never in the world would he forget him for doing this. Someday, he'd pay him back.

He tore off his prison clothes and shoes and tossed them into the carton. Grabbing the new clothes, he quickly put them on. Placing the bills back into the small box, he shoved it into his pants pockets and then heaved the carton of his prison clothes into the bushes

Now, to the key.

Lifting the front seat out, he placed it on the ground. With the gas tank exposed he ran his fingers over the top of the cap and felt the lump of tape. Ripping it off, he removed the key, replaced the seat on top of the tank and shoved the key into the ignition. He ran back to the prison truck.

Jumping into the seat, he put it into gear and aimed the headlights toward the thicket on the opposite side of the clearing. Spying a space free of trees, he drove straight into it at high speed. The truck bounced over the first clump of bushes. At a small dirt embankment the wheels spun in the dirt and the engine sputtered, threatening to stall. He gunned the motor again, forcing the wheels up over the mound. The truck shot forward, climbing over gnarled roots and dense brush. After twenty yards he pulled to a stop, turned off the headlights and leaped out.

Tossing the key into the inky darkness, he sprinted back to the edge of the clearing and ran to Avery's car and leapt in. He'd have to get into the swing of using three pedals again.

"Hmmm, left pedal for the gears, right pedal to brake, center for reverse." He also noted the spark and throttle-levers.

He reached under the steering wheel to the brass quadrant and set the spark level on the third notch. Twisting another lever on the dash, he turned the headlights to bright and raced the engine until it sounded right. He pulled on the throttle, released the handbrake and rammed down hard on the left pedal. With a roar the car lunged forward across the clearing, shaking and shimmying down the bumpy, potholed road. Avery was right. He really souped it up.

At the exit he slowed and scrutinized the cross street. Pulling out, he shot the car forward in high gear and turned left on St. James. He watched for Petersburg, and then turned onto Broad Street.

The guard at the pen would have alerted the camp by now, and Jeb would have set things into motion. Cops would be swarming not only the Main Street train station but also the Seventeenth Street freight yard behind it. He'd throw them off by heading straight to the riverfront. There, he'd find the James River line coming up from Fulton Yards.

While the cops would also cover the riverfront, the extensive length of track along the riverbank would be to his advantage. They couldn't possibly cover every bit of rail, nor would they know whether he was planning to hop a freight going east, west or south. That would spread them out.

According to the timetable, a train came along at eight-fifteen. He'd take whichever one got there first and in whatever direction. Later, he could transfer to one headed for Utah. Everything sounded good. Then, he swallowed hard.

"Don't get too cocky, Ed Bowman.

"You're not safe yet."

CHAPTER 32

~~~

Fear thick as molasses formed in Ed's throat as he snaked the car through the ill-lighted section of the waterfront. An eerie sheath of gray fog shrouded the deserted streets of grungy buildings and weathered storefronts. Everything exuded the smell of damp, rotting wood. Ahead, smoke-smudged industrial plants loomed dark and secretive.

Ed clenched the steering wheel and peered through the thick mist, scrutinizing every shadow and intersection. Anxiety riddled his nerves like a bombardment of well-aimed bullets. He expected cops to jump out any second.

Alert for any unusual sounds, he leaned his ear close to the open window—cops could be waiting ahead. But the only noise he heard was the hoarse blast of a steamer's whistle. He was close to the harbor. East of it were the tracks.

Turning right on Dock Street, he searched the gray skyline until he saw the shadowy outline of the Mayos Bridge, then watched for the vacant lot Avery mentioned. He saw it between two antiquated warehouses. He idled the engine for a few seconds, cautiously studied the brooding shadows for any suspicious movements, then pulled in and turned the engine off.

Quietly opening the door, he slid out and donned his overcoat. Pulling his coat collar up around his neck, he hid the car key beneath the seat, grabbed his gunnysack and left the lot.

Loitering in dark doorways and hugging building fronts, he skirted down alleyways until he reached the riverfront and spied the wharves. He knew exactly where to head from here. Once he hopped a freight he'd be on his way to finding Buford. He could only hope it would prove to be heading to Utah. Then his breath caught.

A police car cut through the mist heading in his direction. An officer leaned from the car window with a spotlight. Ed's heart revved. The lightning-like beam pierced the fog, flashing into every nook and cranny of the building fronts facing the docks. Adrenaline jolted him.

He immediately ducked inside the alcove of a storefront and crouched down. He looked about, his mind catapulting into panic. He saw nothing to hide behind—or did he?

An oversized garbage can sat near the front of the entranceway. He inched forward on his haunches, extended one hand, and dragged the container into the alcove. He removed the lid. The putrid smell smacked him in the face. It was nearly a third full of rotten food and stunk worse than any cage he'd ever been in. No doubt maggots, too.

Climbing over the rim, he stomped on the foul-smelling garbage and scrunched down as far as he could into the can. Maneuvering the lid over the opening, he left it slightly ajar for air and covered his nose and mouth with his hands to stifle his gag reflex.

The cruiser moved closer, slowing in front of the entranceway. The spotlight swept through the darkened recess sending small slivers of light streaming into the open cracks around the lid. Ed recoiled and drew his body into a curled-up knot. After what seemed an eternity he heard the patrol car move on.

Ed raised the lid slightly and gulped in the fresh air. Peering over the edge, he then climbed out and shook the clinging garbage from his clothes. Sidling to the front of the alcove, he looked down the street in both directions. All clear. He skulked forward.

Within fifteen minutes he found the tracks. A freight would be coming soon. It would have to reduce its speed on the uphill curve before heading onto the viaduct. He only hoped it would slow enough for him to hop on easily. He tied his gunnysack to his belt.

Then, he heard it. The whistle.

He broke into a sprint, running like a mad man along the rails. He had to reach the curve before the train did. Whether the tracks were curving or not, he couldn't tell. At least his lungs told him it was uphill. That was good.

The train grunted sluggishly along the uphill curve. Ed dashed up the tracks, fear and desperation tearing through his insides. *Please, no cops...no cops.*

Another fifty yards and his bony chest heaved, his breath coming in painful pants. His lungs were killing him and his legs hurt clear to the bone. With his strength drained, he had to stop. He leaned forward and dropped both hands on top of his thighs. He looked up.

Through the gray mist he saw the black hulk bearing down on him. He fell to the ground and lay flat to avoid the engineer seeing him.

The engine chugged by, steam hissing and billowing from beneath its huge wheels, its rotating headlight barely missing him. The coal cars and gondolas came into sight. Next should be the boxcars. Ed instantly leapt back up and watched for them.

The first one moved into view. He jogged alongside keeping pace, gasping, wheezing, his gunnysack bouncing against his body. He watched for a ladder. He spied the first one and extended his arms. He missed. He tried again and nearly fell. With one last burst of energy he reached out for the next ladder and managed to leap high enough to grab hold of the third rung with both hands.

With feet dangling midair he strained to pull his weak frame up and manage his right knee onto the bottom rung. Tightening the grip of his left hand, he let loose with the other and grabbed the rung above it. Exerting everything he had, he swung his left knee onto the bottom rung.

Puffing and winded, he clung to the ladder. The train picked up speed on the viaduct. Ed closed his eyes, letting the cold, damp wind rush into his face.

He made it!

He spent the night in a collapsed state on the small platform between the end of the boxcar and the brake wheel. Sometimes he slept but other times he just stared into the darkness unable to believe his good fortune.

He fantasized the excitement in camp once everyone heard, especially Moose and Duff. Mostly, he pictured Jeb fuming and spouting off his venomous hatred, his face contorting over the humiliation at being outsmarted.

"Ah, yes," Ed said with a grin, reaching into his gunnysack and biting a chunk from an apple, "the humiliation. Now, there's a bit of satisfaction."

A phrase suddenly popped into his mind from a Jack London

novel his mama once read to him. The main character of the book, describing his escape from a cruel villain, had shouted, "Goodbye, Lucifer!"

"Goodbye, Jeb!" he yelled to the wind.

He shook off the dread that police might be waiting for him at the end of the line. He couldn't worry about that now. He was completely tuckered.

He fell asleep to the rhythmic clickety-clack, clickety-clack of the wheels.

Chapter 33

~~~

The train's massive wheels screamed against the rails, and the ear-splitting screech of grinding brakes and hissing steam shuddered the small platform at the end of the boxcar. Ed jolted awake. It took him a few seconds to register where he was.

Another hard lurch hurtled him to one side of the platform. Grabbing the edge of the brake wheel he clung on tight as the boxcars, one by one, collided like dominoes down the line in a repetitive clatter.

He gazed around. The early morning rays of the sun stretched across the vast flatland. Birds twittered in the shrub grass, interrupted only by sporadic caws of blackbirds.

Ed leaned over the side of the platform and glanced to the front of the train. Burning specks of coal lifted into the air and drifted back over the top. The acrid smell of steam and oil filled the air. Maybe a town ahead? He saw no railroad workers hopping off. Not yet, anyway.

He needed to look for an open boxcar and get out of sight until he figured what was going on with the train. He couldn't chance any bulls spotting him. No way was he going back to prison. Come hell or high water he'd make it to Utah and find Buford.

The wheels ground to a bare crawl. Ed swung around the end of the boxcar, grabbed hold of the ladder, and jumped to the ground. Keeping pace, he trotted alongside.

The next boxcar rolled by. Reaching up with both hands he gave the large door a sideways tug. It wouldn't budge. He tried the next car. No luck.

He looked back toward the front of the train and his breath caught. A worker had left the engine and was climbing up the side ladder to the top of the boiler. He had to find a boxcar fast before the caboose rolled into sight. His pulse raced.

Two more cars passed before he spied a two-by-four protruding from a small opening at the bottom of one of the doors. The train picked up speed, forcing him to move faster. Reaching into the narrow opening he struggled to pull the heavy door open. It began to slide. One inch, two... It was coming.

The door abruptly slid all the way open with surprising ease. A hand reached out and grabbed Ed's wrist. The person on the other end gave a vigorous tug and Ed flew through the air and landed inside on the splinter-worn floor.

From his prostrate position he gawked up into two glaring, steel-gray eyes. The man's face was covered with a bristly black beard, and his wild, unkempt tangled mop on his head reminded Ed of a lion's mane. Heavy-set and muscular, the man's open shirt exposed a mass of dark chest-hair. The guy looked menacing.

"Thanks," Ed said, nervously getting to his feet.

"Ain't nothing," mumbled the raspy voice. "Saw you hop on last night."

"Well, my name's Ed."

"We don't use no names," came the terse reply. "Ya oughta know that."

"But," Ed began, "I appreciate what you did."

"Okay. Call me anything you like." Ed mentally decided on Blacky, but was hesitant to get any friendlier.

Blacky walked back over to the open door. He poked his head outside, checking the front of the train, then the rear. Nudging the two-by-four back inside the car with his foot, he shoved the heavy door shut then shuffled over to a space between two stacks of boxes. He sat down and scooted back until all Ed could see sticking out was the bottom half of his legs. He gave no indication he wanted to talk. That was fine with Ed.

He examined the car's interior in the morning light that streamed from a small window near the ceiling. A narrow aisle about three feet wide cut through the middle of the car from the sliding door to the opposite wall. On both sides, cartons were stacked nearly to the ceiling.

The train gave a sudden jerk. Ed zigzagged down the aisle toward the back wall. Using Blacky's strategy, he rearranged some cartons and made a cubbyhole large enough for his body and deep enough to be out of sight of the door in case any railroad worker or bull might look in. He let out a long exhale. Would the day ever come when he would feel safe?

Grabbing a hunk of cheese from the gunnysack, he broke off a piece. Most of the apples were bruised but he decided to offer some of both to Blacky. He crawled out of his hiding place and walked down the aisle. Leaning over, he peered into the cubbyhole and stretched out his arm.

"Thought you might like an apple, although it's pretty banged up. Got some cheese, too."

Blacky eagerly reached for the food. "Thanks." He hungrily took a bite out of the apple at the same time scrutinizing the reddish scar on Ed's wrist.

Ed quickly pulled his shirt cuff down and asked, "Where you headed?"

"Nowhere," came the short reply, "just ridin' the rails."

"I'm sorta new at this," Ed said. "How far does this freight go? I'm headed for Utah—Wendover, to be exact."

"Yeah?" The man looked up. "I once thumbed a ride through there on the way to California. The place is in the middle of nowhere. But ya won't get there on this train." He took another huge bite from the apple, exposing a missing front tooth.

"This freight only goes as far as Clifton Forge. You'll need to get off there. I'm jump'n at Balcony Falls, so watch for Greenlee, Buchanan and Eagle Mountain. Clifton Forge comes after that." He gulped the last of the apple down and stuffed the hunk of cheese into his mouth.

"That's where they change crews," he continued between chews, "and break up the train, get rid of cars, and add on others. They'll probably hook on another engine to help pull it across the Alleghenies. There'll be two or three more stops doin' the same thing. After that, you'll need to change trains about every hundred miles." He swiped his hand across his mouth and wiped away the remnants of the apple and cheese.

"If you're smart, you'll get off before it pulls all the way into each depot. Then circle around, go to the opposite end and catch it when it heads out. That way you avoid the bulls. Normally, they only check boxcars when the train is in the yard."

Keeping his eyes focused on the man, Ed periodically nodded his head to give the impression he was getting it all. He hoped he'd remember everything.

"Uh huh, go on."

"At Cincinnati," he continued, "change to the New York Central. After that, ya hit St. Louie and change to the Wabash. When you get into Kansas City, transfer to the Union Pacific. That'll get you into Salt Lake City. From there, you're on your own."

"Wow," Ed marveled. "You really know your rails."

"Spent most of my life on 'em," Blacky responded matter-of-factly. "Just remember," he added, "on the next switch you may have to ride a gondola. Boxcars are usually sealed. For some reason this one wasn't."

Nodding his thanks, Ed returned to his enclosure, mentally using acrostics to memorize the train connections. He scooted in, leaned back against the box and crossed his arms behind his head. Thank his lucky stars Blacky pulled him into the boxcar.

Lucky stars? He raised an eyebrow. Or could it be part of his mama's God-sees-that-everything-works-together-for-good, thing? He weighed the possibility with a critical squint.

Nah, considering everything he suffered the last four years—nearly five—it would be too late in coming. On the other hand, he mused, did God use birds? He stared pensively while the question hung in the air. The seagull at camp?

Well, whether it was God, a providential lucky-life-thing, or his own fantasy, the seagull worked and he escaped. If God had anything to do with it, he'd probably never know for sure. Maybe, if everything came to a perfect ending like a Perry Mason novel, some day hindsight might reveal the answer. He brought his knees up close to his chest and wrapped his arms around them, wondering where he would be when and if that hindsight came? Would he be a free man, convinced God saw justice win out? Or back in prison with the realization that no one watches over anyone? He tilted his head inquisitively. No way to figure it out. He needed his mama's faith for that one.

Late in the afternoon his eyelids sagged. He was more tired than he thought. He drifted into the darkness of sleep, slipping in and out of confused dreams and fantasies. The monster with the hydra heads soon moved in with its tendril-like fingers grabbing at him. One of its heads slithered down its body with its face transforming

214

into Jeb's. Next, Ed heard the buzz of ravenous horseflies swarming onto his bloody body, then the scraping of shovels and sounds of dirt being thrown on top of him.

He wrenched awake with a series of reactive shivers at the thought of being back in Jeb's clutches.

Could his dream be a sign the police were waiting for him at Clifton Forge?

CHAPTER 34

<center>~~~</center>

The clickety-clack of the train's wheels rolled on at their usual speed. Ed purposely fought sleep, not wanting a repeat of his ill-omened dream. Scooting out of his cubbyhole, he glanced down the aisle to where Blacky slept. No legs were in the aisle—Blacky had already left!

He leapt to his feet. He had no idea how close the train was to Clifton Forge. Had he missed it? Fear shuddered through him. If he messed up on his train connections and was caught, Jeb would put him six feet under and Buford would never be brought to justice.

He scurried to the door and slid it open. The cool breeze whooshed through the opening, whipping his trousers about his legs. Anxiously watching for signposts along the track, he was relieved when Buchanan and Eagle Mountain whizzed by. Clifton Forge should be next.

He bolted back to his cubbyhole, remembering Blacky's caution. To avoid the bulls, he had to jump before the train pulled into the station, then circle around to the far side of the station and hop back on when it left.

He grabbed his gunnysack with nervous flutters dancing in his chest. Donning his overcoat, he felt for the moneybox and checked the ID papers taped to his chest. Bounding back to the open door he sat down on the edge, let his legs dangle over the edge, and watched fields of green cabbage and red chard sweep by.

Hypnotized by the rhythmical thud, thud, thud of the wheels hitting the track seams, he slumped his head onto his chest and stared unseeingly at the ground that zipped by beneath his feet, thinking of Sarah—her laughter, scent of her skin, their romantic lovemaking wrapped in "golden butterscotch." He imagined having her again and the floodgates opened. The night at the *Clarion* replayed, Sarah's powder-blue blouse…her blood-matted hair… the pool of red on the hardwood floor… her whisper, "*Darling, so glad it wasn't you.*" Then, feeling her body go limp in his arms and the shock of her sea green eyes fixed in a vacant stare. The memory of that night could never be expunged.

He raised his head just in time. The Clifton Forge sign rushed by. The brakes sounded, wheels screeched, and the train began to slow. He saw the depot ahead. His palms grew clammy. He had to jump.

Leaping to the ground, he picked himself up and streaked toward a nearby cornfield and hunched down behind a scrub tree where he meticulously scrutinized the loading docks and area around the station—especially the tracks outside the other end of the station where he would hop on.

He waited an hour while the crew changed and cars were switched. He saw no bustle of activity suggesting police were there.

A signalman waved a white flag and two long bursts of the whistle sounded. The locomotive belched, wheezed, and slowly chugged forward.

Waiting until the signalman was out of sight, he sprinted forward and barreled across the field, running like a mad man between the withering cornstalks. Struggling up the graveled track incline, he rushed for a gondola full of crushed rock. Grabbing on to the ladder, he scrambled up and dropped inside. Scrunching down out of sight, he sagged in relief.

Made it.

CHAPTER 35

~~~

The train traveled over the Alleghenies. Once in Cincinnati, Ed changed to the New York Central, and at St. Louis to the Wabash, but all his train changes were not without problems. He missed one, barely managed to evade a couple of brakemen and a yard bull, and panicked a few times when he couldn't find the right train. At Kansas City he managed to find the Union Pacific headed for Denver. Pleased, he gave himself a jubilant grin. He was getting to be a pro.

In Denver he'd hop off and replenish his food supply with Avery's money. He looked down at his grungy clothes. He'd also buy some clothes at a thrift shop, clean most of the stink off him at a gas station, get a map of Utah, then hop a Western Pacific and ride straight into Salt Lake City.

Every lap of his journey was moving him closer to Buford—but would he find him in Wendover? Four and a half years had passed. If still there, would he recognize him? The guy had probably dyed the white stripe in his hair and done other things to change his looks. With no picture of him, all he had was his memory from the day in court.

He also had a bigger dilemma.

How would he *prove* the man's identity to the police? What kind of hard evidence could he possibly find? Without it, his word as a prison escapee would carry no weight. He felt the bile rising up into his throat. Got to quit worrying. His mama was right. *Don't trouble trouble until trouble troubles you.*

Rearranging smaller pieces of crushed rock to make a backrest, he leaned back as the train picked up speed.

He glanced up into the sky and spoke softly, although not expecting to hear anything back.

"Sarah, I'm going to find Buford or die in the attempt."

Fence-encircled farmhouses soon dotted the landscape. Next

came scattered lean-tos and clumps of inexpensive houses, the run-down kind usually found near railroad tracks. Ed spied the main hub of Denver about a mile ahead. Buildings glistened in the noon sun and church steeples rose high in the air. A canopy of blue sky arched above.

Ed jumped to the ground before the train reached the city center and followed a worn path along the edge of a locust-buzzing field, enjoying the warbles of Meadowlarks mingling with the lusty voices of nearby farm hands. He sucked the tang into his nostrils of new mown hay and barnyard smells. He grinned. Who could believe manure could smell so wonderful? All of it was breath and music to his soul—the wondrous sounds of uncomplicated, everyday living. Someday, he'd have it all back.

Emerging onto Denver's traffic-filled streets, he found a Salvation Army store and bought a pair of khaki pants and a brown plaid shirt, then headed for a gas station to wash up and change.

There, he picked up a map of Utah and spread it open.

Wendover lay far to the west of Salt Lake City, on the Nevada border. He stared, unable to believe the miles and miles of desolate desert either side of the small town. Surely, no train went across that formidable wasteland. Blackie said he thumbed his way there. He'd have to do the same.

He folded the map, and as he did he noticed a brochure on the counter. *Visit Temple Square in Salt Lake City. Home of the Mormons.* Curious, he reached for it.

It was a rare person in Virginia who hadn't heard about Mormons. Did they really have horns, he wondered, and live in stockades? On the front was a picture of a multi-spired cathedral, obviously a tourist attraction. Ed read part of the leaflet.

"Hmm," probably plenty of tourists there. Just the place to beg a ride with someone. He shoved both the map and brochure into his jacket and hustled toward the train station.

Waiting in a field by some willow trees, he studied the train. It sat idling on the track with the engineer inside the cab, the red and brown boxcars behind extending a ways out from the terminal.

Sweeping a cautious gaze for any railroad workers, he headed for the tracks and scrambled up the embankment taking a quick look-see at some boxcars to see if any appeared open. He saw the alloy discs crimped over the wires that hooked the hasps. They were sealed.

Sprinting toward a gondola, he tossed his gunnysack over the top and pulled himself up the ladder, grateful for the balmy weather. Crawling atop the contents, he settled down in a shallow corner and scrunched down to avoid being seen.

He pictured Salt Lake City and Temple Square, finding a motorist, and then arriving in Wendover. But the same problem bugged him. He only had what Avery relayed from Buford's ex-con friend, Billy Farnsworth, who mentioned Wendover. He had to admit it was a long shot Buford went there and stayed. His whole venture might end up a total goose chase. If no longer there, where would he have gone? That thought sent a discouraging chill through him.

What a tragedy if he made it all the way to Wendover for nothing.

CHAPTER 36

~~~

Ed stood in the doorway of the boxcar enjoying the spine-tingling rush as the train entered Salt Lake City. Its wheels squeaked and groaned, then slowed to a crawl. It pulled its load first through the poorer part of town consisting of congested clumps of brown, tumble-down houses, laundry hanging askew on lines, and yards filled with old washing machines and rusted car frames.

The train soon moved into the industrial district where sawmills hummed like beehives and debarking machines expelled the pungent smell of timber.

Despite his previous concerns, he determined to stop worrying. He now felt strongly he would find Buford in Wendover. He had to remain positive. He crooked his lips into a one-sided grin. The guy had no idea the reporter he thought he killed was about to bring him to justice.

Considering the number of tourists he expected to see at Temple Square, he foresaw no problem in finding a ride to Wendover. And if he watched his Ps and Qs, no policemen would single him out in the crowds. He now wore regular-looking clothes and could pass for anyone walking down the street.

The train rattled over a railroad crossing where a line of automobiles waited for the red and white gate-arm to lift. Now, close to the city center, Ed could hear the soft drone of traffic.

Shading his eyes with one hand, he looked towards the center of town. He saw the multi-spired temple rising high into the sky. One didn't normally see a building with so many steeples. According to his mama, temples only existed in Bible times. This definitely piqued his curiosity. He'd kill two birds with one stone. See the temple and find his ride.

Rolling up his gunnysack of clothes with his one remaining apple, he crammed the sack inside his jacket, jumped to the ground and headed toward town. His thrill at being this close to his four-year long goal acted like an intoxicant. The sun warmed his back, and a blue pallet of sky arched above with mashed-potato-heaps of cumulous clouds. At that moment, all seemed right with the world. Maybe everything was working for his good after all.

His enthusiasm, however, didn't last long.

He pulled one corner of his mouth down into a crimp, thinking of the map. Find a ride? Who on earth would be driving across that desolate desert? The vision of hitchhiking 100 miles with no cars coming along, stymied him. What then? Any attempt to answer the question only resulted in tangled-up, knotted thoughts, like pieces of chewed string.

However, the clamor of traffic and other exhilarating diversions yanked his thoughts away and his qualms improved by the time he approached the hub.

He marveled at the granite buildings, the wider-than-normal streets, men and women in business suits rushing along sidewalks, and the shrill clang of streetcars tolling their warning to pedestrians.

Moving further into the heart of the city, he rounded a corner and blinked with surprise. White and gray seagulls were everywhere. They glided overhead, strutted on the sidewalks, and weaved about people's legs unbothered by the clusters of pedestrians or the squeak of newspaper carts rolling by.

The sight of so many made Ed recall the seagull back at camp that gave him the go-ahead to leave—and they were also here. It was like the powers-that-be were acknowledging he had been led to Salt Lake City. Providence? God? Luck? Some day he'd have that figured out.

He waited at a crosswalk for the signal's semaphore arm to change, elated no one standing by was eyeing him with suspicion. He gave himself an omniscient grin. With more people in Salt Lake than he expected, plus tourists on Temple Square, he could forget his doubts about getting a ride. He'd find someone, regardless of any APB that existed. Everything was indeed looking up. Soon, Buford would be behind bars, he'd be exonerated and have his life back at the *Clarion*.

A young woman with long hair like Sarah, short skirt and high heels, hurried past him. Looking away, he refused to give in to the memory. Instead, he focused on two seagulls sitting on the curb. He studied their webbed feet and strange side-to-side gait, but it was no use.

He glanced after the woman, now a half a block ahead of him, and everything rushed in. Sarah breezing in through the door, her burnished mahogany hair fluttering about her shoulders, her silky, hip-clinging tan skirt and the navy high-heels that made her legs look so great. He heard her voice, "*Hi, sweetie.*" His eyes went liquid as he felt the softness of her arms wrap around his neck and her yielding to his kiss. All of it pinched his heart until it was almost more than he could bear. He felt the quiver at the back of his throat. *Buford will pay.*

The signal changed and he crossed the street. Turning on North Temple, he circled the large concrete wall surrounding the complex and spied the wide entrance with its sign, *Welcome to Temple Square.*

Tourists, decked in summer regalia, strolled in and out, most of them with small box cameras hanging around their necks. Others were squatting to take close-up pictures of the seagulls that strutted about their feet.

Ed cautiously looked about for police and saw none. He headed for the entrance. Here he'd find his ride to Wendover. Barely had he taken a few steps inside the gate when he stopped.

He sucked in a gasp of surprise at the blinding explosion of brilliant yellows, blues, pinks and violets. Gold and purple pansies bordered emerald, lush lawns. Trees radiated rainbow splashes of red, yellow, and deep oranges. Myriad daffodils, tulips, and dahlias suffused the scene in a harmonious kaleidoscope of colors.

Towering skyward near the back of the square to his right stood the magnificent temple glittering in the sun. The gray, granite edifice with its needle-like spires reached higher than any building he had ever seen. A statue stood atop. A man blowing a horn. It had to be Gabriel.

To his left stood a white chapel also with numerous steeples. It reminded him of a gothic church he'd once seen in a picture book. A little distance beyond was another building. Unusual, it had a round-shingled roof resembling the top half of an eggshell.

A sudden sound made him swing his head to the right. A door burst open and slammed back against the wall of a small building identified as *Visitors Center.* A large group of chattering tourists exited through double doors and down the steps. Scattering in all directions, the majority headed for the egg-shaped building. Only a middle-aged man and his wife remained at the bottom of the steps. Ed noted the man pulling keys from his pants pocket. Now was his opportunity.

He pushed toward them sending a few seagulls at his feet hopping out of the way.

"Pardon me. I'm looking for a ride to Wendover. Would you be going in that direction?"

"Sorry," the woman said. "We're going toward Ogden—opposite direction."

Ed ambled toward a young man in his twenties who was reading the inscription on a pole-like monument topped with two bronzed seagulls.

"Excuse me," Ed asked, "I'm headed for Wendover and looking for a lift."

"Was born there." The man chuckled. "Sure wouldn't want to go back."

Ed stared. Was he joking?

He approached some parents who knelt by a bed of flowers showing their two small children the intricacies of a crimson tulip.

Ed cleared his throat. The couple looked up. "Sorry to bother you. I'm looking for a ride to Wendover." They smiled politely and shook their heads.

Receiving the same response from others, Ed shrugged. Perhaps he'd have to hitchhike after all—but across a bleak desert with maybe no prospect of cars? Even if one or two came along they might ignore him. Not everyone was willing to pick up wayfarers.

He spied a couple of granite benches on a gravel walkway a short distance from the Visitors Center. With heavy steps he sauntered over to one and plopped down. Placing both elbows on his knees, he cupped his chin in his hands. Things looked pretty glum.

Squinting against the sun he saw a woman with a cane standing on the steps back at the Visitors Center. She spoke to a man standing next to her. Shading her eyes with one hand, she pointed with the other across the short distance to the bench across from Ed. The man took her arm and they moved down the path.

The woman appeared about Ed's age. She had a round face, and her auburn hair might have been red in her childhood. Despite her plumpness she was rather pretty in a wholesome way. Ed figured she probably needed to rest and wondered what happened to make her lame. The man, short and stocky, wasn't particularly handsome but struck Ed as honest-looking. He'd ask them.

They reached the bench. The man remained standing while he steadied the woman as she sat down. She immediately looked at Ed.

"I was telling my brother," she reached up and patted the man's arm, "that I couldn't help but overhear you asking people if they might be driving to Wendover."

"Yes." Ed nodded. "I'm looking for a ride."

"Well, we live there."

Ed expelled a soft breath.

"This is my brother, Harry."

"Glad to meet you," Ed responded. "Would you consider a passenger?" He studied the man's face. She might be willing but her brother might say no.

Harry gave Ed the once-over and rubbed his chin for a few seconds. Ed tried to quell the churning inside his stomach.

"Sure, we'll be glad to give you a lift."

Ed flashed them as big a grin as he could. "That's really nice of you, considering I'm a stranger and all."

Harry let out a guffaw. "Oh, you look decent enough."

"We do like to help people out," his sister interjected. She scrutinized Ed's gunnysack now peeking from the inside of his jacket. He quickly tucked it back inside.

"It would certainly cost you to ride the Greyhound that distance," she continued."

Ed had no idea a bus even went there.

"Got friends in Wendover?" Harry asked, raising an inquisitive eyebrow. Ed shook his head.

"Nope. Just traveling cross-country. Got curious about the salt flats. Thought I'd check them out."

"Well, you both wait here," Harry said. "I'll pull the car around." He took off down the gravel walkway and disappeared through the front gate.

Ed looked at the woman, then down at his feet. His breath momentarily stalled in his throat. It had been years since he'd talked to a woman.

"My name is Maureen Fisher," she offered, breaking the ice."

"Oh, my name is Ed Bo... His heart leapt. "Uh, Ed...Riley." He gripped the edge of the bench with his fingers.

"I always enjoy coming to Salt Lake with my brother," she began. "He takes care of business at the Western Pacific office. I can't drive, you know." She glanced down and pointed to her leg, and then looked back up.

"So," she gestured with a sweep of her hand, "what do you think of all this?"

"Well," Ed said, "the grounds are spectacular and the buildings certainly unique. I was hoping to take a look inside the temple but don't see any tourists going in."

"Oh," she said, "non-Mormons aren't allowed to go in—even some members can't."

"What's the deal?" Ed asked, feeling a tad more comfortable.

"Sacred ordinances, supposedly," she said. "The reason some members are barred is because they have to pass a test. If their answers are satisfactory, the bishop gives them a special piece of paper called a Recommend. That's what gets them in."

"What's the test about?"

"Oh, I don't know. Part of it is they can't smoke, drink alcohol, tea or coffee, and have to tithe ten percent of their income, although I hear more is required."

Ed raised one eyebrow. "Whew! I take it you're not a member?"

"Heavens no!" she exclaimed, throwing up her hands. "The missionaries gave me their lessons once but I have too many reservations. They're persistent though." She laughed. "They still keep coming around. They're sociable—probably because there's nothing much else for them to do. A small place like Wendover can get pretty boring at times."

Ed shifted his position on the bench. "So, tell me about the town."

"Not too much to say." She reached over and repositioned her cane against the side of the bench. "In a nutshell," she continued, her blue eyes focusing on him again, "the town is in the middle of the desert surrounded by salt flats, sagebrush, and straddles the Utah-Nevada borderline. Population is small, a little under two hundred." Ed took an inward gasp at the size.

"What keeps the people there?"

"The potash plant and the WP—" She twisted around on the bench. "Oh, there's Harry."

Her brother hurried half way up the path, stopped midway, crooked his finger and motioned to them.

"C'mon," he called. "Car's parked out in front. If we leave now, we'll make it before dark."

Ed stood and followed them toward the gate noting Maureen did pretty well keeping up with her cane.

He really lucked in with this ride. After years of hoping to find Sarah's killer he was on his way. But only two hundred people? Even Hannigan was bigger than that. All the more chance Buford, if there, could recognize him—probably try again to kill him. Yet, on the other hand, his own appearance had changed. He was certainly a lot skinnier. Four plus years in prison and working on a chain gang changed a person's looks. Besides, Buford thought him dead. He relaxed.

"Prepare yourself," Harry said as they exited the gate and headed for a blue Ford sedan parked next to the front curb. "It's a loooong drive. A good two hours or more—124 miles to be exact."

"That's okay." Ed climbed into the back seat. "I can't thank you enough for giving me a ride. You're really both more than generous."

Maureen slid into the front seat. "People from out-of-state are always puzzled by Utahan hospitality." She twisted half way around in her seat to face Ed. "But this is just the way we are. Besides, you seem nice." She smiled. "We've gotten so we can pretty well size up a person. Never been wrong yet."

Harry closed the door after her and then scuttled around to the driver's side.

Ed thought about the long drive, and apprehension set in. He would be two or three hours in the car with them. What if they asked too many questions? If he refused to answer they could become suspicious. If that happened, he supposed he could jump out of the car if going slow enough, but where would he run? Nothing but sagebrush and salt flats.

Harry climbed in behind the wheel and slammed the door

shut. Ed's breath quickened. Something eerily signaled a warning and a huge pulse of anxiety beat inside him. He should have bowed out and taken the bus. Dread and regret pressed in on him like a two-ton weight.

Harry gunned the motor and pulled out onto South Temple. "Wendover here we come!"

It was too late.

CHAPTER 37

~~~

Harry weaved his car through North Temple's heavy traffic to head for the highway to Wendover only to be forced to reduce his speed due to road construction and men pouring asphalt. The stench hung heavy in the air for more than a mile.

The gassy smell struck a bad chord with Ed—the day the gang poured tar on the road and Jeb whipped him because he hadn't sweat enough. Having the memory crop up while in the car with Harry and Maureen gave him a queasy feeling. Could it be a premonition he made a wrong decision to ride with them?

They seemed like nice people but he didn't know them. Now he was helplessly under their control for 124 miles and something unforeseen could jeopardize his safety. He bit the inside of his cheek. How could he have been so stupid to get himself in this fix? He should have taken the Greyhound. He slumped back against the seat.

Once past the construction, Harry zoomed the car onto the main highway and headed west.

"How long do you think you'll stay in Wendover?" Maureen twisted half way around in her seat and looked at him.

Panic slithered through him. His cheeks flushed hotter than the hot wind that blasted through the open windows. They had only been on the road fifteen minutes and she was already asking questions.

"Not sure..." His mouth went dry. Did she plan to keep this up for the next two hours? A huge pulse of unease hit him. What if he stumbled too much in his answers and they became wary? They might cover up their suspicions during the ride, but then go to the police when they arrived in Wendover.

"Well," she said, "the drive won't offer you much scenery. After we go through Grantsville it's nothing but flat, uninteresting desert. And for Wendover, it's a treeless place consisting mainly of dirt and barren rock. But," she added, "it has salt flats of beautiful snow-white alkali."

"Got to watch out for those salt bears, though," Harry interrupted with a sober face. Maureen rolled her eyes and slapped him on the shoulder.

Ed knew about black bears but not salt bears. Did she slap Harry because she didn't want him to know about them? He didn't relish encountering one.

"There's the Great Salt Lake," Harry called out, pointing over to the right. "Did you know you can't sink in it? Twenty-five percent salt."

Relieved the subject changed, Ed stared out the window in wonderment, feeling a tad more comfortable.

Thirty minutes more and Harry entered the outskirts of Grantsville and slowed the car to the speed limit. Was this his chance to jump out? What reason could he give? They would probably become all the more suspicious and report him for sure.

"This is Grantsville." Maureen laughed. "Where everyone is practically related to each other. It'll be the last bit of excitement you'll see for the next two hours."

They drove down Main Street and exited the other end of town, which took less than five minutes, then on to a narrow, two-lane stretch of highway flanked by desert on either side.

"By the way, Ed," Harry asked, looking at Ed in the rearview mirror, "where you from? No doubt the South judging by your accent." Harry's question sent a reactive shiver through him.

"Vir...ginia. "

"Yeah? What part?"

Ed's insides tightened.

"Oh...different places." Tension edged his voice. He looked out the window. Harry politely dropped the subject. What other questions might be asked? He had to be prepared. *Think, Ed.*

"We're on Highway 40 now," Harry offered, "the old Victory Highway. It'll be pretty dull from here on—"

"Except for you know what," Maureen interrupted. "If Ed has never seen them before, they'll keep him from getting bored."

"Oh yeah, I forgot." Harry smiled. "After we hit Knolls—a small spot in the road that used to be an old siding for the WP Railroad— you'll see what she means."

His curiosity piqued, Ed watched. For what, he didn't know. Salt bears?

Twenty minutes later he saw a road sign with three puzzling words. He muttered them aloud. "*Say, big boy....*"

"Well, that doesn't make sense," he said, grateful for something to take the focus off him.

"Just wait," Maureen chuckled.

Soon he saw a second sign. "*to go through life...*" He waited for the next two. "*How'd you like...a whiskered wife? Burma Shave.*"

Ed laughed in spite of himself and it felt strangely good. Soon he was reading all the signs aloud. "*Grandpa's beard...was stiff and coarse...and that's what caused...his fifth divorce.*"

Harry pointed to both sides of the road, calling attention to the cracked landscape. "Since you said you were curious about the salt flats, there's 159 square miles of them. It's a natural salt bed, Ed, just like the Dead Sea in Palestine. It used to be covered by Bonneville Lake, then gradually receded leaving deposits, some of which are three to twelve feet thick."

"Well," Ed forced a smile into his voice, "since you obviously can't grow anything, what are the flats good for?" He'd keep them talking.

"Well, besides Bonneville Ltd., Wendover's potash plant, when summer comes speed races are held on it. I guess Wendover's only other good feature, if you can call it good, is it keeps the town isolated. Of course, that factor attracts vagrants and those seeking anonymity."

Ed's nerves prickled. Did he say that on purpose? Did Harry suspect he had something to hide? That he wasn't who he claimed? His insides shook.

"Which means," Maureen interjected, "Wendover can't boast as having the most savory characters. But they come and go—never stay for long."

"In the really olden days," Harry continued, "the town was the jumping-off place. Police in Salt Lake City and California dragged skid rows for undesirables and gave them a one-way ticket to Wendover just to get rid of them. This doesn't happen anymore, although transients do wander in now and then. Since the railroad and potash plant always need workers, they hire most drifters without asking questions. Ed picked up on that.

"Yep. No one pays much attention to vagrants," Harry added, "including Kevin. He's the sheriff."

Fear ricocheted like ping-pong balls through Ed's bones. He studied Harry's eyes in the rearview mirror for any unusual expression. Was Harry deliberately watching for his reaction?

"Harry...?" Maureen began in hesitant tones. Ed detected concern.

"Did the Salt Lake office tell you exactly when you'll be... leaving?"

"Now, don't you worry sis. I've still got another week." He reached over and patted her arm. "I'll have everything caught up including the yard work, and I'll ask Kevin to check on you now and then."

Maureen responded with a barely perceptible sigh, leaving Ed to gather she didn't want him to leave. No indication where he was going, or if it was permanent or temporary.

"In town today, sis, I spoke to Mr. Monroe about my replacement. So far they don't have anyone, but they want me to go ahead and leave anyway. Otherwise, you know I'd stay longer." His tone was apologetic.

Ed felt a stir of excitement. Replacement? A job would be great cover while looking for Buford. Avery's money wouldn't hold out forever.

Harry glanced up and caught Ed's eye in the mirror.

"Sorry, Ed, didn't mean to leave you out of the conversation. I work for the Western Pacific Railroad and I've been promoted to Bridge and Building Inspector. They're sending me to the Feather River Canyon in Northern California—a place called Keddie. Snows like heck there in the winter. It's too cold for sis, which is why she's staying behind." He smiled and shrugged his shoulders. "You may have gathered she doesn't want me to leave."

Maureen didn't respond.

Ed leaned forward. "You say they're looking for a replacement?"

"That's right."

"I might be interested."

"Really? You ever work on a railroad?"

"Uh...for a while." His reply caused a guilty chill.

"Yeah? Where was that?"

"Oh...Virginia...like I said." He winced. He needed to be more convincing.

"Yes sir," he continued with as much know-how in his voice he could muster, "I've laid some tracks and ties in my day. Levees in Virginia often give way causing a lot of washouts, so I've done a lot of re-ballasting and covering bridge stringers with sheet iron to prevent fires from hot clinkers falling from engines—also know enough to use treated stringers, or the tops end up rotting underneath and the metal has to be ripped back up."

It was the first time Ed was glad the pen had leased him out to the railroad. He hadn't actually done all the work he was describing. It was only a brief stint as "water man," but he knew enough from watching the workers and listening to inmates talk about the work when back in their cells.

Harry raised his eyebrows. "Well, they'd start you out as a track laborer on one of the section gangs first. That way you'd get a feel for the kind of work required in the desert. In the summer, flash floods sweep across the flats so ditches have to be kept free of water or the ground under the gravel gets soft and undermines the rails. You're definitely interested?"

"Yeah, I am. I have a letter of recommendation from the company I used to work for. It went out of business." Ed nervously pressed his chest to feel the tape still in place.

Harry looked briefly over his shoulder and flashed Ed a quick grin. "Well, they'll be mighty pleased to get a replacement this fast. He tapped Maureen on the arm. "Sis, reach into the glove compartment and get one of those blank applications and a pencil."

Withdrawing the application, she handed it back to Ed.

"Fill that out, Ed. I'll talk to Hutch, the track supervisor, as soon as we arrive and give it to him. The railroad has section houses for workers, so housing won't be a problem for you. They're nothing fancy but it'll be a roof over your head. Later, you can rent a place in town if you like."

"Sounds good to me." Ed's heart leapt. He couldn't believe how this was coming together. He began filling it out, putting down a fake address in Newport News.

"Oh, look," Maureen said, "here comes more Burma Shave signs. This one is my favorite.

Ed read it aloud. "*No lady likes...to dance or dine...accompanied by...a porcupine.* Yep, that's a good one, for sure."

"Well, now." Maureen grinned, turning completely around in her seat and looking Ed squarely in the face. "Didn't those signs make the trip go faster?"

"Sure did." Nevertheless, his laugh felt stilted. He studied her. Her expression was genuine. Nothing seemed amiss. He relaxed a bit more and found himself feeling more comfortable, but felt the caution not to get too chummy. He glanced out the window hoping another set of billboards would come up so the conversation wouldn't shift back to him.

The next sign appeared, but not a Burma Shave. "*A-1 Star Café and Casino. Good food—Drinks –Slots - lodging. Over the hill in Wendover, Nevada.*" Ed blinked with surprise. "I thought Wendover was in Utah."

"It is." Harry laughed. "The town straddles both states. Half of Wendover is on the Utah side—the other half in Nevada."

"We're fortunate to be on the Utah side," Maureen said. "Nothing much on the Nevada side, except the A-1 Star. We call it A-1 for short. It also has an auto court with a few cabins out in back for tourists. Some of the employees rent them, but there's more to it than meets the eye. There's gambling with lots of drinking. It's where the tougher element of town goes. Some of the railroad men go there in their off hours. I think there's only been one shooting out there during the last two years. Still, that's one too many."

Maureen pointed out the front window. "There's Wendover coming up. Now, just as we enter if you look closely at that large rock formation on the right you'll see the shape of a giant lizard."

Ed studied it. He made it out but it wasn't easy.

In a few seconds they entered Wendover, a gray, colorless town with low, hill-like mountains bordering to the north. Ed took note of the Western Café on his right as they passed. Four rough-looking men slouched near the entrance. A few others stood around two gas pumps. He looked for a head of dark hair with a white streak. One of the men wore a conspicuously large cowboy hat that shaded his face so he couldn't tell. Besides, he was too skinny.

"Hey sis, look who's there. Cowboy! Wanna stop and say hi?"

Maureen threw him a cold stare.

Puzzled, Ed turned his head back and took an extra look out the rear window at the man with the ten-gallon hat.

236

Further on, there were a few diners, two more gas stations and a sparse scattering of auto courts. Ed saw no church steeples and thought that strange

"I'm giving you the grand tour, Ed. See that tall rock mountain?" Harry directed Ed's gaze to the right. "That's Needle Point. If you look closely you'll see a vertical slit in the very top of the peak—just like a real needle. Now I'm going to drive you clear to the end of town. Just don't blink or you might miss something." He laughed.

In less than two minutes they had reached the end of town. Ed's stomach rolled to the point of nausea. They had told him Wendover was small but he didn't expect it to be *this* small. Fear attacked once more. Strangely, one of his mother's Bible-quotes popped into mind. She had rehearsed it to him the first day he started working for the *Clarion* and was so nervous. "*Remember son, God hasn't given you a spirit of fear, but a sound mind.*"

He sure didn't agree. No way did he have a sound mind at this moment. If identified before he found Buford, everything would go down the tube and he'd be back in prison. The only way he could eliminate fear and develop a sound mind would be to know for sure Gunther Buford still thought him dead and wouldn't recognize him.

"There on the left," Harry pointed, "is the Stateline Hotel. Most of the building sits on the Utah side. Rumor has it the owner is going to extend more of the building onto the Nevada side and build a casino."

"Well, let's hope not." Maureen sighed. "It's bad enough with the A-1 being so close. I'm glad we have a sheriff, Ed. Kevin is a close friend of ours." Ed's breath caught.

"Nothing much beyond the A-1," she continued, "except the town dump out on the Lincoln Highway that goes to Ely."

"What do you do for real entertainment?" Ed forced a casual tone.

"Well, you can drive on to Elko—another 140 miles. Or locally, you could go cave spelunking if that interests you. Lots of arrowheads found around here. If you're into swimming, Blue Lake is out on the flats.

"Maybe you'll wish you hadn't taken the job," she said, turning around to face him. "It might get a little boring for you."

"Oh, no." He soberly glanced at the dismal surroundings. "I think everything's working out the way it should." Inwardly, he groaned. No way to be inconspicuous like in a big city.

He visualized Kevin capturing him, sending him back to the chain gang, and Jeb burying him out by the kennels, but not before torturing him first. Squeezing his eyes shut, he forcibly shoved the thought away.

He had to be positive. After all, what could really go wrong? At this point, the ride had gone better than he expected and no one in town should suspect him. He had a new name and would soon have a legitimate job. All he had to do was keep a low profile and maintain a cautious relationship with Harry and Maureen. That would give him plenty of time to look for Buford…if here.

Still, it wouldn't be a cakewalk. The guy was dangerous. If he recognized him as Ed Bowman, the reporter, he'd try again to kill him.

Whatever lay ahead, he only hoped Wendover wouldn't prove to be a dead end for him.

…in more ways than one.

CHAPTER 38

~~~

Harry veered the car off Wendover's main drag and drove down a dusty stretch of road full of bumps and ruts. The ride through the residential area didn't encourage Ed. There were a couple of whitewashed houses with junk strewn in the front yards, a huddle of wooden lean-tos, and a cluster of wood-structured dwellings that looked more like chicken coops than houses, obviously erected by someone who knew nothing about building.

"I'll stop at the railroad depot first, Ed, talk with the supervisor and give him your application. I'm sure the job is as good as yours. He'll give me the key to the section house you'll be staying in and we'll zip over there."

Maureen pointed out the post office and jail as they drove by. To Ed, both buildings looked straight out of an old western. He was going to live here? Nevertheless, he congratulated himself. After a 124-mile ride, they indicated no concerns about him—at least not yet.

Harry pulled into the train yard, parked, and hopped out. He returned in less than ten minutes.

"It's all set, Ed. Even though tomorrow is Friday, you'll report to the supervisor for an interview. That'll give you the weekend to get settled. Your place," he pointed with a sweep of his hand, "is straight down that road paralleling the tracks." He pulled the car out.

"There it is." Maureen pointed out the front window as Harry pulled up in front of the section house. It had taken them less than two minutes.

Ed took a furtive glance through the window at the clump of cottonwoods further down the block to see if a police car might be hiding.

"It's not much to look at," Harry said, opening the car door, "and the railroad tracks are practically in your backyard. You may not like living so close to the noise."

239

"No, I'm sure this will be fine." Ed forced an unnatural stretch of his lips, giving him a wooden smile. He climbed out while Harry walked around the car and helped Maureen.

Ed studied the house. He had to agree with Harry. It wasn't much to look at. Made of railroad ties, it sat directly on the ground with no foundation. Reddish-colored roofing shingles layered the outside, a few of which were ripped off revealing black tar paper underneath. The yard wasn't much to look at either. He scrutinized the tufts of dry weeds and dandelions poking up from the baked ground. No grass. No flowers.

Nevertheless, he checked his criticism. It wasn't the Biltmore Hotel, but still a palace compared to the filth and squalor of the cages—and a dang sight better than the barracks. He'd also have privacy and his own bathroom instead of a thunder bucket—at least he hoped there was indoor plumbing. Forgetting his previous concerns, Ed felt a twinge of excitement. A place he could finally call his own. He looked forward to seeing the inside.

"Really appreciate you getting the job for me and permission to move in so quickly."

"No problem at all, Ed." Harry forged ahead to the front door. "It's not locked, no need to do that here, although I do have a key for you."

Ed slung his gunnysack over one shoulder, throwing another cautious glance back down the road. How long before the sheriff would materialize? Could he bluff him as well as he did Harry and Maureen? What if he had to hightail it out? Not easy with one hundred miles of barren desert either side of the town.

They walked inside.

The front room contained a green, upholstered chair with wooden armrests, and a worn couch with a bulge on the seat indicating a spring close to breaking through. In the center of the linoleum floor lay a yellow and purple rag rug. Off to the right sat a wood-burning stove and stack of kindling.

"When the weather turns cold," Harry said, "you can bank up the stove at night with coal. It's hot now, but we're sure to have frost by Halloween." His comment served as confirmation to Ed. Harry had no reservations about him at this point.

Maureen eased herself down on the couch while Harry led Ed

into the kitchen where a huge swamp cooler filled the window. Beneath it sat a small table covered with a red-and-white checkered oilcloth. Next to it, a white-enameled gas range and a brown, wooden icebox.

"Follow me." Harry said with a wave of his hand. Ed trailed behind him down a narrow, green hallway to the bathroom.

Ed couldn't help but beam when he stepped inside. He stared with delight. An old-fashioned tub with lion's feet. He pictured hot water up to his neck. He also noted Harry's mouth curve slightly, obviously amused at his reaction.

"You might have problems if you flush it too many times," Harry commented, pointing to the commode. "We only have cesspools here and the water table is high. There's an outhouse just in case it backs up."

Cesspool...bad flushing...outhouse...who cares? It was better than anything Ed had seen for a long time.

Harry motioned Ed back into the hall and down to the bedroom. A stack of fresh sheets and blankets sat on top of a blue, four-drawer wooden dresser that stood against a wallpapered wall of bright yellow flowers and swirls of green ivy. On the other side of the room sat a cot with metal-link springs and a rolled-up tick mattress tied with twine. Another swamp cooler was in the window.

"This is great, Harry." Ed's mouth formed into a wide grin. After nearly five years in prison this was luxury he hadn't seen for a long time.

"And," Harry added, turning on his heel and leading the way back into the front room where Maureen sat, "you're close to the Pastime Club. If you missed it on the drive, it's back down the road from here. You'll see it on your way to the depot tomorrow. Besides being a pool hall, it has a barbershop. There's also a chinaman who claims to be a healer, just in case you need a doctor." He laughed.

"And," Maureen interjected, "right by it is our one-and-only store, Jensen's Tri-State Mercantile for clothing, groceries and other sundries. She waved her hand in the general direction. "We just call it the 'Merc.'"

"Fortunately," Ed patted his hip pocket, "I have enough money to see me through until payday."

"Nevertheless," Maureen said, getting up from the couch, "we'll give you some food to help out until you can get to the store and stock up."

Harry motioned toward the kitchen. "I'll also bring you some ice for your box. And sis?"

"Oh, yes." Maureen glanced at her watch. "We'll be back to pick you up at six—you're having dinner with us tonight."

"You're gonna do all that?" Ed gaped, wide-eyed. "I mean, invite a complete stranger into your home?" While shocked at their generosity, he felt his insides shriveling.

Could their niceness be a ruse covering an ulterior motive? Invite him to dinner and then pump him for information? They could pass on whatever they learned to the sheriff, since they were friends. He tensed all the way to his feet.

Maureen laughed. "I suppose it does seem rather crazy to outsiders but, like Harry said in the car, we're Utahans and we do what we can to help. Besides, Harry's elated to have found a replacement for his job and wants to show his appreciation. Anyway, we won't take no for an answer."

"We'll let you get settled, now," Maureen said walking toward the door. With that they left.

Ed, still in a quandary about them, stood in the doorway and watched them drive off with a cloud of gray powder trailing behind. He shut the door.

The prospect of being pinned down with more questions unnerved him. He didn't want to go but couldn't very well refuse. He arched one eyebrow and thought about it for a second.

On the other hand, he could also draw information out of *them*. Since Harry had mentioned criminals and transients coming to Wendover, he could find out if in the past few years there had been any fitting Buford's description. If he picked up any sudden change in Harry and Maureen's attitude from something he might say, he could always leave after dark. There's no way he was going to chance going back to prison. If no night freights to hop, he'd go up to the highway and hitch a ride with a tourist heading to California.

But what if Buford is really here? He jutted his bottom lip forward, walked over to the easy chair and sank down. The question hung in the air.

He had to stay and find out. This is what his escape was all about. If he left Wendover too soon, he'd never know. His fingers drummed against the wooden armrest. Wendover was the only lead Avery provided. He'd be a fool not to follow through. Yes, he'd hang in.

Tonight, if he carefully watched what he said, he foresaw no serious problems. Good luck had been with him so far, although that's not how his mama would look at it. Maybe it would continue. He had no way of knowing how his stay in Wendover would turn out until he could look back with hindsight. He only hoped it wouldn't be from a prison cell.

He ambled into the bedroom, emptied his gunnysack of clothes into the dresser drawers, then sauntered back down the hall, through the front room, and to the back door.

Stepping outside into the late afternoon sun, he surveyed the small yard. Harry was right about the tracks. They were fifty yards from the house, complete with a loading dock and corral.

Shoving both hands into his pockets, he moseyed through the knee-high weeds disturbing a couple of horny toads that scurried out of the way.

He reached the rails and peered down the tracks to his left. A half-mile down was a smattering of a few other red-shingled section houses. Beyond that, he could see the roof of the train station where he would report tomorrow.

Turning his head to the right, toward the Nevada side of Wendover, he saw an orange and white-checkered water tower atop a small bare hill. Past it, the hills were too high for him to see further into Nevada. Probably more desert and sagebrush.

He breathed an exasperated sigh. Really a desolate place. Nevertheless, he thanked his lucky stars he finally reached his destination. Regardless of all the risks, he needed to maintain a positive outlook for his own sake. After all, who knew but what something favorable would happen concerning Buford.

He strolled back toward the house deep in thought, watching his feet to avoid stepping on any lizards. Reentering the house, he paced from one room to the other rehearsing evasive answers to every question he could possibly think Harry and Maureen might ask at dinner. They already knew he was from Virginia. What more could they drag out of him that would prove his undoing? Well, although a tense situation, he'd bite the bullet and hope for the best.

Then a new thought made his heart rate climb. They were friends with the sheriff.

What if they invited him to dinner?

CHAPTER 39

~~~

Ed waited in the front yard with needling apprehension. The evening was hot and the town quiet except for the nearby bark of a dog responding to some yapping mongrel across town. He looked at his watch. Five-fifty. His stomach tied in shoelace-like granny knots. Harry and Maureen said they would pick him up at six o'clock...any minute now.

Plunging both hands deep into his trousers pockets, he clenched his fists still worried over the questions he might be asked. Even though memorizing answers to what he thought they might inquire about, he had a nagging feeling things wouldn't go well. He scowled, feeling like a schoolboy fearing an F on his paper even though prepared.

He stared down at the straggles of yellow dandelions and weeds, thinking about the consequences of one slip.

Talk about walking the knife-edge of danger, he thought. There was one more possible fly in the ointment. He still worried whether they would invite the sheriff.

He lifted his flushed face into the balmy breeze that now blew in from the west, hoping it would offer relief from his anxiety. It didn't.

He whipped his gaze up when he heard the car. Harry's blue Ford sedan turned the far corner and came down the road swerving to miss the ruts. Ed looked at his watch. Six o'clock. They were prompt.

Harry pulled up in front.

Hi there, Ed. Climb on in."

Ed forced a smile, nodded to Maureen who sat next to Harry, then opened the back door and slid into the seat.

"You ready for a scrumptious meal?" Harry asked.

"Yep, sure am." He grabbed the door handle and pulled it shut.

"Maureen's some cook, you know."

"Now, Harry, I'm not that great," Maureen chimed in. "If you

245

say things like that, Ed's going to expect too much."

"I'm sure Harry knows what he's talking about, Maureen. It's really nice of both of you to do this."

"Ah, think nothing of it," Harry said. He shoved in the clutch, pushed the gear stick forward and took off.

During the four-block drive, Ed glanced up and down each crossroad studying the residences. A scrubby neighborhood. Most of the houses were made out of railroad ties with added wooden, lean-tos. Others were somewhat better but not by much. No lawns or flowers either, except for dandelions. It was as if nobody cared. He focused on everything he saw—anything to get his mind off worrying if he was going to flub up, or if the sheriff would be there.

Harry turned the corner and pulled up in front of a neatly painted, white and yellow wood-framed house. Ed, raising his eyebrows in surprise, taking it all in with one huge eye-gulp.

A large cottonwood leaned in over the fence from the street shading a lush green lawn. Edging the yard were assorted red geraniums, yellow daffodils and vibrant, purple Iris.

Walking into the yard, Ed recognized varieties from Sarah's garden—lavender and orange dahlias, daffodils, roses, and two-toned columbines.

"How did you manage all this, Harry?"

"Just hauled in a lot of top soil from Tooele with my truck. Too much alkaline in the ground to grow anything unless you do."

"Too bad others don't bother," Maureen interjected. "Sure would make Wendover prettier. Although," she added, "there's a widow lady down the street who has a whole backyard full of gorgeous flowers. Hers and ours are the only houses with flowers.

"Harry, you entertain Ed. I'm going inside to start dinner." Using her cane, Maureen limped up the narrow concrete sidewalk to the front porch and climbed the four wooden steps. Pulling the screen door open, she disappeared inside.

Ed saw no other dinner guests around and breathed a sigh of relief. A warm breeze wafted over the sun-lit yard and Ed began to feel better.

"Follow me," Harry said. "Let's grab some lawn chairs." He led Ed around the side of the house and into the backyard.

"That's sis's pride and joy," Harry said, pointing to a vegetable garden, "but I do most of the work. She can't because of her leg—had polio when she was a child."

Ed searched for an opening to bring the subject up about past criminals in Wendover. Harry reached for three folding chairs leaning against a tree, and handed one to Ed.

"C'mon," he said. "We'll sit in the front yard until dinner."

Ed followed him back around the side of the house. Placing the chairs on the grass beneath the overhanging cottonwood, Ed settled back into his chair. Now, he would ask his questions. He opened his mouth but was too late. Harry started in.

"This place will grow on you, Ed. In fact, I'm going to miss it. Still, I'm looking forward to my new job in Keddie—right in the middle of the Feather River National Forest. Not bad, eh? But lots rougher terrain than here...and more dangerous."

Ed winced at his statement. Harry had no concept of real danger.

"Well Harry, sounds like you have an important job. Guess you have the experience, and I suppose it pays you well enough to make up for the risks. And speaking of risks, Wendover seems like such a quiet place it's hard to picture criminals ever coming here—you know, like the ones you mentioned in the car. Have there been many in recent years? Any near arrests where maybe somebody got away?"

Before Harry could respond, a green Chevy turned the corner and pulled up in front. The driver, his arm resting in the open window, stuck his head out.

"How ya doing Harry?" He had a round face, deeply set furrows between his brows, and a bushy mustache. His head was nearly bald except for a narrow rim of thick, brown hair encircling the base of his scalp. He reminded Ed of a medieval friar.

"Fine," Harry said, getting up from his chair and ambling over to the front gate. "Kevin, I want you to meet Ed Riley."

The sheriff? Ed rose from his chair with shaky legs. Caterpillars wriggled in his stomach on the verge of metamorphosizing.

Kevin reached his arm out the window, extended his hand, and studied Ed with a deadpan expression.

Ed squirmed as he shook his hand.

"New in town, huh?" Kevin asked.

"Yeah. Just hired on with the railroad." Ed swallowed hard against the golf-ball lump in his throat.

"Got any family with you?"

"Nope...single." Ed began to sweat.

Kevin maintained his steady gaze. "Where you gonna be stayin'?"

Ed fidgeted. Why was he asking so many questions? Did he already suspect? Was he recognizing my face from a Wanted poster?

"Well, Harry fixed me up..." His voice trailed off. His butterflies increased in speed. He could almost hear the flapping of their wings.

"By the way, Kevin," Harry interrupted. "Have you heard I'm goin' to Northern California?"

Ed took a couple of steps back toward his chair, relieved at Harry's rescue-effort. At least that's what it looked like.

"Yeah, sure did. Don't take long for news to get around, especially down at the Beanery."

Kevin glanced back over at Ed, his expression a bit more friendly. "Well, welcome to Wendover. If you need anything, Harry can always tell you where to find me." He waved, shifted gears and pulled away.

"He sure doesn't smile much," Ed managed in a casual tone.

Harry laughed. "Oh, he's okay. He always puts on a serious front for newcomers. Likes to impress them with his position."

Ed sat down and leaned back in his chair, his heart still thumping. Harry didn't seem to notice.

Maureen opened the screen door. "Dinner's ready."

Ed rose to get up from his chair when an unexpected squeal of brakes came from down the street. Kevin was backing his car up to the gate. He leaned out the window. Ed sat back down and white-knuckled the two armrests.

"Hey, Maureen!" Kevin called, grinning with a mischievous look on his face, "how's it going with Cowboy? Seen him lately?"

Maureen's face reddened. "You're full of baloney, Kevin. You know I haven't." She looked away and focused her gaze on Harry and Ed. "Come on in you two and wash up. Dinner's ready."

Kevin threw his head back, bellowed a roguish laugh, then

gunned the motor and took off down the street.

Ed followed Harry up the steps, hoping for some way to shift the subject.

"What was that all about...with Maureen and Cowboy?"

"Why don't you ask sis?" He chuckled. "She can explain it better."

"Say," he paused at the screen door and cocked his head looking squarely into Ed's face, "you looked a little nervous back there."

Ed shrugged his shoulders. "Nah. Guess being from a big city it just seemed strange for someone to ask so many questions. City people...are pretty private."

Moving through the doorway, the aroma of Maureen's cooking couldn't help but take Ed's mind off things. Entering the kitchen, Ed gawked.

A white linen tablecloth covered the table, decked with blue and white patterned china dishes heaped high with food. Shiny silverware lay neatly on folded, white linen napkins beside each plate. A large plate of roast beef sat in the center encircled with mashed potatoes and decorated with sprigs of parsley. A tureen of soup, a bowl of rich brown gravy, fresh buttered carrots, beets, homemade bread, radishes and pickle-relish.

He stood in stunned silence. Was this the way people normally ate? He had forgotten. Yet, how could he fail to remember what a good cook Sarah was and how she fussed so over how the table looked? Harry gave him a shove toward a chair.

Bowl after bowl was passed and Ed awkwardly filled his plate. Harry and Maureen were treating him like royalty. He felt himself slowly becoming convinced they were genuinely nice people with no intention of pumping information out of him—at least not on purpose.

He spooned a modest helping of buttered carrots on to his plate. No, their hospitality was certainly not a subterfuge—he was the one guilty of that. Pangs of guilt struck him as he brooded over his deception. They had no idea he was an escaped convict, police were after him, or his reason for being in Wendover. Further, that his name wasn't Ed Riley.

He tried to clear his mind by reaching for his silverware and start eating, but his furling thoughts tossed him up and down out of reality like a yo-yo. The silvery shine of the spoon catapulted him into a mesmeric state. He was back at camp picturing his tin spoon he dare not lose under threat of being put in the box. Other images rushed in—Squeaky's high-pitched voice, Jeb's blubbery belly, the sweatbox, picks digging into his legs, burying Benny, and his promise to tell his mother what happened. Would he ever be able to keep his word? Now, what did Benny look like? Oh, yes, yellow hair…like his dog.

"Dessert?" Maureen's distant voice pierced his thoughts. "It's freshly baked apple pie—alamode if you want it that way. You sort of look like the radishes were too hot. Sometimes they get that way." She laughed. "The ice cream will fix that."

Jolted from his daze, Ed nodded, unable to speak for a few seconds, but then managed to regain control and change the subject.

"Who's this Cowboy I keep hearing about?"

"Oh, no one important," Maureen said shyly, her cheeks flushing. She scooted her chair out and headed for the icebox.

"Yeah?" Harry gave Ed a wink. "Well, he thinks he's important—to you, anyway."

"Oh, Harry," she snapped with a toss of her head, screwing her face into an expression of disgust. Reaching into the freezer, she pulled out a carton of ice cream. "You know there's absolutely nothing going on. I'm not interested in *that* kind of man even if he does wear a fancy hat."

Ed remembered the man with the ten-gallon hat in front of the Western Café. He wasn't very respectable-looking.

"Cowboy—that's the name he goes by, Ed. He's a guy who took a shine to sis." He waved away a bothersome fly and snickered despite Maureen's imploring looks. He hooked one elbow over the back of his chair, obviously enjoying her discomfort.

"We were sitting at a booth in the Stateline Hotel's restaurant. The waitress, a gal named Lil, tripped over sis' cane. Down she went, dishes clattering. Cowboy, who was sitting at a table, knew Lil and jumped up to help."

"Maureen spent so much time apologizing," Harry clucked, tilting his chair back on two legs and locking both arms behind his head, "before it was over Cowboy was paying more attention to Maureen than Lil." He let out a hearty laugh. "He walked us out to our car afterward and ended up asking sis for a date. He still telephones."

Maureen frowned as she placed the ice cream on the sink counter. Tugging at the lid, she half-turned toward Ed.

"He's about as rough as they come, Ed. It was embarrassing. He's a blackjack dealer at the A-1 Star and has certainly been around the block. I'm just plain not interested in his kind."

"C'mon, sis. You got to admit you were flattered."

Maureen giggled, gesturing with one hand in acquiescence. "Okay, but only because he was a man who didn't seem to mind dating a woman with a cane." She jokingly gave a hip-cocked pose and primped her hair in place like a beauty queen.

Harry let loose with a loud guffaw.

Ed politely smiled. It was difficult to adjust to this kind of conversation and life. He could only hope he had plenty of life ahead of him. Right this minute, Kevin could be back in his office thumbing through Wanted posters and might show up before the evening was over. He reached for the dish of ice cream Maureen handed him. If he did, it would be the end of everything.

After dessert Maureen cleared the table and motioned with her hand for the men to go outside. Ed followed Harry into the front yard where they sat in the lawn chairs. The sky was a grayish orange with the sun on the verge of dipping below the horizon.

"By the way, Harry, if I'm thinking about staying in Wendover, what about those undesirables...and criminals you said sometimes come here? Does a small-town sheriff like Kevin catch many of them?" His insides felt like a squeezed accordion. It was labor to get that much out.

Harry got up out of his chair and leaned over to reinforce the chair legs into the grass. Ed stiffened and waited. Was he ignoring his question?

"Don't you worry," Harry laughed, giving the chair frame a shake with his hand to check for sturdiness. He sat back down. "I haven't heard of any crimina—"

"Oh, Harry," Maureen interrupted, flipping on the porch light and walking down the steps, "don't bother Ed with a subject like that. Let's enjoy the evening." She sat down in the empty chair and the opportunity was lost.

Maureen started prattling about the ranchers who lived near Pilot Peak who come by to visit when they happen into town, told about neighbors, town activities, and described the Mormon Ward in the next block.

"The Stake missionaries will be back again to visit this week. They drop by, mostly just to chat. They're nice. I think they're still hoping to convert me. Aside from being missionaries, Ed, it would be great for you to meet other people. When I know they're coming would you like me to let you know?"

"I'll...think about it." Ed felt his whole insides sag. He wasn't interested in meeting anyone else, especially missionaries. At that moment, all he could focus on was the sheriff, fear of being caught, and guilt over deceiving Harry and Maureen.

Struggling with conversation the next ten minutes, relief came when Harry elaborated on his new job.

"I'm going to be *the* big boss over all the bridge and steel gangs," he said proudly. "The WP is a great company to work for, Ed." He then launched into a long recap of the Western Pacific Railroad and its history at Wendover.

"Interesting," Ed periodically chimed in, pretending interest. Actually, nothing Harry said was registering. His voice, a monotonous drone, was made even more indistinguishable by the sound of a neighbor down the street cranking his car engine over and over. It kept dying and starting up again. The whirring and rhythmic up and downs sounded like the throbbing tempo of the chain gang chant. He could hear the old Darkie moaning out the words. Shovels up...thrust 'em down...a long steel rail...then, Jeb's venomous voice at the mess hall shouting, "Come by me...come by me, I want to smell you!"

He waited for a break in Harry's monologue, and then slapped his palms down against both armrests and rose from his chair.

"Maureen, dinner was great—you're really a good cook. But since tomorrow is my first day of work I should turn in."

Maureen had already gotten out of her chair. She raised her index finger to signal him to wait, then scurried up the front steps. She opened the screen door, leaned over and grabbed a large sack sitting inside. Moving back down the steps, she walked over and shoved it into his arms.

"These few groceries will help you out a little."

Ed widened his eyes and took the sack. "I can't believe it. This too? You're both doing way too much."

Maureen grinned and waved his comment off. "Harry can drive you back."

"Thanks, but unnecessary. I remember the way. It's only a few blocks and it's still light." Avoiding a drive with Harry would evade any last minute questions.

Giving them both a farewell wave, he pushed the gate open and sauntered down the street in the direction of the tracks. He needed to walk. His head and neck ached from the tension.

Within five minutes he reached his section house and ambled inside. After brushing his teeth and undressing, he plopped down on the bed hoping to sink into oblivion and forget the whole evening.

No such luck. One anxiety after another rolled through his head—his miserable flashbacks during dinner, concern about deceiving Harry and Maureen, and the sheriff's scrutiny of him.

There could, of course, be a chance APBs were not sent to small towns like Wendover. But what if the sheriff's curiosity piques and he checks with Salt Lake City? Would Kevin come pounding on his door tomorrow to interrogate him?

He spent a miserable night tossing and turning.

What would the next day bring?

CHAPTER 40

~~~

Urgent pounding on the door at five a.m. jolted Ed awake. Disoriented, he bolted upright, and then plunked his feet over the side of the bed onto the linoleum floor. Squinting against the glare of the early morning sun streaming through the window, he rubbed his eyes and glanced about expecting to see Moose and Duff sitting on the edge of their cots. "Oh yeah…Wendover." The pounding on the front door persisted.

Grabbing his robe from the foot of his bed, he slid his arms into the sleeves. The stink of his sweaty body swished up into his nostrils. He glanced over at the swamp cooler still thumping away. It was anything but effective. He teetered through the bedroom door, bleary-eyed.

"I'm coming. I'm coming!" He barreled down the hallway drawing the opening of his robe together and tying the belt in a half granny.

He stopped mid-stride with a paralyzing thought. The sheriff? He stood for a full thirty seconds before logic came to his rescue.

The sheriff wouldn't be knocking. He'd have broken down the door. Besides, if the sheriff checked him out after he drove off from Harry's yesterday evening, he'd have come back and done it last night. His panic subsided.

Stumbling into the front room he glanced at the clock. He had plenty of time before reporting for work, so who was it this early? He reached for the doorknob, hesitated, and then pulled the door open.

A young woman stood on the porch. Her chest heaved from running, and her frizzy, ash-blonde hair stuck straight out like stickweeds.

"I should have gotten here earlier," she said, breathlessly, "but my car broke down. I'm Eadie…the Call Girl." Ed's eyes bugged out.

She snickered at his shocked expression. "That's what we're called. I'm a crew-caller. Sorry such short notice, but you need to

255

be at the trainmaster's office for your interview an hour earlier than planned."

"I'll be there."

"Good." She scribbled something down on her notepad, wheeled about and left.

Shutting the door, Ed hurried back down the hall, his stomach churning. Why an hour earlier? Had the supervisor become suspicious of the information he put on his application? What if he couldn't offer satisfactory answers this morning? Would the man call the sheriff?

He scurried into the bathroom, whipped his robe and pajamas off, jumped into the tub and turned on the faucets. If he had to escape the last minute, how would he manage that?

He grabbed the bar of soap and shifted his focus. He was worrying for nothing. Luck had brought him this far. That had to mean something. He also had Harry's recommendation, and workers were hard to come by and usually grabbed up. All he had to do was try to impress the man and have a perfect story ready for any questions.

After a quick wash he stepped out of the tub, grabbed a towel and dried himself, still unable to quiet the worms that slithered through his gut.

Moving to the washbasin, he stared at his face in the mirror and parted his mouth into what he hoped passed for a self-assured grin. Fake and stupid. He twisted his mouth into a sour expression. He hadn't smiled for so long, he didn't know how. He straightened his posture, pulled his shoulders back and tried again, this time showing more teeth.

"Hi, I'm Ed Riley, from Richm…" Nope. He couldn't say that. His application said Newport News. So did Scratch's letter from Mason's Furniture Company.

Well, if asked to elaborate, he'd mention Chesapeake Bay and tell them he shucked oysters there. No one in Wendover would know enough about oysters to question anything. If pushed for more particulars he knew enough about it as a kid when he went there with his dad the summer before he died. He pictured the sun glistening on the seawater, smell of salt in the air, and the muted cry of seagulls. It was a time with his dad he would never forget.

He scrutinized his face again in the mirror, turning his head from one side to the other, sliding both hands down over the sides of his cheeks and his short beard. Better keep it. Any picture appearing on a Wanted poster would show him clean-shaven. He rehearsed his story again.

"Hi, I'm Ed Riley...from Newport News on the lower James River...down on the coast." Yes, his smile appeared more confident now.

Finishing up, he hustled into the bedroom and dressed, then swallowed down a quick bite of breakfast. He threw a couple of peanut butter sandwiches together from Harry and Maureen's supply and stuffed them into a small sack. Grabbing his duckbill hat, he rushed out the front door and headed down the road toward the depot.

The early temperature indicated a hot day ahead. He could handle dry heat—he only hoped he could handle his interview.

He looked down a side street and saw a small, tarpapered house with a roof made of old gasoline cans beaten flat. He surmised it probably dated back to Wendover's early days as a shantytown.

The rest of the few houses he passed were pretty much alike. No grass or flowers, the ground hard and cracked. Each had its own particular debris—empty cans, boxes, rusty bedsprings, pop bottles, and one house with lots of cats milling about. None were as nice as Harry's, but the house with the cats might place second.

In the next block, he passed the large, white clapboard building on his left with a wide front porch Maureen had mentioned. A sign extended across the front. *Tri-State Mercantile Co.* Wendover's one-and-only store, he thought, recalling Maureen's remark. Next to it was the Victory Garage with a single gas pump. Next to it, the Pastime Club.

Down a side street to the left of the Merc, he noticed the post office Maureen had pointed out. Next to it was a small stone building marked, "Jail." The very sight made his knees spongy. Quickening his steps, he focused on rehearsing his new identity.

"Ed Riley...Newport News...on the lower James River..."

Arriving at the station within a few minutes, he immediately checked the yard for the sheriff's car. He didn't relish running into Kevin. Everything looked okay.

257

He circled around to the front of the brown, two-story wood building sitting parallel to the main tracks and stepped up onto the wood porch. The trainmaster's office door was clearly marked in black letters. He let out a full breath, steeling himself against any unexpected questions, and strolled in.

J. J. Dugan, according to the sign on his desk, sat behind a pile of cluttered papers with telephone in hand. He briefly nodded to Ed and pointed to a chair. Acknowledging the gesture, Ed sat down to wait.

From what he could tell from the telephone conversation, Mr. Dugan was having problems coordinating train orders with the movement of a motorcar. It sounded fascinating, and the exciting reality of his new job set in—that is, as long as he didn't do anything to mess it up with the supervisor.

A tall, wiry man entered the office. His thinning gray hair outlined a tanned, leathery face. Mr. Dugan, still on the telephone, motioned him toward Ed.

The man, following Dugan's cue, walked up to Ed and offered his hand.

"Bob Hutchinson, 'Hutch' for short. I'm the supervisor."

Ed tried out his smile and shook his hand. "Pleased to meet you."

"Understand from Harry you've worked track before."

"Yep, some." Ed fumbled in his pocket and withdrew Scratch's letter and handed it to him.

"My railroad work was in my earlier days. I worked mostly at this furniture factory. You'll see I have a good recommendation."

Hutch studied the letter. "Hmm, ten years with Mason's. Pretty stable. Why did you leave Virginia? And why apply for a railroad job instead of seeking out another furniture company?"

"Well," when Mason's went out of business I shucked oysters for a while, but left because I've been in Virginia all my life and wanted to see what the west was like. Actually, I hadn't thought about working for the railroad until I met Harry and he told me about the job."

"Well, Mr. Riley," he said, looking Ed over, "you look a little frail to me. You sure you can handle it? The work's not easy."

"Yes, sir." Ed pulled himself up tall and struck a confident pose.

"I'm stronger than I appear."

"Well then, let's sit over there." He pointed to a small bench in the hallway. "I'll give you a thumbnail sketch of our little operation here and what you'll be doing. After that, I'll show you around the yard and then drop you off with the track crew. Sorry I had to have you come in earlier, but something unexpected came up and I have to leave soon.

Ed followed the supervisor into the hall, breathing easier. So far, so good. Scratch's letter passed scrutiny, and no questions about his oyster job. Hopefully, that was the last of it. They sat on the bench.

"We service and refuel both passenger and freight trains—those coming from Elko in Nevada," he said, gesturing with one hand to the west—also from Salt Lake." He pointed in the opposite direction.

"Each gang, like the one you'll be on, covers ten miles of track fixing whatever needs to be repaired—inner-rail fissures, bad sand-blows, nicks and gouges caused by inexperienced spikers, sun kinks and pull-a-parts. You'll be re-surfacing, re-ballasting, tamping gravel and putting in new rail—whatever it takes to remedy a situation.

"Working on a section gang," he said, looking Ed squarely in the eyes "is not unimportant, menial work. It's serious business. Hog heads, the engineers, rely on us. They watch the track but can only spy a problem seconds before they run over it. At that point, it's too late. That means if we don't do our job right, there'll be a derailment. Somebody could be killed and it will be our fault." He pulled out his pocket watch.

"C'mon, I'll show you the yard. On the way back, I'll give you a quick look-see in the beanery. Three meals a day if you want. Food isn't bad. And by the way, you'll need to get a telephone."

"That means I've got the job for sure?"

Hutch grinned and nodded. "We're glad to get a replacement this quick. If you knuckle in and stick with it you'll be able to work your way up the ladder."

Ed followed him down the hall to the back of the building. Hutch shoved the rear door open. Stepping into the yard, they were greeted with the clamor of switch engines, boxcars coupling, and a steam locomotive puffing its way into the roundhouse on a spur track.

Ed took another glance around for Kevin's car. Still okay. He'd feign interest in everything he was shown.

Hutch walked him toward the roundhouse. "Take a gander inside," he said.

Ed didn't have to pretend interest. He widened his eyes, amazed at the giant turntable in the center of the floor. Above it was a colossal crane for lifting engines the size of which he'd never seen. On the periphery were eight stalls of machine and blacksmith shops with men busy at work.

He tried to zero in on the individual men, hoping to see someone resembling Buford, but they were too far away and the duckbills of their caps were pulled low over their faces. Hutch motioned to him and they left.

Ed accompanied him around the rest of the yard, listening to Hutch point and comment on various operations.

"By the way," he said, "our yard crew also takes care of the town's needs. When there are mud holes in the roads we patch them. When the mosquito population runs amuck we oil-spray the rainwater pools and any overflowing septic tanks that breed insects. And on pay day, when the squatters and prostitutes come in from Wells and Ely to set up their shacks on the hillsides, the yard crew tears them down."

Hutch angled their walk east of the depot toward two large buildings.

"And here," he said, stopping and proudly folding his arms across his chest, "is the Deep Creek Railroad station office—begun in 1917. Right over there, he pointed, "is the old *Cannonball*. Two locos pull it to Gold Hill, a small mining town southeast of here. During the Great War, ore from there was used to make gunpowder. The track is deteriorating now, so the train can only go fifteen miles per hour. It'll be phasing out soon. But here's what I saved to show you last." He gave Ed an omniscient smile and led Ed inside the other building.

With face beaming, he gestured with a wide spread of his arms. "Feast your eyes on that! It's an 1895, sixty-foot long Pullman. Years ago, this served as the *Cannonball's* passenger car. Go on. Look inside."

Ed mounted the steps, stuck his head inside, and peered down the long aisle of the mahogany interior with its plush, red velvet seats and fancy brass trimmings.

"Wow. I never saw anything this elegant."

"Thought you'd like it." Hutch grinned. "Now, we're off to the beanery."

He ushered Ed back across the yard, rounded the front of the station, and approached a screened door next to the trainmaster's office.

"Gus—he'll be your track boss—ought to be in here." It was then Hutch's voice turned flat and inflectionless.

"Gus?" Ed said, raising an eyebrow.

"Yeah, Gus Mooreland," came the short response. There was no expression on his face Ed could interpret. He mentally shrugged. Maybe some work-related problem between the two of them.

He followed Hutch through the doorway, curious to meet his new track boss.

CHAPTER 41

~~~

Ed followed Supervisor Hutch out of the trainmaster's office and onto the wood planked porch that extended across the front of the building. While he looked forward to meeting his track boss, Gus Mooreland, he was puzzled at the change in Hutch's demeanor. Was the foreman difficult to work with?

He felt a sickening sensation in his gut. If he got on the guy's bad side it could prove the end of his job. He couldn't let that happen. He thought of his mother's words about not troubling trouble. The Beanery was the next door to their right.

Hutch yanked the screened door open, pushing Ed ahead of him into an avalanche of sense-drenching aromas of hot biscuits, coffee, and bacon sizzling on the grill. Ed decided he'd definitely try a meal after work. Burning with curiosity to see which one might be Mooreland, he looked the place over.

There was the typical long counter where three railroad workers sat on green, leather-covered swivel stools sipping coffee. A cook stood at the grill frying bacon, eggs, and flipping pancakes. Behind the counter were the usual restaurant paraphernalia of coffee percolators, carafes, utensils, and stacks of white ceramic dishes. Tables filled the middle of the room, and booths lined along a cocoa-brown wall were filled with workers talking in loud tones. Which one was Gus?

A waitress stood behind the counter, focusing her attention on one particular man. Ed judged her a little older than himself. Her face was heavily made up but not bad looking...not bad at all.

"We call her Queenie—a *friendly* person," Hutch said with suggested meaning, his tones now back to normal. "Come on over, and I'll introduce you.

"The man she's talking to is the Section Foreman, Gus Mooreland. He's the boss over the crew you'll be on. He's not working today. It's his day off. He's okay, but on your first few weeks you may feel like you're walking on eggshells."

263

Hutch maneuvered his way in-between a couple of tables to the counter. "He and Queenie," he added in low tones, "have something going. Be careful about that."

"Hi there, Gus. Got someone you need to meet."

The man swiveled around on the stool, his large belly seemingly glued to the top of his thighs, then stood.

"Gus, meet Ed Riley. He's new on the gang and starts this morning."

Rather than fat as Ed first surmised, his beer belly somehow flattened out when he stood. He was tall, slender, and surprisingly quite muscular. His face, deeply browned from the sun, sported a pencil-line mustache and his jet-black hair meticulously cut.

Gus extended his hand, giving Ed a close scrutiny.

Ed squirmed as the man's protruding eyeballs studied him.

Was Gus trying to place him? Could he be Buford? He pictured the scuffle at the *Clarion* and Buford wearing a ski mask. All he really had to go on was his view of the back of him sitting at the defense table, and the white streak in his hair.

He gave his thoughts an elbow-jab, recognizing how difficult it would actually be to identify Buford. He would probably look at every man he met with suspicion. He couldn't let his imagination run wild. Whoever turned out to be Buford, if he was in Wendover, the man believed he killed reporter Ed Bowman, so wouldn't be anticipating him to show up.

Ed shook his hand. "Glad to meet you."

"Same here." Gus responded with a slow drawl.

Ed did a mental double take. A southern accent. But it could mean Alabama, Tennessee, Kentucky... He looked at Gus' hair. No white streak. Of course, he could have dyed it. Besides, Gunther Buford's physical build at the time of the trial was far huskier—almost a sloppy fat. Gus, on the other hand, had a mustache, was slender, and not at all reminiscent of the man. Nothing about him looked familiar.

"And, Ed," Hutch continued, "this here's Queenie, who makes the best dang java and beans you'll ever eat."

Queenie gave him a seductive smile. "Happy to meet you, Ed." Leaning forward, she placed one elbow on the counter, rested her chin on her hand, and looked up at him.

Ed's gaze immediately traveled from her face down the smooth lines of her neck. Her blouse fell open, revealing more than he'd seen in years. Embarrassed, he jerked his eyes up.

"Glad to meet you," he sputtered, noting that Queenie's flirtatious gestures were not lost on Gus who glared at him.

Hutch quickly cut the conversation short. "Well, c'mon, Ed, the track crew should be close to leaving."

"Nice meeting you both," Ed said, his voice strained.

"Yeah, here too," Gus replied, his cold eyes belying the hospitable drawl of his words.

Outside, Hutch stopped and placed his hand on Ed's shoulder.

"Just a word of caution. Gus isn't the easiest fellow to get along with, but he's the section foreman. That means he's your boss and you're going to have to do your best to put up with his ways. Just don't cross him. And judging from what I sensed back there, play it cool when it comes to Queenie. That's what I meant about being careful."

"Yeah...thanks. Appreciate the heads-up. By the way, it seems Gus has an accent."

Hutch let out a guffaw. "Look who's talking. Yep, he's from the South. Think he said he was from Georgia, but maybe it was some other state—can't recall."

He followed Hutch out to the main track where a crew of men waited by two small rail cars. After brief introductions, Hutch motioned for Ed to slide in next to a young man he introduced as Jake. Ed noted his blonde hair. Mentally, he winced. Like Benny's. Had his mother found out yet her son had died? Or would she never know until he told her?

"Jake will show you the ropes, Ed."

Ed nodded and squeezed onto the seat.

"Okay!" Hutch shouted. "Joe's in charge today. Get those Doodlebugs going. Gotta beat the *Scenic Limited*."

Ed stared in astonishment as the rest of the men piled into the two gas-driven rail cars. There was no counting off...no threatening remarks by superiors...no inspection of pocket contents...no padlock on the car door...no guards...no dogs...no guns—and the men were saying anything they wanted, even joking and laughing. He immediately forgot about Gus and Queenie.

This could be the start of a great job. His heart rate climbed. Just the cover he needed while he poked around town for Buford. He could be a bartender at the A-1 Star, or maybe a black jack dealer, remembering Maureen's remark about Cowboy. He'd also check the Stateline Hotel and the Pastime Club as well. He might even be a cook or waiter at the Western Café. Harry also mentioned a club near the Indian village on the side of the mountain. He'd leave no stone unturned. He'd also check the potash plant.

The rail cars putted the twenty-two miles to Shafter with the men laughing and chatting. The ages of the other five men, Bart, Dennis, Charlie, Joe and Bill, ranged from twenty to sixty. Bart was the oldest.

During the ride Ed relaxed and stared out the window. He visualized his capture of Buford, receiving his long overdue pardon for Sarah's murder, then returning to Hannigan and getting his old job back. What a story he could write. A real exclusive. His dream of investigative journalist at the *Richmond Times-Dispatch* could still become a reality.

The rail cars stopped at Shafter and the men piled out. Jake pointed to an old baggage car parked on a spur.

"Inside contains all the tools we need, Ed—shovels, tamping picks, post-hole diggers, track jacks, claw bars, tie plugs, everything."

Under Jake's guidance, Ed spent the morning pumping sand and cement into roadbeds, stabilizing soft spots, tearing up and replacing rails, and tamping gravel dropped off by a ballast train.

The men worked hard and that impressed him—particularly since there were no guards with shotguns making sure they did. Any one of them could stop for a few minutes, stretch, and eyeball as many jackrabbits as they wanted and not be punished. It was strenuous work, certainly lots different from working on the chain gang, but he enjoyed it, especially because there was no lick to keep.

He liked Jake, guessing him about twenty-five, and felt comfortable with him. He was a talker and volunteered information about Gus.

"Yeah, he's one tough hombre," Jake grumbled. "In my opinion he's not a good section boss. He has an obsession about authority and ordering men around, but we've learned to endure him."

"That bad, huh? How'd he get to be foreman? And why do they keep him?"

"Simple enough," Jake replied with a look of disdain. "He gets the work done. Also, it's hard to get workers to stay in Wendover, so the supervisor doesn't care how tough or mean he is to the men as long as the job gets done on time. Sometimes the men have run-ins with him but it doesn't last long. We know we have to put up with him in order to keep our jobs."

Ed didn't like the sound of that. If the men couldn't get along with Gus on routine work, what chance did he have considering his bad start with Gus' apparent jealousy over Queenie? Well, he'd simply keep his nose to the grindstone, prove himself a good worker, and maybe Gus would forget it. He knelt down to install some interlocking bolts and looked back up at Jake hoping to finagle more conversation.

"Do you find it hard to work in such hot weather? It's already September and the sun is still blistering hot."

"Aw, this ain't really hot—nothing like July and August. Hard work builds my body. Besides, I'm getting a sexy tan. See?" He took his shirt off, laughing as he did, and flexed his biceps. "Muscles turn my girlfriend Nancy on. We're planning to get hitched soon, and then we're..."

Charlie, who was eavesdropping, lifted his head and yelled down the line. "Hey, guys! Jake's gonna get hitched to Nancy. They're finally gonna make it legal!"

"To who?" Bill yelled back.

"Naaaanccccy!"

The men hooted and hollered.

If I were you, Charlie," Jake fired back, "I wouldn't shoot off my mouth so loud. I heard about you and that gal Lil from the Stateline. Heard Cowboy stole her away from you."

Ed perked his ears up.

"Soooo, Charlie," the men razzed, taking their focus off Jake. "Let's hear more about *that*? Did sweet Lil break your poor little heart?"

Charlie's face turned red, then purple. "Shut up!"

The men laughed and resumed their work.

Weary and sweaty at the end of the day, Ed signed out in the office glad it was Friday. Dinner smells were coming from the Beanery. He'd stop by, grab a bowl of chili and coffee, and save him fixing something at home. He would also remember to play it cool with Queenie.

Sauntering into the Beanery, he chose a table instead of the counter, thinking it would minimize contact with Queenie, just in case Gus came in. Unfortunately, she had other plans.

Overly friendly, lowering her voice into a sultry tone, she didn't hesitate to give him the eye and kept flipping her dark, shoulder-length hair for added effect. Every time she passed his table she plagued him with questions. He answered them as vaguely as possible—where he came from and if he had a family. At the same time, he couldn't help notice that despite her attempts to seduce him she did have a likeable quality about her. But all the while he nervously eyed the door, fearful Gus would show up. Growing antsy, he hurriedly gulped down the last spoonful of chili, paid his check and left.

Crossing the yard, he started his trek home, looking forward to the weekend to settle in. He turned the palms of his hands up and examined his sores. He had two fluid-filled bubble-blisters on each one. He'd find something sharp at home, puncture them, let the fluid drain and slap a bandage over them. Blisters were nothing, compared to being slugged in the back with a rifle butt. He'd stop by the Merc and get a few first-aid supplies.

Arriving home, he found a note from Maureen thumb tacked to his door.

Would you like to come over to our house around eight tonight to have ice cream and cake? Sorry, you'll have to walk. Harry's Ford is in the shop until tomorrow. He's having it fixed up so he can leave it with me when he goes to California.

A second invitation?" He couldn't believe it. Maybe what they said was right. In Utah, that's just the way people are. He'd go. He now saw an advantage to establishing a stronger relationship. His tie with them could avert suspicion with the sheriff. He couldn't chance being arrested and sent back to prison before he found Buford. He finished reading Maureen's note.

Harry will be taking the train to Elko tomorrow, so if you need to go to the Merc or other places you're welcome to borrow the truck. It'll be ready by ten o'clock. We'll ride together since I need to get some things too.

Maureen

Shopping for groceries sounded good. He still had some of Avery's money left, and also needed to buy work gloves.

He took a shower and put on a clean shirt and pair of pants. Combing his hair, he thought of Maureen. With her pleasant disposition and good cooking, it was strange she wasn't married. Despite using a cane, a man would be fortunate to have her for a wife. She wasn't bad looking, either. Maybe there weren't many eligible men in Wendover.

Obviously, she was picky for she certainly had no taste for the likes of Cowboy's caliber. That made him all the more curious to get a closer look at the guy. That would be a streak of luck if Cowboy turned out to be Buford.

He'd have to handle it just right—manage everything inconspicuously so not to tip him off. The guy would be set again on killing him if he knew he was Ed Bowman. The real challenge would follow—finding convincing and irrefutable evidence he could take to the sheriff without jeopardizing his own arrest.

His mind was so weary of thinking, he wrested his thoughts about Cowboy. Tonight, he would enjoy a leisurely evening with Maureen and Harry, their ice cream and cake. No telling how many more peaceful evenings like this he'd have to enjoy.

Tonight might be the lull before the storm hits.

CHAPTER 42

~~~

At seven forty-five Ed left his section house and sauntered down the dimly lit road to Harry and Maureen's for ice cream and cake. The air was balmy and tranquil with only the white noise of insects and whisper-like rustle of cottonwoods.

He passed houses where the fragrant aroma of fried chicken and homemade bread floated in the air. He smiled. It reminded him of Hannigan, where everyone knew what their neighbor was having for dinner. He also detected the muffled radio voices of Amos and Andy—Sarah's favorite program.

He looked up at the cobalt sky with its gradual emerging of stars. Harry and Maureen didn't quiz him during dinner the other night. He now trusted them, so looked forward to a relaxing time and amiable conversation. This evening, nothing could possibly go wrong.

Turning the corner to Harry's street, an under-foot crackle sounded behind him, like someone stepping on a broken tree branch. His prison instinct made him whirl about. He saw no one.

Crazy, he thought. He took a relaxing breath. No one would be following him. After all, he had barely arrived in Wendover and no one really knew him yet. But could the ex-con who Avery bribed, Billy Farnsworth, have tipped Buford off about leaking information about Wendover? He cocked his head.

Nah. The guy wouldn't want Buford to know he did that. His spirits picked up. Besides, Buford may not even be in Wendover. He hoped to find that out soon and then move on. He didn't want to waste time here, although where to go next was a problem. Yet, he had a gut feeling Buford was here.

The crunch of dead wood sounded again. He spun around and squinted into the shadowy clumps of cottonwoods. Should he run? Maybe it was someone after his wallet—one of Wendover's transients Harry mentioned.

What if the guy has a gun? He listened for the distinct click of a pistol being cocked. A suffocating weight clamped down on him. He lengthened his stride. Only a block to go.

A deep growl sounded, then evolved into a bark. Ed sagged his body in relief. Someone's dog out for its nightly pee. He gave himself a lop-sided grin. He had to quit being spooked over every little thing.

Rounding the corner of Harry's street he was relieved to see their front yard lit up by the porch light. He moved closer but stopped short and gave an incredulous stare. Agitation etched across his face.

A man and a lady were there—people he didn't know. He hadn't counted on this. Who were they? He didn't relish socializing with someone new and dealing with more prying questions. Even with carefully guarded remarks, Wendover's small-town mentality would guarantee a repeat of everything. Kevin would hear it, too.

Maureen saw him and waved. He swallowed hard. So much for an evening of quietude.

Sauntering up to the gate he undid the latch, noticing Maureen smooth her hair into place as she smiled. Did she do that for him?

"Ed," she said, "I thought you might like to know a couple of our residents. I'd like you to meet Don Peterson and his wife Lila. Don is the Mormon bishop in town." Ed cringed. He remembered what Maureen said on Temple Square about the missionaries always trying to convert her. He hoped they wouldn't try it with him.

A middle-aged, well-built man with high forehead and thick brown hair rose from a lawn chair. His wife, an attractive woman with auburn hair, did the same.

Ed offered his hand. Don pumped his hand far more than necessary, during which time Ed studied his face, watching for any expression revealing an intended subterfuge.

Ed took the vacant chair next to Maureen, noticing as he did the soft powdery fragrance she wore.

"I understand, Mr. Riley," Don began, "you just started with the WP. We'll probably be running into each other. Besides being bishop, I'm also the Train Dispatcher—"

"That means," Harry interrupted, "he oversees the movements of all trains."

"Yep, I enjoy my job," Don continued, "and also Wendover. Lila and I have lived here for ten years and wouldn't think of living anywhere else. The desert grows on you. Even a place as bleak as Wendover." He laughed.

Then, as Ed expected, the questions began.

"Do you have any family with you?"

Ed's mouth went dry. "No—my parents are dead. I'm an only child. But," he managed a smile, "I have lots of cousins scattered across the country." They couldn't report anything from that.

Don and Lila stared at him and waited, expecting more. Ed felt a flush of heat rise to his face and the moment turned awkward.

Maureen immediately stood and reached for her cane.

"Time for ice cream and chocolate cake," she announced. She limped up the steps and into the house. Harry followed, leaving Ed alone to struggle with conversation. However, as the minutes drew on he decided maybe having a Mormon bishop as a friend could prove useful when and if a showdown ever materialized with the sheriff.

Over ice cream and cake, everyone drifted into a more comfortable conversation about Wendover's environment, how great it was for raising kids, and what was happening in town—the new Dairy Freeze, the Stateline Hotel expanding onto the Nevada side, and everyone laughing over the last train wreck on the flats and how many canned goods the townspeople were able to confiscate before railroad detectives showed up with their backhoes to bury everything.

After an hour, they left, but not before Don pumped his hand again and invited Ed to church.

"Now, don't be a stranger, Ed. If there's anything you need you can always call on me. Everyone knows where I live. I may be bishop of the ward but I also consider non-members as part of my flock in this small town since there's no other church. During the day you can find me in my office at work—down the hall from Hutch's."

Yes, Ed decided, who knew but what he might need this man when he nailed Buford. He bet anything, that with Don being a religious man he could discern he was telling the truth about Sarah's murder and his unjust conviction. Not that he was about to share it with him now—only if he found himself in dire straits.

Ed stayed a courteous fifteen minutes after the two left, and then stood.

"I should go. Maureen, your cake was really good." He turned toward the gate and whipped a glance down the shadowy street, hoping he wouldn't be spooked again.

Stepping through the gate, he glanced back over his shoulder.

"I'll come by tomorrow," he said, "to pick up the car so we can go to the store."

Maureen nodded. "I'll be ready." She gave him a radiant smile and a blush rose to her face. Ed's insides fluttered for a split second. Sweet, like Sarah. She had the same color hair but of course they didn't look anything alike. He started down the road, lit only by a single streetlight.

Nearing the corner to his house, he paused. The hairs on the back of his neck strangely stirred. His imagination? Recalling his earlier encounter with the dog, he berated himself and resumed walking.

A needle-sharp sound sliced through the quiet. This time goose bumps prickled down his spine. He didn't plan to wait and see if it was a dog or not. He picked up his pace and moved his legs faster. Only a short distance to go.

A shot rang out. A bone-jangling imperative lurched him forward just as a bullet thudded into the dirt beside him. He raced the remaining distance to home, his legs pounding the ground.

Whirling into the front yard, a second shot ricocheted off the side of the house missing him by a whisper. Charging through the front door, he slammed it shut just as the third shot nearly found its mark. He threw the dead bolt and crouched down.

Scooting on all fours to the window, he reached up and cautiously pulled the edge of the curtain aside. He studied every spectral shape and shadow. Nothing moved. For ten minutes he remained at the window peering into the dark while hammers in his head banged out the Anvil Chorus.

He crept from the window and felt his way across the floor on his hands and knees. Crawling up onto the couch he huddled in the dark waiting for his breathing and thumping heart to regain normalcy. With no telephone yet he couldn't call the sheriff. Better he didn't. The less contact with Kevin, the better.

Who was the shooter? His gut told him it was not one of Harry's transients. If after his wallet, the person would have confronted him on the road with his gun, not chase him all the way home and try to kill him. If not a vagrant, who?

Would Gus do something like this? Surely he wouldn't try to kill him over one innocent encounter with Queenie in the Beanery. Jealousy wasn't strong enough motive for murder, unless...

Could he indeed be Buford? Maybe after detecting his Southern accent he saw him as a threat to his cover. Again, his imagination was taking over. Gus just didn't look like Buford. From what little he remembered from the trial there was absolutely nothing about him that even looked familiar.

Logic kicked in, making him lean more toward Cowboy as the shooter. If Cowboy was Buford and found out from Billy Farnsworth that he had let it leak about Wendover, he could have been watching for any newcomer coming to town. If not that, considering the man's attraction for Maureen he could see his visits to her house as a new man in her life. Still, was Cowboy the kind of guy who would resort to murder over that?

He pulled himself up from the couch and, keeping low, felt his way through the inky blackness and down the hallway to the bedroom. He kept the lights off. Whoever was out there may have left but he wasn't going to chance it.

Sitting on the edge of the bed, he tried rubbing away his headache, wishing he were a braver man—like heroes in the movies who feared nothing. But he knew his limits. Like most men he didn't want to admit things like that. The truth was, while dealing with inmates at the pen he quavered inside all the time. When he fought Buford at the *Clarion*, he only instinctively acted bravely because Sarah was involved.

Should he mention the incident to Maureen and Harry? He ruminated on that. No, they'd tell Kevin and he needed to avoid him. What about Jake? He liked him, but the guy was a talker and it would get around.

He leaned forward with a groan, planted his elbows on his knees and dropped his face into the palms of his hands for a few seconds, then pitched his torso backwards across the bed.

He studied the shilly-shallying shapes and shadows of willow branches outside the window that fluctuated eerily on the ceiling.

Maybe he should hightail it out of Wendover after all. He let out a frustrated sigh. No, he couldn't. How would he ever know if Gunther was here or not? Further, how could he leave Maureen? With her leg the way it is, she'd need help around the place after Harry left for California. It was the least he could do since Harry arranged his job and they had turned out to be such nice friends. He undressed, slipped into bed and pulled the covers up.

Twisting around on the bed from one position to another, he tried to make sense of everything that happened. Cowboy could be Buford...or someone he hadn't even met yet. He slid into a vague, half-sleep, dreading Monday morning.

If Gus' jealousy over Queenie hadn't simmered down, he'd be in for a bad day.

CHAPTER 43

~~~

Monday morning, Ed hoofed down the long dirt road toward the station, oblivious to the lukewarm sunlight that promised a modicum of relief from yesterday's crushing heat. He had more on his mind than the weather. Anxiety filled his every step.

Last night, one of the bullets nearly got him. If he didn't find out soon who was behind it, he could count on getting shot at again. He pinched his lips into a thin line.

So far, he had two suspects. Cowboy rated number one. Jealousy over Maureen could definitely be a motivating factor considering his type of caliber. Gus came in second, but only because Gus was aware he was from the South and might be threatened by that, although nothing pointed to his being Buford as far as looks went. Gus would be back supervising the gang today. Would he forget about the episode with Queenie? He dreaded reporting to work.

He passed the house with cats, the Merc and Pastime Club, and plodded into the depot yard. He sniffed in the oily fumes coming from the round house and listened to the throbbing racket of machinery and clanging of blacksmith's hammers. It certainly didn't help his headache any.

Approaching the trainmaster's building, he stepped up on the wooden porch and ambled toward the office. Pushing the door open, he stepped inside hoping he wouldn't run into Gus before he had to report to work. He glanced around.

Workers were signing in, a few were studying the schedule board, phones were ringing, conversation buzzed, employees sharpened pencils, and others ran about with dispatches in their hands. He looked for Gus. He spied him in the hallway coming from the direction of Hutch's office. His adrenaline rose.

Gus saw him, scowled, and shot him a stony glare. Ed felt icy shards slide through his veins. The guy's jealousy was still apparent...or was he upset to see he wasn't dead? He held his breath as Gus barreled by him without breaking stride, his voice flat and inflectionless.

"I have to go to Elko today. Joe's in charge."

Ed nodded without responding, and watched him plop his duckbill hat on and lumber out the front door. Uncomfortable as their brief encounter was, it still left him in the dark whether Gus could be behind the shooting or not.

Well, at least today he wouldn't have to put up with the guy's belligerent attitude. Maybe the man would simmer down by tomorrow. He sauntered over to the sign-in desk, and had barely scribbled his name and the time when he heard a familiar voice.

"Hey there, Ed!"

He turned back to see Bishop Don Peterson advancing in his direction. He held half a donut in one hand while his other hand wiped powdered sugar from his mouth.

"Ed, good to see you again." Lila and I were just thinking about you this morning. We'd like to invite you to dinner. How about this Friday night?" He plopped a hand on Ed's shoulder and gave him a double pat. He arched his eyebrows and waited.

Ed winced. It was the last thing he wanted to do, but reminded himself he had determined it would be good to have a Mormon bishop in his corner.

"Sure. Sounds great, Bisho—"

"Ah, no need to call me that. Don will do just fine, Ed." He beamed a warm, inviting smile. "Six o'clock?"

Ed managed to stretch his mouth into a wide grin. "I'll be there. Harry mentioned where you live."

"Fine. See you then." Don turned and headed for J. J. Dugan's office.

Ed exited the office and stood outside on the wood deck for a few seconds. What could he expect during dinner? More detail about him other than what they learned at Maureen's?

Glancing at his watch, he hustled down the porch steps and headed for the Doodlebug idling on the track. Most of the men were already aboard. He quickly slid in next to Jake and the rail car took off.

At noon Ed ate his lunch on the track siding with Bart, the oldest member of the gang. The fragrance of his pipe tobacco reminded Ed of his dad. Six feet tall with a beefy build, his leathery skin had turned the color of chocolate from years of working in the sun. His deep-set facial lines, suggesting he'd grappled with many of life's problems, made Ed feel comfortable confiding in him. He related the story of the shooting.

"Well, what do you think, Bart?" He took a bite of his peanut butter sandwich. Bart laughed, giving him a friendly slap on the back.

"Ed, a lot of target shooting goes on in town. At the gravel pits for example, just below Needle Point and a little south of the pig pens, kids go there, sit around the top edge of the pits with their guns and shoot at lizards and rattle snakes. It's a favorite pastime. Even when home, if anything moves in the brush they shoot at it.

"I'd relax if I were you. Probably some kid with his gun and a few shots went wild. I wouldn't lose any sleep over it."

Ed didn't buy it. It was just too late at night for kids to be doing that. Further, the shooter followed him all the way to his house. He couldn't have been mistaken for a lizard.

"Thanks, Bart." He faked a look of relief.

The proof of whether Bart was right or wrong was if the gunman tried again. He had a sneaky feeling there would be a repeat performance. Friday, when he went to the bishop's for dinner, he'd take a different route—one with fewer trees for someone to hide in.

Friday after work, Ed chose the treeless road by the orange-and-white checkered water tower, and angled over to the bishop's street.

He approached the two-story white gabled house, which he assessed wasn't quite as nice looking as Harry's. Like the majority in town, it had no lawn, just gravel on both sides of the sidewalk that led to the door. He knocked.

"Hi Ed, c'mon in." Lila answered the door displaying a cordial smile, then turned and called. "Honey, Ed is here."

Don scuttled into the room, greeting him like he was a long lost brother, shaking his hand with the usual four or five, up-and-down pumps. Ed guessed maybe all Mormons did it that way.

By the time the bishop was through exclaiming how pleased he was that he came, he introduced him to their children—all eight of them. He and Sarah had planned on five.

They sat down to a sumptuous meal of glazed ham garnished with red cherries, buttered carrots from their garden, mashed potatoes, and homemade ice cream for dessert—all without asking prying questions of him. Ed decided he was glad he came.

After dinner, he listened to Don launch into what the Mormon Church believes, including the importance of family and eternal marriage in the hereafter for those married in the temple. Ed thought of Sarah and decided the latter sounded pretty good. He politely asked questions, much to Don's delight. Later, he thanked them profusely for a great evening and said his goodbyes.

He liked the man better now. He felt he would believe his story and support him if it came to a predicament with the sheriff over Buford. A character recommendation coming from the bishop in town would definitely carry weight.

Ed took the same route back home. No mysterious shooter. Could Bart have been right about it being kids?

Inside, his gut said no.

Saturday morning, he meandered the four blocks to Maureen's house. The gray-green leaves of the cottonwoods twisted and turned in the warm breeze, and the sky was radiant over the chestnut hills. All in all it was a beautiful day and he felt on top of the world. With all the tension he'd been through, today would give him a needed break. He'd postpone his visit to check out Cowboy and other men in town until tomorrow.

Harry had left for California and Maureen was in the midst of canning. He told her he would come over and help. Good therapy, he thought. It would get his mind off Gus and Queenie...and the shooter.

He looked forward to the visit, and didn't even notice Maureen's lame leg anymore. She had a delightful sense of humor and he could see why Cowboy had taken a shine to her. He also planned to clean up her yard, something he knew she couldn't do.

When he approached, she was in the yard watering the roses. Her face lit up.

"Ed, you are so sweet to do this." She gave him a big smile. "I hope you know how much I appreciate your help."

"Ah, it's nothing." Ed felt the wash of red rise from his neck as he closed the gate behind him. "Glad for the exercise. Just tell me what needs to be done first."

She handed him a list from her apron pocket and he went right to work pulling weeds in her vegetable garden, raking the back yard and filling up the back of Harry's truck with debris and driving it to the town dump. Maureen periodically kept sticking her head out the back door to keep thanking him. That delighted him.

When through picking apricots from the trees in the backyard, he carried the load into her warm, spicy-smelling kitchen and helped her mash them for jam.

"Okay, now shoo. I can do the rest."

Four hours later, Maureen had all twenty-four bottled jars of jam lined up on her sink and Ed had finished in the yard. She let out an exhausted breath, plopped down on the Chesterfield and motioned Ed to do the same.

"Is there anything else I can do for you, Maureen?" He thought about Sarah. If she were alive, he'd have done more of these same things for her. "I can come over tomorrow morning, Sunday, to—"

"Oh, Ed, you've already done more than expected. With Harry gone, I couldn't have accomplished it all." She smiled at him. "You're really quite wonderful, you know."

Ed felt his heart soar, but only for a second. Inwardly he flinched at her last remark. He felt guilty over her assessment of him, recalling how he participated in whipping Benny. He wasn't the great guy she thought. Further, he hadn't kept his promise yet. Benny's mother had to be frantic, writing letters to the prison, trying to figure out where he was. At some point, he had to find a way to let her know what happened without revealing his location. Her address was indelibly imprinted in his mind. Madge Yates...531 South Eighteenth Street...near the Franklin Street Open Air Market.

"So, Ed…you should be rewarded."

"Oh, no, Maureen…"

"Hush," she interrupted. "I don't mean anything big, just a special outing. Besides—and I don't want to pry—you look troubled."

"Oh? Didn't know I looked that way." He made a dismissive gesture with his hand. "Just pressure from trying to learn my new job." He laughed, but knew it didn't sound genuine.

"Well," she said, passing over his remark, "you need to do something relaxing, like going to Blue Lake before the cold weather sets in. You'll never know how to get there unless I show you, so tomorrow morning we'll go. The drive will do us both good.

He knew she appreciated what he did and didn't want to take that away from her. He'd postpone his jaunt to the A-1 once again.

Ed grinned with enthusiasm. "Sounds great." He relished the idea of an outing far from town where he could relax without worrying about being shot at.

Nothing could possibly happen at an isolated lake out on the salt flats.

CHAPTER 44

~~~

Sunday morning Ed hustled to Maureen's house, and in no time at all they were in Harry's truck speeding out of town on the Ely highway toward Blue Lake. The salt flats were a blinding white and a hot breeze blew through the open car windows.

Ed indulged himself in a private smile. Today, miles from Wendover, he'd enjoy an afternoon at a quiet lake—a slice out of time—where he could shove all his stress into the background.

He hated to admit he couldn't cope with what was going on in his life, but the aftereffects of enduring his years in prison and the chain gang, not to mention the maddening injustice of being accused for something he didn't do, had taken its toll. Further, he now had to deal with Gus' jealousy over Queenie, hope the next shot in the dark wouldn't find its mark, was on pins and needles every time he saw Kevin, and had to determine if Buford was really here. Sometimes, it was more than he could deal with.

Today, however, would be different. Peace awaited him. He could already hear the tranquil water lapping at his feet.

"Here's where we turn." Maureen jutted her hand out waving it in front of Ed's face. "There, to the left."

Ed slammed on the brakes and veered off the blacktop. Following her directions he drove over the weedy flats and parked near a mud dune. Maureen grabbed her cane, opened the car door and slid out.

"Out there," she exclaimed, limping to the front of the car and pointing, "is Pluto Rock—that small mountain in the distance. If you look hard enough you can make out the dog's head."

Amazed at the strange pride in her voice, Ed scooted out from behind the wheel and stared. Is this how one became in a small town? Conjuring up something like a Pluto rock for excitement? He also remembered the Lizard rock she had pointed out when they first drove into Wendover. For a brief moment that kind of life, droning as it sounded, struck him as appealing. But life couldn't be like that for him now. He tensed his jaw. He had a criminal to catch and a life to regain.

Maureen pointed to a narrow trail. "That will take you to the lake. It's about a ten-minute walk from here. Don't be surprised if you're the only one out there.

"I do need to warn you, though," she added, turning back to the car and shooting him an apologetic smile. "There are flies, so you'll have to clip right along or they'll eat you alive. They'll be gone by the time you get to the lake. I can't walk fast enough to outrun them because of my leg. I'm perfectly content to sit in the car and read a book until you return."

Outrun flies? No doubt she loved to exaggerate. "I'm okay with that, Maureen. Sorry you can't come," he said. "I won't stay too long."

He gave a friendly wave and started down the worn path, hoping the lake would remind him of Hannigan. He needed to recapture good memories of Sarah...the day they went canoeing, the thicket they made love in, how he held her, kissed her...

After ten minutes of walking, flies zoomed in like a squadron of planes. Not just flies, but deer flies. With sharp needle-like stings they struck anywhere Ed's bare flesh was exposed, ankles, wrists, neck, ears. They were as bad, if not worse, as the ones at camp.

Flinging his arms to shoo them away, he broke into a run, hurtling down the path as if hell-bent. By the time he reached the end of the trail they mercifully disappeared.

Angling off to his right he saw the lake and sucked in a pleased gasp. The beauty of the sun glistening on the water was more than he expected. It indeed lived up to its name. Intensely blue—bluer than any lake Ed had ever seen.

He made his way through a few clumps of tall, thick-bladed grass and headed with anticipation toward the twenty-yard square clearing in front of the water's edge. But surprise gripped him. Someone else was there. His features fell. So much for time alone.

A young man and woman sat on a blanket, looking out at the lake. He followed their gaze and saw a large raft made of railroad ties. A boy of about twelve, evidently their son, was diving off. Ed curved his mouth into a lop-sided smile. Nothing he had to worry about from them. Good family fun. His day could still turn out okay.

"Hi," the man on the blanket called, turning his head in Ed's direction. Exceptionally thin, he wore brown, horn-rimmed glasses.

"Hello," Ed returned, grinning awkwardly. "My first time here. Thought I'd wade in and see how it feels."

The man nodded, waving him on. "Be our guest."

Ed took off his shoes and socks, rolled up his pant-legs and walked to the water's edge. The boy, he noticed, had quit diving and was lying on the raft sunning himself.

Wading out a few feet, he found the water surprisingly warm, and delighted in the soft, velvet-like mud squishing between his toes.

Standing motionless in the sparkling water with the sun wrapping its warmth about him, he listened to the profound silence. No sound of buzzing flies or cars from the highway, no squawk of birds, not even sounds from the couple on the blanket behind him. He gazed into the turquoise sky that arched above him, still amazed at the quietness.

Then, something unexplainable happened. It seemed as if the whole world abruptly stopped and hung in suspended animation. He lost all perception of his individuality as his whole being strangely immersed with everything around him—the blue water, radiant sky, air, and the hazy purple of the distant mountains.

Everything, including him, melded into one rapturous moment of inexplicable tranquility and harmony, and his spirit expanded into a glorious feeling of being part of, also wrapped in, the whole universe—like he had entered an alternate reality where no past, present, or future existed, and was being embraced by "something."

He didn't know what or who. It didn't matter. Whatever, or whomever…it was magnificent, and an inexplicable confidence settled on him—an assurance he was where he was meant to be and all was well. Was the "something" telling him the attempts on his life would stop? Was it telling him he'd find Buford? Was it God?

The experience began to fade, and he quickly squeezed his eyes shut hoping to make it linger but had no control over it.

He heard the sudden slap of water and looked over to see the boy diving off the raft again. What did it all mean? He turned and waded back to shore.

The man on the blanket stood and offered his hand. "My name is Bill." He introduced his wife, Helen, an attractive woman with blonde hair swept high into a ponytail. She invited him to share their blanket. Meaningless chitchat began, followed by a few questions.

"Yeah, I just hired on to the railroad," Ed said, describing his job on the gang.

"Bill is manager at the potash plant," his wife offered. "I work as a maid at one of the auto courts."

The conversation proved relaxing to Ed, but concerned he'd left Maureen alone too long he rose to his feet and rendered a good-bye.

"I should go. Have a friend waiting for me in the car."

"Nice meeting you," Bill said, rising and shaking Ed's hand again. "Maybe we'll see each other around town."

"Probably." Ed smiled. "Glad to have met both of you."

Turning, he ambled across the clearing, headed for the narrow footpath and stepped through the clumps of long-bladed grass.

He paused to gaze toward the far end of the trail, dreading another encounter with the flies. It was then he spied four people hiking in single-file—two men and two women.

Squinting his eyes against the blinding sun, he focused on the man in front. A wave-spume of panic hit. *The sheriff.* He didn't relish seeing Kevin. He didn't want him becoming too familiar with his face.

Peering more intently, he identified the second man who lumbered behind. His heart pounded even harder. *Gus.*

A woman he didn't recognize came next, and then Queenie brought up the rear. All he needed was for her to start making eyes at him. He stood statue-stiff. The trail was too narrow to proceed.

"Hi there, Kevin," Bill called, as the small party approached the clearing.

Kevin responded with a friendly hello and dropped a blanket onto the ground. The lady with him set a picnic basket down. Gus, Ed noticed, didn't say much. Queenie, however, didn't hesitate to flash him her usual seductive smile.

"Those deer flies," Kevin said, "are something else, aren't they?" Looking at Ed he formed a puzzled smile as if unable to place him.

"Oh that's right, you're Harry's friend. Good to see you again. Ed, isn't it? This sweet gal here is my wife, Patti." Ed nodded. She returned a demure smile.

"Do you know Gus and Queenie?"

"Yeah," Ed replied, "we work together. Hello, Gus...Queenie."

Gus grunted an icy "hello" and gave him a cold eye.

Queenie sashayed forward to help Kevin's wife smooth out the blanket. When they finished, she slowly slipped off her dress revealing a way-too-skimpy bathing suit that left little to the imagination. She leaned over to examine an imaginary speck on her leg, bending over long enough so Ed could see her well-pronounced cleavage spilling over the top of her suit.

She coyly looked up. "You going in swimming, Ed?"

Gus immediately shot a smoldering look in Ed's direction.

Ed panicked. He needed to get out of there—fast.

"Ed," Queenie repeated her question. "Are you?"

"No," he responded, his voice cracking slightly. "Already been in." He tried to steady his voice. "I got to, uh, go now." His pulse hammered in his ears and a nerve in his face twitched. "Maureen," he managed, "insisted I see this place." He quickly directed his comment away from Queenie to Kevin.

"Did you see her sitting in the car, Kevin?"

"Sure did. The wife and I talked to her while Gus and Queenie unloaded the car. Sounds like Harry likes his new job."

"Seems so," Ed replied. "Well, enjoy the water." He pivoted on his heel and started toward the trail, his stomach rising and falling in nauseating waves. So much for a stress-free afternoon.

Stepping onto the trail, he heard Queenie call. "Hey, Ed!"

He turned back to see her point a camera at him. He cringed at the sound of the click.

"Just thought I'd add you to my rogue's gallery." She laughed.

Gushes of desperation hit hard. The last thing he needed was his picture taken. *Play it cool.*

"You should have warned me," he laughed, "or I would have posed." He waved as nonchalantly as he could, then turned away and plodded forward, his nerves tightening at the back of his throat.

What could come of this? He knew the answer. Gus could

get the photo from Queenie and prod Kevin into submitting it to Salt Lake City authorities to have him checked out. The thought paralyzed him.

But that would only happen if he's Buford. And if he is, would he risk authorities coming here? He also supposed that even if Gus weren't Buford, he might do it, hoping to eliminate him as a competitor for Queenie.

Buzzing swarms of flies zoomed in. One gave him a vicious bite on his neck. Flailing his arms he broke into a run and bolted down the path, his thoughts running at the same speed.

Even if Gus turned his picture in, it looked nothing like his clean-shaven, prison photograph. With his new beard and weight loss he didn't look the same as four years ago. Despite rationalizing, dread still shuddered inside him.

Sprinting down the last leg of the footpath, he left the deer flies behind and hustled onto the flats. Reaching the truck, he opened the door and slid into the driver's seat. Maureen looked up from her book.

"Glad you had some company. Did you have a good time?" He nodded, his body still jangling.

"It was everything you said." He turned the key, shoved his foot on the clutch, and eased the truck toward the highway.

Maureen opened the envelope resting in her lap. "This is Harry's letter. Would you like to hear it?"

Ed gave a vague nod, his scrambled mind still on the photo. If authorities identified his picture and he had to explain to Kevin why he escaped prison, he doubted he could convince him. He gripped the steering wheel. And he couldn't suggest Gus or Cowboy might be Buford without proof. He could kiss his mission in Wendover goodbye.

His thoughts flitted to the strange experience he had in the water. Was there some mechanism in the universe that already knew everything would turn out well—that he was indeed where he was supposed to be? Could he take that as a sign Queenie would stuff the snapshot in a drawer and forget it? Would Gus forget about it, too?

"Ed, Harry's letter?"

"Oh, sorry, Maureen. Go ahead."

Maureen slipped on her glasses and began reading Harry's descriptive portrayal of lace-like ferns, lush green forests, pine trees, and twisting railroad tracks hugging canyon walls.

"Sweet, sweet Harry." Maureen giggled. "Now, that's really something isn't it?" Ed nodded, feeling guilty for not paying attention, and faked a smile.

"This is the last page," she said.

For the next few minutes he forced himself to listen, and found himself marveling at her ability to read so fluently. He speculated on how many suitors she may have turned down. Harry said Cowboy still telephoned her. He felt certain she would only be content with someone as educated as herself.

"Harry claims he's landed in paradise," Maureen concluded, folding the letter and placing it back in the envelope. "Sounds like it's really beautiful in Keddie."

"Not like Wendover, that's for sure." Ed feigned a laugh.

"I sure miss him." Maureen gazed out the side window at the sagebrush whizzing by. "We've been together for so long. Of course," she said, turning back and looking directly at Ed, "you've sure filled the gap."

"I haven't done much," Ed said, surprised but pleased at her comment, yet wishing she wouldn't smile at him like that.

They drove the rest of the way home in an amiable silence during which Ed considered how to implement a plan.

How would he get the picture from Queenie without her telling Gus and raising suspicion? He bit the inside of his cheek.

His next thought sent an electric chill through his nerve endings. It wasn't enough to get the picture—he also had to ask for the negative.

How one earth would he manage that?

CHAPTER 45

$\sim\!\frown\!\sim$

Decked out in his Sunday best with the noon sun warm on his back, Ed sauntered toward home after the Ward church meeting. Slipping his jacket off, he slung it over one arm. Don, as he was told to call him instead of bishop, invited him. He was glad the service was over. The sermon was dry as talcum powder.

At first he felt a little twitchy about attending, even guilty, knowing Don anticipated his joining at some point. He had no such intentions. Nevertheless he went, believing it a good way for church members, as well as Don, to know him better. It would cement his image in the community and throw off any possible suspicions about him.

There was, of course, another advantage. If something unfortunate happened during his hunt for Buford, and the sheriff didn't believe his story, Don and the church members, with all their handshakes and friendly slaps to his back, would support him. They exhibited a strong kinship with each other, almost family-like, that seemed to include him. He enjoyed that, but no matter how hard Don pushed for him to join, he had more important things to occupy his mind than religion.

Last night, he went to the Western Café to see if he could spot "Cowboy." Disappointed, he saw no one with a ten-gallon hat. He also had to deal with his upset over the snapshot taken of him at Blue Lake, and rehearse the right words when he approached Queenie on Monday to ask for both the snapshot and the negative. It would be tough, but he had to move fast before Gus got them from her. The snapshot might be easy, but the negative? He let out a long, audible breath.

Tugging at his necktie, he loosened it from around his neck. His splintered thoughts were wearing him out. He looked for something along the street to distract him and angled over to a white picket fence near the end of the block. A widow lived there. She was the only one in Wendover with a whole yard of flowers—

even more than Maureen's.

He poked along the fence line, bending here and there to breathe in the pungent blooms of roses, yellow honeysuckle, and admire her pink ruffled iris. That's when he changed his mind about going home.

He'd stop by Maureen's first and tell her about his experience at the ward. Get her thoughts on things, although he knew she had no interest in joining the Mormon Church. "The Bible is enough for me," she once told him. Nevertheless, he felt she'd be interested. He was right.

"Of course, I'm interested, Ed." She invited him into the front room and they sat on the couch. "Tell me everything," she said, propping her elbow on the arm of the sofa.

Ed rehearsed everything. The impressive, 2-1/2 minute talk given by a child, Don's boring sermon, Joyce Anderson's Sunday school class, which he admitted he liked, and the potluck afterward.

"Of course," he said reassuringly, "I don't plan on joining."

"Well, regardless of my stance," she said, "you're a fine man, Ed Riley. If joining the Mormon Church would make you happy then I'd be the last person to ever say anything to discourage you." She rearranged the pillow behind her back.

Ed's heart soared. It was the first time she'd ever volunteered she thought he was a "fine" man. Her words were balm to his soul. He almost forgot the wrong things he did in prison.

After an amiable chat and a cup of coffee he left, still feeding on her comment. *"You're a fine man…a fine man.*

But in thinking about her, his mind somersaulted back to the snapshot. What if Gus got the picture before he could ask Queenie for it? If it led to his arrest, Maureen would sure change her mind about his being a fine man. She'd find out he was a prison escapee— worse yet, convicted for murdering his wife. He shuddered. He would hate to have her find out about his participation in Benny's death.

He decided to stop by the Post Office and bypassed his house. Naturally, he didn't expect anything but wanted to clear his box of junk mail. Besides, the sun was shining through the cottonwoods, white cumulous clouds were piling up like mashed potatoes, and he simply wanted to enjoy the peace and tranquility. His jumbled-up insides needed it.

He ambled past the house with the cats. Today, there were only nine. Approaching the Tri-State Merc, he noticed the store was closed but several men sat on the steps smoking cigarettes and drinking beer. One huffed away on a harmonica.

A man, tall and angular, sat slouched on the top step. His dishwater hair looked like torn up shredded wheat. Glancing up as Ed neared, he set his beer can down and stood. Grabbing up the ten-gallon hat hanging on the railing post, he plopped it on his head. It didn't take much to figure out who he was.

Ed gave him a quick once-over. Maureen was right. He sure wasn't her type. His left eyelid drooped over a rough, unshaven face that was lined with gullies etched from a life of whiskey and beer. A cigarette dangled from one corner of his mouth. Nothing about him resembled Buford. He was simply too tall, skinny, and ugly.

The man moseyed down the steps. To Ed's surprise, the man lengthened his stride and sidled up alongside him.

"New in town, ain't ya?"

"Yeah." Ed tried to hustle ahead of him.

The man kept pace as Ed cut over toward the post office. "Better be careful. You might be treading on someone's territory where you oughtn't." He grinned a sickly smile, revealing tobacco-stained teeth.

"Don't know what you're talking about," Ed mumbled, walking faster.

"Well, you best think about what I'm saying," he warned. "Wouldn't want you to do anything stupid. Might get yourself hurt." Cowboy slowed his steps, letting Ed push ahead.

Ed reached the front door of the weathered post office and quickly entered. Once inside, he glanced furtively through the window. Cowboy was sauntering back to the Merc.

That was an ominous threat if ever he heard one. Cowboy obviously was not Buford, so the threat had to be about his jealousy over Maureen. Gossip in Wendover traveled faster than wild fire, and Cowboy probably heard how much time he was spending with her. He exuded a dramatic sigh. That's all I need—Gus jealous over Queenie, and Cowboy green-eyed over Maureen.

He twirled the combination of his mailbox, fingered through the junk mail, and then threw it into the trash receptacle. Exiting the building, he cautiously examined the street. All clear. He started home a different way, kicking a few pebbles in front of him. How dangerous was this guy? Monday, he'd have to pump Bart for information about him.

"Oh drat." He pressed his tongue between his teeth and made a tsking sound. Tomorrow was a holiday with only a skeleton crew. Bart wouldn't be there. He also remembered Queenie saying she was taking off for Vegas. She wouldn't be there either. A whole day, lost. What if Gus already got to her before she left?

That night in bed, he hardly slept. In the blackness behind his eyelids he kept seeing Cowboy's ugly face. How much more of his seeing Maureen would set the guy off? What would he try?

Then a chill started at the base of his neck and traveled to his feet.

The shooter had to be Cowboy.

CHAPTER 46

~~~

Cowboy flung open the screen door to the Tri-State Merc, tripping the jingle of a small bell. Barreling across the threshold, he bumped into a small boy at the counter eyeing a glass jar of purple jawbreakers. A few pennies in his hand dropped and scattered onto the floor.

"Sorry," Cowboy mumbled, barely breaking pace. He angled toward the center aisle and strode toward the back wall cutting a swath through ladies toiletries, blue jeans, and pipe tobacco. His steel-like gray eyes riveted on one thing. The gun section.

Perusing the shelves, he clamped his fingers around a box of .38 shells. His face went rigid. Gus was one mean taskmaster. This time, he wouldn't miss. He'd get it done.

He couldn't imagine a man being so obsessed with a gal like Queenie that he'd hire someone to murder any man who looked at her. After all, her kind were a dime a dozen. At least he guessed it was because of Queenie. He reached for a second box.

Gus never spelled out his reason for asking him to do the job. He had simply put two and two together. Whatever the guy's reason, he didn't care. Gus always paid well, and he had to take this job—his last—although Gus didn't know that. This last time was imperative. He needed the bankroll to carry out his own plans—pay off his gambling debt at the A-1, and then get out of Wendover. He'd been here long enough. More importantly, he also owed money in Chicago and desperately needed to pay it off. Time was of the essence before they came looking for him. He didn't dare underestimate the Borgata mob.

Doing Ed Riley in would be no big loss. It would actually work in his favor—give him another chance at Maureen. He envisioned her leaving Wendover with him.

Why he was so taken with her, he didn't know—unless it was because she was so different from the women he was used to. She just had a way about her, even with her cane.

"We're closing in five minutes!" Mr. Jensen called.

Cowboy squiggled past a husband and wife examining flannel shirts, and moseyed toward the front of the store. He dropped the boxes on the counter and plopped two dollars down.

Mr. Jensen snatched up the bills and rang the amount up on the cash register. Digging his fingers into the open till he handed him back some coins. "I'll put them in a bag—"

"Never mind," Cowboy mumbled. He swept up the two boxes and thrust them into his jacket pocket. Exiting through the door, he let the screen door slam behind him and strode across the wooden porch and down the steps.

Yanking the door of his Ford pickup open, he slid in and shoved the key into the ignition. Reaching across to the passenger side he pulled the glove compartment open. A revolver lay inside. He placed the two boxes of shells on top of it, slammed the compartment shut, and then snatched up the can of Kreuger beer lying on the seat. Puncturing the top with a church key, he took a swig and then started the engine. The sooner he got the job done, the sooner he'd get paid.

Gunning the motor, he grabbed hold of the stick shift, shoved it into gear and took off down the dirt road, spirals of blue smoke curling behind him.

CHAPTER 47

~~~

Monday, after work, Ed ambled down the road toward Maureen's, his shoulders drooped low. Nothing stirred in the breezeless air, not even the cabbage-colored leaves hanging on the cottonwoods. His frustration felt like a millstone in his chest. His search around town last night for someone resembling Buford had once again proved negative. He felt a sodden dullness of failure.

Maybe trying to recognize Gunther Buford after all these years was too much to expect. He might not even be here.

He thought of Gus. He certainly had the temperament of a guard—aggressive, controlling, superior attitude—but looked nothing like he remembered from the trial.

He reached up and pressed his knuckle hard against the bridge of his nose. Frustrated? That was putting it mildly. Somehow, he had to find something productive, or his whole venture in Wendover would prove a lost cause.

He gave a hard kick at a small rock on the ground, shooting it directly into a clump of pigweeds. Stinkbugs, their shiny black derrieres hoisted high, scurried away. Spiny, horny-toad lizards also scampered out. They darted in front of him swift as dragonflies, stopping every few feet to eye him before skittering away.

Ed watched them with curiosity. Maureen said stroking their stomachs would put them to sleep. Well, he wasn't about to catch one to find out.

His biggest concern was tomorrow—his dreaded encounter with Queenie to ask for the snapshot and how he was to manage the negative as well. He had rehearsed what to say so many times his brain was worn out.

Visiting with Maureen would cheer him up. Being with her meant more to him every day. No romantic thoughts. Nothing like that. It was more of a comfortable kind of deep caring that existed between them. She provided a quiet stability in the midst of his tumultuous roller-coaster life. Sometimes he admitted he'd like to have a closer relationship with her, but right now his life was too complicated.

Approaching her house, he pulled the gate open, cringing as the hinges emitted an irritating screeching noise. He studied it. A good shot of oil should fix it.

He moved up the sidewalk to the front steps, looking forward to a respite from his woes. He also anticipated something else and wasn't disappointed as the tantalizing smell of cinnamon and nutmeg wafted through the screen door.

The aroma tugged at past memories—to an uncomplicated time. A time before he turned into someone else who did things he wished he'd never done. He longed for the Sunday afternoons in the hammock...sunbeams slanting through ash trees... Sarah bringing a pitcher of sweet tea and cookies.

He knocked, then gently pulled the screen door open and poked his head inside. Maureen was in the kitchen, potholders in both hands, bending over in front of the oven. She looked up.

"Come on in. I'll just be a minute." She pulled a pan of pumpkin cookies out and set them on top of the stove.

"You're just in time." She smiled. Grabbing a spatula she scooped up a few, slid them onto a dish, and offered him one. "Watch it, they're hot." She motioned him with one hand toward the couch. "Make yourself comfortable."

Ed took a cautious bite of the cookie and plopped onto the couch. While he nibbled, he watched Maureen remove her apron, place it on a hook, and then smooth a few stray hairs back from her forehead.

What if, God forbid, the Virginia police should track his whereabouts before he nailed Buford? Would she believe him innocent? He couldn't bear that. He unknowingly let out a troubled sigh.

"What on earth is wrong, Ed?" She gave him a quizzical look as she set the plate of cookies on the coffee table and moved to the other end of the couch. "You look tense. No, troubled is a better word."

"Oh, do I?" A nerve at the corner of his mouth twitched. He wasn't covering up well. He forced a smile.

"I've got just the thing." Maureen grinned. Reaching over to the end table, she grabbed her purse and rummaged inside it. Whipping out a stick of gum, she unwrapped it and thrust it at him.

"There, chew on that. It'll loosen up your face."

Ed popped the stick into his mouth.

"Thanks, Maureen, but I'm not sure Black Jack gum mixes with pumpkin." He laughed. He needed to convince her he wasn't troubled.

"You know," he said, leaning back and swinging one arm across the back of the sofa, "Don Peterson has been at me to join the church."

"Oh, is that what's troubling you?"

"No. Not really. Just thought I'd mention it." He shrugged. "The way Don explains it, baptism is supposed to forgive every sin one has ever committed." He rolled his eyes good-naturedly. "I suppose that means I won't have to worry over any bad stuff I ever did…and won't go to hell." With a slight inclination of his head he raised his eyebrows making it a question instead of a statement.

"That's what the Bible says," Maureen offered. "It's like being born brand new again." She gave him a fond smile as she adjusted the pillow behind her back. "But I'm sure you don't have much bad in your life."

Ed felt his features go slack. He thought of Benny. He doubted baptism could wash away the fact he contributed to a person's death. Sometimes the remorse and guilt swelled up from so deep inside of him, the anguish was more than he could bear. How would she view him if she found out? He bet anything if Don knew, he wouldn't let him be baptized—not that he was considering it—but in this close-knit town it would get back to the sheriff and he'd be back on the chain gang before he even had a chance to find Sarah's killer.

"Now, there you go again Ed. I don't know why you still look troubled." She reached for the plate of cookies. "Have another cookie—take two. While you're chewing on those I have something exciting to tell you that will lift your spirits." She grinned like a cat that had swallowed the proverbial canary.

"I'm all ears, Maureen." Ed leaned forward. He was ready to

hear anything. She looked ready to explode.

"Well," she exclaimed, fanning both hands out to the side, "they just put up two new Burma Shave signs on the highway. A neighbor told me about them. So, speaking of hell..." She cleared her throat and giggled.

"*Special seats...reserved in Hades...for whiskered guys...who scratch the ladies.*"

"Yeah, pretty cute, Maureen." *That was it?* He could only dream of the day when something that boring would excite him.

"Listen to the other one," she said. "*She kissed...the hairbrush... by mistake...she thought it was...her husband Jake.*"

"Now, didn't those lift your spirits?" She beamed a radiant smile, reached over and patted his arm. To Ed's surprise his heart strangely leapt.

They spent the next two hours around the radio munching on cookies, listening to Gene Autry's Melody Ranch and chuckling over quips between Charlie McCarthy and Mortimer Snerd.

Ed looked at his watch, and then stood.

"You don't need to leave yet, do you?" Maureen raised her eyebrows and looked up at him. "The Texaco Star Theatre will be on soon—Fred Allen's pretty funny. Of course, if you like something more sinister, Inner Sanctum will be on although it's a little creepy for me." Hesitating, she strung out her next sentence with intermittent pauses. "But...I'll let you...take...your pick."

Maureen seemed nervous. She had been relaxed all evening but now there was tension in her face.

"You okay, Maureen?"

She pursed her lips and dropped her gaze.

"Is anything wrong?" He wracked his brain. "Did I say something to upset you?"

She shook her head and looked up. "I'm just being silly. It's just... Well, Cowboy came by today pressuring me to go out with him again. He even started asking questions about you, like where you came from."

Ed bristled, but before he could quiz her on specifics, Maureen looked down at her crippled leg.

"Heaven knows, I don't know what he sees in me."

"I certainly know," Ed said, momentarily brushing aside his irritation with Cowboy. "Any man would be proud to be seen with you."

She snickered and then blushed. "Why, Ed, what a sweet thing to say. But I guess it's no big deal," she said, waving off the subject with a dismissive gesture. "All I have to do is keep telling him no, and sooner or later he'll give up."

Ed grimaced. He didn't look like a guy who gave up easily.

"But maybe," she continued, looking up into Ed's face with a demure smile, "I'm just mentioning it as an excuse to keep you here longer."

Keep me here? Ed's heart turned over. He didn't know what to say. It pleased him, but further involvement would complicate things.

"Thanks..." he stammered, "for the offer...to stay for the radio programs. I'm sure I'd enjoy them. It's going to turn dark soon, and I have to get up early tomorrow morning."

His words were stilted and he knew it. Noticing the disappointment on her face, he grasped at any excuse he could think of.

"The *Exposition Flyer*, the one that took the *Scenic Limited's* place, is coming through from Salt Lake and we have minor track work to do before it travels on to Frisco."

He stood, shoved his hands into his pockets, and looked up at the ceiling. "And since the Deep Creek Railroad's track to Gold Hill is torn up, we have scrap to haul away..." His voice trailed off.

"That's sad," Maureen said, lifting herself up from the couch and reaching for her cane. "That little railroad lasted twenty-two years and now nothing will be left to show it ever existed."

"Well," he said, feeling more at ease with the new subject, "guess I never thought about it that way. Hutch also wants me to spend the day with some guy in the yard before going out with the crew. Says he wants me to learn how to repair things like defective frogs. Not sure I know what they are but guess I'll learn."

"You're coming right along with the lingo." Maureen laughed. "Harry explained them to me once. They're switch hinges that look like frog legs."

"Yeah?"

"Sounds to me," she continued, "like they're thinking about promoting you. You're due for it."

"Don't know about that," he replied, giving her a lop-sided smile, "but wouldn't that be something?"

Actually, it would mean more than Maureen realized. It would mean he'd be off the track gang and out from under Gus' thumb and mean looks.

"Well," Maureen said, walking him to the door, "from the look on your face a promotion obviously meets with your approval."

Ed nodded and glanced through the screen door at the street. He was safe—not dark enough yet for the shooter.

Reaching the door, Maureen propped her cane against the doorjamb and surprised him by reaching up with both arms and giving him a hug.

"I hope you get the promotion, Ed," she whispered close to his ear. "You deserve it."

Ed's face flushed. A thousand firecrackers shot off inside him and his legs turned rubbery. He wanted to hug her back but was at a loss. *Can't get involved...*

"Uh...thank you," he stammered. "Gotta...go now."

Maureen smiled as he stumbled out the screen door, navigated down the steps and out the front gate.

Rushing onto the road, the glow of her hug coursed like warm fluid through his body. He should have hugged her back. No, maybe she didn't mean anything by it. Still, he knew she liked him. Last week she said he was a fine man. His kaleidoscopic emotions nearly made him dizzy.

He pushed down the road, picturing her face the moment she reached up and put her arms around him. *Yep, she definitely likes me.*

Arriving home, he undressed and crawled into bed. He didn't dare let the situation go any further. He couldn't. Not without telling her the truth.

Neighborhood dogs began barking. A reactive shiver tightened his stomach. Was someone out there? Cowboy? Buford? He held his breath, anticipating a shot crashing through the window any moment. Five, ten minutes passed. The dogs quit howling.

A frustrated breath wisped from the corner of his mouth as

he rolled over onto his side. His mind hurled in all directions—Cowboy's motive in pumping Maureen about him...the possibility of the law catching up with him...searching the clubs again for anyone resembling Buford...what kind of proof he should look for to prove whether Gus might be Gunther or not...

What he needed was a more up-to-date picture from the trial instead of the old one that came through at the *Clarion* from Buford's employment file fifteen years previous. Did he dare contact Mr. Casey for it? He dismissed that idea. Police would be keeping tabs on him. Bob Wilkinson? "Hmmm." They had hit it off pretty well at the trial, and he had an instinctive feeling Bob would believe his story.

If he contacted him and requested a more current picture and it nailed someone in town as Buford, he'd offer Bob an exclusive. He doubted the man would still be at the *Virginian Pilot*. He mentioned a transfer to Richmond, but which paper?

Well, first things first. His focus tomorrow had to be on Queenie and getting the picture and negative. She'd be in a good mood after her fling in Vegas. He squeezed his eyes shut. He could only hope Gus hadn't got to her first.

If he did, he was a goner.

CHAPTER 48

~~~

Ed trudged into the yard toward the trainmaster's building, his eyes bloodshot. He had lain awake practically all night, half his thoughts romantically on Maureen, the other half worrying about approaching Queenie. When he asked for both picture and negative would she become suspicious? He swallowed hard against the lump in his throat. Worse yet, would she tell Gus?

He let the early morning racket from the roundhouse invade his senses, hoping the noise would rattle his sleep-deprived brain. Workers yelled and blacksmith hammers clanged. Diesel fumes wheezed from a nearby loco. Its exhaust smarted his nostril like a stiff whiff of ammonia. Just what he needed.

Rounding the side of the trainmaster's building, he peered around the porch at the tracks. The doodlebugs were gone. Gus wouldn't be back until four. He had a clear shot at Queenie before reporting to Alex, the Yardmaster.

Opening the screen door to the Beanery, he glanced about. Two waitresses were clearing dishes from tables. Queenie stood stuffing napkins into a holder. He headed for the far end of the counter and slid on to the stool.

"What'll it be, hon?" She smiled, her voice sensual and inviting as usual. Ed instinctively tensed. She had a way of flirting with those eyes of hers that was hard to resist.

"Just a cup of coffee, Queenie."

"Sure thing, Ed." She grabbed a cup and a carafe and began pouring.

"Say, Queenie, know that picture you took of me at Blue Lake? Sure would like one."

"Yeah?" She looked back. "I'll get a copy made."

Ed smiled nonchalantly. "Hate to bother you. Why don't you just loan me the negative and I'll get it. No sense you going to the cost."

"Oh, no problem at all." She set his coffee in front of him. "Say, why don't you drop by my apartment some evening for dinner and you can pick it up then. I'll cook dinner and…" her crescent-shaped eyelashes lowered, "I do serve a delectable dessert."

Ed took a quick gulp of his coffee without responding, feeling his cheeks flush hot. Good thing Gus was out with the gang.

He supposed he should be flattered she had a thing for him, but she couldn't compare to Sarah. To Maureen, either. There was something vibrant, almost glowing about Maureen. He couldn't quite put his finger on it. Whenever he mentioned it, she would smile and say, "Maybe it's because I'm a Christian." He couldn't see what religion had to do with it. But, whatever, it was compelling.

A customer at the opposite end of the counter banged a spoon against his coffee mug signaling a refill.

"Back in a minute, Ed."

He watched her move down the counter swaying her shapely hips more than usual as if to let him know her invitation would be worth his while. He knew she had more than dinner on her mind. It was chancy, especially if Gus found out—but he had to get the negative. Well, as soon as he did, he'd devise some excuse to leave early before she dragged him off to the bedroom. At least her invitation let him know Gus didn't have the negative.

Queenie sashayed back. "Sound good to you, Ed?"

"Yeah. That's fine, Queenie. I can always use a home-cooked meal."

"I'll look forward to it, Ed." She sensuously stroked a few strands of hair back behind one ear with her fingers, and then flipped the bulk of her hair back. Ed smelled the scent of her shampoo. She then slid her hand down the side of her neck, then casually down the front of her blouse as if checking the buttons. A lot of woman, Ed thought.

"One problem, Ed." She threw him a wounded look. "I'll be out of town the next couple of weeks. My sister in Vegas is having health problems. How about when I get back?"

Ed felt relieved. Even putting it off two weeks, Gus couldn't get the picture while she was gone.

"That's okay, Queenie." He forced a smile, slid off the stool, and placed a dollar bill on the counter. Moving toward the door, he looked back over his shoulder.

"I'll check with you when you return, Queenie."

"You be sure and do that, Ed."

Swallowing hard, he shoved the screen door open and stepped out onto the wooden porch.

Gus, his face clenched, stomped out of the roundhouse and headed toward a silver, corrugated shed. In one hand, he held a clipboard of inventory papers. Hutch had yelled at him again about his report being late. He crimped his mouth, kicking himself for having procrastinated, so today he put off going with his men to bite the bullet.

He spent all morning with roundhouse department heads checking and compiling their inventories. He only had one sheet left to fill in and he'd be done. He hated paperwork, but it was important he keep Hutch happy. He had to get that transfer to California.

Shoving the clipboard under one arm, he fumbled with a large ring of keys and plodded to the shed door. Singling one out, he thrust it into the padlock, twisted the U hinge open, and stepped inside the dark interior. He yanked on an overhead string and the shed filled with light.

Trudging over to a huge bin, he begrudgingly grabbed a pencil from his shirt pocket and started counting all the post-hole diggers, shovels, tamping picks, claw bars, plus a multitude of bolts and tie plugs.

After an hour, he breathed relief, shuffled out of the shed and locked it behind him. Tramping across the compound, he entered the trainmaster's building and dropped the forms into Hutch's inbox, then headed toward the Beanery. He needed to double-check with Queenie on what time he should come over tonight.

His pulse raced at the thought. Erotic memories of the other night with her ignited sexual undercurrents that spread from his loins upward through his body until his face flushed hot. Strangely, it didn't last. His mental vision was interrupted with the image of the warden's daughter. He clamped his teeth tight and shook the scene away. He had to quit thinking about Sue.

Smoothing both sides of his hair at the temples, he licked one finger and ran it over his pencil-line mustache, and then pulled the screen door open and stepped across the threshold. He swept his gaze around the room, and then stopped short.

Tornadic anger tore through him. Queenie stood at the far end of the counter with Ed. The look on her face said it all. Why did she have to be such a flirt? And Ed? He was obviously enjoying it.

Whirling about, he rushed back onto the porch letting the screen door slam behind him. He bolted down the porch steps and hustled to the rear of the building. Loathing for Ed rumbled deep inside. He quickly sidled in-between two corrugated tin sheds to wait.

He wasn't going to let this newcomer interfere with his relationship with Queenie. She was the best thing he'd had since Sue. He clenched his hands into fists.

It was time Ed Riley learned a lesson.

CHAPTER 49

~~~

Ed exited the Beanery with mixed emotions and stood for a moment on the porch staring out at the flats. He felt good that Queenie hadn't balked when he asked for the negative, but he certainly didn't expect her to invite him to her apartment for dinner. And he knew what she meant about serving a "delectable dessert." He hoped he could handle things. And what if Gus finds out? Regardless, he had to get that negative. His life depended upon it.

Turning, he ambled over to the trainmaster's office and shoved the door open. He had to meet Alex at the roundhouse. He'd take his usual shortcut, cut down the office's back hallway, drop his lunch bucket into his locker, and then exit the rear of the building.

Angling between the desks, he moseyed down the hall past Don Peterson's open door. Don sat hunched over his desk.

"Morning, Bishop...I mean, Don." He gave a casual wave as he passed.

Don looked up and gave him an "old buddy" kind of grin, and tossed a wave back. "See you Sunday morning?"

"Yeah, I'll be there." He enjoyed Don's friendliness, but resented how pressured he made him feel. But yes, he'd definitely put in his appearance at church. He'd settle for another one of Don's mind-numbing sermons. He at least enjoyed Joyce Anderson's Sunday school class. He was learning a lot he never knew before, although it wasn't what he remembered his mama teaching him. Nevertheless, he would keep the relationship going with Don who claimed important connections with government officials both in the county and at the State capitol. It could work to his advantage if he got into a scrape with the sheriff. He placed his lunch bucket in his locker and exited the rear door.

He stopped short, paralyzed in his tracks. Gus stood by two nearby sheds slamming one clenched fist into the palm of his other hand. Ed felt a sickening sensation. It only took seconds for panic

309

to whirl Ed about and head back for the rear door of the building.

Gus bolted after him, grabbed him by the shirt, and pulled him between the two sheds. He slammed him against the metal, corrugated wall.

"Stay away from Queenie!" he growled. He shot his fist forward into Ed's stomach. Ed doubled over, gasping for breath, and then received a hard uppercut to the chin that flipped his head backwards against a sharp edge on the metal shed. He went limp and slid to the ground. He felt blood flowing down the side of his face. It only took seconds for his prison instincts to kick in. Balling his hands into a fist he came up fighting.

His swing connected a strong blow to Gus' chin. Gus staggered, didn't fall but recovered, and lunged forward. Grabbing Ed, he spun him around and shoved him face-forward into the wall, pressing his own body against his back and twisting his arm behind him until Ed thought it would break.

"Now, you listen, I seen the way you ogle Queenie. You stay away from her. Got that?"

Ed's breath came in sporadic bursts. "Listen...Gus," he wheezed, "I have no...interest in Queenie."

"Not the way it looks to me," Gus snarled, shoving Ed's arm up higher and forcing a yelp out of Ed.

"Gus," Ed blurted in pants, trying to catch his breath, "I'm interested...in another woman...not Queenie.

Gus, still breathing hard, remained silent for a few seconds. Gradually, he relaxed his grip. Ed turned and faced him, blood streaming from his nose and down the side of his head.

Gus stepped back a few inches "That may be, but count this as a warning with worse to come if ya mess with her." He shook his fist in Ed's face, and then narrowed his eyes.

"There's something else about you that makes me doubly not like you. Just can't put my finger on it. In the meantime..." he gave another tough jab in Ed's groin, "keep away from my girl." He turned and stomped off.

Ed, his body shaking, slumped against the shed. He touched the side of his head, winced, and staggered back into the building and entered the restroom. He moved unsteadily over to the washbasin. Leaning forward, his hands on each side of the sink, he closed his eyes for a few seconds and then raised his head and looked in the mirror.

He looked awful—three abrasions on his face, a discolored lump beneath one eye, and a gash on the side of his head. His ribs hurt too. He soaked some paper towels in cold water and gingerly wiped the blood off.

It wasn't so much getting beat up over Queenie that bothered him, although that was bad enough, but he couldn't forget what Gus said—there was something else about him he couldn't put his finger on.

Was he Buford and his memory was kicking in from the trial? But there was no way he could have picked him out from all the reporters in the packed courtroom—and Buford faced the judge most of the time.

Unless... He felt the tingles and sucked in a quick breath. Unless it was from the night they fought at the *Clarion*. Even though Buford thought him dead, his memory could be pulling it up. That sounded more logical.

He had to watch his step from now on and keep recognition at bay. He'd keep his head down when they passed each other in the office or yard. On the gang, he'd keep his back to him as much as possible. He'd also keep a low profile at the Beanery. He couldn't afford to get into another scrap. Others might see it and call the sheriff.

Gus' remark made part of him feel overjoyed at the thought that he might be Buford. At least that told him Wendover was where he was meant to be.

Now, more than ever, he needed to get that picture from Bob. Saturday, he'd call the *Virginian Pilot* for sure.

When Queenie returns from Vegas, he'd get her to promise not to let Gus know about their dinner date. Yet, he knew she enjoyed making Gus jealous.

If she promised, could he count on it?

CHAPTER 50

~~~

It was still light when Ed turned the corner toward Maureen's house. Wisps of warm air rustled through the cottonwoods, and the pink tinge of early evening spread across hilltops.

Nice, he thought, but that didn't help how he felt. Every step jarred pain in his ribs from his fight with Gus. Since then, he was leaning more toward the notion Gus could be Buford—in fact, he was almost positive. Something in his gut rang true. His dilemma was how to prove it. He needed absolute, conclusive proof. Saturday, he'd call the *Virginian Pilot* in Norfolk to see if Bob Wilkerson still worked there or if he transferred to Richmond. He'd ask him for a more current picture of Buford.

He felt hesitant about calling and letting his whereabouts be known, but if he could convince Bob of his innocence and promise him an exclusive when Buford was caught, it should influence him to play along.

But would a picture be convincing enough, he wondered? A man can do a lot to change his appearance. Loss of weight alone dramatically changes a person's face. He had to find something more besides a picture—evidence beyond all shadow of a doubt.

He strolled through Maureen's gate. They planned to listen to the radio shows this evening. He clamped his right arm tight against his ribcage so the porch steps wouldn't jar the pain. He also pulled a few strands of hair down over the gash on the side of his head hoping to make it less noticeable. If she said anything about his bruised face, he'd pass it off by changing the subject and asking her what the latest was with Oxydol's Ma Perkins and The Romance of Helen Trent. That usually got her going. Oh yes, and Pretty Kitty Kelly.

He thought it strange how she became so caught up in the lives of fictitious radio characters. Maybe listening tonight to the Great Gildersleeve with his crazy, warbling laugh sliding up and down the scale, and Fibber McGee letting everything fall out of his closet in clunks and thuds would get his mind off things and make him laugh. Heaven knows he needed more of that.

He gingerly climbed the steps, noticing the dust mop sitting on the porch. Now and then she cleaned late in the day because of not feeling well. Lately, she really didn't look good. Maybe her leg bothered her more than she let on.

He peered through the screen and gave a light tap.

"Hold on a minute," she said. Her hand shot out, holding the door part way open while she leaned over to straighten a rag rug lying askew near the threshold.

Ed began talking while she bent over, trying to make his voice sound as upbeat as possible to keep her from paying attention to his face.

"You just might be right, Maureen."

"What do you mean?" she asked, still bent over.

"You know...about my being considered for a promotion. I'm being shown everything to do in the yard—how to maintain switches and, of course, those frogs." He laughed. "Also, I'm learning how to throw and alter switches...'Bending the iron' they call it." He took a deep breath. He was talking too fast.

Maureen motioned for him to come in while she fussed with the rug. Ed stepped inside.

"And how'd your day go with the soaps?" he continued.

"Which one?" she chortled before straightening up. "Now, we could start with the Guiding Light...

"Good grief!" she exclaimed. She reached up with her hand and touched his cheek. "What on earth happened?" She turned his head to one side. "And there's a gash on the side of your head!"

Ed flinched. "Oh that? Just...took a bad fall. Guess I sort of banged myself up a little." He forced a broad grin.

"A little? You march right over here and sit down while I get some medicine and bandages." Grabbing him by the arm, she pulled him over to the couch, and then limped off in the direction of the bathroom.

In a few seconds she returned with a metal box. Sitting next to him, she flipped it open, took out some cotton and hydrogen peroxide, and tenderly dabbed his bruised face. Mercurochrome came next.

Ed winced, but loved every minute of it. It had been so long since anyone had touched him like this. All he'd known for so long had been brutality.

Watching her face, he studied her angelic sympathy and concern. Now and then she looked up at him with such a caring smile it melted his heart.

She finished by taping a bandage over the cut. Ed took her hand.

"Maureen, thank you..."

She looked up and smiled. "Oh, it's nothing, Ed. Really. I'm glad to..."

There was a long hesitation. Ed looked into her eyes. Something inexplicable was transpiring. He knew she felt it too.

What occurred next he couldn't explain. He felt as if his spirit left his body and melted into hers. Leaning forward, he followed the direction it pulled him. She responded. Their bodies converged and his arms enfolded her. Wrapped in a close embrace they held each other for what seemed like an eternity.

Ed was the first to move. He lightly brushed his mouth along her cheek, and then with one hand lifted her chin. Their lips met and they tenderly kissed. Before he knew it he heard himself saying, "Maureen, I love you..."

"I love you, too, Ed," came the soft reply.

Ed's heart soared, but then he reluctantly pulled away, struggling for the words he knew he had to say.

"Maureen," he said, turning his head away, "for reasons I can't explain now, I can't offer marriage...maybe in six months. There are, uh, some things I need to take care of." He turned back and looked at her. "In the meantime...could we consider ourselves just engaged? I'll get you a ring. We can drive to Tooele next weekend to get it."

A quizzical look spread across her face. She nodded, pausing a few seconds before she spoke.

"Ed, I know there's something going on in your life you haven't shared with me, but I can wait. When you're ready, you can tell me."

He closed his eyes in relief.

"C'mon," he said. "Whatever else you need done in the house,

I'll help. I've been worried about you lately. You don't seem well."

"No, you're hurting from that fall," she said in a sympathetic tone. "You can do the easy stuff, like the dishes."

She led him to the sink, handed him the dishrag, and then tripped off with the broom humming a tune.

"I'm going to call Harry in the morning," she called from the bedroom, "to tell him the good news."

"That's great, hon."

Ed shoved the rubber plug into the drain hole and turned on the faucet. Watching the sink fill, a thought jostled him.

If he spread the word about his engagement, Queenie might stop flirting with him. She could even call off dinner at her apartment and hand him the negative directly. In addition, Gus' jealousy might end. He didn't know if it would put the kibosh on Cowboy's infatuation with Maureen or not. He might prove to be a sore loser. He grabbed the box of Oxydol, sprinkled some into the water and churned it to suds with his fingers.

Time seemed to be of the essence now. At some point, Gus' memory would click in and he'd guess his true identity. He submerged two soup bowls into the dishwater when an idea zinged through him so suddenly it was like a dislocated joint had slipped back into place.

His brow immediately creased at the thought and dismissed even considering it. Nevertheless, it kept ricocheting inside his head. He had to pay attention.

Could he actually do something like that? Break into Gus' house? He shuddered. What if he were caught? Yet, being a convicted murderer already, he wouldn't be in any worse situation with the law. Besides, he might find paperwork proving Gus was Buford. Yes, it was paperwork he needed. Then, he'd have concrete evidence to take to Kevin. He thinned his lips. He'd do it. Desperate times call for desperate measures.

After chores, he and Maureen sat on the couch and talked about future plans and never got around to listening to the radio shows. It delighted him to see Maureen's excitement. They hugged and kissed a while, until it was time for him to leave.

By the time he arrived home, his body really hurt. Tomorrow, he'd stay home from work. He'd call Hutch and feign illness. He'd also telephone Alex and assure him he'd be there on Monday for his instructional tour.

In bed that night he smiled. He was actually engaged. Never in his wildest dreams did he think he'd find someone he could care for again and who would return the kind of love he so longed for. She constantly fussed over him, baked special treats, and made him feel like a king. Yes, he did love her, but it was different from what he had with Sarah.

How would their engagement affect Cowboy? If he was green-eyed before, think what he would feel now? Would the shootings resume? He pulled the covers up and gingerly rolled onto his side.

His main concern, however, was Gus. He'd make sure he, and everyone else, heard about his engagement by telling Queenie first thing Monday morning.

Nevertheless, before he could marry Maureen, he knew he had to bring Buford to justice and exonerate himself. His first step would be to contact Bob Wilkerson.

Tomorrow, he'd call Norfolk and find out which newspaper he transferred to. If Bob meant what he said in his letter to him at the pen, about finding it difficult to believe he was guilty, he had a good chance of his believing his explanation of innocence and more readily keep his whereabouts secret. A creeping uneasiness came over him.

Could he really trust him?

Calling him would be the most risky thing he'd done since he escaped prison.

CHAPTER 51

~~~

Ed crawled out of bed. The sun had been up for an hour, and the moist air drifting through the window screen reminded him fall was approaching—but he had more on his mind than the weather. Today was the day. He was excited, but filled with dread.

He slung on his bathrobe. Could he do it? Stumbling into the kitchen, his chest was so tight he could hardly breathe.

He dawdled at the breakfast table, glancing at the telephone sitting only three feet away. Contacting Bob Wilkinson was chancy. He wrenched his eyes away and back to his bowl of Wheaties. He shoveled another spoonful into his mouth while he studied the picture on the back of the cereal box.

Johnny Mize, the Cardinal's first baseman, stared back at him, his image encircled by bursts of orange and yellow suggesting a spectacular man of courage and grit—almost God-like. *Breakfast of Champions?* Ed narrowed his eyes in annoyance.

All the guy has to do is play baseball and they honor him like some conquering hero. It didn't compare with what he had to do—call a man who might not believe him and who may not keep his whereabouts secret. If that happened, it was back to prison. It would literally be the end of him and Buford would never be brought to justice.

He glanced at the telephone again. He took a deep breath and let logic take over. His first call to the *Virginian Pilot* should be nothing to get nervous about. It wasn't like he was going to hear Bob's voice on the other end on his first call. He was sure he didn't work there anymore. He just needed to find out where he transferred.

Sliding his chair over to the telephone he arranged a pencil and tablet, then curled and uncurled his fingers to release the tension. He lifted the receiver and dialed zero.

"Information please," came the singsong voice.

"I need the number for the *Virginian Pilot* in Norfolk, Virginia."

"One moment, please. Here is that number. Portsmouth 69875. Would you like me to connect you?"

"Yes, thank you." Ed's voice cracked and he cleared his throat. He pressed the receiver to his ear while the connection went through, then tensed when he heard the voice.

"*Virginian-Pilot and Ledger-Dispatch.* May I help you?"

"Can you tell me if Bob Wilkinson is still at your paper?" He stopped breathing.

"Well, no, he isn't," came the reply. "He left a couple of years ago. He's now with the *Richmond Times-Dispatch* in Richmond. Would you like that number?"

"Yes, I'd appreciate it." Ed grabbed the pencil and wrote it down.

"Thanks so much." He hung up the receiver, sagged back into the chair, and let out a labored sigh.

"Whew! Step one done. And now..."

He picked up the receiver again as shudders eddied through him. With hesitant fingers, he dialed.

"*Richmond Times-Dispatch,*" came the voice on the other end.

"Bob Wilkinson, please."

"One moment, I'll connect you."

"Bob Wilkinson," came the deep voice on the other end. Fear shot through Ed. He swallowed a couple of times.

"Hello," the voice repeated, "Anyone there?"

"Bob..." His voice quavered. "I don't know if you remember me—Ed Bowman...from the...Gunther Buford trial?" The voice on the other end went silent for a moment. Ed went stiff, feeling anxiety etch across his face.

"My God, Ed! Yes, of course I do. Where are you?"

"First things first," Ed managed. "Remember the letter you wrote to me in the penitentiary? You said you found it hard to believe I was guilty?"

"Yes, of course. But, your escape made it look like—"

"Bob, I assure you I'm innocent. And that's what I want to talk to you about." His armpits grew clammy. "But first, I have to have your word if I reveal where I am, you'll keep it secret. In return I promise to give you an exclusive when this is all over." A huge pulse of trepidation engulfed him.

"Yes, I promise."

320

Ed's heart soared. "That's great. This means a lot—"

"But what do you mean," Bob interrupted, his voice rising in increments, "when it's all over? You mean you're going to turn yourself in?"

"No, Bob. The reason I escaped was to find the real killer of my wife and—"

"I read the report when you were first arrested," Bob interrupted. "You claimed Buford killed her."

"That's right, and it's a long story. To make it short, I escaped prison to track him down. I believe I've found him but need more proof to identify him. So, I need a favor from you."

"Sure, Ed. Anything."

"I need you to mail me a picture of Buford taken at the time of the trial. The one I had at the *Clarion* was from his sixteen-year-old employment record. I was arrested before a more recent one came through the AP Wire. I don't feel I should call Mr. Casey. Police may be keeping tabs on him. Can you send me one?"

"Sure, Ed. I can dig it up. Where do I send it?"

"You've, uh, got to assure me, Bob, you will destroy the address after you mail it so no one will accidentally come across it on your desk—also, swear you won't tell anyone." His emotions plunged up and down like a tidal wave.

"You have my word, Ed." The tone in his voice resonated genuineness.

"Okay. Here it is." He paused. "Ed Riley—my fake name—P. O. Box 73, Wendover, Utah." He waited during the silence while Bob wrote it down.

"Whew, Ed. You must have had an inside lead to end up that far away."

"Yeah. I'm hoping it will pay off. How soon can you send it?"

"By tomorrow." He paused. "Will you keep in touch?"

"I sure will, Bob. You have no idea what a relief it is to have your help."

"Do you need me to come to Wendover?"

No. I'll phone you if I come up with anything worthwhile."

"Great, Ed. I'll get right on this and mail it from a different location. I won't put any return address on it. I'm sure you'll receive it okay."

"Thanks so much, Bob.

Ed hung up the receiver and slumped back into his chair. Would the picture look exactly like Gus? It had been nearly five years since the trial. He grabbed the edge of his robe and wiped the sweat from his forehead and back of his neck.

All he could do now was wait.

Ed knelt alongside the bathtub as he filled it with hot water. Sprinkling Rinso in, he tossed in his laundry and began scrubbing his work pants and shirts against a corrugated, glass-ribbed washboard, agonizing over his guilt in not telling Maureen everything.

She had already asked about the scars on his wrist from the hitching post. Fortunately, he was able to pass it off and she didn't push. Now they were engaged. This made things different.

Should he tell her the truth—including how he contributed to Benny's death? That thought induced a bone-jangling effect. He hated to have her know that side of him. He swished his clothes around in the water, wrung them into tight wads, refilled the tub with clear water, and tossed everything back in for rinsing.

The truth could shock her so much she might call off their engagement. If she did, would she tell Kevin? After all, the sheriff was a long-time friend. His throat closed spastically, but then he strangely relaxed.

Something in his gut said she would understand—even about Benny. That, of course, didn't make him feel absolved from what he did. Could God ever forgive him? Heaven knows he'd prayed and asked forgiveness just like his mama taught him. She had told him even if one's sins were scarlet-red they were forgivable. To him, red meant Benny's blood.

On the other hand, he thought of Joyce Anderson's class. She said God only forgave "most sins." Which ones didn't he forgive? There were times when Mormonism didn't quite sound like what his mama taught him.

Dunking his clothes up and down to make sure all the soap was rinsed out, he twisted them tight and then carried them into the kitchen and draped them on the back of the kitchen chairs to dry.

Moseying into the front room, he plopped into the easy chair. Yes, Maureen definitely needed to know about his prison record.

He'd do it after lunch. But, all of it?

Maybe he only need tell her he was sent to prison for a crime he didn't commit. He wouldn't have to say it was for murder unless pressed. Maybe he'd even leave out about Benny...maybe not. He would show her the scars on his back and legs and simply say he had to escape to get away from Jeb and the tortures, and that his pursuit for evidence to exonerate him led him to Wendover. He wouldn't name Gus directly and didn't think she would push for more.

He smiled at the ripple of relief. Then he worried if she physically could handle being told that much. Last week he became concerned. She hadn't felt well again and knew it couldn't be her leg.

He could only play it out and see what happened.

Ed stood in the archway between the living room and the kitchen trying to subdue the waves of acid that tore through his stomach.

"Hon, I have something to tell you."

Maureen stood at the kitchen sink and stopped what she was doing. She looked up. "You sound so serious."

"First," he began, "I want you to know I'm hopelessly in love with the most beautiful woman in the world."

She reached for her cane, crossed the room and planted a big kiss on his cheek. A warm glow spread through him.

"I'm glad, dear," she cooed. "But I don't know about the beautiful part. I bet you say that to all the girls." She chuckled, then paused and cocked her head. She studied his face. "You're really serious about something, aren't you?"

Dread nearly suffocated him. "Yes, dear. Come and sit down." She followed him to the couch.

Gently placing her hand in his he explained everything he had rehearsed, all the while watching her facial expression. Before he knew it, he spilled other details he hadn't planned to tell her yet, including Benny.

"Well, that's it, hon." There was a long silence before she spoke. He held his breath.

"Dear," Maureen said softly, despite obvious shock on her face, "all I know is you are the sweetest, kindest man I've ever known. I believe you when you say you are innocent—and you certainly didn't deserve the kind of treatment that awful man Jeb gave you. The evidence to exonerate you must be here in Wendover or you wouldn't be here. So, who or what is it?" She raised her eyebrows. "Can I help?"

"Shhh." He placed his finger on her lips. "Trust me, Maureen. It's best you don't know too much."

"Well...alright, dear. I'm very much in love with you and it's not going to make any difference. I'm glad you told me this much. I'll never tell anyone—not even Harry. But," she said, wincing her face into concerned lines, "are you in any danger?"

"No, no, hon. I assure you I'm not." His stomach knotted.

Without rehashing the subject again, they played cards for the remainder of the evening and listened to the radio until time for him to leave.

Walking home, he exulted with joy. She believed him about everything! His mother was right. All things were working together for his good. He had escaped Jeb and the chain gang, Maureen had come into his life, and he didn't think Gus would beat him up a second time as soon as he heard about his engagement.

Cowboy was another matter.

By Saturday, word had spread through town like wildfire. Wendover was small and news of a death, wedding or engagement whipped gossip into a frenzy. It didn't take long for it to trickle back to Ed.

"Did you hear? That crippled Miss Fisher is getting married? And to a drifter, no less."

"Disgraceful," said another. "She should have her head examined."

"Yes, and I heard she broke off an engagement with that Cowboy fellow," added another. "You know, the one from that awful gambling place over the hill?"

In spite of the gossip, Ed couldn't have been happier. At work, the men good-naturedly slapped him on the back and wished him well. Ward members were excited, although expressed disappointment he and Maureen weren't going to join the church and get married in the temple. The bishop just smiled like he knew better.

Monday, at work, Gus cornered him.

"So, I hear you're engaged now," he snapped. "But, that don't mean nothin'," he hissed, wagging a finger in Ed's face. "If I see you making eyes at Queenie again, you can expect a repeat of what I gave you before." Ed simply nodded and walked away.

Could he count on their apparent truce—if it could be called that? Yet, later in the day fire still smoldered in Gus' eyes when they happened to run into each other, as if he were still trying to place him from somewhere. At some point Ed knew the night at the *Clarion* was bound to register. He had to work fast.

The daring idea that had come to him earlier, prodded him. Yes, breaking into Gus' house seemed his only option for finding paperwork to identify him. It was dangerous, but he had to risk it. First, though, he'd wait until Bob's picture arrived and see if it was conclusive enough.

At the end of the day, Ed ambled back across the yard with Alex, the Yardmaster, to clock out. Every bone in his body was tired. Alex had taken him on the pump trolley four miles out on the track to show how to identify problems with under-maintained tracks, when to adjust and lubricate switches, and how to clear talus fallen from the cut faces of inclines. He hoped he made a good impression. He needed a promotion—anything to get out from working under Gus on the gang.

They approached the porch, and Alex stopped.

"By the way, Ed, I almost forgot. I signed you up to ride the nine o'clock helper engine Monday morning. Not that we're thinking of making you an engineer—just to give you a thorough understanding of the whole operation which includes the run to Elko over the Silver Zone grade. Helper engines hook on to trains that need additional power going up and down steep grades. You'll be riding with Bruce. That's the helper over there." He pointed.

Ed studied the huge engine. "What's that man doing on top of the boiler?" he asked.

"Oh, that's Jerry. It's his turn to put the chemical cakes in the water tanks. The cakes neutralize the hard minerals. Without them the water will foam and prevent steam from forming. Are you familiar with why, and how serious it is if they don't?"

"Yeah. Bart told me about one of the engines blowing up on the pass some years back due to the water's mineral content being high. Killed the entire crew."

"Yep. What happens is the crown sheet melts and the water flashes into steam. At 200 psi, the water expands about sixteen hundred times its own size. The explosive force not only shoots steam into the cab scalding everyone to death, but also lifts the boiler up from the rear where it'll go spinning end-over-end down the track for hundreds of feet." Ed cringed.

"So," Alex said, "it's pretty serious business if the cakes are forgotten. If it ever happens again, another engineer will have yanked his last whistle cord."

"Well, I'm looking forward to it," Ed responded. And he meant it. Riding an engine was every kid's dream. He was no exception.

On his way home, Ed wondered what it would feel like to be blown up.

At the same time, he felt a kind of deja vu but shook it away.

CHAPTER 52

~~~

At midnight after work, Gus jumped into his dark blue Chevy, gunned the engine and shot over to the main highway. His nerves were fraying to the breaking point. He hired that dumb Cowboy to do the job and he hadn't done it. Ed Riley had learned his lesson about Queenie from the beating he gave him, but his hailing from Virginia posed a continual threat to his identity and plans. Nothing could mess that up. Getting rid of him was the only solution. White-knuckling the steering wheel, he raced past the Stateline Hotel and sped over the hill to Wendover's Nevada side.

He pulled up to the A-1, slammed on the brakes and skidded his truck in the gravel up to the front entrance. He turned the ignition off.

Stretching his body across the seat, he grabbed a rolled-up uniform and a box labeled, *Chemical Cakes,* then shoved the door open and climbed out. He wished he could figure out what else bugged him about Ed. There was something...yet, there was no way he knew him back in Richmond. He slammed the door shut and stormed up to the cafe's front door.

He paused and took a deep breath. *Simmer down—don't draw attention.* With the palm of one hand he casually shoved the door open to the aroma of coffee and clatter of dishes.

He navigated across the restaurant floor, pacing his gait with as much control as he could muster, and strode toward the back of the diner. Pulling aside some purple drapes, he entered a smoke-filled room where the noise of slot machines and clanking of coins greeted him.

He squinted through the smoky haze at Cowboy who stood behind the green-felted Blackjack table nimbly stacking chips. A lone man sat in front of him studying his cards and debating whether or not to hit his hand.

Gus caught Cowboy's eye. He shot him a scorching look and motioned with his head to follow him out the rear door, marked "exit."

Cowboy groaned, finished his deal, then signaled to another man who stepped up and took his place. He hustled across the room to the back door and pushed it open.

No sooner had he stepped outside then Gus exploded, shaking an angry fist at him.

"You haven't done your job!"

Cowboy leaned against the building and lit a cigarette. He took a deep drag.

"Look, I'm doing what you wanted." Not my fault I missed the night I shot at him. It was dark and—"

"You're not being paid to fail."

"Don't worry," Cowboy snapped, "I'm still keeping tabs on him and I'm gonna try again. But tell me something, Gus." He blew out a gray puff of smoke. "I don't understand. The guy is engaged now. You don't have to worry about him and Queenie no more."

"Shut up. I got reasons that don't concern you. Just remember, I'm paying you plenty to do this." He flashed him a seething glare.

"Okay, okay. Don't get into a hissy fit." A condescending look of exasperation etched its way across his leathery face. Gus noticed, but let it go.

"Here's my plan," he growled, "since I have to do all the thinking." He thrust the box and bundled uniform into Cowboy's stomach.

"You're to put this uniform on tomorrow morning. He pulled a folded piece of paper from his pocket and moved beneath the light bulb that dangled over the doorway. Cowboy leaned in to see.

"This is the marking on this here helper engine you're to go to. It'll be parked on the spur track next to the roundhouse. Climb up on top and place this box on top of the engine so that anyone watching can see you doing it. That's where you open the top of the tender. All you got to do is drop the dummy cakes in."

"Yeah, I know what to do. Remember I worked there a short while. But what's this got to do with Ed?"

"Never you mind. If it works, you'll get your money. And you gotta do this on the early morning shift. Six a.m. sharp. Keep your head down but make enough noise so someone notices you up there. And don't wear that stupid hat of yours or you'll be identified for sure. "No more slip-ups, ya hear?"

Cowboy took an angry puff on his cigarette, flipped it into the dirt and ground it out with the heel of his boot. "Don't worry."

"Don't let me down this time," Gus snarled. Whirling about on his heel, he disappeared around the corner of the building.

Cowboy reentered the building mincing his lips. Gus and his maddening schemes. It made no sense why he still wanted to get rid of Ed. He certainly wouldn't be interested in Queenie now that the man was engaged. Not that he minded doing the job—Gus paid well—but his demanding personality rubbed him the wrong way. He wanted to be through with the job and with him. Then, he'd hightail it out of Wendover, get back to Chicago with the money he had saved and pay off the Borgata mob. He only had a short time on the note he signed before they'd be on top of him.

Further, getting rid of Ed would benefit him. His engagement to Maureen had riled him to no end. With Ed out of the way he was sure he could convince Maureen to go to Chicago with him.

CHAPTER 53

~~~~

Ed came out of the office and squinted against the blinding glint of the morning sun.

"Hey, Ed!"

Shading his eyes with the palm of his hand, Ed looked across the yard. Alex stood by the roundhouse waving his arm, trying to yell over the roar of the compressors.

"Bruce is pushing the train over Silver Zone in a few minutes. Be sure to be on it!"

"Yeah," Ed returned, with a wave of his arm, "I haven't forgotten. Looking forward to it." Like all kids, he still carried the dream of riding a locomotive. Today was going to be exciting.

He strode across the wood-planked platform, nervous about his upcoming dinner date with Queenie. Will she cancel since she heard that he's engaged? If she didn't, could he count on her promise not to tell Gus?

He also worried if Bob's forthcoming picture of Buford would nail things or not, and concerned with the risk he was taking in burglarizing Gus' house. One run-in with the law and he'd be sent back to prison—his whole mission down the tube. Could he count on his mother's, everything-is-going-to-work-together-for-his-good, scripture? *Relax Ed. One day at a time.*

He moved down the steps, focusing on how good the warmth of the sun felt on his back and lengthened his stride across the yard toward the helper engine that sat idling on the tracks behind a caboose. The Pusher, as the helper was referred to, sounded like a panting, throbbing beast pawing at the ground anxious to get going. Ed felt the same way.

He saw Bruce, the engineer, lean out of the cab window and look questioningly at him. Ed hustled forward, yelling as loud he could over the noise.

"I'm coming!"

He grabbed hold of the ladder's rungs and pulled himself up

into the cab. Bruce was busy setting controls. Jerry, the fireman, was already aboard and in position near the boiler and firebox. Ed stood in wonderment, gawking at the myriad gauges, metal rods and cranks that filled the interior.

"I watch the gauges," Jerry offered, noting Ed's engrossed expression. "I regulate the amount of air intake for the fire, shovel in more coal when needed, and keep an eye on the boiler." A quick smile curved on his face. "I'll be moving up to engineer soon."

Ed grinned and gave him a thumbs-up, then turned to watch Bruce maneuver the throttle and inch the engine forward to couple onto the rear of the caboose. A crewman on the ground dropped the locking-pin in.

Bruce leaned out the cab window and looked up ahead. "All we're waiting for now, Ed, is the signal."

Ed followed Bruce's gaze. A man at the front of the train raised and lowered a flag.

"Ah, there it is." Bruce pulled his head back in.

The lead locomotive started up, each car jerking in succession. Bruce began turning valves and advancing the throttle forward. The train chugged out of the station gradually picking up speed.

Ed leaned out the opposite cab window, letting the hot wind rush into his face. He enthusiastically returned the wave of three children who ran alongside the road trying to keep up.

How many times had he done the same thing? At four o'clock every day he ran pell-mell through Benton's Hollow and up the ridge to the tracks just so he'd be there in time to wave to the engineer. What a thrill when his wave was returned. After the train disappeared into the distance, he'd run back home to be greeted by his mama. She always said the same thing. With hands on her hips, a faded blue apron tied around her waist, she would shake her head in mock dismay.

"Land O Goshen, child, I have no idea what you see in running lickity-split just to see a train."

Ed smiled at the memory and continued waving to the three children until they were left far behind.

The train chugged by the loading corrals behind his section house, then picking up more speed, whizzed past the orange and white-checkered water tower at the edge of town and shot over to the Nevada side of Wendover and onto the desert.

"Looks like you never rode a loco before," Bruce called over the din of the engine, observing Ed's rapt look. "You're right about that," Ed shouted, exhibiting a broad grin. "Especially a helper engine."

"We use these Pushers," Bruce explained, "when a train doesn't have enough strength to pull itself up over a steep pass. On upgrades there's the risk of coupler failure, so a push by us from the rear solves the problem. Whistle signals from the lead loco tell me when to apply power, drift, or brake. If I should misunderstand his signals and I push while he brakes, we'd undergo a violent bunching of cars and possible derailment. We also stay hooked on for the downhill ride on the other side. That way, we can provide a degree of braking in case the train becomes a runaway."

"Whoa!" Ed exclaimed. "That would sure take your breath away. Of course," he said sheepishly, "not that I want that to happen." He gave an apologetic smile.

Bruce let out a chortle at Ed's child-like enthusiasm. "Well, relax and enjoy the sage brush. Not much else to look at. We'll reach the pass soon."

Ed remained glued to the cab window for the next twenty minutes. Bruce was right. Nothing but stretches of sagebrush-covered desert, rock-strewn gullies, and straw-colored tumbleweeds.

"We're starting up the grade, now,"

Ed pulled his head back in to watch Bruce masterfully control the water gauges and steam valves. Jerry shoveled more coal into the firebox.

"Say, Bruce, Alex told me about the chemical cakes that go into the boiler to prevent foaming. Are any with us so I can see what they look like?"

"Sure. Go ahead." Bruce motioned with his thumb over his shoulder. "The supply is in that box over there. It should be open."

Ed stepped toward the rear of the cab, and then called back over the roar of the engine. "Hey Bruce, the box is sealed. Okay to rip it open?"

"What do you mean it isn't open?" Bruce widened his eyes in alarm.

"Must be a new box," Ed yelled.

Bruce whirled about. "Jerry—check that box!" Ed instinctively jumped back.

Jerry dropped his shovel, rushed over and examined it. His mouth dropped open. "He's...he's right," he shouted over the roar of the engine and rumble of wheels. "None's been taken out!"

"Jumpin' Jehoshaphat!" Bruce's face paled.

Ed suddenly became fearful, too—over what, he didn't know. "What's the matter?" he croaked.

"As of yesterday, this box was our last one with just enough for today's run plus two or three. The new supply is coming in tomorrow. The fact it hasn't been opened means only one thing. No cakes were taken out and put into the water tank this morning. Explain that, Jerry!"

"Bruce," Jerry spluttered, "I phoned Bradley last night knowing I'd be delayed this morning. He said he'd do it. When I arrived this morning and checked with him, he said when he went into the yard to do it someone else was already on top of the tender taking care of it. He saw him drop the cakes in. But since the box hasn't been opened, that means the guy Bradley saw must have been doing something else—certainly, not putting any of *these* cakes in."

Bruce's face went white. The vein in his neck pulsed. "Let's pray the crown sheet isn't melted!" he shouted. "Jerry, check the gauge cocks and glasses for the sheet's water level."

Ed's toes curled in his shoes. He remembered Bart and Alex's account. "You mean...we could explode?"

"You better believe it," Bruce exclaimed. "If the boiler blows and lifts up from the rear, hot steam will shoot directly into the cab. No way we'll survive that kind of scalding.

"We're nearing the top of the grade now. I'm going to signal ahead for the engineer to stop before we start down the other side."

He leaned out the cab window and stared up the long line of boxcars to the front of the train where the lead loco was just disappearing over the top of the grade. He began yanking the whistle code. He cocked his head and listened. Nothing.

"Oh, Lord help us now!" he gasped. "It's out of hearing range."

Ed gulped spastically. "Can't you put on our brakes and stop the whole train?"

"No. We only have an independent brake for this loco, but

I'll try it anyway. Maybe the head-end brakeman up front in the doghouse—that small shelter on top of the tender—will feel the resistance. That's exactly why we keep these trains short. He can stop the entire train with his brakes—that is, if he gets the message. Thank God for continuous brakes instead of the old stem-winders. Hang on!"

The locomotive's brakes tore into the iron wheels. Sparks shot from beneath the sides of the engine and the piercing shriek of metal-against-metal filled the cab.

Wide-eyed, goose flesh riddling Ed's body, he hung on for dear life. He pictured the train derailing any second.

Bruce furiously adjusted the controls and then abruptly turned and peered straight ahead into the window of the caboose ahead.

"There," He pointed, "the conductor and rear brakeman!" Ed looked and saw two men enter and turn to climb up into the cupola, the lookout cabin on top.

"Ed," Bruce yelled, "stick your head out the window. Get their attention. They won't be able to hear you—just wave your arms. Do something...now!"

Bruce let out a series of short whistle blasts as Ed lurched to the window, hung on to the top edge of the casing with one hand and leaned his body out. Waving one arm he began yelling, but the wind caught his words and blew them back into his face.

The two men in the caboose had barely entered the cupola when Bruce's whistle blasts startled them. The conductor looked up.

Ed waved his arm frantically. Then he did the only other thing he could think of. He whipped one finger across the front of his neck indicating the threat of death.

The conductor stared. Panic crawled over his face. He jerked his thumb up in acknowledgement, whirled around and rushed back down into the caboose with the brakeman following. Through the lower window Ed saw them disappear into the boxcar ahead of them.

"They got the signal!" Ed yelled at Bruce. "They're heading up front to tell the engineer. What do we do now?" His whole body trembled.

"Pray," Bruce replied breathlessly. "I'm putting on as much

brake as I can. We're at a bad place on the grade and the head loco is out of sight. We might be able to stop if the conductor gets to the engineer in time."

Ed's body went rigid while the seconds ticked away. He envisioned the boiler exploding, with huge chunks of blackened metal and scalded pieces of their bodies shooting into the air like Roman candles.

The wheels on the boxcars ahead of them squealed, groaned, and began slowing. "They did it!" Bruce shouted.

After what felt like an eternity, the train came to a complete stop. Ed, his heart pounding, leaned back against the cab wall and crumbled onto the floor.

Bruce, his face red, took a tremulous breath and wiped the perspiration from his face with his sleeve. "We haven't had an incident like this since the early thirties."

"Jerry," he turned to face him, "whatever Bradley said he saw makes no sense. The only supply would have been in this box." He thoughtfully tapped his chin. "Maybe this was deliberate. I don't know what those box cars up ahead contain—maybe something vital someone doesn't want to reach its destination."

"You mean...sabotage?" Ed stared at him.

"Could be. Wouldn't be the first time. But of course that was back during the Great War."

Bruce leaned out the cab window and glanced toward the top of the grade.

"Engineer's coming alongside." He threw Jerry a quick look. "You know what needs to be done." He scrambled down out of the cab, jumped onto the ground and hurried forward.

Ed, stunned, remained hunched on the cab floor. "Jerry, we all could have been killed."

"Yeah," was all Jerry could manage. He leaned over and ripped the box of cakes open, reached inside and looked at Ed. "I can't help but wonder why Bruce would think sabotage. It would make sense if the war were still on, but nothing of major importance is being shipped now—at least that I know of."

He pulled some cakes from the box. "Be back in a sec." He climbed out of the cab, grabbed hold of the ladder and hustled atop the tender.

Ed sat for a few minutes in prolonged trembling. A grim

thought ricocheted through him and boomeranged against every nerve in his body. Another attempt to kill him?

Gus had to know from the schedule board that Alex had assigned him to this train. He stared pensively. But the dummy cakes? Who put them in? If Gus, Bradley would have recognized him. Besides, that wasn't Gus' job. Cowboy? But he doesn't work for the railroad and wouldn't be knowledgeable about boilers.

Bruce finished talking with the engineer and climbed back up into the cab just as Jerry dropped down into the cab from the tender.

"New cakes are in, Bruce, and the crown sheet is okay. Water level, too. We caught things in time. We can continue on."

"No." Bruce shook his head. "We're heading back. The engineer agreed. Can't take the chance of going over the pass now. We need to check everything out on this engine. Who knows what else we might find." Adjusting the controls, he yanked the whistle, and then leaned out the window to listen for the return code, after which the train moved backwards down the grade.

By the time they pulled into Wendover, Ed's nerves were at full stretch, convinced the sabotage was a plan to kill him. Too many threats and close calls were happening in his life to call it a coincidence.

What he needed was someone else on his side—someone who could provide more information on Gus and Cowboy without his revealing why he wanted to know. It could only be Bart. He'd think of some explanation.

Ed entered the trainmaster's office, scribbled a note, and left it in Bart's call box.

Meet me at seven o'clock tomorrow morning beneath the corrals behind my section house.

Come alone!

CHAPTER 54

$\sim\!\!\sim\!\!\sim$

$\mathbf{A}$wake before sunup, unable to sleep, Ed hurriedly dressed anticipating his covert meeting with Bart at seven o'clock. Gobbling down a quick breakfast, he hurried outside to the tracks and waited under the corral's loading ramp, smoke-blackened from hobo campfires.

Bart was his only hope for an ally in Wendover. With his long-time connections with workers and office staff, he could possibly provide inside information on Gus and Cowboy. But would he believe the little he intended to tell him? He glanced at his watch. Never had it ticked so slowly.

"Over here, Bart!" Ed jumped out from beneath the ramp and waved his arm.

The pungent aroma of Bart's pipe tobacco preceded him as he approached.

"What on earth is all this cloak and dagger stuff?"

"C'mon," Ed motioned, "scoot under here and I'll explain." They hunkered down beneath the ramp's creosoted oak ties.

Bart leaned back against one of the posts, raised his eyebrows and waited. Ed took a cavernous breath.

"You got to swear to me, Bart, you won't tell anyone about this conversation."

"Ed, you've got my word. But for heavens sakes, what's this all about?"

"Well, uh...someone's trying to kill me."

Bart's mouth dropped open, letting his pipe fall out. With a quick movement of his hand he grabbed it before it hit the ground. He leaned forward. "Who? Why? Are you positive?"

"Yep. Too many accidents to chalk it up as coincidence."

"Well, let's hear about it." Bart stuck his pipe back into his mouth and folded his arms across his chest. "I'll shut up. You talk."

"I'm not exactly sure who it is. It's either Gus, or a guy named Cowboy—or both.

"I know who Cowboy is," Bart interjected. "Most everyone does. Not a good reputation. He'll do anything if his palm is greased well enough. But as far as Gus, are you sure you're not reading too much into the guy? He definitely has a mean streak—but try to kill someone? And why?" He gave Ed a long, quizzical look.

Ed slid both legs beneath him, Indian style. At that moment it felt so good to have someone genuinely interested, he was tempted to share everything—his conviction for Sarah's murder, his escape, suspicions about Gus being Buford—but caution checked him.

"It all started with Queenie flirting with me."

"Uh oh." Bart winced. "But even though Gus has an unruly temper, jealousy isn't enough to make him want to kill you. Especially since you're engaged now."

"First," Ed continued, slamming his fist into the palm of one hand for emphasis, "he got me behind the tool shed and beat the living tar out of me. Next, when I was walking home from Maureen's, before we became engaged, someone shot at me in the dark. Barely missed me—"

"Shot at you?"

"Sure enough—and it wasn't kids target-practicing late at night. And then—"

"There's more?" Bart blinked his eyes with incredulity.

"Yeah. Last week, Cowboy was on the Merc steps when I walked by. He came right up and threatened me."

"What'd he say?"

"That I might be treading on someone's territory, and if I wasn't careful I could get hurt. He didn't say *his* territory, but *someone's* territory. Now, he could have been speaking about someone else, or referring to himself in third person. But it was the way he said it."

Bart stroked the side of his face and slowly shook his head. "I don't understand what his interest in you is. Gus, I can understand because of Queenie, but—"

"Well," Ed interrupted, "before I showed up on the scene, Cowboy was pestering Maureen to go out with him."

"Hmm." Bart gave a few swift puffs on his pipe. "Cowboy is one tough hombre. Still, you don't try and kill someone over that."

"There's more," Ed blurted. "You heard about the incident at

Silver Zone yesterday?"

Bart nodded. "Yeah, it's the talk of the yard."

"Bruce suspected sabotage, but admitted it made no sense. He knew of nothing significant the boxcars were carrying."

"And you think it was intended to kill you?"

"Bart, there's no doubt in my mind. But who can it be? Gus? Cowboy? Are they in this together?" He made a helpless gesture.

"Could there be any other possible reason beside their jealousies?" Ed slumped his shoulders and waited, holding his breath hoping Bart would offer some tidbit.

"Good questions," Bart mused, removing his pipe from his mouth and knocking the tobacco out against the tie footing. "But at this point it's hard to say. They both have motives for hatred, but what's so illogical is Gus would want to kill you over Queenie since you're engaged now, or Cowboy over Maureen, even if they came out on the losing end."

"Unless," Ed offered, "Cowboy is the kind who carries a grudge to extremes."

"Could be." Bart glanced at his watch.

"I'm really sorry, Ed. I've got to get going." He crawled out from under the ramp.

"But I do agree," he said, straightening up. "Something's fishy. I'll nose around and see what I can find out. In the meantime, watch your back."

The rest of the day, Ed did exactly that. He eagle-eyed every scenario that could possibly pose danger.

At noon, Ed slipped away to the post office to see if Bob Wilkinson's picture of Buford had arrived. His breath nearly stalled in his throat. It had. With shaky fingers he tore open the manila envelope and slid the picture out.

Yes, it was Buford, from what little he remembered from the trial, but the more he stared at it the more it didn't look like Gus. Although a slight resemblance, the face was much fatter, and the half-closed eyes were puffy and bleary like a man on a drinking binge. It definitely wasn't enough to convince the sheriff. His disappointment felt like a chunk of concrete in his chest. He had to find more evidence. Burglarizing Gus' house was the only answer.

He hurried back to work and had barely reached the perimeter of the yard when he heard his name.

"Hey, Ed!"

Looking up he saw Bart motioning to him. He stood by the old Cannonball building. Ed hurried forward.

"Been hoping to catch you," Bart said.

Ed spoke in low tones. "Have you found something out about Gus or Cowboy?"

"Yeah." He glanced warily about.

"Okay, let's hear it."

Bart looked around again to make sure no one could hear. Ed felt everything go silent inside him, and impatiently shifted and re-shifted his feet.

"I did find out some stuff about Gus," Bart said, lowering his voice. "First, I got a look at his employment file. He lists no relatives at all.

"Second, while we already surmised he was from the South, I found someone who said he recalled Gus mentioning he came from Richmond and had bragged about working in law enforcement for fifteen years."

Ed gulped. *Richmond and law enforcement. That could mean prison guard.* He didn't dare let Bart know the significance of that.

"Still," Bart continued, "I don't know how that particular information helps. But it's more than we knew before."

"Probably doesn't help much," Ed said in as casual a tone as he could, "but it fails to explain any motive for why he's targeting me—that is, aside from his jealousy over Queenie. Anything else?"

"Well," Bart countered, squinting his eyes and then cocking one eyebrow, "one thing appears peculiar to me."

"What's that?" Ed mentally crossed his fingers.

"Why, after fifteen years of service," Bart gestured with his pipe, "would a man quit a job, especially during the depression when employment is scarce, and come to a place out in the middle of nowhere to hire on as low man on the totem pole? And if he had a job for that many years with law enforcement, why didn't he put the capacity he served in on his application? You'd think he'd want to offer it as a plus. There were no letters of recommendation in his file either."

"Yeah, strange. But maybe he skipped town because he owed

342

a lot of money. If so, certainly not a motive for trying to kill me. What about Cowboy?"

"That's the interesting part." Bart paused to tamp some tobacco into his pipe. "Before the Silver Zone mishap, I went up to the casino the other night to play the slots. Hoped to corner Cowboy in a casual conversation when he was through at his table—buy him a drink or something and see what I could find out. Just as I was about to, who should walk in but Gus with a box tucked under his arm."

"That's nothing unusual," Ed said nonchalantly, "a lot of the men go there to gamble." His interest nevertheless piqued. He hung on to Bart's next words.

"Gus didn't sit down at any of the gaming tables. He gave Cowboy the eye, and Cowboy immediately turned his table over to another dealer and followed Gus out the rear door. Both had serious looks on their faces. Now, doesn't that seem unusual to you? They're definitely involved in something together."

"Hmmm," Ed rejoined, gesturing for Bart to continue.

"Gus never came back in but Cowboy did, carrying the box Buford brought in. You should have seen the look on his face. He was fuming. It looked like Gus had pressured Cowboy into doing something he didn't want to do. Maybe like...kill you?"

"But," Ed asked, shaking his head in mock puzzlement, "why?"

"Personally, Ed, I think it's the jealousies they both have in common against you. But," he shrugged, "I only suggest this because I can't think of anything else."

Ed pulled his mouth in at the corners. He wanted more. *Think, Bart. Come up with something else.*

"That may be, Bart, but from what I heard the crew say, Lil is his girlfriend now. And Gus? Like you said earlier, why should he be jealous over Queenie since he knows I'm only interested in Maureen? Any ideas?" Ed tried to quell the churning of his insides. "Or could you have been reading too much into their meeting?"

"Perhaps, but you can bet your bottom dollar if they're in cahoots, whatever they're involved in isn't good. And it obviously had something to do with the box."

"Bart, I've got to thank you. That's more information than I had before. Whether it's going to add up will remain to be seen."

Bart gave Ed a reassuring slap on his shoulder. "I'll still keep my eyes and ears open. In the meantime, keep a careful eye peeled."

"Sure will, Bart."

The rest of the day, Ed processed the new information. *Gus from Richmond and in law enforcement.* In his mind, that pretty much nailed Gus' identity. He now felt even more confident about his earlier idea about Gus' motive. Anyone from the South could recognize him because of the trial's notoriety. Yes, it was all coming together. Fortunately, Gus hadn't connected him with Ed Bowman, the reporter—not yet, anyway.

But what was Gus' confab with Cowboy about at the A-1 Star? What were they hatching up? It couldn't be jealousy on either of their part. If it was about the box, what was in it? He cocked his head. *Think, Ed. What could possibly be in it that would connect to you?* Then revelation hit him with sledgehammer force.

Fake chemical cakes!

Now he was really on to something. Further, since Cowboy had the reputation of being a man for hire, it meant only one thing.

Cowboy had to be Gus' hireling.

CHAPTER 55

~~~

Saturday morning, Ed shuffled across Maureen's front room to the kitchen sink, nearly tripping over the vacuum cleaner bag that needed to be emptied. He plunged his hands into the soapy dishwater. Maureen was sick again and he was spending the day helping out. Nevertheless, he couldn't quit thinking about the narrow escape at Silver Zone and wondering what Gus and Cowboy would think up next.

"Ed," Maureen called from the bedroom where she lay on her bed, "did I already tell you how sweet you are to do what you're doing?"

"Yes, you did, hon. And I'm happy to do it. Some day I'll be sick and you'll do the same for me. You keep resting sweetheart. Tomorrow the new diesel arrives, and I know how badly you want to see it. I want to be sure you're up to it."

"Thanks so much, dear. No way do I plan to miss the new 5,400 horsepower diesel. Who would ever imagine steam engines becoming obsolete? Maybe one more hour," she called, "and then I'll get up."

Ed walked into the bedroom. "You look yellowish."

"Honey," she laughed, waving him away, "everyone's color changes when they come down with something. My fever is no longer up and I'm beginning to feel better. I think its run its course. Besides, the doctor might put me in the hospital. You know how doctors are."

"Yeah." Ed nodded. "Now, I know how much you want to see that engine—we all do—but hon, regardless of that please let me take you to the doctor in Tooele." He leaned over and gave her a kiss on the forehead.

"Oh, just give me a little time and I'll be back to my old self. Stop worrying, dear." As always, Ed gave in.

Nevertheless, he continued to worry. The last two weeks her health continually fluctuated. First, she would feel fine, and then

345

she'd be down with what she called a flu bug. Suffering fatigue and lack of appetite, she also complained of joint pains and headaches. He thought about Gus and Cowboy, worried if something happened to him there'd be no one to take care of her.

He finished the dishes, grabbed a towel and dried his hands, then ambled over to the couch and sank into it. He squeezed his eyes shut. He had to quit being so tense. After all, the plan to blow him up failed, and thanks to Hutch giving him a promotion, he didn't have to worry about it happening again. He was no longer on Gus' track gang.

"Your natural talent," Hutch said, flashing Ed a smile, "leans more toward mechanics. So, your new job is Track Inspector and Motor Car Maintainer. You'll cover the area west, between Wendover and Winnemucca. Pay increase, too."

Ed smiled. He'd be on the road with a new, yellow-paneled truck and nothing around him but stretches of barren desert. Even knowing Gus and Cowboy were in cahoots and would try again, there was no way one of them could creep up on him out there without his seeing them.

The drive would also give him more relaxed time to work out details for breaking into Gus' house. Regardless of how little Bob Wilkinson's picture looked like him, he was confident Gus was Buford. He couldn't delay. He needed real proof.

He reached for the *Deseret News* lying at the far end of the sofa. Grabbing it up, he thumbed through the classifieds. An ad by a California company caught his attention.

Send your letters to us and we'll mail them for you. Your address remains private. All information kept confidential. Send for details.

He widened his eyes and pulled the newspaper closer. What a perfect way to keep his promise to Benny. Sending a letter with a California postmark to his mother couldn't be traced back to Wendover. Her name and address were still emblazoned in his memory, *Madge Yates, 531 South Eighteenth Street, Richmond.*

He got up and angled over to Maureen's small desk. Withdrawing a clean sheet of stationery from a drawer he wrote a short letter to the company requesting details. Sealing it in an envelope, he stuck it in his shirt pocket. He'd mail it on his way home tonight. He scooted back to his chores, emptied the vacuum bag, and began sweeping the kitchen floor.

Should he tell Maureen about his upcoming dinner at Queenie's apartment? Unfortunately, even after hearing about his engagement she didn't want to cancel. While Maureen would understand why he had to get both the picture and negative to protect his identity, she'd worry he'd succumb to Queenie's wiles.

He smiled. He was in love with Maureen.

No chance of that.

CHAPTER 56

~~~

The slender fingers of dawn stretched yellow and orange streaks across the salt flats, then moved through the town's underbrush and crept up the trunks of the cottonwoods. Ed ambled down the road toward Maureen's house, the air crisp and tangy with heady smells.

In an hour the new diesel would arrive from Salt Lake. Maureen was naturally excited, but he wasn't.

Considering tonight's daunting task, and what he planned to do at midnight, diminished any excitement over the diesel. To say he was nervous about breaking into Gus' house was putting it mildly, despite the pleasant sound of tree swallows and tanagers twittering in the trees.

Normally, he enjoyed early mornings. No yowling cats, no voices from neighborhood houses, or cars starting up. The only sound might be a gentle breeze snapping sheets left overnight on a neighbor's clothesline. But no enjoyment for him this morning. Not with so much on his mind. What he wouldn't give to magically transport himself back to a Hannigan morning—back to when he had no troubles at all.

There would be roosters crowing at dawn, the smell of magnolia blossoms in the air, and warm caresses of sunny afternoons in his hammock with casual conversations between he and Sarah over a glass of sweet tea. They would watch goldfinch and purple martins splatter in the birdbath and then flit by with their iridescent feathers looking like ribbons of blurred color. It was a kind of otherworldliness. If he could only take a slice out of time right now and forget the harsh realities of the present. But he couldn't. All he could think about was Gus. Nothing could deter him from what he had to do.

Midnight, Gus would be on the night shift. Somewhere in his house had to be incriminating evidence nailing Gus' true identity. Nothing should go wrong—he had gone over every detail.

Nevertheless, he shoved his hands into his pockets as he approached Maureen's street picturing the abyss that loomed before him if caught. A reactive chill shivered down his spine. The gloomy thought, like a dark premonition, grabbed him in a strangle hold.

Squaring his shoulders, he forced his thoughts in a different direction—the new diesel arriving this morning. Gus would also be there to see the train. What kind of reaction could he expect from him since the Silver Zone explosion failed?

Turning the corner, he saw Maureen eagerly waiting on the front porch. Returning her wave, he entered the yard and angled toward Harry's truck parked in the driveway.

"This is something we certainly don't want to miss," Maureen said, scurrying down the steps and over to the truck. "Sure wish Harry were here to see this." Ed opened the door for her.

"Oh, he'll see it alright," he said, relieved she was feeling back to her old self. "I'm sure the train will travel the Feather River Canyon route. He'll see it when it comes through Keddie."

The sun was barely up when they reached the depot. Word traveled fast. Railroad buffs from Wells, Ely and Tonopah were already there waiting along the track. Guests from the Stateline Hotel came roaring down in elegant Carson-topped Chevy Cabriolets and fancy Fords with v-shaped grilles. A frenzy of excitement and tension hung over the crowd of jubilant observers as they waited on pins and needles for a glimpse of the new innovation.

Ed glanced around for Gus. He was nowhere in sight.

The sound of the locomotive grew nearer. The crowd's eagerness accelerated.

"It's coming! It's coming!" They stretched their necks and peered eastward down the track.

Within minutes the black hulk, exhaling ill-smelling diesel fuel, thundered into the station with its long line of cars behind. Everyone eagerly pressed forward, sprinting up and down the track to examine every inch of the beast.

"This is history in the making!" one shouted.

"I'll be telling my grandkids about this!" another shot back.

"Isn't it marvelous?" Maureen exclaimed.

"Yeah, sure is." Ed stretched his face into a wide grin. "But not quite as exciting as watching an old steam-wheezing, gear-grinding loco." Maureen gave him a playful jab in the ribs.

He looked again for Gus. *Uh oh*. He spied him standing by the front door of the trainmaster's office puffing away on a cigarette. Ed held him in an analytical gaze. Gus, rather than exhibiting interest in the diesel, had his eyes glued on trainmaster Dugan and the office clerk who were leaning over looking beneath the train wheels. Gus quickly opened the front door to the office and slipped inside.

"I'll be back in a minute, hon." Ed kissed her on the cheek.

Circling around to the rear of the building, he entered the back corridor near the restroom. Hugging the wall, he quietly inched forward. Around a corner, he could peer directly into the front office. Gus was fumbling through a cabinet drawer. Ed recognized where Hutch had placed his personnel file.

Withdrawing a folder, Gus flipped through the papers. He paused at one page. At the slant Gus was holding it, Ed could make out a bold logo at the top. It looked like his Mason Furniture letter. What did Gus think it would tell him?

The sudden roar of the diesel outside rattled the building. Gus whirled about and looked out the front window. Shuffles of feet sounded outside on the porch steps. The office staff was returning. Irritation rippled across his face. He yanked the letter from the folder, stuffed it inside his shirt, and replaced the file in the drawer.

Ed, sensing Gus would probably leave through the rear door, swiveled around and barreled down the back corridor. He quickly slipped into the restroom and rushed into a stall. Breathless, he leaned against the wall. If Gus came in, he'd be nonchalant and give no indication he'd seen him.

Seconds passed before he cautiously emerged. Tiptoeing over to the door, he pressed his ear against it. He heard the diminishing rumble of the diesel leaving the station on its way toward Nevada, then the sound of the front door bursting open. Personnel piled into the office, their excited voices echoing down the hallway.

Next came the door slam of a metal footlocker and hurried footsteps of a single person sweeping past the restroom and exiting through the back door. It had to be Gus.

What did Gus plan to do with Scratch's letter? Should he be concerned? What could the man *really* do? Mason's didn't exist, so he couldn't check it out. Neither would it reveal his *Clarion* background. However, it would confirm Ed Riley worked in Richmond for ten years prior to transferring to Newport News. His throat went tight. That would set Gus' teeth on edge for sure.

Ed opened the door a crack and peered out. All clear. He stepped into the empty hallway and left the building. Gus was nowhere in sight. He probably put the letter in his locker for safekeeping until quitting time. Circling around to the front of the building, the urgency to break into his locker and steal it chewed at his gut.

"There you are," Maureen called. "Where have you been all this time?"

He swallowed hard and smiled. "Oh, just taking care of something in the office. C'mon, I'll drive you home. No need to bother with breakfast for me. I'll stop by my place before I go to work. Sure glad you're feeling better."

He dropped her off at the house and parked the car, all the while his thoughts in a dither. Aside from Gus knowing he once lived in Richmond, could there possibly be anything in the letter itself to tip him off it was fake? Logic told him there was no way. Nor would it reveal his identity. Nevertheless, the stress started his insides shaking.

"Bye, hon." He kissed her on the cheek and hurried out the gate. His breath rushed out of his chest harder than usual. Even if Gus could figure the letter was bogus, it wouldn't make him surmise he was Ed Bowman, the reporter.

Nevertheless, he needed to take every precaution. Gus would take it home later this afternoon and scrutinize it before returning for his night shift. That meant he had to get the letter somehow.

An idea swiftly jostled its way into his head. He narrowed his eyes as it took root. The padlock hinges on the lockers were thin. He could easily break into it—and he had a bolt cutter in the shed. Gus would naturally suspect him when he discovered it gone, but wouldn't be able to prove it. Nor could he report the theft without admitting he'd stolen it from the office. Yes, breaking into his locker was his only option. He'd do it this morning while Gus was out with the gang.

Arriving home with his emotions a jumbled mess, he hurried into the kitchen and forced down a bowl of shredded wheat and piece of toast, made a sack lunch, and then scuttled back down the road toward the depot.

So much had happened. First, shots in the dark, the near explosion at Silver Zone, Gus and Cowboy conspiring at the A-1, the need to get the negative from Queenie. And if that weren't enough to do him in, Gus stole his letter and tonight he intended to burglarize the man's house. He let out a long, tortured breath.

I'm not cut out for this.

CHAPTER 57

~~~

Ed hurried down the road toward the depot. Everything was quiet when he entered the yard except for the pounding of his heart. The roundhouse machinists and blacksmiths hadn't arrived yet, and only one man crossed the grounds near the old Cannonball building.

He walked as casually as he could toward the truck shed. He knew right where he placed his bolt cutter.

Approaching the shed, he singled out a key from his key ring, undid the padlock and pulled the weather-beaten door open. Stepping inside he closed it behind him and then yanked on the string that hung from a ceiling bulb.

In the dim, yellow light, he marched directly to his truck's storage compartment. Opening the lid, he grabbed the bolt cutter and shoved it into his duffel bag. He took a couple of deep breaths and leaned back against the garage wall to wait for his heart to slow down. Wiping his sweaty palms on his trousers, he left.

Hustling to the rear entrance of the trainmaster's building, he slipped inside and listened. All he heard from the front office were a few voices. He tiptoed and moved down the hall to the green, metal footlockers. Fear shifted up his jugular. He took a quick glance around. No one. He moved silently along, checking the name labels.

Ah, Gus Mooreland.

With shaky fingers, he unzipped his duffel bag and withdrew the bolt cutter. Carefully positioning the jaws around the hinge, he squeezed. The hinge broke with a snap that resounded down the corridor. He froze. He listened for any office chairs scooting away from desks. Nothing. He carefully removed the padlock and opened the locker door.

Inside was a shapeless gray jacket stained with grease, a duck-billed hat, a pair of work gloves and some girly pictures. Ed pulled the jacket out and thrust his hands into the pockets. Empty. He

355

reexamined the inside of the locker. His body sagged. No letter. Gus had it with him. He fought against the disappointment.

This meant he definitely had to get inside Gus's house tonight and find it. He flinched, visualizing his arrest and extradition back to the chain gang if caught. He felt like a knotted rubber band inside him was about to break and catapult him into the arms of the sheriff. It also didn't take much to picture the whipping post, the sound of shovels scraping in the dirt, the buzz of horse flies swarming over his dead body and Jeb looking down with fiendish delight.

Replacing everything in the locker, he eased the door shut, wincing at the squeaky hinge. He repositioned the broken padlock, then with cushioned steps moved back down the hall, slipped out the rear door and crossed the yard.

At the end of the day he stopped by Maureen's house to check on how she was feeling. She was lying on the couch complaining of a heavy feeling in the right side of her stomach.

"It's giving me a little pain—but not much," she quickly added, noting his concern.

"You're starting to look yellow again, Maureen. The diesel was too much for you. You've been losing weight. Too much. This isn't normal. Whether you like it or not," he insisted, "I'm going to ask Jane Tuttle to come over and check you."

He immediately left and returned with the school nurse, a blonde, slender woman of about thirty-five.

"I'm not a doctor, Maureen," Jane said after examining her. "But from your symptoms, your color, and especially the place in your abdomen that hurts, I suggest you get to a doctor as soon as possible." Ed watched Maureen's face drop.

"Now, I'm not trying to alarm you," she continued, "but you know it's ninety miles to Tooele and roads will be turning icy soon.

"Doctor Farley is the one I work with. If you like, I'll call him when I get back home and tell him you're coming in. How about tomorrow?"

Ed shot a quick glance at Maureen. He was surprised to see her agree.

"He'll probably want to take tests," she added to Ed at the door, "so I'd plan on staying in town for more than a day." With that, she left.

"Hon," he said, returning to her side, "don't worry. The doctor will simply give you medicine to bring home, and it will do the trick. We'll be back by tomorrow night."

Ed stressed over her condition, but he also became frustrated with the delay for breaking into Gus' house. He forced a slow inhalation. Ransacking Gus' house tonight would definitely have to wait. Maureen came first. During that time, he could only hope Gus wouldn't detect the letter's forgery.

An hour later, Jane called to say she made the appointment.

"Be at Doctor Farley's office—ten o'clock tomorrow."

"Okay," Ed responded. "I'll sleep on the couch tonight and keep an eye on her. We'll head out first thing in the morning." He hung up, and then called Hutch, explained the emergency, and asked for the next day off.

Early the next morning he stuffed apples into a sack, made peanut butter and jelly sandwiches for the trip, and arranged a bed on the back seat for Maureen.

During the long drive to Tooele he kept glancing at her in the rear view mirror. Her color was worse and her stomach still hurt. All he could think of was how he'd never be able to handle losing her. He pushed harder on the accelerator.

"Slow down, dear," Maureen said, "I'm not dying, you know."

CHAPTER 58

~~~

Gus was fit to be tied. The Doodlebug, much to his frustration, putted into the station at noon instead of eleven-thirty. They had been slowed down by the head inspector's three-wheeled Velocipede riding the track in front of them. The guy could easily have taken the machine off the track and let them go ahead of him. That rankled him. All he could think about was Ed's recommendation letter and getting home to examine it more closely before he had to return for his late shift.

He jumped out of the railcar as soon as it came to a stop and headed for the office. His work boots thudded across the wooden planks of the porch and into the office where he signed out and then left and bolted across the yard toward his car.

Had Ed really worked for that company—in Richmond and Newport News? Could he check it out? Even though the company was defunct, maybe he could find a way to contact John Squires, the man who signed the letter. He could pretend he was a WP Supervisor asking for references. If Ed lied about working at the place, he could report it to Hutch. His throat went tight. Problem was, Hutch liked Ed. Well, he thought, who knew what it might lead to.

Sliding into the seat of his Chevy he sped out of the yard toward home, his eyes glaring with anger. So far, all his attempts to get rid of Ed had failed. Yet, there was something else about the man that strangely bugged him—like he knew him from somewhere. He pulled his brow together in creases. No faces from the pen rang a bell. As guard, he pretty much knew all the convicts. Ed simply wasn't one of them.

Why was Ed at Wendover in the first place? And all the way from Virginia? This was too much of a coincidence. Could he be an undercover cop? He sure didn't look the type. He reached home in all of five minutes.

Home was in the east section of town, consisting mostly of

trailers and a few houses. He was proud he lived in one of the better-looking houses. No living in a tar papered section house anymore for him. He tore into the driveway and could hardly get out of the car fast enough. He raced up the front path and through the door.

Dropping into his easy chair, he turned the switch to the lamp that sat on the end table. Reaching into his shirt pocket he pulled out the letter from Mason Furniture and leaned in under the light.

"Hmm. Eight years in Richmond, and only two in Newport News." Living in Richmond, he had to know about his trial. Every newspaper blared the story. Of course, that didn't mean he now recognized him as Gunther Buford. He slouched deeper into the chair. A defunct company. Can't follow up on that unless I can locate John Squires.

He read and reread the letter, then jerked his head back. He did a double take at the signature line. *Respectfully, John Squires, Manager.* He widened his eyes.

Squires...Squires...

He grabbed the pack of cigarettes lying on the table, pulled one out and lit it. Taking a deep drag, he leaned his head against the back of the chair and blew a couple of smoke rings into the air. The name sounded so familiar. Why?

It only took a few seconds. The face of an inmate with white hair and slanty, pointed eyebrows came into focus.

All inmates and guards at the pen knew Scratch. He faked official-looking passes and documents—anything a prisoner or ex-con needed, often signing the name of John Squires on his bogus papers. When finished he'd slip them to certain guards, of which he was one, to smuggle to a con or deliver to a parolee on the outside. Gus was more than willing to participate. Inmates and ex-cons paid Scratch dearly for his service, so his cut as middleman was considerable. Why Scratch was stuck on using the name of John Squires, he didn't know.

He got up and sauntered into the kitchen and swaggered over to the sink, proud of what he figured out. Filling the coffee pot with water, he dumped a scoop of coffee into the perforated basket. Clamping the lid down tight, he lit the burner and then ambled over to the kitchen table and sat down.

He stared out the window, reflecting on the days he sat in the county jail for killing the warden's daughter. He'd probably still be rotting in jail, or else been strapped in old Sparky, if it hadn't been for his having smuggled a set of Scratch's "John Squires" papers to Billy, a parolee who still owed him for it. He had leaped at the chance to help him escape and have his bill paid in full. Bribing the jailer to get word to Billy to visit him was sheer genius.

Good ol' Billy. His lips formed a smug smile. Always pays to have someone in your back pocket.

The rapid sound of percolating coffee drew his attention. He glanced over and checked the color through the glass top. Pretty close. He got up and shuffled over to the cupboard. Grabbing a mug, he poured the steaming liquid in, plopped in a couple of sugar cubes in, then blew across the top. His thoughts still focused on Scratch.

He had no idea where the man went when he transferred out of the pen. Rumor said he'd been relocated to a chain gang.

"So," he said aloud, grabbing a spoon to stir his coffee and angling his way back into the front room, "how do Ed Riley and Scratch know each other? What's the connection? How would he come by one of Scratch's letters since he didn't remember Ed being a prisoner at the pen?

No sooner had he placed the mug on the end table and eased himself into the chair when he bolted upright. There was only one answer.

Ed must have been a prisoner transferred from some place else to the same chain gang as Scratch. His heart thumped against his rib cage. That's it. He's an escapee! He's here because he heard about Wendover through the underground grapevine.

He absorbed the revelation in stunned silence, thinking back to when Ed first started laying track. He shuffled in small steps, a habit no doubt acquired from wearing shackles. He grinned and folded the letter up.

"Well, Ed Riley," I got you pegged.

"Now, what I need is that picture Queenie took of you at Blue Lake."

CHAPTER 59

$\sim\!\sim\!\sim$

Shaded by giant elms, the white-stuccoed office building of Dr. Raymond Farley sprawled across a green, rectangled lawn. The sky, typical of November, was cloudy and dismal during Ed's drive from Wendover. He worried it might depress Maureen. But upon arriving in Tooele, the sun shone bright enough to cause them to squint against the blinding sparkle of the silver specs of mica embedded in the concrete walkway that led to the front door. Ed took the sun and the silver glitter as a positive sign.

"Everything is going to be fine, hon." He squeezed her hand. "Medication will fix your problem." Maureen face remained glum. All is well, hon," he continued. "The sun is out now. Listen to those sparrows chirping in the trees. See them?" He pointed. Maureen looked in the direction of the birds, nodded and smiled, but said nothing.

Pushing through the building's double glass doors, they checked in at the desk. They hadn't waited but a few minutes when a nurse whisked Maureen away down a white, sterile corridor leaving Ed to cool his heels in the waiting room.

For over an hour Ed sweat it out, perturbed by the calmness of others who nonchalantly sat in the lobby reading magazines. To pass the time, he studied the green and white pattern in the floor, mentally tracing the lines with imaginary fingers. Then he alternated by staring out the window watching the sun periodically duck in and out behind clouds. One minute the sky was blue, then gray.

He looked at his watch thinking of his plans to break into Gus' house. Maybe the doctor would be through in time so they could be back in Wendover before midnight. Or was the town nurse right? They might have to stay overnight.

He reprimanded himself. Maureen, of course, came first—but they had no future if he didn't find the evidence to exonerate himself. Ten more minutes passed. To his relief the nurse appeared.

"Mr. Riley, will you please come with me?"

His leather shoes squeaked conspicuously against the tiled floor as he followed her down a cold, long white hallway with the sharp smell of antiseptic prickling his nostrils. The coldness of the hallway made him shiver like he'd walked into a meat locker.

Fear needled him about what the doctor would find, but he quickly forced a more positive mind-frame. He didn't dare let himself imagine it to be anything serious. One prescription and they'd be headed back to Wendover.

The nurse ushered him into a room, then left.

Maureen sat on an examination table slightly bent over, one arm pressed against her abdomen. Ed felt his facial muscles instinctively tighten. His nerves skittered about inside him like a pinball machine.

"What have they come up with?" He gave her a tremulous smile.

"Don't know yet, honey," she said. With one hand she motioned towards a chair for him to sit. "The doctor thought I might have some kind of liver problem and is putting a rush on the tests. That's all I know. He did say for me not to be overly concerned until he sees the results." Her tone seemed reassuring.

"He also mentioned there might be the possibility we'll have to go into Salt Lake for more tests."

Ed grimaced. "I don't like the sound of that."

"Oh, don't be a worry-wart," she smiled. "I also explained that since we're engaged you would be in on my medical decisions."

At that moment, Doctor Farley opened the door holding a clipboard with papers.

"You must be Mr. Riley." He smiled and extended his hand.

Ed shook it, studying the doctor's face for any hint of bad news. Nothing.

"Miss Fisher," he said, sitting down in one of the chairs, "my examination, plus the limited tests I've run, indicates you have hepatitis. Only more tests can narrow it down and confirm the exact type." He looked down and thumbed through the papers on his clipboard.

"Because of the location of the pain, your color, and the length of time this has gone on without treatment, I'm pretty sure your liver is involved." He looked up, his face stoic, no expression one way or the other. "You should be prepared this may mean cirrhosis—on the other hand, it may not."

Ed felt like a thunderbolt struck him. *Hepatitis...cirrhosis? But cirrhosis is what alcoholics got. Maureen never touched the stuff.* Numbness immobilized him. He glanced at her. She appeared unmoved.

"I'm sending you to Salt Lake to see a specialist, Doctor Heinz, at the University of Utah Medical Center. His offices are in the County Hospital on Twenty-First South. I've made an appointment for you this afternoon at two o'clock. Is that convenient?"

"Yes. Thank you, Doctor," Maureen said politely. "You've been very frank and I appreciate it."

Ed searched Maureen's face. She was playing it cool, but he caught her jaw muscles flexing.

"Do you have any questions?" Doctor Farley turned to Ed.

Ed shook his head feeling totally helpless. Could the doctor be withholding anything from them?

"I think, Mr. Riley," Doctor Farley continued, "you should be prepared to stay in Salt Lake over night. Doctor Heinz will probably put her in the hospital for a couple of days. Do you have a place to stay?" He arched his eyebrows. "Or you may prefer returning to Wendover until the tests are—"

"No!" Ed exclaimed, "I'll either get a motel or sleep in the car. I'm not leaving her."

They left and headed for Salt Lake City.

Within the hour they arrived and found the hospital a huge, uninviting colorless complex of buildings spanning three city blocks.

They parked in a huge concrete parking lot and ambled across two more before reaching the main steps. Pushing through a heavy door, they entered the building and inquired at a large circular desk. The receptionist pointed to the elevator.

"Go to the third floor. Turn right. You'll see his office. His name is on the door."

Ed held Maureen's hand as they rode the elevator. They said nothing. They only stared at the changing floor numbers on the

365

monitor, until it stopped at the third floor where they stepped into a pale green corridor reeking with the acrid smells of medicines and antiseptics.

Maureen used her cane but Ed kept his arm hooked through hers refusing to let go, even when they sat on one of the hall benches to rest. Lab technicians and nurses hurried by in a steady stream while others pushed patients in wheelchairs.

"Sort of a forlorn place," Maureen commented. Ed, grim-lipped, said nothing.

She stood and motioned she was ready to continue. Rounding the corner at the end of the hallway they saw the doctor's name on the door and walked in.

"Please come in," Doctor Heinz said, smiling and shaking their hands. Short, with graying hair and horned-rimmed glasses, he radiated warmth and reassurance. Ed felt better already.

Motioning them to two chairs, Doctor Heinz moved to his desk and came right to the point.

"Doctor Farley telephoned the results of the preliminary tests. Did he mention you might have to stay for more tests?" He paused, and waited.

Ed and Maureen both nodded.

"Well, then if you're prepared, I'd like to do that. We'll start the tests tomorrow morning." He turned to Ed.

"Mr. Riley, we're not going to know anything right away, so you could comfortably return to Wendover. The tests will take all day tomorrow and there's nothing you can do here. Maureen can keep in touch with you by telephone. As soon as we have the results she can let you know when to drive in and get her."

Ed looked at Maureen, confused about what to do. She reached over and reassuringly patted his arm.

"In the meantime, Miss Fisher, take this paper to the receptionist and she'll get you checked into a ward. It's a long walk back to where you need to go. So, if it won't embarrass you we can offer you a wheelchair."

Maureen hesitated, and then nodded in the affirmative.

A lump formed in Ed's throat. She felt worse than she was letting on.

A nurse wheeled her down a maze of corridors. Ed followed

behind. At the ward she handed Maureen a gown.

"Please wait out in the hall, Mr. Riley."

Ed sat on a bench. Leaning forward he massaged his temples. *Cirrhosis.* Doctor Farley mentioned medication. That means it's curable. He felt a ripple of hope, but it only lasted a few seconds as he stared at the drab, slate-colored floor.

Twenty minutes passed before the nurse stuck her head out the door.

"You can come in now."

Ed jumped up and hurried into the room. The shock of seeing two other patients in nearby beds looking so sick alarmed him. She shouldn't be in here with them. He moved to her bedside.

"Now, dear, I want you to go back to Wendover," Maureen urged, lifting herself up from the mattress on one elbow. "You need to get back to your job. Doctor Heinz is right. What would you do here all day but sit while I'm off doing tests?" She smiled. "Stay at my place. I'll call you tomorrow and let you know exactly when to come and get me. Okay?"

"I just don't know what to do," Ed said forlornly. "I just can't leave you."

"Yes, you can," she said. "Besides, if you return home you can call Harry. In fact, I'd really like you to do that for me. He needs to know. Will you?"

Ed remained quiet for a few seconds. "Okay," he reluctantly agreed, pulling a chair over to the bedside.

He stayed until the nurse insisted visiting hours were up. Giving Maureen a hug, he walked toward the door, hesitated, and then spun around on his heel. Rushing back, he gave her another squeeze.

"Love you, hon."

"Love you, too, dear."

He moved slowly out the door, but not before turning to take one last look.

The ride back to Wendover proved difficult. His thoughts whirled a mile a minute. Could Maureen's sickness be punishment for the things he'd done in prison, especially his part in Benny's death? Further, he hadn't kept his promise to contact his mother, but should be hearing from the California people soon. Maybe after all he did in prison God didn't think he deserved her.

His logical side quickly kicked in, reminding him he'd done everything he could to live a good life since he escaped. Nevertheless, he argued. He did violate the law by breaking into Gus's private locker. And what about his plan to burglarize the man's house? But wasn't he justified? How good did he have to be?

Arriving in Wendover, he drove straight to Maureen's house, telephoned Harry and explained what had happened.

"Can you come, Harry?"

"Ed, I would if I could, but I'm needed in the canyon. It's a disaster. There's a massive slope-slide about thirty miles west of Keddie. Rain is filling up the canyon at Bucks Creek and we have landslides on the track with boulders as big as freight cars. But keep me posted on sis's condition. In case I can't be reached at home, here's the telephone number at the Keddie office. Call collect if you have to. I'll alert them you might be calling."

After Ed hung up, Don and his wife Lila dropped over to inquire about Maureen. Speaking in his role as bishop, Don was especially consoling. "I'll see that Maureen's name is put on the prayer list in the temple, Ed."

It was no time at all before women from the Relief Society came with their casseroles and salads, all of them sympathetically expressing concern and promising to remember Maureen in their prayers. Ed felt encouraged. Mormons were indeed proving to be good friends—like his second family.

That night, Ed lay in Maureen's bed trying to buoy his spirits. It only made sense they had to run tests to see which medicine to give her. Everything would be okay. He'd head for Salt Lake as soon as Maureen called. With a prescription, everyone praying for her, and her name in the temple—which he supposed was a wonderful place—she'd get better. She'd be back in time for Thanksgiving. He berated himself for entertaining the worst.

By morning, he felt in better spirits and went to work. He let everyone know at the yard. "She'll be coming home today. I'm sure of it. I'll be receiving a call any time."

He waited all day.

Maureen telephoned early that evening and described the different tests she underwent.

"How's the ache in your side—lessened any?" Her split-second hesitation worried him.

"Everything's fine, dear. The doctor says you can come in tomorrow morning." Ed perked up.

"That's great! But what did the tests show?"

"So far, I'm in the dark. He probably wants to wait so we can both hear them together."

Ed started to speak but Maureen interrupted.

"I'm sorry, Ed, I can't stand here at the telephone any longer. The pain in my side is a little worse right now—probably from all the tests. I'm sure it will get better once I'm on medication. Miss you."

"Miss you too, honey." He hung up the phone.

He walked into the kitchen and headed for the icebox. Why was she still in pain? Oh yes. A smile spread across his face. Doctor Heinz hadn't given her the medicine yet. That would quickly take care of it. He reached into the icebox and grabbed some lunchmeat.

He could hardly wait until tomorrow.

CHAPTER 60

~~~

At daybreak Ed hustled out of Maureen's house, breathing in the raisiny wet scent clinging to the cottonwood leaves from an earlier shower. The November morning air was nippy, and rich pinks slowly crept in from the salt flats and spread across neighboring yards. The fresh fragrance and cloudless sky, plus his exuberance over bringing Maureen home, promised a perfect day. A warm kernel of happiness triggered a smile. Nothing could mar it.

He headed for Harry's truck. After Maureen came home and was situated, he would embark on his previously postponed midnight venture of breaking into Gus' house. He had thought of everything down to the smallest detail, but worried about botching it. He pictured himself sneaking through the dark. Things could go wrong. Nervous fluttering pricked his chest and he felt panicky, like a chicken knowing it's going to have its head chopped off.

What if he were caught? Or what if he didn't find anything? A sickening sensation plowed through his gut. With no real evidence—and Bob Wilkinson's picture not looking like Gus looks now—no way would the sheriff believe Gus was Buford. He emitted an agonizing moan and shook the distressing scene out of his mind. *Don't think about it right now. Got to keep my nerves steady*. His major focus today was getting Maureen back home. One thing at a time.

Sliding into the car seat, he backed the car out of the driveway and drove to the main thoroughfare. Passing the Highway Patrol Station, he sped the car out onto I-40, his midnight undertaking still clawing at him. So much hung on tonight. Like it or not, he had to give it attention—get it out of his system before he reached Salt Lake. With 123 miles to go, he had plenty of time. He replayed all the details again.

He arrived at the hospital only to have the nurse inform him Maureen had been moved to a different ward.

"But first," she added, "the doctor wants to see you in his office." Shattering icicles plunged down his spine. Her tone triggered apprehension.

"Mr. Riley, please come in." Doctor Heinz looked up from his desk as Ed entered. He pointed to a chair. Ed sat, his body brittle with tension.

"Mr. Riley," he said, "I wish I had better news for you." Ed's stomach went queasy.

"Maureen," he continued, "has Hepatitis B. This kind can evolve into two forms—acute hepatitis, which rarely results in liver failure, and chronic hepatitis. In Maureen's case, numerous tests confirm the latter has occurred.

"Unfortunately," he continued, "it has advanced to HCC, hepatocellular carcinoma, the most common kind of liver malignancy. In other words, Mr. Riley, she has liver cancer."

Ed widened his eyes. The shock hit him with sledgehammer force. He swallowed hard. "Does this mean... she's going to...die?"

"I'm sorry, Mr. Riley. With Doctor Farley's tests and my initial examination of her when she first entered, I already surmised this but wanted to wait for more tests. I anticipated she would have about two months but our tests have suggested less time."

"How...long?" Ed choked, tears filling his eyes.

"Well, it's not that simple anymore." He paused, looked down at his desk and methodically straightened a small stack of papers. He looked back up.

"Early this morning she took a turn for the worse. Her pain became quite severe and we had to administer painkillers. Later, she went into a coma. So, there's no way she can come home at this point."

Ed's insides froze. He leaned forward. "How soon...will she be out of the coma?"

"Mr. Riley, there's no guarantee she will ever come out of it, although some do. Look at it this way. She has cancer, she's in pain, and while she's unconscious she isn't feeling anything."

"I want to see her."

"Of course, Mr. Riley. However, I need to warn you she won't know you're there. However, rest assured everything possible is being done for her. I'll have someone take you. She's in a private room now." Stepping into the outer office, Doctor Heinz called for an aide.

Ed waited for fifteen excruciating minutes before an older woman in a pink jacket exhibiting a pleasant smile appeared. She motioned for Ed to follow her. It took another ten minutes to reach her room. Pausing before stepping across the threshold, he turned to the lady.

"When someone's in a coma," he ventured, "do they ever come out of it?"

"Sometimes they do," she replied kindly. "But remember this. Even though a person is unconscious, many claim if you talk to them they can still hear." Ed walked into the room.

A long, tan curtain hung from a circular track in the ceiling around the bed. He stepped forward and gently pulled it aside, then stopped abruptly as if someone had slugged him in the chest. Although Doctor Heinz told him what to expect he was unprepared for the reality of her condition.

A tube extended from Maureen's nose. Bottles of fluid dangled above her from metal mobiles. Needles were taped to her arms. A cold, metallic gray table held bottles and boxes, cotton swabs and syringes. A pendulous bag hung near the bottom of her bed with a tube leading up under the covers.

He moved near the head of her bed and stared down at her jaundiced face. It was a horrible orange. He dragged a chair over and sat. Reaching for her hand, he held it tenderly. Could she really hear him if he spoke?

"Hon, I'm here," he said softly. "I know you're in a coma but they say you just might be able to hear me.

"Now, listen—you *can't* leave me. You've got to fight this. You know how much we mean to each other."

He stroked her hand longing for something, an eye-flutter, a finger movement, anything to show she heard. His eyes never left her face.

"I talked to Harry. He would have come but there's a terrible storm in the canyon and he can't leave. In fact, he doesn't even know yet you're this bad off."

Unable to check his grief any longer, tears oozed from beneath his eyelids and he buried his face in the edge of the blanket to stifle his moans. "Please...please, Maureen, don't leave me."

Between sobs he looked up, searching for some change—some indication she maybe heard and was reviving. Nothing. She lay still, oblivious to the tube in her nose, her orange-colored face expressionless, her breathing labored. He knew he should call Harry but couldn't bring himself to leave her.

He spent much of the rest of the day praying, pleading, imploring and then bargaining. "If you'll let her live, I'll be a better person." He thought of Don's remark about putting Maureen's name in the temple. "I'll even join the Mormon Church...any church." Finally, he was worn out.

One of the nurses came in.

"Go to the cafeteria, Mr. Riley, and get yourself something nourishing. You need to keep up your strength. If anything serious happens, I'll be sure to send for you." Ed decided she was right.

After grabbing a bowl of soup and a sandwich, he found a telephone in one of the hallways and placed a collect call to the Keddie office. A clerk answered. Ed explained the situation.

"I'm sorry, Harry is still out at one of the tunnels. The canyons are really bad. We've had more slides. I imagine he'll be out all night so I may not hear from him until morning. I'll give him the message as soon as he checks in."

Ed hung up, went back into the cafeteria and purchased a salad to take back to the room for later.

Evening came and Ed kept a constant vigil holding Maureen's hand and continuously talking to her.

"Visiting hours are up," the nurse said, stepping into the room.

Ed was reluctant to leave—even angry—but rules were rules.

Exiting the building, grief and confusion weighed like chains. Would her name in the temple prove effective? Would a miracle come through?

He reached the parking lot and threaded his way through aisles of parked vehicles until he came to his car. Warming up the engine, he pulled out onto Twenty-First South to look for an inexpensive place to spend the night.

He found a small auto court, checked in, and dropped into bed exhausted. He felt a tad better away from the depressing atmosphere of the hospital, even began entertaining positive thoughts. He felt strongly that when he went back to the hospital in the morning he'd receive a wonderful surprise when he walked into her room. Maureen would be sitting up in bed smiling. He pictured Doctor Heinz's puzzlement.

"Well, Mr. Riley, looks like I was wrong and we've had some kind of miracle here."

Ed crossed his arms behind his head. Surely, if the Mormon priesthood has the power Don claims, her name in the temple should do the trick.

Chapter 61

~~~

Ed awoke around five thirty a.m. He took a quick shower and arrived at the hospital at six-fifteen fearful he'd be kicked out for showing up before visiting hours. He strode down the long hallway toward Maureen's room imagining the scenario again.

Maureen would be sitting up—well, maybe lying down. She would smile and say, "Hi, dear, I can hardly wait to get home." She wouldn't know she'd been in a coma and he'd have to explain. She'd probably say something about how messy her hair looked and how she hated for him to see her that way. He grinned at that. Of course, the doctor might insist she stay for another day and he'd reassure her. "It's okay, hon. Just a necessary precaution."

Three more doors to pass. Two more...one.

"Mr. Riley?"

Turning, he recognized the nurse who had talked him into going to the cafeteria. She rushed up and took hold of his arm. Before she could speak Ed heard a noise and quickly turned back.

Orderlies were pushing carts out of Maureen's room. Doctor Heinz appeared next and stopped when he saw Ed. Handing his clipboard to a nurse, he walked toward him. The nurse in the hall dropped Ed's arm and left.

Ed stood motionless, a horrible feeling forming in the pit of his stomach.

"Mr. Riley, I don't know how to make this any easier." An electric chill swept through Ed's bones.

"Maureen has unfortunately...expired. I'm so sorry. Everything possible was done. We didn't know how to reach you. She developed breathing problems during the night and...well, she went quickly."

Ed's mind tailspinned, unable to believe what he was hearing. Engulfed with panic, he pushed past the doctor and raced toward Maureen's room. Hesitating in the doorway for a second, he stared at the tan curtain hiding her bed from view and then inched forward. With trembling fingers, he pulled the circular drape aside.

Maureen lay peacefully on her pillow, arms down at her sides. The nasal tube had been removed, along with the apparatus from under her blanket. The medical supplies on the stand by her bed were gone. Everything was neat, orderly, and quiet.

He stared into her face. He felt a nerve at the corner of his mouth twitch. He moved closer, studying her eyelids for any movement. He reached for her hand and slowly lifted it. Lifeless. He touched her forehead. It felt cold. Clammy. Different.

"God," he whispered, "how can I function without my sweet Maureen? How can my world be the same without her?"

Loss and grief collided, hitting him with a double-whammy that convoluted into a collage of confusing images. Maureen's face suddenly shifted into Sarah's. He was back at the *Clarion* looking down at her body, her powder blue blouse covered with blood, hair draped across one cheek, hearing her last words to him.

Maureen had no last words for him.

His eyes went liquid, and all the broken pieces of his heart rose up into his throat, nearly choking him.

"Mr. Riley?" Doctor Heinz stood behind him. "We need to know your plans for the…arrangements."

Ed turned to face him, fighting back his emotions. "I…don't know," he said, his voice cracking. "We never talked about something like this. We live in Wendover and there's no cemetery or mortuary there. I just don't know what to do." His voice trailed off.

"Then may I suggest the Tate Mortuary in Tooele? Most Wendover residents use their services."

Ed nodded.

"I know this is a shock, Mr. Riley. You have my deepest condolences. I'll have the nurse take care of the initial arrangements. Please feel free to stay in the room as long as you need—no one will disturb you." With that, he left.

Ed slumped into the chair by Maureen's bed and hardly moved, struggling to grasp the reality and disentangle the two traumas from his mind of losing both Sarah and Maureen.

After an hour of reaching no understanding why God would do this to him a second time, or why her name in the Mormon temple didn't work, he reluctantly left the room.

Shuffling through the sterile corridors in a daze, he passed two nurses chatting at the desk. They appeared oblivious to him and his tragedy. Hadn't they heard?

He moved by patients sitting on hall benches talking with relatives. He heard the sound of orderlies wheeling metallic tray tables down the hallway, one of which had a defective wheel. *Thump, thump, thump.* All the hallway noise and blurred voices sounded hollow, discordant, as if he were drifting slow motion in a vapory dimension where no one could see him.

He went down the elevator, drifted past the Information Desk to the entrance, and pushed the heavy front doors open. Stepping into the chilly November air, he pulled his coat collar closer around his neck. He stood for a moment and studied the grounds.

Somehow he expected everything to look different. It didn't. The trees and shrubbery lining the front walk were still there. He could hear the rush of traffic on Twenty-First South, visitors walking up the concrete steps talking about mundane things, cars entering and exiting driveways. The world was continuing as if nothing were amiss. It seemed wrong. He gazed upward, resenting the morning sunlight. How could God let it shine today?

Sauntering through the parking lot, he passed two men leaning against their cars exchanging idle conversation. One of the men let out a hearty guffaw that cut through Ed like a knife. He wanted to grab him by the throat and say, "Don't you know, the woman I love just died!"

He reached his car and fumbled with the key in the door until it opened. Sliding into the seat he started the engine, then stared through the bug-splattered windshield.

Why was it whenever something wonderful happened in his life the rug was always pulled out from under him? First, his sweet Sarah murdered. Now, Maureen dies. Everything had been taken away from him. Everything. Further, he was no closer to Buford's capture. Why was so much against him? He wiped his eyes.

Putting the car in gear, he pulled out of the parking lot, turned onto Redwood Road and headed for Tooele.

Four hours later he arrived in Wendover feeling drained, not only from the long drive but the somber atmosphere of the funeral home, selecting the casket, arranging the service, and tediously going over financial details. He knew Harry would help. The funeral would be held in the mortuary's chapel, the burial in Grantsville.

Pulling into the driveway, he trudged into the house, and then telephoned Don who immediately left work and came over.

After offering his condolences and giving him a sympathetic look, he cocked an inquisitive brow. "What date and time have you decided for the services? The weekend is best so those who work can make it. And of course, I'm available to conduct the—"

"Bishop...I mean, Don. I hope you won't be offended. Maureen would not want a Mormon bishop conducting her funeral. Are you okay with that? The funeral director in Tooele said he would do it."

Don nodded good-naturedly, but when he left Ed detected a wince of displeasure. He also forgot to ask him why Maureen's name in the temple failed. He now had the unpleasant task of telephoning Harry. Fortunately, Harry was in the Keddie office when he called.

Stunned, Harry stammered, "I'll...try to make it, Ed. But I'm up to my ears taking care of...these slides." His voice quavered. There was a long pause. Attempting to control his feelings, his tone shifted from emotional to business-like.

"There's forty thousand cubic yards of granite and rock on the tracks and highway. To avoid another slide I have to coordinate the boring of a three thousand-foot tunnel through solid rock." His voice slowed. "I'll call San Francisco right away...see if they can get someone to replace me."

"That's fine, Harry."

"Ed—" Harry's voice broke. "I'll make it if at all possible, but there's a chance I might have to stay. You understand?" He dissolved into tears.

"Of course, Harry. Maureen would, too."

Unable to say goodbye, Harry hung up.

Three days before the funeral, a steady flow of visitors came to the house. Ward members expressed sympathy, all of which he needed, and Relief Society women brought their casseroles. Alex and Hutch came by after work, including Jake, Nancy and their toddler.

When Bart arrived, he motioned Ed off to a corner.

"Ed, I saw Gus and made sure he knew."

"What was his reaction?" Ed tilted his head.

"Well, he was taken aback and silent for a few seconds, then weakly mumbled something about being sorry and walked off."

Ed expelled a deep breath. "Maybe, in view of everything, he and Cowboy will lay off of me for a few days."

"Let's hope so," Bart said.

Ed hoped so, too. It would give him a breathing spell until he got through the funeral and could reorganize his thoughts about breaking into Gus' house. Right now, he couldn't focus on much of anything.

The stream of people continued throughout the day. Queenie telephoned from Vegas, surprising Ed with a more tender side to her.

"Ed, honey, so sorry about Maureen. We'll reschedule our dinner date. I have to stay in Vegas a couple more weeks to take care of my sister. She's recuperating from surgery."

Relief spread through him. At least with Queenie gone Gus couldn't get the snapshot or negative from her.

That evening, Harry called.

"I feel terrible, Ed. In spite of all my efforts to arrange for a replacement, there's no way I can take time off. This is the worse storm we've had in years."

"Sure. I understand Harry."

At the graveside service in Grantsville, Ed absorbed very little of what was said. The remarks about a future resurrection offered no consolation. Adding to his grief was the cold weather, the drab, gray cemetery with its spindly, skeletal trees devoid of leaves, and Maureen's casket being lowered into the near-frozen ground.

After everyone left, he lingered at the grave trying to exert a Christian perspective of life-after-death like Maureen and his mama had. It was futile. He also struggled over what Don and Lila told him the night he had dinner with them. "*Those who die and aren't members of the church, do not go to heaven to be with Jesus but are consigned to a spirit prison.*" Prison? The image ripped him apart. At the funeral, Don had put his arm around his shoulder and confirmed it.

"Maureen will be freed once her temple work is done. Ed, all the more reason why you should join the church."

Who was right about heaven—Maureen and his mama, or the bishop? All he could do was puzzle over the fact Maureen loved and knew her Bible and felt positive she would go to heaven—not to prison.

Taking one long last look at the grave, he ambled back to his car and started the long drive back to Wendover.

Maureen's house was appallingly still when he walked in the door—more than he could bear. Her opened Bible lay facedown on the couch. On the kitchen sink sat a new box of Aunt Jemima Pancake Mix, also an unopened sack of Gold Medal flour ready to make his favorite pumpkin cookies.

He moved with slow, heavy steps into the bedroom and looked in the closet. Her dresses hung straight and formless. He buried his face into one of them, breathing in the scent of her perfume. He wanted every last vestige of her. He would move out of his section house and rent Maureen's house from Harry.

That night, he lay awake in Maureen's bed staring in the dark at the shapeless shadows playing on the walls and holding the blankets close to his nose to hold on to whatever was left of her smell. If he happened to doze, he dreamed he was running through a labyrinth of hospital corridors disoriented and panicky, trying to find Maureen's room. At one point he tried forcing the dream to change by picturing himself back on the chain gang being beaten at the whipping post.

Nothing worked.

He took three days off from work and scrubbed the kitchen floor, waxing it shiny like Maureen insisted, cleaned the house, and listened to her radio soaps as if needing to keep up on them for her sake.

When he returned to work, he plodded robot-like through the motions, overlooked maintenance orders, and often forgot to take tools to a job. He couldn't even think about breaking into Gus' house yet.

Every night, he came home to silence. Maureen's excited

chatter was not there to greet him or update him on the Romance of Helen Trent or Pretty Kitty Kelly. Neither was she sitting in the evenings, happy and contented, laughing with him at Baby Snooks and Fibber McGee and Molly.

Slumping into his chair, he stared into space. Tonight, like so many others, he didn't bother eating. His soul ached with loneliness. He yearned for Maureen's radiant smile, entertaining antics, and the way she looked at him with adoring eyes and said, "*You're the most wonderful man in the whole world.*" His grief ate away at him like a cancer.

Once in a while he jerked his head up and glanced about the room expecting to see her, until it finally filtered through she was never coming back. He leaned forward and held his head in his hands.

"Dear, sweet Maureen," he sobbed. "You're gone forever...just like Sarah."

CHAPTER 62

~~~

Ed plodded down the road to work under a heavy drizzle of rain, his thoughts on Maureen. Overhead, dark clouds unfurled and picked up force, threatening a downpour. He scowled. Of all days for Harry's car to have a flat tire. Further, he still didn't know when he'd feel up to the business at hand—breaking into Gus' house.

The clouds split open just as he arrived at the yard. The drenching rain hit the ground like a thousand needles. Ducking his head against the spitting barrage, he pulled his jacket up over the top of his head and broke into a run toward the trainmaster's building. He spied Hutch taking cover beneath the overhang of the porch and bounded up the steps to join him.

"We're in for a good one today," Hutch said, looking at the angry sky through the sheets of water cascading over the lip of the roof.

"Yeah, a real gully-washer," Ed said. He moved to the edge of the porch and scraped the mud from the bottom of his shoes.

"Ed, I need to talk to you about something." Ed looked at him.

"I hate to say this, Ed, but you're not focusing on your job like you should. I do understand and am sympathetic, but think you need more time off. You look terrible with those dark shadows around your eyes."

"I know." Ed shrugged. "I haven't pulled myself together very well since..." His voice trailed off.

"Well," Hutch said, giving him a friendly pat on the back, "you have vacation time coming. How about finishing up today, and then taking next week off? He cocked one eyebrow and waited while his question hung in the air.

"Yeah," Ed nodded. Hutch's tone was more a mandate than suggestion. "Maybe another week will pull me out of this. Thanks, Hutch. I'm headed inside to pick up my check. I'll let the clerk know. He gave his wet jacket a couple of shakes and stepped toward the office door.

He knew he was flubbing up at work. While admittedly it was over the loss of Maureen, it was also due to his pressing need to break into Gus' house but not feeling up to it yet. He had to get it done yet also needed time to grieve. Both were tearing at him. Now that he had a week coming, maybe he could get it done.

He'd check the board for Gus' work schedule. He should be working the late shift next week. If he broke in and found no evidence proving him Gunther Buford, he had no idea what his next move should be. Maybe his escape from prison would end up a lost cause.

He pushed the office door open, and gave a start. Gus stood at the front desk. He turned and looked at Ed, giving him a disdainful, half-twisted smile—almost smug-like. His expression gave Ed a bone-jangling effect. What did it mean? His thoughts flushed hot. He could come up with only one possible answer—Scratch's letter.

Even if Gus figured out it was bogus, he reasoned, it certainly didn't reveal he was Ed Bowman. Nevertheless, to be on the safe side, he'd look for it when he burglarized his house. Nodding an awkward hello, Ed maneuvered past him.

In the clerk's office, he sauntered over to the work board hanging on the wall. Running his gaze down the scheduling he looked for Gus's name. There. His late shift would be every night next week and end at two a.m. Perfect.

"Sorry," the clerk called, "checks didn't make it. They'll be here tomorrow for sure."

Disappointed, Ed moseyed back into the main office. He hesitated in case Gus was still there. He saw him give a thumbs-up to the man at the front desk and reach for the outside door to leave.

"Yep, gonna have a great weekend. Leavin' for Vegas tomorrow for a couple of days to hit the high spots." He closed the door behind him.

Good, Ed thought. He could break in sooner.

He reached for the door just as Bart came in with water dripping from the brim of his hat. They paused to speak in the doorway.

"Ed," he said in low tones, "I thought you should know Gus and Queenie have broken up."

Ed gave a start of surprise. "You sure?"

"That's the scuttlebutt. Maybe he'll let up on you now. Cowboy, too."

386

"Really? Thanks, Bart." Ed doubted they broke up.

"Scuse me." A voice came from the porch. "You guys are blocking the doorway and it's wet out here." A man pushed between them.

"Sorry." They stepped aside. Bart gave Ed a departing nod, and Ed stepped onto the porch to watch for a letup in the downpour.

He'd break in Monday night for sure. Since Queenie was back, he'd schedule their dinner date for Sunday, the night before, and get the picture and negative. He had to get Queenie's picture first. He wanted them before he ransacked Gus' house. Once Gus discovered Scratch's letter gone, he would definitely be his first suspect and try to get the picture from Queenie and send it to Salt Lake authorities.

He thought about his Sunday date with Queenie. Now that Maureen was gone, he doubted that his mentioning he was still in grief would stop Queenie from trying to seduce him. He'd have to figure up a good-sounding excuse for not staying long. Gossip spread fast in a small town. He didn't want anyone seeing him there too long and thinking he was shacking up with her. He'd give her a ring later and set it up.

He waited on the porch ten minutes for a break in the downpour and then hustled down the steps. Sprinting across the yard, still concerned about Queenie, he raced down the road toward home hoping to avoid a further cloudburst. What if she gives him the picture but refuses the negative? What then?

Ed barreled through his front door, beating the imminent downpour of rain. He had barely shut the door when the phone rang. Racing into the kitchen, he grabbed it up on the third ring.

"Hi there," came the sultry voice. "Just got back from Vegas today. I have your picture. How about dinner tonight?"

Ed's breath stalled in his throat. This was sooner than he planned.

"Tonight? What…what about…Gus?"

"No worry. He and I split up. Besides, I understand how hard it is to lose someone you love. I went through it once myself. We'll simply have a nice evening and talk. I know you're still hurting."

Her reassuring expression of sympathy warmed him. Was she telling the truth about Gus?

"Well…okay. But how about Sunday night instead? Gotta spend time on Harry's car, fix a flat tire and other things."

"Sure, hon. See you then."

CHAPTER 63

~~~

"C'mon in, Ed." Queenie smiled as she opened the door. She wore a low-cut blouse pulled down low on both shoulders, and just far enough to reveal her full cleavage. The bottom of her blouse was tucked into the waistline of a black taffeta skirt that rustled above her hose and high heels. She motioned him to come in. Ed took a full breath, stepped inside and looked around.

Queenie's cinderblock apartment was one of many clumped together at the base of Needle Point. Her apartment was exquisitely decorated with low-lit lamps, jet-black oriental figurines, and blonde furniture sitting on a blood-red carpet, all of which seemed out of place in Wendover. Yet, its other-worldliness captivated him. The only thing not blending with her décor was a black and white Felix-the-cat clock hanging on the wall with its swinging, pendulum-tail and synchronized eyes tick-tocking back and forth.

"Have a seat, hon," she said, pointing to a chair at the dining room table. "Dinner is ready. You just relax while I bring everything out."

She disappeared into the kitchen. Ed immediately scanned the top of every piece of furniture for a single snapshot or a yellow Kodak envelope. Nothing.

Queenie made a couple of trips to the kitchen and back. Soon, the table was loaded with a delectable feast—roast chicken, gravy, dressing, and biscuits.

"I'll get the picture for you after we eat," she said, scooting out a chair and sitting down.

It was a sumptuous meal and Ed ate with gusto, including two pieces of lemon meringue pie. He had to admit it was the best he'd had since Maureen died. He hadn't realized how much he missed the companionship of a woman and a home-fixed meal.

When finished, he helped her clear up the table. Queenie donned an apron and filled the sink with soapy water.

"Tell me more about Maureen," she said. "I didn't know her

well. Seemed like a real nice lady."

Relaxing, Ed told her about how they met, and how she contracted polio when a child. Queenie, he noticed, appeared genuinely sympathetic. It felt good to be around someone who cared. Maybe the evening wouldn't turn out as bad as he feared. Yet, a nagging inside suggested otherwise. He pushed it aside.

He continued to share his and Maureen's future plans, her death, the funeral, and Don explaining the necessity of Mormon temple work to get the dead person out of spirit prison. He even mentioned Don wanting him to join the Mormon Church. He deliberately threw that in, knowing Queenie wasn't the church type. It might work as a deterrent to any further plans she might have about a future with him.

"Have you decided?" she asked.

"Nope. Got to figure some things out in my mind yet—especially that spirit prison thing. Then, there are all those angels appearing to Joseph Smith. Not sure whether I believe that or not."

They finished the dishes, and then sauntered into the front room. With dinner over, he knew he'd better plan his exit. Ed patted his stomach.

"Queenie, it was a great dinner but I really should be going. I'm, uh, expecting an important telephone call later this evening. So, if you have the picture? And about the picture, I was wondering if—"

"Oh, Ed," she said with annoyance. "Don't be in such a rush." She walked over to a spindle-legged desk, pulled open a small drawer and pulled out the snapshot. She shoved the drawer shut but not before Ed recognized the yellow Kodak envelope inside. The negatives had to be in it.

Moving back to the couch, she placed the photo on the end table, out of reach.

"Now, c'mon, hon," she purred, nudging him down onto the couch. She reached for a decanter and poured two goblets of an alcoholic drink over crackling ice cubes and held one out to him. "Just a few minutes and then you can go." She sat down next to him. Ed hesitated.

"Don't be such a prude, Ed." She ran her smooth fingers down the side of his face, ending with a small tug at the collar of his shirt.

The knot in Ed's stomach crunched tighter. Her touch felt good. Even with all her sympathetic talk, he knew the bedroom was next on the agenda, yet he needed to play along for a few more minutes. He couldn't leave until he had the negative.

He glanced at Felix. Its eyes shifted back and forth as if shaking its head and rhythmically ticking a warning him. No...no...no...no.

Stupid, he thought. *It's just a clock.*

Ed took the goblet. Joyce Anderson's Sunday school lesson about the evils of alcohol and tea keeping one out of heaven leapt out at him. *Crazy,* he thought. He wasn't a member. No reason to feel guilty. He'd take a little—just enough to pacify Queenie. He took a few sips, but it had been so long since he'd indulged he immediately felt a rush of wooziness.

"Whoa, Queenie. This is really something!"

She laughed. "In Vegas, we call it a Scorpion. Really yummy." She downed her glass, then poured herself another and then another, growing drunker by the minute.

Ed's opportunity came when she rose unsteadily from the couch, her speech slurred.

"You'll 'scuse me a minute, won't you?" Leaning over, she ran her fingers through his hair, pulled a lock down on his forehead and dragged one finger over his lips.

"I'll be right back," she whispered, bending down even closer. Ed gawked as she sauntered away, her voluptuous hips swaying beneath the swishing folds of her taffeta skirt, her perfume hanging heavy in the air.

Once gone, Ed's mind cleared. Leaping up, he sprinted across the room and pulled open the desk drawer. Grabbing the Kodak envelope, he opened the flap. There were at least ten or more negatives. Which one? No time to hold them up to the light. Taking them out, he crammed all of them into his hip pocket, replaced the envelope, and closed the drawer. He darted back to the couch just in time.

Queenie reappeared in the doorway, paused for effect, and then seductively glided into the room.

Ed sucked in a gasp. His eyes traveled from her bare legs gleaming white through the opening of her black, silk robe, and then up her shapely form to the low neckline of a lacy, black negligee. Her breasts were barely covered by the sheer chiffon, and their creamy white curves rhythmically rolled and undulated as she sensuously moved toward him. A flush of heat crept through him.

"Getting late, honey." Her voice came low.

She sashayed closer and leaned over, letting her negligee fall open even more. "Why don't you stay the night? Wouldn't it feel good to be held...caressed? You've been through so much pain," she cooed. A pulsing ache started in his loins. His face felt hot.

"I should be going..." He made no move to rise. He pictured holding her, feeling her naked body next to his, making love. Could he capture what he had hoped to consummate with Maureen—close his eyes and pretend? He struggled with the burning tidal waves that surged through his body. Then a numbing thought tore through his head, making his skin prickle.

What if Gus put her up to this? What if she lied about breaking up with him? Maybe he concocted a plan with her to get him to stay the night then, while asleep, a swift knife to the throat...

"I've got to go!" he blurted. Jumping to his feet, he grabbed the photo from the table and rounded the end of the couch, knocking over a chair in the process.

"Good grief, Ed," Queenie snapped, her face crimped in annoyance, "I don't bite, you know!"

Ed had already yanked the front door open and bolted outside. He rushed to his car, at the same time shooting a quick glance into the surrounding shadows for Gus. He saw no one. Yanking the car door open, he jumped into the seat and started the engine. With tires spinning in the gravel, he peeled out.

Speeding across town, the air whipped through the open window cooling his feverish face. He just may have saved his life—literally. At least he had the picture and the negatives.

He pulled into Maureen's driveway, parked the car in the garage, and barreled into the house. Once inside, he slumped onto the couch.

He pictured Gus' reaction when Queenie told him their plan fell through. That is, if they were indeed in cahoots. He hoped he was wrong. Who knew?

He hoped no one saw him leave. Wendover's grapevine traveled with lightning speed. His reputation would be the talk of the town, not to mention the ward. He sure didn't want that. He couldn't jeopardize his friendship with Don. He needed him in case of a possible showdown with the sheriff.

Not knowing for sure what connection, if any, Queenie and Gus had, he needed to avoid her. Could he be that strong? He took a deep breath. She had a way about her that was hard to resist. Tonight was a good example. It also told him a lot about himself.

Undressing, he fell into bed, only to toss and turn. When he closed his eyes, all he could see was Queenie in her black negligee. If she and Gus really did split up, she was fair game. He was lonely, and...

Am I crazy? He bolted straight up. It would foul up everything. There was only one way to get Queenie off his mind—dream of Maureen.

He tried.

It didn't work.

CHAPTER 64

~~~

Monday, the dreaded evening came. Ed was on pins and needles waiting for midnight. The time loomed nearer and nearer. He checked the clock. 11:15 p.m. Tonight was his Rubicon. He would prove whether Gus was Buford or not.

He rehearsed his plan, making sure all the tools he needed were in his bag, checked the dark clothes he had on to be sure they were dark enough, timed everything so he'd be through before Gus got off work at 2 a.m., and where to look once inside his house so as not to waste time.

What if Gus' schedule changed the last minute and he came home and found him? His insides clenched to the point of nausea.

He got up from the couch and paced around the kitchen, then through the front room and back again, bolstering himself with the fact that if he found what he was looking for it would all be over. Gus would be sent back to prison. Sarah's death would be avenged. He'd be exonerated and have his old life back.

He dropped onto the couch and looked at the clock again. Thirty minutes to go. Twenty...ten...

With nerves at full stretch, he left the house precisely at midnight, zipping his jacket against the chilly breeze. Only a few stars glittered overhead.

He wore black pants and a navy blue windbreaker, the darkest clothes he could find, and clutched the handle of a small bag containing a flashlight and tools. To say he was apprehensive was putting it mildly.

Despite the pall of trepidation hanging over him, he had worked all the details to perfection and felt confident he would not only get Scratch's letter back but also find paperwork linking Gus with Gunther Buford and the murder of the warden's daughter.

Snaking from street to street, he peered through the thick shadows listening for sounds. Aside from the faint sighing of cottonwood limbs eerily hanging over the shadowed street, all was quiet. Not even the howl of a dog.

He knew exactly where Gus lived—the east side of town near the black water tower. Gus' house was in the old section. In a small town everyone knew where everybody lived.

The neighborhood dated back to when the railroad first came to town in the early 1900s. It consisted of congested conglomerations of trailer homes and shacks shoved so tightly next to each other it was a wonder there was any air in-between to breathe. The dirt roads and pathways were rutted, ill lighted, and meandered in and out like streams of water following the path of least resistance.

Fixing his eyes ahead, he skulked across the clearing in front of the post office, slithered past the Tri-State Merc, rounded the corner and sinuously moved down the road passing the water tank and Bum's Jungle where hobos built their campfires.

One more block to go.

He crept through the narrow spaces between trailers and shacks with their rusty, corrugated roofs, breathing in the last remnant of fried chicken and smell of cigarette smoke and beer. Weaving through the darkened yards he kept close to the willows until he spied Gus's house.

The single-story stuccoed building was better than the other residences. Definitely not the Waldorf, but for this section of town considered pretty good. Not much could be said about the yard, but that was normal for Wendover. He checked for Gus' car—nowhere in sight. The windows were dark.

Dread, like a vice grip, tightened his chest and for a split second fear froze his feet to the ground. He took a slow, deep breath, and moved forward with resolve. Skulking into the backyard, he sidled from tree to tree, studying every shadow and listening for sounds.

Squatting close to the ground, he crabbed forward on all fours to the back entrance and carefully inched the screen door open. He grimaced as the coiled spring creaked, piercing the dark quiet of the air. Slowly, he turned the knob to the door. Unlocked. Not uncommon. He wouldn't have to use his tools. Good. Less noise.

He pulled the flashlight from his bag. Flipping it on, he eased into the darkness of the kitchen. Keeping the beam low to the floor, he inched his way across the linoleum and tiptoed through the house until he entered the front room. The stale smell of smoke and ash immediately rushed into his nostrils.

With a flick of his wrist he swept the light across the room to the fireplace that contained smoldering remains of a fire. At the same time, he spied a card table with a pile of loose papers on top. He bolted forward.

Holding the flashlight at an angle, he spread the papers apart on the table with one hand, and with the other fingered through receipts and bills looking for Scratch's letter and anything else of importance. Nothing.

He slunk over to the end table by the easy chair and pulled the small drawer out. Nothing but a pack of cigarettes, matches and nail-clippers. He swung the beam around the room and studied the blue, wallpapered walls. No pictures to hide anything behind.

He moved silently into the bathroom whipping the shaft of light around at the pink and mauve-painted walls, then to the basin. He gave a pleasant start of surprise. On the counter sat a bottle of black hair dye. If he remembered anything from the trial it was Gunther's streak of white hair. But it wasn't proof enough for the sheriff.

He navigated back into the front room and moved quietly toward a nearby door that stood ajar and inched it open. The hinge squeaked in the black silence.

Inside stood a rumpled bed and a dresser. Shirts and trousers were draped over two chairs and dirty socks were strewn about on the floor. He hurriedly went through every pocket of the shirts and pants. Nothing.

Hustling over to the dresser, he pulled each drawer open and dug his hands beneath everything. Only underwear, socks, work pants and toiletries. He scrunched his brow, perplexed.

Now, if he were Gus where would he hide Scratch's letter?

Ah!

He bolted over to the bed and hurled back the blankets. Lifting the top corner of the mattress, he held it in place with his shoulder while he ran his arm in as far as he could. Working his way down to the foot of the bed, he felt something. Withdrawing a manila envelope, he let the mattress drop back down.

Propping the flashlight on the bed covers, he opened the envelope and pulled out an eight-by-eleven sheet of paper. He immediately recognized Scratch's letter. Relief washed through him. What else? He gaped in surprise—a snapshot of a woman. Former wife? A daughter?

He thrust his hand back into the envelope and retrieved a small object. An earring. He turned it over in his hand and scrutinized it. Encrusted with some kind of black gunk, he rubbed some of it off with his finger. A large emerald with rubies graced the center with a border of mother-of-pearl encircling the perimeter. He raised one eyebrow.

Why would Gus have a lady's earring—and only one? Had he been married? Why take the pains to hide it? Somehow, he puzzled, it had to be connected to Buford.

It didn't take long before he widened his eyes, recalling the day at the courthouse when he eavesdropped on the conversation between the attorneys.

"The sales clerk claims to have sold a one-of-a-kind set of earrings to Buford that supposedly matches the single earring left on the victim's body."

Ed stared at the object. Could this possibly be the missing one?

He rubbed more of the gunk off. Was this dried stuff, blood? Could be. He gave himself a jubilant smile. *I got you now, Gunther Buford.*

But even though a great find, as far as the sheriff went, an earring wouldn't prove Gus' identity. Neither would a bottle of black dye.

He placed the earring and Scratch's letter back in the envelope, folded it and shoved it into his jacket pocket. He needed something more concrete. Some kind of paperwork—a birth certificate or proof of employment when Gus was a guard at the pen. Would Gus still keep something like that around? *No, he'd destroy it.*

Sprinting back to the fireplace, he shined the flashlight into the mass of ashes. Had that been the purpose for the fire? He knelt and leaned in, letting out a cough as the smoky odor rushed into the back of his throat.

Half holding his breath, he saw a few curled-up, scorched sheets of paper with the corners unburned and still intact. He looked closer and detected fancy scrollwork at the edges. A birth certificate? He remembered the one Scratch forged for him with a similar border. Pulling out his penknife, he carefully moved some of the delicate ashes. He grimaced. They fell apart.

He continued poking around, carefully lifting the blackened sheets aside with his knife, only to have them crumble. His heart sank. All of them were beyond salvaging.

He started to stand when he noticed the burned remains of a single sheet of paper blown off to one side by the chimney draft. About a fourth was left unburned. It appeared salvageable. He carefully examined it and made out the last part of one word...*rion*. Below it was part of another word, *circula*... Goose bumps formed. His *Clarion* article? He was sure of it. He pulled the manila envelop from his pocket and gingerly slid the piece in.

But why did Gus feel the necessity to burn this since there were no pictures of him in the article to identify him as Buford? Further, he was positive Gus didn't suspect he was Ed Bowman. He must have decided to simply get rid of everything that connected him to Virginia.

A muffled noise sounded outside in front of the house. Ed jerked his head up. Did a neighbor see his flashlight through the window? Had Gus left work early? Panic seized him.

Jumping up, he rushed across the front room, shot through the kitchen and out the back door. Scrambling across the yard, he ducked behind a shed and peered around the corner. He saw no one. Nevertheless, he needed to get out of there fast.

He moved with lightning speed between the shadowed cottonwoods, bounding from trailer-yard to trailer-yard like a rock skipping on water, then past the tower and Bums Jungle until the conglomeration of homes was left behind.

Tearing down the main road, rain started pelting his face. He passed the Merc, turned the corner, and cut in front of the Post Office. Four blocks yet to home.

Three...two...one.

He flew through the front yard gate, zipped around to the back and yanked the screen door open just as volleying claps of thunder shook the house and rain fell in torrents. Locking the hook-and-eye latch behind him he sank to the floor, his chest heaving.

After tense minutes of regaining his breath, he felt his way in the dark on hands and knees through the kitchen and into the front room. Pulling himself up onto the couch he leaned back into the cushions and relaxed—or at least tried to. Gus would discover the theft when he got home and know for sure he did it.

Nevertheless, despite the trauma of his undertaking, he felt pleased at what he found—the bottle of dye, Scratch's letter, and evidence the *Clarion* article and other documents possibly identifying Gus as Buford had purposely been burned. His most important find? The missing earring. He felt strongly it had to belong to the warden's daughter.

He pulled the envelope from his jacket and carefully slid his fingers to the bottom. Withdrawing the earring, he leaned forward and studied it in the stream of moonlight coming through the front window. If it was in fact *the* earring, what could he do about it?

He couldn't take it to Kevin and explain it might be the missing earring from a five-year-old murder that occurred in another state... that he wasn't really Ed Riley but Ed Bowman, a reporter unjustly convicted for his wife's murder that Gunther Buford committed... or that he escaped prison to prove Kevin's friend, Gus Moreland, was actually Buford and guilty of not only one murder, but two.

Kevin could jump to the wrong conclusion by his being in possession of the earring—that *he* was the murderer, and that his motive was to frame Gus to eliminate him as a competitor over Queenie's affections. He slumped forward.

No, there was nothing he could do about any of what he found. It could all work against him. But, at least his suspicions were validated. Gus Moorland was Gunther Buford.

At work tomorrow he would come face to face with Sarah's killer.

The man who destroyed his life.

CHAPTER 65

~~~

Tuesday morning Ed trod across the yard toward the trainmaster's building, arriving mid-morning to pick up his delayed check. His stomach felt like a volcano about to erupt. No way did he want to run into Gus. Not after last night. The thought he might, nearly unglued him.

Breaking into Gus' house produced an unsettling effect on him. Yes, he got Scratch's letter back and now had the bloodied earring of the warden's daughter, Sue Davis. At least he assumed it was hers. If right, Gus would have an even stronger determination to kill him and get it back.

He reached the wood porch and took the first step up when he spied Gus across the yard. He was leaning against the old Deep Creek Railroad building. Ed's breath went shallow. He looked like a thundercloud and stared at him with a smoldering, threatening kind of look.

Shudders jangled through Ed all the way to his toes. Why wasn't Gus out with the gang?

He looked away from the venomous gaze and climbed the rest of the steps onto the porch feeling Gus' eyes still drilling into his back. He glanced back. Fortunately, Gus remained where he was and made no move.

Ed shoved the office door open. He needed to hide what he stole. What if Gus broke into Maureen's house while he was away on one of his drives to Elko and found it? He clamped his mouth into a tight line. He'd have to squirrel it away so well there'd be no way. And he needed to do it—fast.

"Hey there, Ed." Hutch waved from the hallway. "A few days off and you're already looking better." Ed nodded and smiled, returning the wave.

He picked up his check, hurried home and retrieved the envelope hidden in the back of his closet. Folding the envelope as small as possible, he also included the snapshot and negative he took from Queenie's apartment and the picture Bob Wilkinson sent of Buford. He dumped out his accumulation of loose change from a large Sir Walter Raleigh tobacco tin and stuffed the envelope inside.

Hustling through the kitchen and out to the screened-in back porch, he grabbed a crowbar and pried up a loose floorboard. Gus would never find it here.

Dropping the can into the cavity he replaced the board, grabbed one of Maureen's multi-colored rag-rugs and threw it on top. He sagged back against the wall. How might Gus retaliate? He felt nauseous.

He could only wait the week out and see.

CHAPTER 66

~~~

Lil grabbed Cowboy's sleeve and held tight.

"Stop! Don't do it. The money's not worth this."

"Shut up!" He shook away her grasp, his face clenched like a fist, and stomped out the door of the small bungalow situated behind the A-1. Lil followed.

"This time I gotta do it right or Gus says he won't pay me. I'm fed up to the teeth with his overbearing tirades, being chewed out, and told I'm incompetent." He strode toward his car, glancing as he did at the sun now smoldering close to the horizon.

"Tonight's it. This'll be the end of my dealing with that man and then I'm outta here."

"What do you mean by that," Lil croaked with a surprised look.

"Never you mind." He yanked the car door open and jumped in. Revving up the engine he shoved it into gear, then took off, tires spinning, leaving Lil swathed in a choking swirl of grit and gravel.

Cutting in front of the restaurant, he gave the steering wheel a hard twist to the right and roared his Chevy onto the highway and sped toward Three Mile Hill. He arrived in ten minutes flat and gunned the car up the steep dirt road leading to the plateau. He parked where he had a birds-eye view of the highway below and could see the headlights of any vehicle driving in from Nevada.

According to Gus, Ed would be returning about now. His yellow-paneled railroad truck would be easy to spot. He glanced at the sky. That is, if the oncoming rain clouds stayed put.

Squirming into one position then another, he tapped his fingers in rapid succession against the steering wheel.

"C'mon, Ed Riley. Time to meet your maker."

CHAPTER 67

~~~

Ed sped his yellow-paneled truck across the last leg of the Nevada desert toward Wendover. Exhausted, he stiffened his arms out and braced them against the steering wheel, pressing his aching spine into the back of the car seat. It had been a tiring trip with maintenance stops at Tobar, Shafter and other places.

He peered through the top half of the windshield at the sky, now a mishmash of slate and mustard yellow, then at the bone black clouds churning over Three Mile Hill that was spreading an aphotic darkness over the landscape. He could smell the oncoming rain.

He felt safe on the open stretch of highway with nothing but flat desert and sagebrush all around. Neither Gus nor Cowboy could sneak up on him without being seen.

That didn't mean they wouldn't try something—even during the night while he slept. He planned to put stick-braces in his windows to prevent them from being opened from the outside.

Cresting Silver Zone Pass, he spied Three Mile Hill ahead. From there it would be a short glide down into Wendover. He loved the hill. It was high up on the plateau where Maureen pointed out the salt flats in the distance to show him the curvature of the earth. He'd stop for a few minutes. Get his mind off things. He wouldn't go to the top, just park along the shoulder. He'd still have a good view.

Slowing down, he pulled off the blacktop across from the dirt road that led up to the plateau. He turned the motor off, leaned back in the seat and took in the panoramic view. As usual, it was spectacular.

For five minutes he watched the lights of houses come on one by one. Extending his gaze to the far side of town, he followed the ribbon of highway leading out of Wendover. The headlights of cars, like scatterings of small stars, moved across the salt flats heading east for Grantsville, Tooele and Salt Lake. He thought of the Burma

Shave signs Maureen enjoyed, one in particular. *He played a sax, had no B.O., but his whiskers scratched so she let him go.* He smiled, pulled out his red bandana and blotted his eyes.

Sliding out from under the steering wheel he moved over into the passenger seat to stretch out his weary legs. He glanced to his left at the darkening road leading to the top of Three Mile Hill. Waves of nostalgia swept over him. The plateau was used as a lover's lane. He and Maureen went up there more than once to sit in the dark and be romantic.

"Ed, God brought us together," she so often whispered in his ear. "He also arranged for you to get your railroad job. And dear, I know he's forgiven you for your part in Benny's death."

He winced about that. He hadn't kept his promise to Benny yet. He'd written a dozen drafts of letters and then thrown them away. He couldn't bring himself to tell his mama he participated in the whipping that led to her son's death. Maybe by the time he received information from the California ad, he'd have the perfect letter written. Perhaps God was waiting to forgive him when he actually mailed it.

The roar of a car's motor sliced through the stillness. Ed whipped his head to the left. He saw the silhouette of a car with no headlights rumbling down from the plateau toward the highway. Ed relaxed and chuckled. *Absent-minded lovers.* The driver would switch them on before he reached the bottom. He'd have to in order to make the turn onto the highway.

Ed kept watching the car as it pummeled down, picking up speed. Ed flexed tight. If the driver didn't switch on his lights soon to make the turn, he'd plow straight across the road and into him.

He flipped on his headlights, grabbed the shift knob and shoved it into first. Stomping on the accelerator he shot the truck back onto the blacktop and headed downhill toward Wendover. Concerned, he slowed, watching in the rear view mirror. If the car didn't make it and wrecked, he'd be close by to help.

The dark vehicle careened down the last leg of the hill, still with no lights, and miraculously hurtled a sharp left onto the highway without tipping over. Ed breathed an audible sigh but kept watching.

"Crazy kids. Why don't they turn their lights on?"

The car came faster. Soon it was tailgating him. From the shape of the car silhouetted against the skyline, it was a Chevy. He made out the darkened figure of a lone man at the wheel. So much for lovebirds, but why doesn't he pass? Ed rolled the window down and stuck his arm out, motioning the driver to go around him.

The car sped up and slammed hard into his bumper. Ed widened his eyes. "Wha... the guy must be drunk." The A-1 Star was another mile. He'd pull in there and let the driver pass him into town. He floor-boarded the pedal. The Chevy did the same.

Pulling alongside Ed's left rear fender, the driver veered a sharp right, smashing into him again. Ed lost control of his vehicle and spun around whipping the steering wheel to the left and right. He tipped on two wheels, skidded off the highway, and zoomed off the road and out across the rough sagebrush.

Jamming on the brakes, he came to a stop fifty yards away and immediately flipped his headlights off. No way could the guy see him now. Too dark. Would the driver come looking for him?

He sat breathlessly trying to quell the hundred-mile-an-hour thumping of his heart. This was no random drunk driver. How stupid to think he'd be safe on maintenance runs when he was dealing with a man desperate to escape the electric chair.

The Chevy looked like Cowboy's, but the outline of the driver's head didn't indicate a hat. It also wasn't Gus' car. Who else could it be? Still, his gut said, "Cowboy." It had to be. Based on Bart's report, they were in cahoots. If killed on the highway, Gus could then get into Maureen's house and search for the earring.

A clap of thunder sounded. The angry shrouds of clouds burst open and a torrent of rain fell in heavy, pewter-griseous drops peltering his windshield.

He watched the highway through the blur of rain. The car's red taillights headed down the grade. He wasn't coming back and his headlights were now on. Would he stop at the A-1 to lay in wait for him and try to finish the job? He kept watching. To his relief, the Chevy continued on into town.

Ed turned his lights on, started the engine, and gave the accelerator a punch. He jounced back over the wet sagebrush and onto the highway.

Driving down the hill he cruised past the A-1 and entered

town, passing the Stateline Hotel. He scrutinized the parking lot and gas station. No Chevy. He examined both sides of the street until he turned right off the main highway onto the road leading to Maureen's house. He checked his rear view. No one appeared to be following.

Pulling up in front of his house he turned the engine off and leaned wearily into the back of the seat. He stared at the rivulets running down the dirt-caked windshield and listened to the rain pulsating on the roof. Once more he'd been lucky. He let out a heavy groan. It wouldn't hold out forever.

Grabbing his lunch bucket off the seat he slid out of the truck, first looking warily about as he did, and then dashed up the walk to the front door.

Once inside, he locked the door behind him and then flipped the light switch on. He stood lifeless for a moment, his back against the door, shoulders slumped. Mentally, he sifted through everything that had happened—not only tonight but since he came to Wendover—the shootings, the boiler explosion, fierce encounters with Gus, then tonight's close call.

He had to face it. His goal to bring Gunther Buford to justice simply wasn't materializing, and he was fast reaching the point where he was tired and worn out from it all.

Fatigue oozed from every pore as he sauntered into the kitchen. He placed his lunch bucket on the sink and sank wearily into one of the kitchen chairs. Leaning forward, he placed his elbows on the table and cradled his head in his hands.

Things were coming down to the wire now. Gus was doubling his efforts knowing he had the earring. Tonight was evidence of that. The next time, one of these murderous attempts was going to prove successful. He straightened up to stretch a kink in his back. Maybe he needed to get the heck out of Dodge.

It was definitely decision time. He needed to face reality. He had failed in his mission to avenge Sarah's death and get his old life back. It simply wasn't going to happen. He was glad his mama wasn't around to see her Bible scripture hadn't worked.

The brooding hurt welled up deep inside. He scooted his chair out from the table and stood.

Yes, he'd leave and get on with his life as best he could. With

Maureen gone there was nothing holding him here. He'd of course need a job. Keddie seemed to offer the answer. He'd call Harry tomorrow and have him watch for an opening. How long it would take, he didn't know. If he could hang in until he heard back, and avert any next attempt on his life, he'd make it. In the meantime he'd move out of Maureen's house and the memories and go back to his section house. It was still empty and would make leaving easier. He'd let Hutch know, and spend two nights after work to make the move.

He sauntered over to the sink and pulled the thermos out from under the wire clamp of his lunch bucket. Dumping out the leftover cocoa, he turned on the faucet, rinsed it out and placed it upside down in the rubber dish rack.

What if nothing opened in Keddie? That would leave him with only one option. He rubbed the back of his neck in resignation. He'd have to split on his own without the prospects of employment and incur the painful scenario of ducking the law and trying to find a new job again. He expelled a bone-weary sigh.

He set the wood braces in the windows, flipped out the lights and dragged himself into the bedroom. Undressing, he dropped exhausted into bed.

Reaching under his pillow, he slid his fingers across the barrel of the new handgun he purchased at the Merc. He imagined Gus breaking in and their having a final showdown. He could shoot him and claim self-defense. That fantasy felt good.

But no—not good. Gus had to be captured alive. It was the only way Ed Bowman could be exonerated. He let out a despondent groan.

He rolled over, closed his eyes and tried to sleep, but his emotions from the night's attack refused to settle down. His decision to leave Wendover also bothered him. He wanted to go, but stared up at the dark ceiling in a quandary about it.

After spending so much effort to track Buford to Wendover, should he stay and hope some break might still present itself?

He rolled over. No. He had followed all avenues to identify Buford and had reached a dead end. Further, he was sick and tired of living this kind of life—worrying when the next shot, explosion, or car accident would do him in.

He dozed off, his hand beneath the pillow resting on his gun, wondering how Gus would react tomorrow when he saw him still alive.

CHAPTER 68

~~~

Friday, the day broke gray and chilly. Now back in his section house, rain, like an artillery barrage, beat a steady tattoo on the roof. It staccatoed against the windows, gushed from the eaves, and gurgled down the metal gutters. With it came the wind. It roared through the chimney and rattled the damper in the flue until Ed thought he'd go crazy from the infernal racket.

Weary from lack of sleep and still nerve-racked over the Three Mile Hill attempt on his life, he readied himself for work feeling like the title page of an obituary. With all the attempts to kill him, and finding nothing to put the clincher on Gus' identity without risking his own freedom, he'd reached the end of his rope.

Well, he had definitely made his decision. Soon, he'd be out of Wendover and away from Gus and Cowboy. All he had to do until then was take extra precautions until he was able to leave. To continue working for the railroad, Keddie was the answer. He needed to call Harry right away.

Moving over to the telephone he lifted the receiver and dialed. Harry answered.

"Harry? Yeah, I'm doing fine. Say, I'm thinking of transferring out of Wendover. Will you keep an eye out and let me know about any job openings in Keddie before they get posted?"

"Sure will, Ed. It'll be great to have you up here."

"By the way, Harry, what should I do about your car?"

"Oh, you can just have it, Ed. Consider it a gift for being so good to sis."

"Wow, thanks so much. And by the way, I've moved back to my section house.

"That's fine, Ed. Think I'll sell the house. I'll keep in touch and let you know about any openings as soon as I hear."

Ed hung up feeling half good and half guilty. Good that he made the decision to distance himself from Wendover and not worry about his life being snuffed out, but also guilty because he was giving up. Again, he was glad his mama wasn't around to see it.

He donned his raincoat and slipped on his galoshes. Gus would probably hear from Cowboy some time today letting him know he failed last night. What disaster would they plan next? A bomb in his maintenance truck?

He snatched up his umbrella, irritated he had to walk to work in the weather. Harry's car had developed a screeching noise in the engine, serious enough he felt he shouldn't use it until it was looked at.

Grabbing his lunch bucket from the kitchen counter, he tread wearily out the door. Claps of thunder sounded and lightning cracked across the sky. Gusts of rain swept beneath his umbrella and showered his face. By the time he reached the dirt road in front of the Merc, the downpour of rain had turned the ground into a mucky lake. The slushy mud nearly suctioned his galoshes off his shoes.

Shivering with the cold, he arrived at the depot. He squished across the water-logged yard in a fast pace toward the trainmaster's building, trying to dodge the pelting sheets of rain that hit the ground like hails of bullets. Despite what had happened and what still might happen, he had to admit he looked forward to running into Gus. He wanted to see his reaction at seeing him alive. It would at least confirm he and Cowboy were working together.

Leaping up onto the wood porch, he moved under the overhang, sniffing in the breakfast smells from the Beanery, imagining he detected Queenie's exotic perfume mixed in with the aromas. He fought the warmth spreading through his body and shook out his umbrella.

No way did he want to see her—not after the traumatic event at her apartment. At least he had the negative and the snapshot. That's all that mattered. He took a tremulous breath, his mind replaying Queenie in her black negligee. One more good reason for leaving Wendover. He entered the office.

Barely had he shut the door behind him when his breath quickened. Gus stood only six feet away from him at the front desk, his back to him. Ed didn't move. Gus would turn around in a minute, and then the look on his face would tell him if he was surprised he was alive.

"Thanks for your help, Scott." Gus shoved one arm into the sleeve of his jacket, pointing with the other to the paper in the clerk's hand. "Just remember, items one through four have to be expedited. The other two don't make no difference."

"Sure thing, Gus. Count it done."

Gus slid his other arm into his jacket and wheeled about. His head yanked back reflexively in a jerk of surprise. His eyebrows shot upward as his eyes met Ed's. He let out an expulsion of breath. It was all Ed needed.

"Mornin' Gus. Wrap up snug. It's a wet one out there."

Gus, despite his startled expression was quick on the pickup.

"Yep…it's a toad-strangler alright." He snapped up his jacket and lost no time pushing past Ed and stepping outside.

Ed headed for the locker room to stow his lunch bucket, giving himself a crisp nod and smile of satisfaction. He needed that confirmation. He hated to be in Cowboy's shoes when Gus chewed him out.

He clocked in. Maybe he shouldn't feel so smug. Gus, most likely, was determined his next plan wouldn't fail. He could be planning something this very minute and he might never reach Keddie. Luck couldn't be on his side all the time. He thought of his handgun and glad he bought it. Gus could try something in the middle of the night.

"Hey, Ed!" Bart's voice called from down the hall. "Got great news for you." He rushed forward, and then paused to look around to make sure they were alone.

"Let's have it, Bart." Ed gazed inquiringly. "I'm in the mood for some."

"Cowboy's gone…left town."

"Whoa!" Ed sucked in a surprised gasp. "That *is* good news. How come?"

"Don't know, except he left suddenly—didn't even give notice at work. I saw Lil at the Merc early this morning and she said he took off. Said he was going back east to look for work."

"Strange she didn't go with him."

"I raised the same question. She said she was through with him and she's leaving too. Gave her two-week notice to the A-1 and plans to move back to Nebraska. That's where her parents live."

Ed couldn't believe what he was hearing. He had a good guess why Cowboy left.

"Thanks so much, Bart, for letting me know."

"Glad to do it, Ed. I just hope Cowboy was the source of all your troubles and not Gus."

"Let's hope so." Ed gave him an appreciative smile.

Bart turned to go, and then whipped back around. He flashed him a serious look of concern.

"Now, Ed, you relax. Cowboy's gone. And remember, Gus and Queenie have split. He gave him a good-natured slap on the arm. He has no reason to be jealous of you anymore."

"Sure, Bart. Thanks again."

Ed exited the rear of the building thoughtfully sucking in his cheeks. Opening his umbrella, he headed for his truck shed. Cowboy being gone was good but that wouldn't stop Gus. It wasn't all about his jealousy anymore—the guy had more at stake than that. Fortunately, he hadn't identified him as Ed Bowman yet, but dollars to doughnuts he knew he was the one who burglarized his house and took the earring. He also remembered Gus' odious words the day they fought behind the shed.

"There's something else about you I can't put my finger on—but it'll come to me!"

Would he ever guess he was the reporter he believed he'd killed? He shuddered. It just might happen.

Reaching the shed he entered and probed under the hood of the truck first to make sure no wires were cut, and then scrutinized the brakes to check for tampering. He focused on all possibilities.

He thought of Bart's statement, *"Gus and Queenie have split up."* Queenie told him the same thing the evening he was at her apartment. Maybe she was telling the truth after all. No difference to him now. He was leaving and needn't worry about further contact. After running out on her the other night and taking the negatives, he sure wouldn't be hearing from her again.

Two days later Ed paced restlessly from room to room. Should he telephone Harry again...this soon? He didn't want to be a pest. Or should he forget Keddie and take off for parts unknown without waiting for his call?

The telephone rang. His heart leapt. He bolted across the room and grabbed up the receiver.

"Harry?"

"Hi there," purred the throaty voice.

Ed's jaw dropped. Queenie was the last person he expected to hear from.

"Hon, I really need to apologize about last week at my place. Guess I shouldn't have come on so strong. But," she teased, "you must know you're some hunk of a guy. Can you blame me?"

"I...appreciate your calling, Queenie." He visualized the night at her apartment, her bare legs gleaming milk-white through the slit in her robe, the top of her negligee falling open...

"I'm, uh, not feeling very well right now," he croaked, making his voice sound as hoarse as he could. "Think I'm coming down with something. Must be this weather."

"Gee, sorry to hear it, hon." Her voice was sympathetic. "I'll check with you later. Take care, and don't worry about the other evening."

"Sure...bye." He placed the receiver in the cradle and drew his eyebrows together in puzzlement.

For some reason she wasn't giving up—and she didn't even mention the negatives. Maybe she hadn't missed them yet. But sure as Carter has little liver pills he knew she'd be calling again. And she was a lot of woman for him to keep pushing away.

He emitted a heavy sigh. He thought of Maureen's warm kisses. What would it be like with Queenie? He had such an aching loneliness to have someone's arms around him...to feel loved. While he knew the attraction was only physical and she could never replace Maureen, could he be satisfied with that? He gave a swift kick at a small wastebasket, shooting it across the floor.

"I'm talking crazy to even think about her," he grumbled. Not only because of the morals his mama drilled into him, but because he was leaving Wendover. He could picture the gossip flying around town. Everyone would know, including Don. Until he left, keeping him on his good side was still a necessity.

Stomping into the kitchen, he yanked open the icebox door and grabbed a couple of eggs. Plopping a pat of butter into a frying pan, he broke the eggs into it, added milk, and began stirring.

Soon, his stirring advanced into a forceful thrashing of the eggs until they jumped over the edge of the pan and dripped into the burner. He wrenched the pan away and slid it to one side.

Why was he having such a difficult time fighting his attraction to Queenie, when his main concern was leaving Wendover and focusing on how to avoid a next disaster from Gus? Queenie would foul up his plans.

His attraction to her, he knew, was only because he missed Maureen's companionship. He was just grasping for a substitute.

He reached into the cupboard for his Breakfast of Champions and shook the Wheaties into a bowl.

Right now, he certainly had more to be worried about than her.

CHAPTER 69

~~~

The doodlebug pulled into the depot after its long day's run. Gus didn't wait for it to come to a full stop before leaping out. All he could think of was his shock at seeing Ed alive. He hustled around the building and across the yard, his face convulsed with anger at Cowboy's failure. This time he'd really chew him out.

Jumping into his car, he sped across town to the A-1 Star. Skidding up front, he hurriedly parked, and then rushed inside the café letting the door slam behind him. The Venetian blinds rattled and customers looked up.

With long strides he hustled toward the purple drapes. Pulling them aside, he entered the room and approached the dealer at the Black Jack table.

"Where's Cowboy?"

"Oh, he isn't here anymore."

"What do you mean," Gus exploded, "not here?" He felt heat engulf his face.

"Yeah, Gus. Surprised you didn't know. Just took off," he said, casually shrugging his shoulders. "In this business they come and go." He waved his hand in a dismissive gesture.

"Well, did he say where he was going?" Gus snapped.

"Nope." The man leaned over and reached under the table. "But he left you this letter—"

Gus grabbed it from the man's hand and stomped over to one of the booths and slid onto the seat. He wiped away the specs of saliva forming at the corners of his mouth and, grim-lipped, ripped open the envelope.

Gus, I'm not going to do your dirty work for you anymore. You're too hard to deal with. I don't mind killing, but that guy Riley has got nine lives. You're on your own.

Cowboy

Slamming his fist down on the table, Gus clenched and unclenched the note into a tight wad before shoving it into his shirt pocket.

417

"So, Riley's got nine lives, huh?" he muttered. Spasms of irritation rippled at the back of his throat. He scooted out of the booth and stood for a few seconds.

He didn't need Cowboy anymore. Knowing now Ed had been a prisoner in the same chain gang as Scratch, he had already notified Richmond authorities anonymously and sent them a picture. Queenie had given him a set of snapshots from the day they were at Blue Lake right after they were developed, including a picture of Ed. He also sent one to the Tooele police.

Once authorities identified Ed in the picture as an escapee, they would close in. He'd be caught and sent back to prison. With Ed eliminated, he'd not only have Queenie back but eliminate having any man in Wendover who hailed from the South—a necessary precaution. He gave himself a dry, one-sided smile, turned and strutted toward the exit.

You, Ed Riley, have breathed the last of your nine lives.

CHAPTER 70

~~~

Ed sauntered across the yard from the roundhouse after picking up a tool he had requisitioned. He started for his truck shed when he remembered Hutch had asked him to sign some papers in the payroll department due to some procedural change. He had time, so headed into the office. So far, he hadn't heard from Harry and the waiting was driving him crazy. He didn't know when Gus would strike next.

The clerk handed him the papers. In the middle of signing, Don sidled up alongside him.

"Great news, Ed."

"Yeah?" Ed turned. "What's up?"

The only time Don had something to say was usually about joining the church. He was definitely a man on a mission. This time, however, his tone sounded different.

Don patted him on the back. "C'mon in my office and I'll tell you all about it."

Ed handed the papers back to the clerk and followed Don, first looking about to see if Gus was around. He felt somewhat puzzled. Ever since Cowboy left town, Gus had ignored him at work—no mean glares and no attempts on his life. Of course this was a relief, but something wasn't right. He knew better than to think Gus had given up.

"Grab a seat." Don pointed to a straight-backed chair in his office and shut the door. Quick-stepping to the other side of his desk, he sat down and leaned forward, his elbows atop the desktop, both hands fisted under his chin. "I think you're going to like this."

Ed studied Don's cat-like Cheshire grin. He looked like he had swallowed the canary of all canaries.

"Ed, you're not going to believe what I received special permission to do in your behalf." He leaned back in his swivel chair, clasped his hands behind his head and purposely waited for a reaction.

His behalf? Ed would play along. It would at least get his mind on something else besides his anxiety over not hearing from Harry. He scooted forward onto the edge of his chair and arched both eyebrows, feigning interest.

"Well, Don, you sure have my attention." Don looked pleased.

"Ed, I have no doubt you're going to join the church at some point—

Ed mentally slumped. He should have known.

"Well, Don, I haven't come to any conclu..."

"Oh, I know all that, Ed." He gave a wave of dismissal. "Just relax. No pressure. I just wanted to tell you something I think will make you happy."

Ed cocked his head, his interest now piqued.

"Once in a while, in special circumstances," Don began, "the name of a deceased person can be sent in for temple work by a bishop even though the person involved, such as yourself, isn't a member yet. With your permission and my signature, this can be done for Maureen. If she accepts the work, she won't remain in spirit prison."

Don's words shocked him with as much intensity as the *zaaap-clack-clack-clack* of a cattle prod. He hadn't expected this. Ed sat speechless for a few seconds.

"But, Don..." Ed scrunched his face into a puzzled look. "You know she didn't want to become a Mormon, although Joyce Anderson did tell me once that when a person gets on the other side and sees the Mormon Church is true they regret having rejected it."

"Yep, Ed. You got that right."

Ed wrestled with both positive and negative thoughts about any consideration of Don's idea.

"Well, all I know..." Ed paused, sat back and sawed one index finger across his lower lip, "...Maureen was pretty adamant about her stand against the church—although I have to admit any talk about heaven intrigues me. What does 'temple work' mean specifically?"

Don immediately shifted into his serious, bishop-tone. He looked Ed squarely in the eye.

"Certain things go on in the temple I can't discuss because they're sacred, but I can tell you a little bit.

"Maureen would be baptized by proxy by a female temple worker. Then she would go through the endowment ceremony and experience everything through the eyes and ears of the temple worker going through in her place.

"She will also receive a new name. When the day comes you join the church..." Don smiled and gave Ed a half wink. "...you'll qualify to go through the temple and be married to her. When you do, you'll be told what her name is so you can call her forth in the resurrection as your wife. We're talking here, Ed, about marriage for eternity. Not just till death do you part.

"There are special rooms through which the endowment ceremony proceeds. First, there's the Garden of Eden room with murals of beautiful landscapes, waterfalls, birds and flowers—all representing the earth before the fall. Next, there are rooms representing the three heavens—the Telestial, the Terrestrial, last of all, the Celestial—"

"But Don," Ed interrupted, "besides looking at beautiful murals what are the rooms good for? I mean, what takes place in them?"

Don opened a desk drawer and withdrew a colored picture of the multi-spired Salt Lake Temple and held it up.

"Ed, in there," he pointed to the picture, "she'll receive special passwords that will allow her to leave spirit prison and bypass the angels who guard the entrance to heaven. No one but those who go through the temple know those words,"

"Now, wait a minute, Don." Ed weighed it with a critical squint of disbelief. "You mean if one isn't a Mormon and they don't know the passwords, they don't get into heaven?" He stared at Don, unbelieving, but didn't wait for an answer. He pushed on.

"First of all," he explained with a wave of his open palm, "Maureen knew her Bible and she didn't say it mentioned anything about needing to know passwords."

"Ah, Ed." Don leaned back in his chair. "The beauty of the tokens, passwords and signs of the holy priesthood can only be appreciated by those who go through the temple and understand modern-day revelation. God revealed to Joseph Smith all the saving ordinances that were too sacred to put into the Bible.

"The ultimate experience will be the Celestial room." He paused as if fighting tears back. "The Celestial room corresponds to entering exaltation in the highest degree of heaven and living in the presence of God for eternity. Like I said, I can't tell you the specifics, but let me describe it.

"It is a large room with softly muted walls and dazzling crystal chandeliers hanging from high ceilings. Architectural arches and fluted columns are trimmed in gold and embellished with clusters of fruit and flowers. There are also luxuriously brocaded couches and chairs. And here's the best part." Don's face flushed with excitement.

"Elegant staircases surround the perimeter of the Celestial room leading to special sealing rooms where couples are married for time and all eternity. In the center of these rooms is an altar with a velvet-padded top and a cushioned kneeling-pad. Dressed in white, they kneel and join hands over the altar. There, they are sealed for eternity by the power of the priesthood to come forth in the morning of the first resurrection as husband and wife clothed with glory, immortality, and all the blessings of Abraham, Isaac and Jacob.

"Now, Ed," he leaned forward, "when the time comes you join the church and go through the temple, you can be married to Maureen. I took the liberty of asking Joyce Anderson if she would stand in proxy for Maureen when the time comes. You will then be sealed as husband and wife for all eternity."

"Now, what do you think about that?" He leaned back in his chair and laced his fingers across his belly. "Would you like to give your permission?"

Ed felt overwhelmed. It sounded beautiful. "Don, I've got to admit it all sounds great. I had no idea the temple did all that. However..." He glanced at his watch. "I'm sorry but I have to get on the road. Got a faulty track switch down the line to repair. Have to get it done before nine o'clock."

Don slid his chair out from the desk, scooted around to the front and placed his arm around Ed's shoulder.

"Shall I go ahead and submit Maureen's name? Remember, when she watches from heaven during the ceremony she still has her free agency. She can always refuse what's done for her—but I doubt she will. Ninety-nine percent of those who pass on without having embraced the true gospel on earth accept what is done for them in the temple." He smiled, waiting for an answer.

Ed's thoughts became higgledy-piggledy, splintering between his reservations about other church doctrines he found difficult to accept, and the exciting idea of being married to Maureen for eternity. Would Maureen see things differently now she was dead? He knew God intended for them to be married had she lived longer.

"Sure, Don. Why not?" He waved his hand in a gesture of acquiescence. "Go ahead...it certainly won't hurt. Like you say, she can reject it if she wants."

"Of course, Ed." Don grinned his Cheshire cat-like grin again. Ed hated that.

"As to my joining the church...that, uh, is still up in the air. Still have things I need to resolve." He smiled apologetically, although he didn't know what he had to be apologetic about.

Whether he wanted to admit it or not, he liked what he heard, but he did question Don's comment that ninety-nine percent of the dead accepted the temple work. How could he possibly know that? He turned and headed to leave.

"I'll set the paperwork into motion," Don said, opening the door for him. "Have a great day. See you Sunday, Ed."

"Thanks." Ed sauntered down the hall and exited through the rear door. He headed for his truck. He didn't see any harm in letting Maureen's paperwork go through just in case it was true. But join? Yet, if he didn't, how could he learn Maureen's new name so he could call her forth from the grave? He wrestled over all of it. Were passwords really needed in heaven? The subject left him bewildered.

All he knew was that right now he couldn't even consider joining. Membership would keep him in Wendover and he had already set the wheels into motion to leave. He just wished Harry would hurry up and call.

Hopping into his truck, he headed out of town and onto the flats. Salt crystals in the drainage ditches alongside the road dazzled like diamonds in the sunlight. He supposed the Celestial Kingdom was glittery like that.

He pulled onto a side road going south to the track with the faulty switch and bounced along the mud and salt-hardened road. Three hours later, he drove ten more miles to visit the siding at

Salduro and check on maintenance-of-way equipment, then drove back to the depot.

Parking his truck in the shed, he clocked out in the office and ambled down the road toward his section house, unable to quit thinking about Maureen becoming a Mormon. Was he being unfaithful to her by allowing that to take place?

As far as his joining, he couldn't allow anything to deter him from leaving Wendover. There was no reason to stay. He had found nothing to nail Buford, and now the situation had escalated and his life was in jeopardy more than ever. Gus knew he was the one who ransacked his house and would want to get the earring back.

Gus would kill if he had to.

CHAPTER 71

~~~

Ed moseyed into the kitchen early Saturday morning, miserable from no sleep. If Harry didn't call soon he'd have to call again. Yet he hated to bug him since he was so busy with the storms in the canyon. He lit the burner under the pot of leftover coffee. Last night's misery was not only from worrying about Harry, but new thoughts.

He was leaning more and more on just taking off and forgetting about Keddie after he picked up his check Monday. Which direction should he go? Did it make any difference?

He shuffled over to the table and slumped into a chair. Nothing seemed to be working for him at all. Waves of wretchedness shot through him as he stared out the window. Life had dealt him a rotten hand, and he didn't know why. He looked up at the ceiling and raised his fist.

"God doesn't work everything out for good! Do you hear that mama?"

He groaned as the whole kaleidoscope of his fractured life rushed in. His sweet Sarah murdered…his conviction…Maureen dying. Everything and everyone he ever loved had been ripped from his life. Further, he had failed to bring Buford to justice, and his escape from prison had all been for nothing.

"C'mon God," he whispered, "let's have a little action. Remember, you're supposed to work everything together for my good." A harsh, choking sound erupted from his throat and he broke into sobs until his chest hurt from the convulsions. The sound of the coffee pot brought it to a halt.

He ambled over to the stove. Grabbing up a potholder he poured the hot liquid into his mug, and with heart-heavy tread staggered into the front room and slumped onto the couch. No one cared whether he lived or died. He felt lonely and worthless. Not even God was on his side.

If Harry hadn't called by Monday when he picked up his check on Monday, he would definitely pack up and take off for parts unknown. But where to? He moped around the rest of the morning in a state of despondency.

Late noon the telephone broke the silence. His heart leapt. Harry?

He reached over to the end table and lifted the receiver.

"Hello?"

"Hi Ed, Harry. Got something for you. First, it's only temporary, but a permanent job will be opening soon after. Interested?"

"Yeah, Harry. This is great news."

"The first job is working with a crew to move boulders off the track near the Indian Falls tunnel. Some may have to be mud capped with dynamite. The permanent opening after that is Signal Operator. You would be setting up and maintaining the signals on the tracks and in the yard."

"Yep, I'm definitely interested. I've already been promoted to Track Inspector and Motor Car Maintainer."

"How soon can you leave?"

"Monday I pick up my check, so probably not until Tuesday."

"Okay. Call me when you get to Quincy. We'll meet there, and I'll take you on to Keddie. I'm in a rush right now, so have to go. I'll see you then."

Ed hung up the receiver, his spirits lifted. He needed to get busy packing.

He scurried out the backdoor to the shed to get some boxes. The sky shone sunny and bright. He took a deep breath. After the night's downpour, the air was a potpourri of rain-wet fragrances and earthy scents.

He stood motionless in the palpable silence for a few minutes inhaling the lime-green smells. He looked toward Needlepoint, where the barest of the orange and yellow sunset, like a gold-laced tablecloth, had draped itself across the mountain peak.

He hurried into the shed and tugged out some boxes, then raced back inside the house and dropped them on the front room floor.

He'd also run down to the station. Even though Saturday, Hutch would be in the office. He'd tell him about the job and ask him to

426

set up the transfer papers. There might even be a chance the checks came in early and he could leave sooner. He'd also ask Hutch to keep it quiet until after he left. Gus couldn't know. It might spur him into immediate action.

One thing he had to do before he left…call Bob Wilkinson and let him know he had reached a dead end. Poor guy, he was probably sitting on pins and needles waiting for his promised exclusive.

Steering his way toward the bathroom, he undressed, tossed his clothes into the hamper, and then stepped into the bathtub. Spinning the faucet, he adjusted the temperature and then slumped back and relaxed in the rising water.

He hated the thought of leaving without having proved Gus was Buford, but he pretty much faced a roadblock when it came to the sheriff. Fingerprints would have been the only convincing evidence. No way he could get those now. He should have thought of it the night he broke in...a drinking glass...something. He grabbed the long-handled brush and began scrubbing his back.

He'd take his Sir Walter Raleigh tobacco can with him. At least he'd have the satisfaction of Gus not getting the earring back. He gave himself a smug smile. That ought to drive the guy crazy.

Twisting both water handles off he barely stepped out of the tub when he shot his eyebrows up with an ingenious idea. Grabbing a towel, he threw it around his shoulders and began seesawing it across his back.

Yep, a great idea.

Once he landed in Keddie, he'd anonymously mail the earring, the remains of the *Clarion* clipping and the photo of the young woman to the authorities in Richmond. He'd tell them his suspicions about Gus being Buford and urge them to see if the earring matched the one found on the body of the warden's daughter. If it did, they would contact Kevin and have Gus arrested and he'd remain in the clear. Maybe everything would work after all.

He hung the towel back on the rack and moseyed into the bedroom, grabbed a set of khaki shirt and pants from the closet and quickly dressed. No telling how soon Gus would try again, although he still remained puzzled.

Gus wasn't paying much attention to him when they happened to run into each other. Only once in a while did he flash a self-

427

satisfied smile. That baffled him. Well, he wouldn't worry. He was leaving Wendover. He felt he could leave with good conscience, having given everything his best shot. He had also given God a chance but he didn't come through. There was nothing more he could do.

He glanced in the mirror and gave his hair a few swipes with a brush. Now, he needed to go see Hutch.

Grabbing up his car keys, he hesitated for a moment and listened. Cars sounded nearby. He slipped his wallet into his pants pockets. Who could that be—guests at the neighbor's house across the street? Sure a lot of them.

A heavy knock at the door startled him, but not as much as the voice that followed. It jolted him into a heart-thudding state of panic.

"Come out with your hands up, Ed! I have a warrant for your arrest."

Kevin! Pulsations of fear mushroomed. He lurched out of the bedroom into the front room and headed for the back door. He froze. An officer's silhouette appeared through the rear curtains.

"Come out peaceably," Kevin shouted, "or I'm coming in on the count of three!"

Ed's mouth went dry. He spun on his heel one way and then the other.

Police were at the back door, Kevin at the front.

He stood paralyzed.

CHAPTER 72

~~~

Ed stood statue-stiff. His breath came in fast, suffocating paroxysms.

"This is the sheriff, Ed. I'm counting to three and I'm coming in!"

"One... two..."

Ed's throat open and closed spastically during the eternity-like seconds between counts. He ran his tongue over dry lips. It was over.

"Thr..."

"Hold on," his voice cracked, "I'm coming..." Stumbling toward the front door, he placed his hand on the doorknob, hesitated a second, then opened the door.

Kevin, his eyes cold and unblinking, stood in full uniform with a .38 pointing at him. Ed's heart pounded so hard he could barely breathe. Any indication from Kevin of their previous friendship was gone, along with any wild hope he might believe his explanation of why he escaped prison. Kevin never looked so hard and unrelenting. How did he find out?

"Hands above your head."

Ed shot both arms up and glanced past him. Three other patrol cars were parked in front with large letters imprinted on the side, *Tooele County Police*. Officers in blue and white uniforms crouched behind their opened doors, automatic rifles aimed. Ed's stomach contracted into a rock-hard ball.

"Ed Riley," Kevin began in an authoritative tone, "serious allegations have been made against you. Are you going to come along peaceably?"

Ed felt near to retching. He nodded, unable to speak.

Holstering his revolver, Kevin whipped out a pair of handcuffs.

"Turn around," he said, his face rigid and unremitting. Ed complied and cold handcuffs snapped onto his wrists.

A paralyzing depression saturated his bones. He was headed

back to prison, to heavy shackles around his ankles, pick shacks digging into his legs...and the whipping post. There was no way now he could send the earring to Richmond. Gus would remain free.

The residents across the street stood in their doorways peering. It wouldn't take long for them to heat up the telephone wires. All his friends at work would know within the hour—Hutch, Bart, church members. Everybody, including the bishop. Would Don stick by him like he hoped? The answer to that question induced a sinking sensation in the pit of his stomach.

"Ed Riley, you're under arrest as a fugitive from the State of Virginia..." The rest of his words were a blur as he shoved Ed toward the patrol car, opened the door and pushed him into the back seat behind the metal lattice. Slamming the door shut, he climbed into the driver's seat, pulled out, and sped down the road. The other three cars followed, red and blue lights flashing, their shrill sirens alerting the town something big was going down.

Who turned him in? He still didn't think Gus knew he was Ed Bowman. Kevin had to have spent all night making calls to verify his identity. But how without a picture of him? He tried to think rationally despite his rattled nerves.

Kevin shot the patrol car down the road, turned left at the Merc, and skidded up to the small jailhouse next to the post office. The other police cars came to an abrupt stop behind him, their tires screeching in the loose gravel. Patrons bolted out of the post office to rubberneck. Ed gravitated lower into the seat.

Kevin turned off the engine and jumped out. Opening the rear door, he motioned Ed to get out, and jostled him toward the small, white-stuccoed building. The other officers jumped out of their cars and followed, rifles pointed. Unlocking the sun-blistered front door with its tattered paint strips that hung in curls, Kevin nudged Ed inside.

The office was the size of a small kitchen. Sitting off to Ed's left stood a battered, roll-top desk with a conglomeration of papers sticking out of pigeonholes. On the wall behind it hung a large, brownish-orange corkboard tacked with police bulletins and Wanted posters. Hanging askew on another wall were yellowed photos of President Roosevelt and J. Edgar Hoover. On the opposite side of the room was a half-opened door revealing a darkened hallway. Ed surmised it led to the cells.

Kevin directed him through the door and down a narrow corridor, motioning with his hand to the other officers to remain in the office. He stopped in front of an empty cell—the only one.

Fumbling with his ring of keys, Kevin unlocked the cell door. Yanking it open, the nerve-jarring squeal reminded him of the hinges on the pie-wagons. Ed pictured being back there. Could he handle all the rotten filth again, bugs, the stench of urine? Kevin undid the handcuffs.

"Okay, get in." He shoved Ed forward, and then slammed the cell door shut.

Ed stood in the middle of the concrete floor and took a quick glance around. The only two things in the cell were a cot and a toilet. He looked at Kevin who stood in the corridor staring at him with his hands on his hips.

"I know all about you, Ed," he said, loud enough for the patrolmen in the office to hear. "Tooele confirmed everything this morning with Virginia. They even had a picture someone sent to them that matched your prison photo."

Picture? Ed's antenna went up. He had the picture and the negatives. Somehow, Gus must have got one from Queenie earlier. Who else with a picture of him would send it to Virginia?

Kevin shook his head. "You sure had everyone fooled— especially with you being Harry's friend and wanting to marry Maureen. Poor woman. Good thing she died before she found out. Were you planning to kill her, like you did your wife?"

Kevin's words cut deep. A protest wavered on his lips but nothing came out. He stood aghast at his own helplessness to say anything. His grief over Sarah and Maureen was too much.

"Just so you know," Kevin continued in an expressionless voice, "the State of Virginia has issued a fugitive warrant for your arrest and is requesting you be returned. I'll be taking you to Tooele in the morning to appear before the judge." He turned and started for the office, then paused and looked back over his shoulder.

"I'll be back in a while to see if you want to give up your rights, make a statement and waive extradition. Think about it." Turning on his heel, he swaggered down the hallway into the office and shut the door leaving Ed in the cold, chilling silence.

He dropped down onto the edge of the cot, sick at heart. Leaning forward he buried his face in his hands, and then began rubbing his throbbing temples. Somehow, Gus was behind this.

He should have left Wendover right after Maureen died instead of waiting to hear from Harry.

It took about two hours before the roaring in his ears subsided and he pulled himself together. He sat for a long time scrutinizing the discolored gouges in the walls—especially the four steel bars at the dirt-smudged window. No way out. He bit the inside of his cheek. Why even think about trying when surrounded by a hundred miles of salt flats?

He shuffled over to the small window and peered out. All he could see was the rear wall of the Tri-State Merc scribbled with graffiti. High above that, a little sky.

He didn't belong in jail. Out there was the world he belonged to. He thought about Wendover, surprised how fond he had grown of the place. While it certainly wasn't Hannigan, he knew every street, alleyway and cottonwood tree like the back of his hand.

He thought of the insignificant things he would miss, and his emotions thickened.

Sitting on his back porch steps in the evenings and watching the cottonwoods bend in the breeze...enjoying the gold and copper flushes of fall...picking up dry, brittle leaves, squeezing them until they crackled into a million shapeless pieces and slid through his fingers. He even appreciated winter with its spindly-looking trees and bare branches poking up against the skyline like brush bristles.

Yes, Wendover had grown on him. He called townspeople by their first name and had friends like Bart, Alex, and Jake. His throat constricted. What was their opinion of him now? Would they dare come to see him before he was hauled off tomorrow morning?

The thought of anyone he knew coming, tore through his gut like a flash fire. He couldn't face them. He also thought of Harry. How would he react? Even as far away as Keddie, he'd hear about it. Gossip had a way of roaring down the tracks and infiltrating every train station from Salt Lake City to Frisco.

"Oh Lord," he gasped. "Ship me out of here quick!" He didn't want to face anyone.

Doddering back to the cot, he plopped down picturing the legal process. First, a hearing before the judge at the county seat in Tooele. After that, extradition to Richmond. What if they returned him directly to the chain gain instead of the pen—to Jeb? A nerve in his lower lip quivered. He knew what to expect from a man whose despotic authority had been defied. On the other hand, maybe they would return him to the pen instead. That wasn't a pleasant thought either.

"Either way," he moaned, "I'm a dead man."

CHAPTER 73

~~~

At noon, Kevin unlocked the cell door and stepped inside carrying a tray with a yellow sack containing French fries, a hamburger, and a Styrofoam cup of black coffee.

"Here. Got it from the A & W."

Ed stood in the middle of the cell where he had spent the last few hours pacing. Much to his relief, Kevin's overbearing attitude disappeared—probably because the officers were gone and he had no one to impress.

"Got a couple of papers for you to sign," he said, placing the tray down at the foot of Ed's cot and reaching into his shirt pocket. It's up to you. You can waive your right to a preliminary hearing, with the understanding you'll be returned to the State of Virginia even if the governor's warrant hasn't been received yet."

Ed's thoughts raced. Any attempt to tell about Gus would fall on deaf ears since the Tooele hearing wasn't about Buford—only his own escape and conviction for Sarah's murder. If he hired an attorney to fight extradition he'd be tied up in the Tooele jail for a long time with no real gain.

He jutted his bottom lip forward, engrossed in thought. Yes. His best chance to nail Gus and be cleared would be a quick extradition back to Virginia. There, he might be able to convince authorities.

Would Michael Payne and Barry Triving, Buford's defense attorneys, still be in practice? They'd certainly remember the case, although any attempt to talk to them would probably be futile. The D.A., Rob Hill, would be the one. He'd be anxious to nail Buford. Would he believe him without any earring to show as proof? It was a long shot.

"Well, are you gonna sign now?"

"Yeah, I'll sign." He sat down on the edge of the cot, scribbled his name at the bottom of the page and then looked up. He would tell Kevin everything but ease into it slowly.

"Say, Kevin," he ventured timidly, "would you mind telling me how you found out?"

"All I know, Ed, is someone from here sent the Richmond authorities a picture of you. It was sent anonymously." Ed figured it had to be Gus.

"You know…I really do like you, Ed, and this was really hard for me to believe." He gave a bland smile. Ed waited a few seconds before speaking.

"Kevin, there's something I think you should know."

Kevin raised his eyebrows. "Yeah?"

"The reason I came to Wendover."

Ed got up from the cot and ambled over to the window. He turned back and looked at Kevin.

"It's because I was following an escaped criminal from Virginia."

"Oh, come on now, Ed." Kevin rolled his eyes.

"It's true. Before all this happened I was a reporter for the *Casey Clarion* in Hannigan, a small town just outside of Richmond. You can check it out.

"I covered the murder trial of a penitentiary guard, Gunther Buford, accused of murdering the warden's daughter. I wrote an article for the *Clarion* that Buford read while in jail. It pretty much stated he was guilty. It riled him so much, he escaped and came looking to kill me before he fled the state.

"He sneaked into my office late one evening with a gun, claiming what I wrote prejudiced everyone against him and messed up his chance of getting an acquittal. When he tried to shoot me, Sarah, my wife, accidentally moved into the line of fire and was killed." He took a tremulous breath. His eyes filled as he studied Kevin's face for any sign of belief. Nothing yet.

"Buford fled, dropping the gun," he continued. "I picked it up, leaving my fingerprints on it. Buford's weren't on it because he wore gloves. So, I was the one convicted."

"Ed," Kevin shook his head in exasperation, "don't try my patience. Practically every guy I arrest has a story. They all insist they're innocent."

"But I have *proof* of where Gunther Buford fled to…and his new identity." Ed felt the flush of heat rise to his face. Would Kevin believe this part? "He's here in Wendover!"

Kevin stared at him for a moment. He made a flippant gesture with one hand and gave a half amused expression.

"Okay, let's hear about the criminal in Wendover—and it better be good." He moved away from the cell door, sat on the end of the cot and waited.

Ed sifted through the risk. Kevin might not believe he found the earring in Gus's house. He'd assume he had it in his own possession because *he* murdered the warden's daughter and wanted to pin it on Gus because of their conflict over Queenie. Ed crossed the cell and leaned against the other wall opposite Kevin.

"Only one earring," Ed began, swallowing hard, "was left on the body of the warden's daughter. I overheard one of his defense attorneys say it was handcrafted, one-of-a-kind. He also said he hoped Buford, whom he admitted was probably guilty, got rid of the missing earring because like other killers he probably took it as a keepsake. Well, I found the earring in Gus' house. I believe it will match the earring left on the body of the warden's daughter." His breath went shallow.

Kevin yanked his head back reflexively. "Gus? he sputtered in shock, his eyes wide. "You mean, Gus…Mooreland?"

Ed nodded. A quick exhale wisped from his mouth. "But I can't prove it yet unless the earring is sent to Richmond to compare with the one left on the body."

"And, Sherlock," Kevin grinned, unbelief still evident on his face, "just how did you get this so-called earring from Gus' house?"

Ed lowered his eyes. "I…I broke in. But along with the earring I found a photograph of a woman who just might prove to be the warden's daughter. I also found something else—part of a clipping of the article I wrote for the *Clarion*. Gus tried to burn it in the fireplace with other papers."

Kevin crimped his mouth. "That's the last straw, Ed." He slapped both hands on his thighs and stood.

"I've known Gus for nearly a year. Yeah, he has a temper, but murder? I don't think so, Ed."

"Kevin, please! Check with the Richmond authorities. The ring is in a tobacco can in my house, along with the newspaper clipping and photograph. It's under the floorboards near the back door." He stared at Kevin in mute appeal. "Please, go get it. There's also an old picture of Gunther Buford."

"Enough!" Kevin shouted. "There's no way I'll believe this about Gus." He marched out of the cell, pulled the door shut, and traipsed back down the corridor to his office.

Ed slumped back against the wall. What did he expect? He thought of the many times before when he had proclaimed his innocence. Hannigan police didn't believe him...neither the Warden...now, Kevin.

He stared down at the meandering cracks in the concrete floor. Where, he thought cynically, did he ever get an idea God sees everyone gets a fair shake? *Ah yes.* From his mama. He gave a half smile. "Yeah, right."

He lay down on the cot, curled up facing the wall, and studied a tiny cockroach crawling along a crack.

Tomorrow, Tooele.

What if during that time Gus grows fearful, thinking I'll tell the Tooele authorities about him? He could panic and take off. There would be no way to bring him in then, let alone find him. Would Gus skedaddle? He rolled over on his other side.

In a slow afterthought, he changed his mind. Gus wouldn't feel the need. Already bosom-buddy with Kevin, he knows he would be believed. Further, his long-time position with the railroad and time in Wendover carried weight. No. He wouldn't leave.

For him, however, the die was cast. He'd take the rest of today to simmer his emotions—prepare for the hearing tomorrow and then his extradition. He needed to accept the way things had turned out.

The dominoes were now lined up, ready to fall into their inevitable sequence.

CHAPTER 74

~~~

Ed lay on his cot in the evening, staring at the ceiling and taking in the smell of the musty cell, the rank stink of his body, and Kevin's cigarette smoke that wafted down the corridor.

Everything, like dominoes, would topple soon in fast order. The first one had already fallen. Domino one—his arrest. Domino two would be his hearing in the morning. Domino three—his extradition. He didn't know what direction domino four would topple, once in Richmond. It all depended if he was successful in contacting Rob Hill.

Rolling his body off the cot, he stood and paced around the cell floor in circles. He thought about Don. Would he show up before tomorrow morning? He pressed the bridge of his nose. Or should he ask Kevin to call him?

With Don's ties to Mormon State officials he could, if he wanted, possibly delay his transfer to Tooele, giving him time to prove his innocence. Would he still display some modicum of their friendship? He winced his face into apprehensive lines and dug the toe of one shoe into a small rut in the concrete floor. He scraped away the dusty crumbles. Should he ask Kevin to ask Don to come?

Something inside him said no. Why?

Evening arrived. Kevin brought him dinner from the beanery and then left. It consisted of two slices of roast beef, mashed potatoes, gravy and corn. Ed assumed Queenie fixed it. He wondered if she felt sorry for him. Gus, on the other hand, had to be ecstatic.

Barely had he finished eating, when Kevin called down the corridor.

"Ed, you have a visitor."

Shudders swept through him. Hutch? Bart? What could he possibly say to them? Queenie? Maybe, Don?

Panic gripped him. He hustled over to the bars and peered down the hall. Kevin led a large figure of a man through the office door. Ed's breath quickened. It was Don.

Despite his fears, hope revved. He would tell him everything. Surely he would believe him. He stepped back from the bars while Kevin unlocked the cell door.

"You can go on in and sit with him, bishop. I don't think you got anything to worry about." Grabbing a straight-backed chair from the hallway, Kevin dragged it in and set it near Ed's cot.

"I'll leave the cell door unlocked. Just come on out when you're ready to leave." He pulled the bars shut and ambled back to the office.

"Hello, Ed." Don angled over to the chair and eased himself onto it.

Ed nodded a greeting. An awkward silence followed.

"Well," Don began softly, "guess we have some things to talk about."

"Yeah, suppose so," Ed mumbled, sitting down on the edge of the cot.

"Is it true what the sheriff says about you?"

"Yep, all true. I escaped prison...but I was unjustly convicted for my wife's murder and—"

"Ed," Don interrupted, "I want to tell you I enjoyed being your friend during the time you actively attended the ward."

"Thanks," he responded, trying to decipher what he saw in Don's eyes. He didn't want to hear anything Don had to say until he could first explain everything. He pushed on.

"I want you to know, Don, even though I have to go back to prison I'm grateful you're going to send Maureen's name into the temple. Whatever happens to me, I'll at least be comforted by the fact her temple work will be done and she'll be out of that prison.

"And I was really thinking hard about joining the church, getting baptized, and going to the temple and having her sealed to me for eternity, even though there are still a few things about the beliefs I don't understand. But you could probably explain them and set my mind at ease.

"Aside from that, can you possibly help me out by talking to Kevin, or the judge in Tooele, and explain I'm really innocent?" He cocked his head inquisitively. "I know you're well connected."

"Well, Ed..."

440

Ed took advantage of the bishop's hesitation.

"Let me tell you the details about what I'm accused of doing. My wife Sarah's death was really an accident. Another man shot her... Gunther Buford. He intended to kill me...the gun went off when she moved into the line of fire..." He ran his sentences together, barely taking a breath in-between, at the same time searching the bishop's face. "I didn't kill my wife, Don. Can you do something to help so I can have extra time to prove my innocence?"

Don, his eyes grave, furrowed his brow.

"Ed, I need to explain something to you."

Ed scooted back against the brick wall. He didn't like the way that sounded.

"First," Don began, "there is no way I can allow Maureen's temple work to go through now. My motive in submitting her name to begin with was based on my anticipation you would be joining the church soon and—"

"But," Ed, interrupted, "what does Maureen's temple work have to do with me, especially since I'm innocent? Can't you go ahead and do it anyway? I'll be exonerated at some point. Maybe you could get Kevin or the Tooele judge to put a hold on things so you could baptize me and I could convince the authorities of my innocence."

"Ed, uh..." Don ran nervous fingers across his temple, smoothing a few hairs behind one ear, and then gave an uncomfortable smile.

A dismal depression pressed down on Ed. He discerned an objection coming.

"You are probably unaware," Don began, "of the church's view on the subject. Even if you wanted to be baptized now, the crime of murder carries a mandatory action of excommunication, therefore—"

"But, bishop," Ed interrupted, "like I explained, I'm innoc—"

"The church," Don pushed, his face taking on a judicial expression, "makes situations like this very clear. Murder is the sin unto death spoken of in the New Testament." He leaned forward, placed his elbows on his knees and steepled the fingers of both hands to a point beneath his chin.

"Although most sins can be forgiven," he continued, "there are some so grievous they are beyond forgiveness. Jesus only died for some sins, not for a crime like yours. In a nutshell, no one who is guilty of murder can ever be allowed to join the church or enter the Celestial Kingdom."

Don's words were like an emotional punch to his heart. Unable to speak, Ed let his mouth hang open.

The bishop cleared his throat.

"The reason is," he said, "the murderer not only cheats the victim of life, but the opportunity to receive saving ordinances in the temple that would entitle him to godhood. Knowing about your criminal background," he said, "I could never permit you to be baptized, go through the temple, let alone allow you to be sealed to Maureen."

"But," Ed spluttered, "I didn't murder my wife. Like I said, it was Gunther Buford. I didn't pull the trigger...you've got to believe me." His voice cracked.

Don gave him a placating smile. "Ed, I'm not here to assess the circumstances. As a bishop and judge in Israel, I have to abide by the rules of the church as well as the law of the land that has already found you guilty. Further, I should let you know that since Jesus' blood doesn't cover murderers, you must eventually pay the full price—if not in this life by legal execution, then after you die."

Ed's eyes transfixed with shock. He couldn't believe what he was hearing. None of it made sense.

"But bishop, even if I were guilty of murder I thought *all* sin was forgivable." He tried to control his voice.

"Not quite."

"Well, if there's no repentance for me, will I *ever* go to heaven? I want to see Maureen...Sarah...my dear mama...also, my dad."

"Yes, you'll eventually go to heaven—but only the lowest heaven. How it works, is after you die your fate will be to spend a thousand years in hell. At the end of that time, if you repent, you will come forth in the second resurrection." His voice trailed off.

Ed's jaw dropped. "But, Don," he gasped, remembering from Joyce's Sunday school class the second resurrection meant the resurrection of the damned, "Maureen read her Bible a lot—so did my mama—and they both said regardless of what a person had done Jesus forgives them and they will go to heaven, not hell. Isn't that what faith, repentance and the cross is all about? I thought the church believed that, too."

The bishop shook his head. "I'm so sorry, Ed. Any exemplary life after this kind of crime, even baptism, carries no weight with heaven. As far as the church ruling about not being able to join the church, the *Doctrine and Covenants* states no murderer can ever enter the top heaven, the Celestial Kingdom. Joseph Smith received the revelation directly from God: '*The murderer shall not have forgiveness in this world, nor in the world to come*.' In view of this, I cancelled Maureen's temple paperwork." Don stared into his lap, avoiding eye contact.

Dejection crashed over Ed like a tidal wave. Was the bishop telling the truth? Did Joseph Smith really receive a revelation from God? If so, Don's proclamation decimated everything he ever hoped for in one fell swoop. Maureen's temple work wouldn't take place and she'd stay in a spirit prison forever. And with no help from Don, he was headed back to prison where he was sure Jeb would see to his death. Then what? To hell for a thousand years while Gunther Buford remained free? He felt the blood drain from his face. All had been a waste...an utter waste. He drooped his head onto his chest, taking a full minute to regain his composure while Don waited.

"I'm sorry, Ed." Don broke the silence, making a feeble gesture with one hand. "The church's stand on the issue can't be changed." Ed looked up.

"Don...you were my last hope. You have no idea what prison is like...especially for someone who is innocent."

He suddenly squeezed his eyes shut, struggling to stifle the strange, heaving emotions that felt like volcanic tremors quaking deep inside him. Molten anguishes of hopelessness roiled in his groin and rumbled in his abdomen. He felt it mount higher into his chest like rising water in a flood, creeping toward his throat. It was a force he couldn't reckon with. Any second, he knew everything inside him would erupt. It was not something he wanted Don to witness.

Leaping to his feet, he grabbed the startled bishop by the arm and wrenched him out of his chair. Yanking the cell door open, he shoved him into the corridor and slammed the bars shut. Turning his back to him, he covered his face with his hands. Any minute he

443

knew it would look as mangled as his insides. He held on as best he could until Don had quietly retreated down the hallway, entered the office and left.

The rising torrent of misery and despair came faster and faster, swelling up into his throat. He dropped to his knees onto the concrete floor with a thud. Then, out it came—a wrenching, banshee-like wail.

"Oh God," he cried in heart-rushing sobs. "Everything...for nothing? And I'm going to hell?" His body heaved with convulsive weeping.

At the end of the corridor Kevin stood in the office doorway where he had stood for the last half hour, listening.

He stepped back into the office and quietly shut the door.

CHAPTER 75

~~~

$\mathbf{A}$ hot, muggy breeze blew through the cell window during the night, wafting in the gagging stench of garbage cans from the alleyway behind the Merc. Ed pitched and tossed on his lumpy, urine-smelling mattress and wrinkled his nose. Wind-gusts also sent the yellow light bulb in the corridor swinging back and forth, casting spectral shapes with ghostly fingers on the gray, pitted walls that only pulled him deeper into the dark abyss of his despair.

In the morning, Kevin would take him to Tooele for his hearing and extradition. After that…prison. Once 2,000 miles away from Wendover, what chance did he have of proving Gus' identity?

He tried to sleep but his mind, in a sepia haze, continually floated back to the *Clarion*. He held Sarah's bloody body, listened to her last struggling words, relived his arrest, heard the snap of handcuffs, the judge's words sentencing him to life in prison, and then his escape from the chain gang. Lastly, he imagined the crack of Jeb's metal-pronged whip vindictively slamming down on his back and horse flies swarming his bloodied body.

With a moan he flipped over on his stomach. He buried his face into the smelly mattress hoping to smother the vision of Jeb's crooked lips and insidious smile welcoming him back to the chain gang. The inevitable *if-onlys* followed.

If only he had found more evidence in Gus' house to identify him as Buford…if only Bob Wilkinson's picture had worked…if only he had left town sooner…if only Don had offered to help. If only…if only…

But nothing could be changed. They were fixed forever.

Next came Don's ill-boding words.

"A murderer can never go to heaven. Your fate is to spend a thousand years in hell. Not even baptism carries any weight for your kind of crime…your kind…your kind…."

Don's words, like an axe-wielding pendulum, swung viciously back and forth inside his head, slicing into his soul and slashing to shreds any hope for redemption, forgiveness for wrongs, heaven, or seeing Sarah, Maureen and his mama again.

In the background, Maureen's voice quoting Bible passages mingled with Don's words. Fading in and out, all the words were staticky, like a radio dial set to the wrong frequency. Who was right? A Mormon bishop's proclamation based on revelation from a possible prophet, or what Maureen claimed the Bible said?

Well, whichever, there was no point in even thinking about it now. Don had to be right, otherwise why would he let his Mormon theology take precedence over their friendship? He also had a hard time understanding why a man, supposedly holding God's priesthood and claiming he had the Holy Ghost, couldn't supernaturally discern he was telling the truth.

He flung his feet over the side of the cot and lurched over to the window hoping to clear his head. The light of a nearby streetlight highlighted the back wall of the Merc with its swirl of graffiti. Ed's eyes traced every geometrical curlicue of paint spray and chalk that meandered about in convoluted design after design, and designs within designs.

The conglomeration of inter-winding configurations seemed to mimic all the complex twists and turns of his life since his conviction—tracking Buford to Wendover, wanting to avenge Sarah's murder, hoping to clear his name, breaking into Gus' house—and barely surviving Gus and Cowboy's attempts to kill him. All for what? Ultimately, nothing. Like the graffiti's structureless, never-ending lines, there was no conclusive end in sight.

The reality of that gripped him and his stomach heaved. With a tortured groan he barely made it to the toilet in time to throw up. Staggering back to his cot, a black aloneness consumed him as he slumped down onto the edge.

Barely three seconds passed when something strange made him raise his head—a phantom-like voice.

"*All is not lost,*" it whispered, "*no matter how hopeless things appear.*"

A look of puzzlement slipped across his face. Did that mean Don would change his mind and he'd be at the hearing tomorrow to alter the course of things—or Kevin would believe him and come through the last minute?

Maybe the whisper he heard was just his own dogged determination refusing to accept facts. He chewed the edge of his tongue. Yes, that was more likely. What else could it be?

He thought of the Pollyanna attitude of his mama. *"There's always something good about any situation if you look hard enough."* He focused, squeezing the lines of concentration between his brows, trying to think of something, but it didn't work.

Reality screamed through the subterranean corridors of his mind.

Pale strands of morning sunlight crept through the barred window. Ed heard the squeak of leather shoes in the hallway. He stiffened.

"Ed," Kevin called, pulling out his keys, "we have to be in Tooele by eight. We need to leave now.

Unlocking the cell door, Kevin sauntered in. "You understand I'll have to cuff you for the trip?"

"Yeah." Ed got up from the cot, turned around and dutifully put his hands behind his back.

Kevin shook his head. "Nah, front is okay. I have breakfast from the Beanery sitting in the back seat. You can eat it on the way." He snapped the handcuffs around his wrists and motioned him down the hall and into the office. Kevin grabbed his car keys from the desk as they exited the building.

Ed glanced about as they headed for the patrol car. It would be the last time he would see Wendover and his friends—if he still had any. Mile-wise, Kevin was bringing him closer to his eventual death at either the hands of heavies at the pen, or by Jeb.

Kevin yanked the car door open and Ed wriggled onto the back seat behind the metal lattice. Hustling around to the driver's side, Kevin slid in behind the wheel. Giving a quick glance in the rear view mirror, he turned the ignition, backed out of the alley, and started up the street.

Ed longingly glued his eyes to every familiar sight as they drove through the neighborhood. Down the street past the old widow's house with her backyard of flowers, and then the house where he and Maureen spent happy times sitting on the couch together munching on pumpkin cookies and listening to radio shows—Baby Snooks, Charlie McCarthy, the Aldrich Family...

He glanced at the front yard, reliving his first evening in Wendover eating ice cream in their lawn chairs, and remembering the way Maureen gently doctored his face after his fight with Gus. He instinctively lifted his cuffed hands and touched the side of his face as if he could still feel the imprint of her fingers. Then there was their first kiss and his asking her to marry him. He shoved the hospital scene out of his mind…the tubes…her yellow face.

The house glided past him. Twisting around, he stared out the rear window unable to tear his eyes away.

"Goodbye Maureen," he whispered.

Rounding the corner, they passed the ward building. My supposed family, Ed thought grimly, taking in the white-framed structure and recalling the warm welcome he always received like he was someone special. Since Don had now rejected him, everyone in the ward would too.

Kevin reached the highway, passed Needle Point, and headed for the edge of town. At the Highway Patrol Station, Ed glanced to the right toward the water tower and the spread of trailers and houses. Somewhere in the midst of those rooftops half hidden in clumps of trees, sat Gus' house.

None of it made sense. Buford remained free and he was being sent back to prison. The injustice of it gnawed at him. His mama's stance made no sense either. The scriptures she quoted were always supposed to work. Well, they didn't. Life wasn't like that. Maybe she knew now.

He supposed his biggest puzzlement was the day at Blue Lake when he stood in the warm water under the cloudless sky and felt so at peace—especially when he received the profound impression that God, or something, was assuring him he was where he was meant to be—like he'd been directed to Wendover. He pulled his mouth in at the corners. Surely, it had to mean something. It was so...so supernatural.

He leaned back against the seat and squeezed his eyes shut. Wake up Ed. None of it was real. He had to quit deceiving himself.

At the edge of town, Kevin stepped on the accelerator and sped onto the salt flats. Ed took one last glance through the rear window.

Fading into the distance was the huge rock Maureen insisted looked like a lizard, recalling how elated she was when he finally said he could make it out. Then, there was Blue Lake's Pluto Rock. He'd miss silly things like that. Three Burma Shave signs whizzed by. *To go through life...how would you like...a whiskered wife?* His eyes filled, remembering her sweet giggles.

He reached down and placed the breakfast tray on his lap and began eating.

An hour and a half later, Kevin pulled into Grantsville and turned on the road leading to Tooele, a ten-mile long stretch of desolate land separating Grantsville from Tooele.

Much to Ed's surprise, Kevin began to chitchat as they drove. Mostly about nothing. Ed figured it was because they were nearly there and, despite Kevin's elation over making a big arrest, probably felt sorry for him.

"Hard to believe," Kevin began, "experimental war chemicals, gas and the like, are stored at the Ordinance Depot way out there." He waved his hand off to the distant right. "Good for our enemies, but bet it sure makes Grantsville and Tooele residents nervous. And did you know the ancestors of the Goshute tribes lived here eleven thousand years ago?"

Ed didn't respond. He didn't feel like talking about poison gas or Indians. He was too busy thinking about his extradition and wondering if he'd be able to locate Rob Hill. He was his only hope.

What if he had since died? An icy chill crept up his back.

Kevin lifted the radio mike to his lips. "Thompson here. Entering town with the prisoner. Have someone meet me at the jail."

Kevin cruised through Tooele's business district, slowed at the old stone courthouse, and then veered right down a side street. In the yard behind the large structure sat an old pioneer log cabin designed for sightseers. Behind it, a small brick jail.

Pulling up to the curb, Kevin rolled down the window and motioned to two officers who stood waiting. Sliding out of his seat, he opened Ed's door.

The officers, one on each side of Ed, took hold of an arm and walked him across the yard toward the uncomely building. Ed noted the jailer standing in the doorway, and the building's two barred windows.

They were led inside and down a short, shadowy corridor. Ed counted ten cells, five on each side. Only two were occupied. The prisoners who were lying on cots immediately raised their heads to scrutinize the new resident.

Kevin undid his handcuffs, and the jailer motioned Ed into the last cell and locked the door.

"Ed, you'll have to stay here until someone comes to get you for the hearing. That'll be in about an hour. I'm going now to file your waiver." Turning, Kevin headed back down the narrow passageway. "I'll see you in the courtroom."

"Kevin!" Ed called, pressing his face against the bars. "Don't forget. You know—what I told you about Gus and the tobacco can I hid under the floorboards?"

Making no response, Kevin left the building. Ed sank onto the cot, disheartened. One hour until his hearing.

Would Don, or anyone, from Wendover be there?

He paced the cell, feeling like an overstressed balloon on the verge of exploding.

CHAPTER 76

~~~

"All rise for the court!"

The judge, white-haired with a slightly ruddy face and black, horn-rimmed glasses, emerged from a door behind the bench. The sparse gathering of spectators rose. Ed stood at the long counsel table facing the bench.

The courtroom looked like most—the bar in front with its swinging gate, the judge's bench, jury box and witness stand, all made from the same colored wood, including a long enclosed workbench covered with red docket books.

He flared his nostrils. The courtroom smelled musty and old, like it hadn't been cleaned for months. It was a distinctive smoky kind of smell, a mix between his mama's dank root cellar and the choking dust after shaking out a vacuum cleaner bag.

He nervously glanced about to see if anyone from Wendover had come. No one—not Hutch or Bart. Neither Don, whom he hoped, for the sake of their friendship, might have reconsidered his Mormon judgment. If not, at least have come to say something encouraging the last minute. No one was there but Kevin who stood beside him staring straight ahead.

"The Superior Court of Tooele County is in session," the Bailiff announced. "The Honorable Benjamin Clifton presiding. Be seated."

Ed lowered himself onto the straight-backed chair and gave a quick side-glance at Kevin, searching for some facial expression indicating a change of mind about Gus being Buford. Nothing. Kevin remained dour-faced. Not even a polite or encouraging smile.

Ed drooped his shoulders. All he could hope for was that he had planted a seed in Kevin that might sprout later—hopefully, not too late in the game.

He stared up at the bench. Judge Clifton looked menacing in his black robe as he browsed through papers in a folder.

451

"I have a copy," he began, "of the fugitive warrant for Ed Bowman who escaped from a Virginia chain gang, based on Virginia authorities verifying Ed Riley as one and the same person.

"I also have a copy of the original judgment which states the defendant was convicted of murder and sentenced to the Virginia State Penitentiary. Included is the initial indictment and warrant for his arrest after Mr. Bowman escaped, issued September 12, 1939.

"I have been informed that Mr. Bowman has waived extradition and the prosecution is offering the defendant's waiver of rights.

"Sheriff Thompson, would you please take the stand."

Scooting his chair out, Kevin walked forward to be sworn in.

Ed noticed he was back to his old swagger. Guess he couldn't blame him. An escapee from a chain gang was a big catch for a small-town sheriff.

"Please state your name and occupation."

"Kevin Thompson, sheriff of Wendover." The fingernails of the court stenographer clicked away at the keys.

"On April 4, did you receive a call from Richmond authorities informing you the defendant was an escaped convict?"

"Yes sir."

"What did you do after you received this information?"

"I telephoned Tooele and spoke with the County Sheriff. I requested backup from Tooele. Four officers were sent to Wendover early the morning of April 6. We then proceeded to the defendant's residence and arrested him."

"Did you advise him of his rights?"

"Yes sir."

"Did he understand them?"

"Yes sir. After the arrest he signed a statement to that effect and waived extradition."

"Thank you Sheriff Thompson. You may step down."

The judge pulled his horn-rimmed glasses down on the end of his nose with his index finger and squinted at Ed.

"Mr. Bowman, the court wishes to make certain you fully understand your rights. You can fight extradition. You have the right to counsel. You also have the right to produce evidence on your own behalf."

452

Ed thought about how to respond. If he wanted to rescind his waiver he'd only be told to hire an attorney, stand trial, and produce evidence he wasn't Ed Bowman. He couldn't very well do that. Besides, a Utah trial wouldn't accomplish what he wanted. The only place he could bring up his innocence and tell about Gus and the earring would be in Richmond.

"Mr. Bowman, do you want to fight extradition?"

"No, Your honor."

"Do you admit to being Ed Bowman?"

"Yes, sir."

"Then, in waiving your rights do you understand I will sign an order authorizing your immediate return to the State of Virginia?" He waited.

Ed's insides quaked. "Yes."

"Very well." The judge shoved his glasses back up on the bridge of his nose. "The court is convinced the defendant understands his rights and finds there is sufficient evidence Ed Riley is one and the same as Ed Bowman who escaped from the Virginia State Penitentiary's chain gang on September 12, 1939. An order will be issued accepting the defendant's waiver of extradition and directing his immediate return to the State of Virginia.

"In the meantime, the defendant is remanded over to the county sheriff until such time as he can be transported back to Virginia. There will be no bail. Court adjourned."

Bringing the gavel down, the judge stood, pivoted on his heel and disappeared through the door behind the bench.

Ed's breath quickened as two armed deputies stepped forward. They each took an arm and led him away from the counsel table. Ed panicked. He had to make one last attempt. Yanking free of their grasp, he whirled around.

"Kevin, I beg you," he said in a burst of desperation, "even if you don't believe what I said about Gus, please get my tobacco can and hold on to it. Authorities in Richmond may contact you later about the earring. Will you do that much?"

Kevin gave him a long, perplexed look and then reluctantly nodded. Ed's heart raced. Would he really?

The deputies grabbed hold of him again. They marched him out of the courtroom into the holding room, down the back steps through a narrow, shadowy stairway, and out the rear exit of the building to the jail.

Sitting in the desolate silence of his cell, Ed did everything he could to emotionally prepare himself for his return to Richmond.

CHAPTER 77

~~~

Gus stepped out the door of the Merc, his arms loaded with three sacks of groceries. The sky was cloudless except for a few fleecy ones in the east, and the air balmy and surprisingly warm. He smiled. The day perfectly matched the exuberance he felt. Ed Riley was now out of the picture and sitting in a Tooele jail ready to be sent back to prison. The guy was as good as dead. He knew what years in the pen could do.

Quickstepping down the wooden steps he placed the sacks into the back of his truck. Grabbing an Oh Henry candy bar from one, he swaggered around to the cab door. Pulling it open, he slid into the seat and tore the end of the candy wrapper open. He sat for a few minutes, exulting. He had plenty to be pleased about.

The threat of Ed hailing from Virginia and at some point recognizing him, was now gone. And the odds of anyone else from Virginia landing in this God-forsaken place to endanger his identity were nil. He rolled the candy wrapper down.

He had, however, to give credit where credit was due. If Queenie hadn't taken the snapshot he wouldn't have had anything to send to the authorities. Later, she told him Ed had stolen the negatives. Then, of course, there was Scratch's bogus letter that tipped him off. Only one thing baffled him. He scrunched his brows and stared through the windshield.

Why did Ed break into his house in the first place? He doubted Ed suspected his real identity. Thank goodness he burned his old papers before he broke in.

Only one thing he could chalk it up to. The guy was a natural thief at heart. After all, that's probably what landed him in prison in the first place.

No sense wondering, he thought. If it hadn't been his house it would have been someone else's. He probably took Sue's ruby earring thinking he could sell it. He did, however, feel uneasy having it out of his possession. Nevertheless, there was no link to Sue.

He took a bite of his Oh Henry and closed his eyes. His saliva glands practically overflowed with delight. Nothing beat chocolate-coated peanuts and caramel.

He gorged down the rest, swiped the runoff from the corners of his mouth, and then jostled the key into the ignition. He needed to drop his groceries off at home before he met with Supervisor Hutch. He had no idea what it was about but had his suspicions. He presumed it was going to be good news. Shifting into reverse, he backed out.

He drove down the rutted road toward his house. He passed Bum's jungle and the red water tower where empty gallon bottles of Tokay wine and Pork and Bean cans were strewn about. Today, even that eyesore didn't bother him. Not only was he ecstatic over getting rid of Ed—and of course, getting Queenie back—but he looked forward to today's meeting.

Hutch had sent word for him to report to his office with no hint as to what it was about, but according to the scuttlebutt a promotion was in the air. He already suspected as much. Last week, Hutch had him meet with the freight car supervisor to learn about the new railroad equipment. That was enough to indicate something was brewing in his favor.

If true, his advancement up the ladder would bring him exactly what he wanted—a position of unquestioning authority and respect. The higher up he climbed, the more it would bring. He'd regain what he had at the pen, and more. He jutted his chin out and gave an arrogant laugh.

He was head and shoulders above the other workers when it came to efficiency. The upgrade would also be to his credit when his transfer to California came through. It was about time things started going his way.

He stretched his mouth into a triumphant grin.

Hutch rose from his chair. "C'mon in, Gus." He motioned for him to sit down. Gus settled into the wood-backed chair next to the desk, trying to mask his anticipation.

"I'll get right to the point, Gus. We have a problem."

Gus flinched. *No promotion?* He managed to hold his composure.

"Yeah? What's that?" He posed his face stoically.

Hutch smiled. "Relax, Gus. The problem is, I actually have two bits of good news for you but it's presenting a dilemma—not only for me, but you."

Gus' stomach knotted. He raised his eyebrows. "Good news…a dilemma?"

Hutch reached down and pulled a file from his bottom drawer. "The transfer you requested came through." He laid it on the desk.

Gus widened his eyes with delight. "That's great. But what's the problem? You also said *two* pieces of good news?"

"Here's what it boils down to," Hutch said, scooting his chair back a few inches and crossing his legs. "Your transfer came through just this morning. Prior to that, I had planned to promote you to Signal and Switch Operator. I'm hoping you'll take the job and decide not to transfer to California." He cocked his head to one side, raising his shoulders in a questioning gesture, and then continued.

"You've had a few years more of experience working the rails and know most of the inspection techniques and safety criteria for track structure. But here's the dilemma for both of us." He rubbed the back of his neck.

"For me, I want to keep you. You, on the other hand, want to transfer out. So here's something for you to consider. The job here would pay you more and be a higher grade-level than your present rating. So, do you want to transfer at your present rate, or stay and leave later at a higher rate?" Which way do you want to go?"

Gus let out a soft expulsion of breath and squinted in thought. *Wendover with more status and pay? Or California at lower pay, but a safer future and dissolving into the large population quicker?* Yet he wanted the promotion.

"The promotion sounds great, Hutch, but I've also been living for this transfer—"

"I know that," Hutch interrupted. He propped his elbows on the desk and formed a small pyramid under his chin with his hands.

"I have to admit California is more attractive than Wendover. And you could leave as soon as next week if that's what you want to do."

Gus raised his shoulders in a helpless gesture.

"Well, Gus, I gave a lot of thought to this in case you opted for

457

the transfer. As much as I hate to lose you, I do have an alternate proposal."

"What ya got in mind?"

"Troy Monahan, the present Signal and Switch Operator needs to transfer to Ohio due to a family situation. If you could stay for another month and a half until he leaves, I could officially promote you to entry-level Signal and Switch Operator with a bump in pay. And if you're still gung ho on leaving, I have a qualified man in Elko who could fill your position after that. During that time you can learn the ropes, and then leave with your new title and salary.

"I know it isn't very long on the job, but you're a quick learner. It'll be a step up for you, and I'll give you a good recommendation on your transfer—which I would have done anyway."

Another seven weeks? Gus scowled. On the other hand, what did he have to lose? With Ed out of the picture things were more relaxed now and his identity was no longer at risk. It would also give him time to sweet-talk Queenie into leaving with him.

"Yep, Hutch. I'll take you up on the deal." He stood and they shook hands.

Anxious to tell Queenie the news, he strode into the Beanery. It might take some doing to get her to leave Wendover, but the glamour of California would certainly appeal to her. He looked about but didn't see her—only one waitress in sight. He saw Kevin sitting at the counter. He sauntered over and slid onto the stool next to him.

"Hi there, Kevin."

"How ya doing?" came Kevin's droll response. "What's new?"

His strange tone pulled at Gus. It wasn't quite as lively as usual.

"Well," he said with a cocky grin, "just got promoted to Signal and Switch Operator. Hey, you sorta look down. You sick? The wife okay?"

"Yeah. Everything's okay. You know, just the job." He waved his hand with a casual dismissal. "Workload can get heavy at times. But say, that's good news about your promotion."

"Yep, but it's not permanent—at least in Wendover." Gus was glad to see Kevin's face change for the better. He glanced toward the end of the counter. "Hey Betty, cup of coffee, here!" He turned back to respond to Kevin's questioning look.

"I'm gonna be transferring out in a month and a half."

Kevin pulled his eyebrows down into a V over his nose and said nothing for a second.

"Well, Gus, I hate to see you go. We've been good friends for some time now." He grinned and emitted a shaky laugh. "Guess I'll have to find another fishin' buddy." Gus observed Kevin's oddly stretched lips.

"Say, the weather's pretty good, Kevin. Tomorrow's Saturday. How about it? I'll get Queenie and we'll take a run out to Blue Lake and see what we can catch. How does that grab ya?"

"Sounds good, Gus. What part of California you moving to?" He raised a questioning brow. Gus winced. He hadn't anticipated getting pinned down about that.

"Oh, not exactly sure yet. It might be Frisco, Sacramento, L.A., Barstow…" He felt relief when Betty approached with his coffee.

"Hey, where's Queenie?"

"She took the morning off, Gus. Should be back this afternoon." She set his coffee down and sashayed away.

Gus gulped down his coffee as fast as he could. He didn't relish any more questions about California.

"Sort of in a hurry Kevin." He slid off the stool. "Shall we shoot for ten o'clock?"

"Yeah, fine. Gus. I'll look forward to it. The gals can pack the lunch."

Gus plopped a dollar bill down on the counter, turned and strode across the floor to the door thinking about Kevin's strange demeanor. He wasn't his usual self. He shrugged. Maybe he and Patti were having problems.

Closing the door behind him, he paused on the porch. He glared with disgust at the desolate flats that stretched in all directions. *Seven more weeks.* Well, having stuck it out this long already, he could certainly handle a few more. Besides, he'd have higher status and a bump in pay when he transferred. That had to be worth something.

With chin hoisted high he swaggered down the steps and scuttled across the yard.

Seven weeks and he'd be home free!

CHAPTER 78

~~~~~

At ten o'clock, two agents from Virginia flew into Salt Lake, borrowed a car from the local police, and sped to Tooele. Upon arriving they wasted no time. They signed the papers, handcuffed Ed, and led him to the car.

Ed climbed into the back seat, his body brittle with tension. He had spent all night struggling to settle his nerves by realizing there was nothing he could do about anything at this point. Unless some miracle happened, he might last a year in the pen, less on Jeb's chain gang. The door slammed shut. An inextricable knot twisted in his chest.

For forty-five minutes, he managed to maintain his cool on the drive to Salt Lake. But his biggest struggle still bothered him— coming to grips with the possibility he might not locate Rob Hill. He sent a few trembly prayers up, unsure if God was listening considering He hadn't helped him so far, but thought it wouldn't hurt

They arrived at the Salt Lake Airport. Checking through the gate, the agents hustled him onto the tarmac. During the few minutes it took to walk to the small, private plane, Ed swept a nostalgic gaze at the Wasatch Range, squinting through the heat waves shimmering from the blacktop.

He pictured Cottonwood Canyon with its fiery yellow and orange foliage. There, he and Maureen enjoyed a romantic picnic. They nearly went all the way with their affections but she, with her strong belief in biblical standards, and he imagining his mama looking over his shoulder from heaven, remained strong. He climbed the steps and boarded the plane.

"Over there," the agent pointed, "next to the window." He sat down next to Ed while the other agent buckled himself into a seat across the aisle. The engines revved and the plane pummeled down the runway and lifted off. Ed watched through the small window as the ground sank away.

High over the city he spotted the spires of the temple. His throat plugged up. Even with his reservations about Mormon beliefs, he imagined the beautiful ceremony that would have sealed Maureen to him forever and his face locked with pain.

The plane climbed higher and Salt Lake City and its temple spires receded into the distance. He pressed his face against the windowpane straining to see, as wisps of grayish blue clouds rushed in over the wings and blocked his sight. He slumped back into his seat.

That part of his world—now gone.

They landed at Byrd Field. Ed stepped out of the plane. The oppressive heat slammed into his body like a blast furnace and he heard the cicadas' familiar, high-pitched screech. The reality of being back buckled his heart.

He looked around and scrutinized the horizon line to get his bearings. Gazing to the south, he pictured Hannigan with its quiet streets of even-rowed elms and maples that whispered in the night breeze through his and Sarah's bedroom window. He'd never see it again.

He looked to his left, knowing the direction of the penitentiary and the chain gang. He wondered about Moose and Duff. Were they still there? He thought of Benny's mother. So much for his letter from California. He'd have to write her from prison. At least he wouldn't have to face her.

Once through the terminal, he waited at the curb with the agents until a squad car pulled up. Climbing into the back seat, he glanced questioningly at one of them, almost afraid to ask the question. The agent discerned his look.

"You'll be going to the jail at the County Detention Facility," he said. He flashed him a greasy smile that jelled into a smirk. "How's it feel to be back in Richmond?" Ed didn't respond.

They drove out of the terminal, turned on South Airport Drive, merged onto I-64, and sped toward town. Twenty minutes later they approached the jail—the same one Gunther Buford ha been held in. Ed barely hung on emotionally.

"What happens next," Ed managed as they parked. The agent twisted around in the front seat.

"You'll appear before a circuit court judge on the new felony charge for your escape. You'll have a court-appointed attorney if you can't afford one. Your escape will necessitate a trial. Based upon the Comeback Law, double time will be added to your original sentence. I understand you were already sentenced to life, so I guess that definitely means no parole. You're still under the jurisdiction of the penitentiary," he added, "so, after your trial you'll be sent there."

"What about…the chain gang?" Ed swallowed hard, wondering if Jeb had already been notified.

"Whether you'll be transferred there later is anybody's guess," he said. They entered the building.

Fingerprinted, Ed was then led to lockup where he stepped into a cold, concrete cubicle. Spasmodic shudders swept through him.

Could this be the same cell Gunther sat in?

That night, Ed was besieged with nightmares. He was back on the chain gang being tortured at the whipping post. Benny's bloodied body was there, as well as all the swarming deer flies.

Then the scene changed and he was racing panic-stricken through fields and swamps, his clothes catching on barbed-wired fences, tripping, tumbling into ditches, slipping in the mud, struggling out of quicksand—all the time, howling bloodhounds barely a snarl away. Captured and dragged back to camp with the hard road ruts pummeling his body, he was thrown down in front of the mess hall and greeted by Jeb's hideous, sneering face. It was a relief when he awoke.

Exhausted, Ed sat on the edge of the cot in the dark gripping his head in his hands. He felt like he'd been run over by a locomotive. The dream was real enough—he could expect that and more. He wished he could talk to his mama.

Why did she fill his head with all those fanciful ideas of everything working for his good? Why did he ever think God was aware of him? Fat chance he'd even find Rob Hill after all this time. Even if Hill were in Richmond somewhere, he'd have to go through his court-appointed attorney who probably wouldn't believe him. It was all a lost cause. In six months to a year, he groaned, "I'll be dead.

He stared through the barred window into the night sky as the darkness of depression enveloped him, imagining Gus at the A-1 Star drinking a beer and rejoicing.

By the time the morning sunlight effused the cell, Ed had pulled himself out of his depression. During the night, one of his mother's dictums kept filtering through his fogged mind. *"Where there's life, there's always hope."* Something about it resonated. Was it because of his desperation? Or did it mean there was a chance his court-appointed attorney might believe him about Gus? He let out a long, mournful sigh. He was grasping at straws.

He thought about Rob Hill and an idea suddenly jostled him. He had forgotten he had one phone call coming to him. No reason he couldn't call the D.A's office and see if he could contact Hill before his attorney arrived. The guy would jump at the chance to nail Buford after all this time. If successful, the wheels would be in motion by the time his attorney showed up.

He called to the jailer through the bars.

"I need to place a telephone call. I have that right, don't I?" He heard a chair scrape against the concrete floor.

"I'll check."

"I also need the telephone number of the D.A.'s office."

"Be back in a minute."

Ed heard the heavy steel door at the end of the corridor open and shut. Minutes later the jailer returned holding a pair of wrist and ankle cuffs.

"You can make one phone call." He handed him a scrap of paper through the bars. "Here's the number. But you're sure not gonna have much luck calling *that* office. It'd make more sense if you called your attorney."

"I don't know his name," Ed replied. "The court appointed him. But I'm sure he'll be contacting me soon."

"Place your wrists near the bars."

The jailer reached in and snapped the handcuffs on. Stooping down, he affixed the ankle chains, and then unlocked the cell door. Ed followed him to the end of the hall. The jailer pointed to a telephone on the wall.

"Ya got three minutes." He sat down in a chair, balanced the chair back on its two back legs and folded his arms to wait.

Ed raised his cuffed hands and dialed. The number rang three times before someone answered.

"Prosecutor's office."

"May I speak to Rob Hill?"

"Who?"

"Rob Hill...the Chief Prosecutor."

"Willis Mucklestone holds that position. But just a minute, I've only been here a short while." He heard her turn away from the phone. "Any of you heard of Rob Hill?" The responses were muffled.

"I'm sorry," she said, coming back to the phone, "Rob Hill is no longer with this office—hasn't been for quite some time. He's now a judge over in Powhatan County."

Ed's heart sank. "Well, who can I talk to then? I'm being held at the county jail. I'm innocent of a crime and I know who—"

"Click." The dial tone sounded.

He stared at the phone, hung up the receiver, and shuffled over to the jailer.

"They hung up on me. How come?"

The jailer shook his head matter-of-factly. "Personnel at those offices are trained to know that when prisoners call they're either trying to get someone to bring them cigarettes, or hope someone will listen to their sob story. You got anything to say, they figure you can tell it to your attorney."

"Well," Ed persisted, "when am I going to hear from him?"

"Give him time," he said wryly, "but don't count on it soon. Most come the day just before the trial. Sometimes you may not see him until you walk into court."

Desperation welled up. Ed's voice rose. "But I have to talk to him before then. Have you any idea which attorney has been assigned to me?"

"Nope...and you can't make any more telephone calls, so simmer down."

Ed's face flushed hot as the jailer led him back to his cell and locked him in. He dropped onto his cot and stared at the floor.

What if his attorney didn't show until the day of the trial? There'd be no chance to tell him his story. Of course, even if he showed up in enough time, there was no guarantee he'd believe him. The only person who might was now a judge in a different county and there was no point in trying to telephone him. Mr. Casey told him once that judges weren't allowed to listen to personal pleas from prisoners. He mulled over what the man in the cell opposite him had told him the day before.

"You might as well forget it, man. Court-appointed attorneys don't care. They just figure you're one more guilty guy who got caught and you're gettin' whatcha deserve."

Ed grimaced. Everything appeared hopeless.

If he could only get to Powhatan County.

A week rolled by and no attorney. Ed paced the floor. No doubt he had been assigned one of those I-don't-care attorneys. Well, he couldn't just stand around and do nothing. Sitting Indian-style in the middle of his cot, he spent an hour devising two plans.

Plan A was to hopefully talk with his attorney—that is, if he arrived in enough time before the trial. If he did, he would ask him to relay his story about Buford to the new D.A., Mucklestone. But if Mucklestone declined to pursue it, or if his attorney didn't arrive in time, he would set Plan B into motion—escape and somehow get to Powhatan County and force his way in to see Rob Hill.

To accomplish that he would need a weapon and a hostage. It would either have to be his attorney or the jailer—whichever opportunity materialized first. If the jailer, he'd manipulate him into his cell by faking being sick. If his attorney, he'd grab him after the jailer opened the cell, move out into the hall with the weapon pressed against his throat, and then lock the jailer in the cell. Once out of lockup, he'd demand the clerk turn over a key to one of the patrol cars. He saw them hanging from a pegboard when he first arrived.

If he hadn't been shot by then, he'd make his hostage drive to the Powhatan County Courthouse. The police would never dream he would head to see a judge. They'd be searching railroad yards and highways leading out of town. He listened to himself, confident it was a good plan, but his insides twisted.

During the ride, he might even be successful in convincing the hostage of his innocence and why he needed to see Hill. But if complications arose and he couldn't get inside the courthouse with the hostage—prickly barbs raced down his spine—he'd drop him off somewhere unharmed, ditch the car, and lay low for a few days until he decided his next move.

The following few days, Ed studied every movement of the jailer, timed the coming and going of guards, and carefully noted the time for lights out.

"Jailer?" he called through the bars.

"Whatcha want?" came the voice at the end of the corridor.

"Any chance I could get a toothbrush?"

"Sure, I'll get you one."

Ed heard the chair scrape against the floor and the steel door open at the end of the hall. In five minutes he returned with a brown, wood-handled toothbrush. Handing it to Ed through the bars, he supplied him with a cup of water.

"Thanks—appreciate it." The jailer nodded and lumbered back to his post.

Ed quietly pulled his cot a few inches away from the wall. Perfect. Just what he was looking for—a cracked brick with a jagged edge.

That night after lights out, he lay face down on the cot with his blanket pulled up close to his neck. Sliding one arm out, he hung it down between his bed and the wall. Holding the bristle end in his hand he began snoring. With each thunderous exhalation he synchronized the scraping of the handle. Up and down he rubbed the sides, rotating the toothbrush against the rough edge of the brick, until sleep overpowered him.

In two nights time, he created a sharp, pointed instrument he could hold at the attorney or jailer's neck. Not that he'd really plunge it into their throat, but they wouldn't know that.

This was his only chance as far as he could figure.

CHAPTER 79

~~~

The jailer's voice called from down the hallway

"Hey, Bowman! You've got a visitor—your attorney."

Ed's stomach rushed up into his throat. He heard the steel door open and shut at the end of the corridor. This was it—Plan A. Now, all he had to do was tell his story convincingly.

The jailer plodded down the hallway. Following behind was the lawyer, a tall, lanky man in his early thirties with a wavy crop of red hair, wearing a gray, pinstriped suit. The jailor unlocked the cell door, placed a chair inside and left. The attorney's cologne floated in with him, a mix of leather and new-mown grass.

"Mr. Bowman, I'm Ray Huxley, your attorney." He flashed a wide smile and extended his hand. Ed took it and managed a return smile.

"I'm here," Huxley began, clearing his throat and sitting down, "to talk about the charges against you. This will be brief.

"In reviewing the documents forwarded from Tooele, plus your fingerprints, there remains no doubt as to your identity. Your trial is set for next Tuesday at ten o'clock. I'll see you then, but just wanted to touch base." He stood and turned toward the cell door to call the jailer.

"Wait!" Ed rasped the word out.

Huxley looked back. "Oh, don't worry," he added, "I'll send over a suit of clothes so you'll look presentable—"

"No. That isn't it," Ed blurted. "There's something I need to tell you." His voice rose to an uncomfortable degree. "Please...sit back down."

The attorney, slightly perturbed, returned to the chair. "Can you make it short? I have another appointment—"

"I realize," Ed cut in, trying to swallow past the lump forming in his throat, "you're probably too young to have been an attorney in 1938, but I know where an escaped prisoner is—Gunther Buford. He was a guard at the penitentiary who murdered the warden's daughter. But he also committed a second murder, my wife, for which I was wrongfully convicted. Michael Payne and Barry Triving were his defense attorneys. The prosecuting attorney was Rob Hill."

Huxley cocked his head. "I know Payne—good man—recently retired." He gave Ed a slow, appraising glance, reached into his breast pocket and whipped out a small notebook flipping it open unconcernedly. "Okay," he said, "let's hear it."

Encouraged, Ed plunged right in.

"A few years before my incarceration, I was a reporter for the *Casey Clarion* in Hannigan." Startled, the attorney looked up. Ed went on.

"My first assignment was to cover the murder trial of Gunther Buford who, as I said, was accused of killing the warden's daughter. On the day before the trial, in a secluded corridor of the courthouse, I accidentally overheard the defense attorneys, Payne and Triving, voicing anger over the prosecution's new witness—a sales clerk who sold a unique pair of earrings to Buford that matched the single earring left on the victim's body. The other one was missing. I also heard them admit they believed Buford guilty but needed to win the case to avoid losing an important client.

"I immediately dashed back to the *Clarion* and wrote my article on what I heard. The story came out in the evening paper. Unfortunately, Buford read my article in jail and realized the contents were damaging to his defense. Deciding he was good as convicted, he escaped rather than stand trial. Before he fled, he came gunning for me.

Huxley calmly wrote in his note pad.

"To make a long story short," Ed continued, upset at Huxley's lack of interest, "he showed up at the *Clarion*." His voice thickened with emotion. "A wild shot aimed at me killed my wife Sarah instead. Buford took off, and I was blamed for her death because my fingerprints were on the gun from having picked it up."

Huxley blinked with surprise. "What about Buford's?"

Ed massaged the bridge of his nose to halt an oncoming headache. "He wore gloves. But there's more.

"After I spent three years at the penitentiary, my fourth on a chain gang, I worked up to trustee and escaped."

"Quite a feat. How'd you manage that?"

Ed launched into his story about Avery and Wendover.

"I determined to bring him to justice. Buford is in Wendover now—if he hasn't taken off—and works for the Western Pacific Railroad under the alias of Gus Mooreland.

"I told all this to the sheriff who arrested me, Kevin Thompson, but because he's friends with Gus wouldn't believe me."

"Got any real proof this Gus is Buford?" Huxley asked.

"Sorta. I broke into his house." Huxley's eyebrows shot up.

"I not only found part of the clipping of the *Clarion* article I wrote, but a photograph of a young woman who may prove to be the warden's daughter. Also, an earring which I believe will match the single earring the police have in evidence—if they still have it." Ed scooted to the edge of the cot and leaned forward.

"During my time in Wendover," he continued, "I used an alias in working for the railroad. Gus didn't know my real identity, but I became a threat to him anyway because he knew I hailed from Virginia. I guess he thought I might recognize him from some newspaper picture from the trial back then. Anyway, he and an accomplice tried to do me in more than once."

"Where's the earring now?" Huxley asked, his pencil hovering over his notepad.

"I left it inside a tobacco can hidden in my section house, including the partial newspaper clipping and the photograph. I didn't take it to the sheriff earlier because there was no way to prove I got it from Gus' house. None of it was conclusive enough. Further, my possession of the earring would have made me look like I was the one who killed the warden's daughter and took it— that I was trying to frame Gus because of a competitive conflict over his girlfriend.

"After my arrest, I begged the sheriff to get it and put it somewhere for safekeeping. I'm hoping he did, but he was adamant in not believing my story about Gus."

Huxley scribbled more on his pad while Ed fidgeted and studied the attorney's face. The man was all business.

"Well, counselor," Ed stammered, "is that enough to convince you and the Prosecutor? If so, the police will have to act fast. I tried calling Mucklestone's office, but didn't get anywhere. I was hoping to contact Rob Hill, the prosecutor at the time of Buford's trial, but he's now a judge in Powhatan County."

Huxley wrote Hill's name down, slipped the notebook back into his shirt pocket, and looked up. Ed saw no hint of anything promising in his expression.

"Well, you've got quite a story," he responded in a monotone. Ed couldn't pick up whether he believed him or not.

"I'll contact the Prosecutor's office and see what the chief thinks. Whether he believes your story is anyone's guess. I'll let you know. If he does, I'm sure he'll act quickly. On the other hand—no offense—but cons do concoct some pretty good stories."

Ed groaned. "Mr. Huxley, that's all I'm asking for. You have no idea what this will mean to me. Besides vindication, justice will be served for the murder of my wife, Sarah whom I dearly loved."

"I'll get back to you."

"When?" Ed pushed, getting up from the cot.

"I'll try to reach Mucklestone this afternoon, but he's hard to catch. I'll let you know by Monday afternoon for sure one way or the other." With that, he left.

Ed collapsed back onto his cot. At least Huxley would follow through, or sounded like he would. However, if Mucklestone didn't buy any of it, and Huxley's waiting as late as Monday afternoon to let him know and his hearing the very next morning, it would force him to put Plan B into motion immediately. The thought nearly unglued him.

Plan B would really be walking the knife-edge of danger. He could only hope his sanity wouldn't give way while he waited.

CHAPTER 80

~~~

Kevin pulled his patrol car up to the front of the jail. It was Sunday, his day off, but he didn't mind. He had to prepare an equipment requisition and mail it off to Tooele on Monday. It should have been done Friday.

Sliding out of the car, he sauntered across the graveled surface toward the door of the jail. He glanced up at the sky. Still a good color but a slight nip in the air. Fall was around the corner and days for outings diminishing. The near-yellow leaves on the cottonwoods verified his prediction. Good thing he and Gus chose yesterday to go to Blue Lake. He felt his face tighten with an unidentified emotion. He stretched his mouth a couple of times to relax the muscles, and unlocked the door.

Upon entering, he paused for a second and stared at the doorway leading into the cells. Only days ago, Ed tried to explain away the killing of his wife and why he escaped prison. What a shockeroo that was. Who would have thought him an escaped felon?

He plodded over to the desk and sank into his chair. He'd get his report done quickly so he could get back home. He didn't want Patti sulking all day. She never did understand how seriously he took his responsibility and that taking one day out of the weekend now and then wasn't the end of the world. This evening, he'd make it up to her by taking her to dinner at the Stateline Hotel.

Picking up a pencil, he started to reach for the requisition form but instead thought about yesterday at Blue Lake. Gus had been particularly jovial, no doubt because of his new position and upcoming transfer. He'd definitely miss him. Fortunately, Queenie seemed to be enjoying his company since Ed was no longer in the picture. Gus told him he was confident he could persuade her to go to California with him.

His thoughts shifted back to Ed's preposterous story. He pressed his lips into a thin line. No way was Gus a murderer. The

473

very thought threatened to suck him down into a place he didn't want to go.

He let out an annoyed sigh and pulled out a side drawer and withdrew the tobacco tin Ed had pleaded with him to get. Well, he did.

Flipping the top open with his thumb, he emptied the envelope and its contents onto the desk. He had looked at all of it before. It was idiotic to think any of it contained evidence against Gus. Gus also confirmed to him that no one broke into his house.

He gently lifted the fragile corners of the paper with burned edges and pulled it out. He looked at the word *...ion. Then, circula....* Obviously a newspaper article but it didn't prove it was about Buford, or that Ed wrote it.

He carefully laid it aside and unfolded the recommendation letter from Mason Furniture. Nothing there at all. Obviously a forgery, since the letter was dated the same time period Ed was in prison.

Reaching for the snapshot of the young woman, he tilted it toward the window light. No telling who she is. He looked at the earring. Strange. Only one. Obviously, a keepsake.

He replaced everything back into the can and placed it into the drawer. Absolutely nothing to incriminate Gus. Ed simply used the contents to bluff his way out of capture and avoid being sent back to prison.

A heavy shadow pressed his spirit. Why couldn't he shake it? Maybe it was because he never questioned Gus in detail for his report. He hadn't thought it necessary at the time.

Yet, considering Ed's accusations, unfounded as they were, perhaps he should have. Technically, it needed to be in his official account. Without it, it could boomerang on him later if superiors called him on it saying he hadn't followed procedure. He had to make it right. Yes, that was what was bugging him.

All he had to do for the arrest record was have Gus respond to a few routine questions and provide paperwork establishing his identity as Gus Mooreland. Surely the guy had a birth certificate. Not for one minute did he think Gus guilty, but since Patti wanted to move to Tooele to live, he wanted his records to be impeccable for when the time came he transferred to his new job. He felt a

474

ripple of relief.

Gus would go along with it when he explained he needed to cover his ass with his superiors. Gus, however, did have a temper. He winced and tapped the end of his pencil against his chin. He processed his thoughts slowly and carefully. He didn't want to offend him.

He glanced at the clock. Gus told him he'd be working overtime Sunday with the Signal Operator to get a start on his new job. It wasn't anywhere close to Gus' quitting time yet. He'd drive to the depot, leave a message in his box, and ask him to meet him early tomorrow morning. Seven o'clock would provide ample time before Gus had to report to work.

Grabbing two sheets of his *Wendover Sheriff* letterhead from the middle drawer, he arranged a carbon in-between and began to write, making sure he worded it well enough so Gus wouldn't be overly concerned.

He reread it and felt satisfied. He locked up, sauntered out to his car, and drove to the train station and placed his letter in Gus' box.

He went to the Beanery, had some coffee, and then went back to the jail to complete his equipment requisition.

Gus gave a good-natured wave to Troy Monahan, the Signal and Switch Operator, as they parted. "See ya on Monday."

He let out a breath of relief. He looked at the sky. It would soon be dark. They had worked overtime on Sunday. Troy was hoping to narrow the time in teaching him so he could leave sooner for Ohio. That might also shorten his own time so he could transfer to California faster. Yet, working that long, his back ached and his feet hurt.

He and Troy walked everywhere on foot, performing on-ground track inspections and evaluating defects to assess the best means of correction. He also taught him how to determine track profiles by coordinating the operation of a track geometry test car. He felt good.

The more skills he gained in the short time before he transferred would help. When he arrived in California he'd be at a higher place on the totem pole and have the respect he deserved.

Only seven weeks—maybe sooner. He visualized an invincible future ahead of him.

Shoving the office door open, he hustled past the desks and headed down the corridor to the locker room.

"Hey, Gus!" He stopped and turned back.

The clerk at the front desk pointed toward the stationmaster's office. "Kevin asked me to let you know he left a message in your box."

Gus raised his eyebrows. "Yeah? I'll get it before I take off."

Sauntering down the hall to the lockers, he wondered what Kevin wanted. Probably to set up another day to do something special. He gave an approving smile. Kevin considered them good friends. At Blue Lake he even said he would miss him. He snickered. All that meant to him was that he had played his cards right and was in solid with Wendover's naïve, hick-town sheriff.

He passed the personnel office where he had taken Scratch's letter, recalling the night Ed broke into his house and stole it back. All past history now. But he regretted no longer having Sue's earring

He reached his locker and grabbed his jacket, grinning at the thought of what Ed was in for—the filth, brutality, the hopelessness, the mummy-like condition prisoners so often went into before they died—unless they were killed by a shiv in the back first.

No, he wouldn't last long. Maybe Ed never would have identified him, but he couldn't take that chance. Good thing he thought to burn his papers.

Snapping the padlock shut, he strolled back up the hall. Entering the stationmaster's office he moseyed over to the pigeonholes, grabbed the protruding envelope and nonchalantly ambled back down the hall and left through the rear door.

Lumbering across the yard, he ripped open Kevin's envelope. Reaching his truck, he scooted into the seat and pulled the letter from its envelope.

"What?" He yanked his head back in surprise and raised his left eyebrow a fraction. *Official letterhead?* Why so formal, Kevin? He began to read.

Dear Gus,

Would you mind stopping by the jail tomorrow morning at seven before you report for work?

476

The case is settled about Ed Bowman, of course, but due to my own negligence I never included questioning you at the time. I didn't feel it necessary, but for the sake of my records I should have, since you were included in Ed's false accusation. This is just to cover myself in case my superiors wonder why it isn't in the record.

It shouldn't take long. Just a few questions. I'd also appreciate it if you could bring some paperwork like a birth certificate to establish proof of your identity. Nothing to be concerned about.

Your friend,

Kevin

Gus gaped at the letter, his mouth hanging ajar. Something intuitive sent a warning. For some reason, he didn't buy Kevin's reason about pacifying his superiors. And a birth certificate to verify his identity? This really presented a problem.

He studied the letter. Could he be reading more into it than he should? He reread it, this time his sense of alarm increasing. A nerve flicked at the corner of his mouth.

"This is not good," he mumbled. The whole scenario radiated danger. What could he do about a birth certificate? He no longer had connections with anyone who could forge one for him. Telling Kevin he lost it would appear suspicionable.

He stared in an unseeing gaze through the dirt-streaked windshield. What to do...what to do?

The answer immediately shuddered through him—the only possible one. It hit with sledgehammer force.

Get out of here, Buford. Now!

Turning the ignition, he threw the car into gear and jammed his foot on the accelerator. Speeding out of the yard, he raced the truck toward home thinking he'd worked two long years for his transfer, including a future with Queenie in populous California where he'd be safe from police, and all his carefully laid plans— down the toilet. He clamped his jaw tight. Resentment, anger and frustration spasmed across his face.

He flew past the water tower without even giving Bum's Jungle a side-glance, and barreled down the circuitous roads through the conglomeration of trailers until he skidded into his driveway.

Leaping out, his nerves at full stretch, he dashed through the front door and rushed into the bedroom.

He could still head for California. He knew plenty of side roads and detours across the desert to avoid the main highways. Once there, he'd lose himself in the urban sprawl but would have to find a different job. That meant he'd have to start all over with a new alias. He groaned. He did it once, and he could do it again.

He would have a good twelve hours head start before Kevin came looking for him when he didn't show in the morning. He pulled out all his dresser drawers, wrenched the clothes out and threw them onto the bed. Sweat ran from his forehead and stung his eyes. Maybe he just might head for Mexico instead.

Scuttling over to the closet, he whisked two suitcases from the top shelf, threw them onto the bed and stuffed clothes into them. Latching the clasps, he streaked into the front room with them and placed them in the doorway. He ran back into the kitchen, pulled paper sacks from a drawer and threw in as much food as he could from the cupboards and icebox. Sprinting out the front door, he loaded them into the truck, raced back to the doorway and grabbed his suitcases.

He gave a quick eye-sweep around to make sure he wasn't leaving anything important behind. Without bothering to shut the front door, he charged back out to his vehicle, tossed the suitcases into the back, and then jumped into the seat. He looked at the sky. It was already growing dark.

He backed out of the driveway and tore down the road past the water tower, his knuckles gripping the steering wheel. At the main highway, he slowed. It took all his will power to keep from flooring the accelerator. He couldn't attract attention.

He passed the Stateline Hotel, then drove over the hill to the Nevada side, zipping by the A-1 Star.

Turning left on the Ely highway, he stomped on the gas and sped off into the night.

CHAPTER 81

~~~

Ed staggered around his cell, worn out from the tension. The whole weekend was spent in a nervous blur waiting for Monday when Huxley would report D.A. Mucklestone's response.

During the time he watched visitors come and go and listened to their endless chatter—tobacco-roughened voices, hyena-like nervous laughs, and women with sobs in their voices—all the time thinking about his arrest in Wendover, Kevin refusing to believe his story, and replaying Don's betrayal of their friendship.

Monday had now arrived, and he had no idea if his attorney or the D.A. believed him. Adding to his alarm was the fact that Huxley should have arrived by now. It was already after two o'clock and time was of the essence.

With sweaty fingers he gripped the toothbrush concealed in his pocket, just in case. If the attorney brought bad news, he'd be ready to shift immediately into Plan B.

At two-thirty, he heard conversation at the end of the corridor. He recognized Huxley's voice. His heart galloped, but as the dialogue moved closer there were more voices than just his and the jailer's. Could it be Mucklestone?

Rushing over to the bars, he frantically peered down the hallway. The jailer was dragging a couple of chairs down the corridor toward his cell. Huxley followed. Behind him an older man, casually dressed in brown slacks and a checkered jacket. Couldn't be Mucklestone. No suit. He felt concern spread across his face Whoever the guy was, it would foul everything up. Huxley had to be alone for him to use as hostage.

Ed stepped back as they approached the bars. The jailer unlocked the door and motioned the two men inside. He set the chairs down and left.

"This gentleman," Huxley said, addressing Ed and turning to the stocky man with thick glasses that magnified his eyes twice their size, "is Bob Jenkins." Jenkins offered his hand.

Ed let go of the toothbrush and pulled out a clammy palm, wiped it on his pants and shook the man's hand. Who was this guy? Why was he involved? Could it be that Huxley was shifting his case to another court-appointed attorney? But he wasn't dressed like an attorney.

Ed lowered himself back onto the cot as the two men sat. He studied Huxley's expressionless face. No indication whether Mucklestone believed his story or not. His only hope to use him as his hostage would be if Jenkins left first, and he came up with some pretense for Huxley to stay afterwards. Of course, the jailer was his other alternative, but the attorney was his best bet for getting into the Powhatan courthouse.

He slid his hand back into his pocket, tightened his grip around the toothbrush, and tensed for the impact of whatever was to come next. Huxley was the first one to speak and introduced Jenkins further.

His unexpected words caused Ed to give a jerk of surprise. He blinked his eyes twice.

He didn't expect this.

CHAPTER 82

~~~

Early Monday morning Kevin sat at his desk arranging a stack of papers. He glanced at the clock. Seven-twenty. Gus was twenty minutes late for their meeting. He stood and sauntered over to the corner, grabbed a broom and dustpan and headed down the back corridor. He wasn't worried. He'd be here soon.

He whistled a tune while sweeping the floor, musing over the note he left in Gus' box. He had worded it just fine. No way Gus should be concerned. His cooperation would sure help cover his butt if his records were examined.

He bent over and swept the dirt into the dustpan, and then shuffled back up the corridor to the office and emptied it into a green wastebasket. He glanced at the clock again and pursed his lips. He'd give Gus a call at home. Maybe it slipped his mind.

He picked up the phone and dialed. The hollow-sounding ring on the other end repeated itself seven times. He hung up.

Maybe Monday was a bad day—his new job and everything. He'd swing by the depot, leave another message in his box and arrange for a different time. He thrust the broom and dustpan into the corner, grabbed his keys and headed for the door when the phone rang. He turned back and grabbed up the receiver.

"Gus? I was just going to—"

"Is this Sheriff Kevin Thompson?" came the voice in his ear.

"Oh…yes. Sorry for that. I was expecting a call from someone. What can I do for you?"

"Willis Mucklestone here, District Attorney in Richmond, Virginia."

Kevin blinked with surprise. "Yes, Mr. Mucklestone. How can I help you?"

"Your county recently extradited a criminal to Richmond, an Ed Riley, alias Bowman, and I was told you were the arresting sheriff. Is that correct?"

"Yes sir." Kevin pulled his body to attention.

"I would like to check out an assertion the prisoner is making about evidence presently in your keeping." Kevin cringed. He knew what that was.

"Sir, I'm guessing you mean the tobacco tin Mr. Bowman, I mean Mr. Riley, claimed contains evidence about another criminal. Let me assure you, Mr. Mucklestone, I have examined the contents more than once and there's absolutely nothing in it remotely bearing on his—"

Mucklestone interrupted. "Except for one thing," he said. "Now, I'd appreciate it if you would assist me." His voice was impatient.

Kevin grimaced. Ed really did a snow job on the Richmond guys. "Sure." His words were flat. "Anything to oblige. What do you need?"

"Bring the earring to the telephone."

"Sure thing." He laid the receiver down. Breathing a tremulous sigh, he reached into the drawer and pulled out the tin. Opening it, he shook the earring out onto the desktop. He picked up the receiver.

"Got it right in front of me."

"Good. I have in my hand the earring obtained from our evidence room left at the scene of a 1938 murder allegedly committed by one Gunther Buford. I'm going to describe it to you. Tell me if they match." Kevin felt a weightless chill.

"The one I have," Mucklestone began, "contains a round emerald in the center surrounded by eight rubies. On the outer rim is a border of iridescent mother-of-pearl."

"Well...yes sir." Kevin's words felt strangled. "They are...a match."

"So," he asked, "can you explain how Ed Bowman came by it?" Kevin drew in a quick breath.

"The only explanation..." His voice trailed off and he began again. "The only explanation I can think of, Mr. Mucklestone, is Ed is the murderer."

"Well, of course, that's possible, but discovery in the trial appears to contradict that. Ed Bowman had no contact with the victim nor did he have a motive. He claims a man in your town, a Gus Mooreland, is in fact Gunther Buford who not only murdered the warden's daughter but also killed his wife.

Kevin shot up tall in his chair. "Sir, there's no way! The man

482

is a hard, honest worker on the Western Pacific Railroad and is a close friend of mine. I can say for sure," he said, waving his hand with a flourish, "that conjecture is wrong. I've known him for some time," he added. "Why, just yesterday we went fishing together..." His voice weakened to a thin whisper and a strange panic whirled through his body.

"Be that as it may," came the terse voice on the other end, "our office would appreciate your cooperation in obtaining the fingerprints of Mr. Mooreland to see if they match the fingerprint on the earring in our possession. If they don't, fine."

Kevin recoiled. How could he ask Gus to do that? Dread raced through him.

"Well, Sheriff Thompson?"

"Yes... Yes, of course. I'll get right to it and get them off to you. Give me your telephone number and where to send them." Grabbing up a pencil, he slid a piece of paper in front of him and wrote it down.

"Thank you, Sheriff. Give me a call when they're in the mail." A click ended the conversation followed by the dial tone.

Kevin hung the receiver up and slumped against the back of his chair. The call totally unglued him. Was there any possibility Gus could indeed be... He couldn't even finish the thought.

He shot his arm forward, grabbed up the phone and dialed the trainmaster's office. He took a quick intake of breath as if about to plunge into icy water. A clerk answered.

"Jay J. Dugan's office."

"Give me Dugan." Kevin fidgeted while he waited, glancing again at the clock. Nine-thirty.

"Hi there, Jay, Kevin Thompson here. How ya doin'? Say, could you tell me if Gus has checked in yet, or if he's on a different time schedule today?"

"Got a problem there, Kevin. Gus should have clocked in at eight this morning. Hasn't shown up. I was just about to contact Eadie and have her run down to his house and see what's wrong. Maybe he's sick."

Kevin took a pained breath and closed his eyes. An uneasiness crept over him.

"Kevin, you there?"

483

"Yeah, Jay. Thanks."

He hung up the receiver and gulped down the saliva that had balled up in the back of his throat. He sat for a few seconds when adrenaline jolted him out of his chair.

He sprang around the corner of the desk, grabbed his keys and tore out the door. Jumping into the patrol car, he gunned the engine and tore off down the road leaving a twisted swirl of exhaust behind.

He turned left at the Merc, his stomach clenching and unclenching, turned another left, and sped down the road toward the red water tower and Gus' house.

There was no way he was wrong about Gus. He was probably ill. Otherwise he would have kept their appointment. There had to be a logical explanation. He struggled against the notion that ricocheted through his head. Oh Lord," he gasped. Was Ed's story right? No. Maybe I'll find him lying unconscious on the floor.

Whipping the steering wheel to the right, he spied Gus' house ahead and noticed the front door wide open. A burglar. His truck wasn't there either. Panic shifted along his jugular. He jounced the car into the rutted driveway and killed the motor.

He leapt out, and streaked toward the front porch. Maybe Gus met with foul play. He withdrew his gun from his holster. With one bound, he vaulted over the three stone steps and entered the front room. Everything was quiet.

"Gus?"

He stealthily moved through the front room, then to the kitchen. A chair was knocked over and the icebox door was open. He looked inside. Cleaned out. He hustled to the bedroom door and cautiously pushed it open a crack. "Gus, you in there?"

He opened the door wider and gawked. Everything was in disarray. Dresser drawers were hanging out, empty. He strode to the closet. No clothes. Empty hangers lay on the floor. He slumped back against the wall widening his eyes as the painful reality hit.

Ed was right—and he'd been played. Gus was Gunther Buford!

He staggered back into the front room sick to his stomach. He moved slowly to the front door and stepped outside. He stood on the top step and took a deep breath.

Gus, his friend, was gone.

CHAPTER 83

~~~

Ed's mind was a collage of muddled confusion at Huxley's shocking words when he identified Bob Jenkins. Ed stared at the older man with the thick glasses and eyes twice their size. He arched his eyebrows in a questioning slant. It made no sense.

"Yes, Mr. Bowman." Huxley smiled. "You're probably wondering why a representative from the Parole Board is here."

Ed knew he'd never be eligible for parole. They certainly wouldn't be making an exception in his case. Even if they were, a parole wouldn't clear his name. Why wasn't Huxley telling him the results of his contact with Mucklestone?

Huxley waved his arm toward Jenkins. "I'll let him tell you about it."

All Ed could do was wait.

"I'm here, Mr. Bowman," Jenkins began in a casual tone, "because the Board has deliberated over numerous letters from Utah sent to the Prison Commission.

"Letters?" Ed asked.

"Yes, from residents of Wendover, all on your behalf. Every letter claims you held a responsible job, were a model citizen, and an admired member of a local church."

Ed knew the letters certainly couldn't be from ward members, or could they—definitely not the bishop. Maybe railroad friends... Hutch? Bart? Jake?

"The Commission," he continued, smiling, "turned those letters over to the Sentence Review Board and that's why I'm here." He pushed his glasses up on his nose, enlarging his eyes even more.

"After taking into consideration your rehabilitation, corroborated by the Wendover letters and the fact you no longer pose a threat to society, a decision was reached.

Ed felt a prickling sensation shimmy up his spine. He relaxed his grip on the toothbrush. Maybe he was getting a parole after all—but that's *not* what he wanted—he needed to be exonerated!

485

Jenkins cleared his throat. "In conjunction with the recommendation of the chairman and the unanimous vote of the Board, the felony escape charge against you has been dismissed and your Comeback time waived."

His Comeback time waived? Ed let out a disappointing exhale. Why did they think this was good news? It would make no difference in his life sentence. He looked up as Jenkins quickly cut back in.

"Please, Mr. Bowman." He scooted his chair forward, scraping the wooden legs across the concrete floor. "Relax. You haven't heard the whole story. I'm trying to handle first things first. The Board also made another recommendation."

Baffled, Ed eyed him curiously but still held on to the toothbrush.

"But first," Jenkins added, "I'll let you hear what Mr. Huxley wants to tell you about his contact with Mr. Mucklestone." Ed braced himself.

"I reached Mucklestone," Huxley began. "And remember, I told you earlier he works fast? Well, he thought your story worth checking out and contacted Rob Hill over in Powhatan County. Judge Hill remembered the trial and said the victim's belongings including the single earring left on the body were still stored in the Evidence Room.

"Mucklestone telephoned Sheriff Thompson in Wendover and inquired about the earring you said was in the tobacco can. Thompson had done like you asked and had it. After the D.A. described the earring over the phone, the sheriff conceded they matched, but since there was no actual proof you found it in Gus Moreland's house he strongly suggested you could be the murderer and proceeded to give excuses why he didn't think Gus Mooreland could be Gunther Buford."

Huxley's words triggered a gush of nausea. Ed tensed against it and waited for more.

"Nevertheless," Huxley said, leaning forward, "Mucklestone insisted the sheriff bring Mr. Mooreland in for fingerprinting, and then send them on to him including all of the tobacco tin's contents. The sheriff, although reluctant, agreed."

Ed shot up straighter at the glimmer of hope, but it lasted only for a second. Huxley's next words were disheartening.

"However, sad to say, Mr. Bowman, Sheriff Thompson was unable to comply with the fingerprinting. An earlier request by him asking Mr. Mooreland to come in and verify his identity caused the man to flee Wendover."

Ed dropped his head and rubbed his forehead. Gone was any chance of bringing Gus in. It was the end of everything.

Before Huxley could continue, Jenkins interrupted.

"I want you to see this, Mr. Bowman." He withdrew a document from his briefcase, held it up and grinned.

"A request was put in to the governor to grant you a full pardon."

Ed dropped his jaw and stared at the sheet of paper.

"Yes, Mr. Bowman," Huxley chimed in, flashing a bigger grin than Jenkins, "you've been pardoned."

"But this isn't making sense." Ed scrunched his forehead lines and looked at both of them. "You said—"

"Well," Huxley broke in, "with the recent arrest of Gunther Buford—"

"What?" Ed nearly choked.

"An APB was put out on Mr. Mooreland—or I should say Gunther Buford. He covered his tracks well by cutting through Indian reservations down through Nevada and Arizona. Nevertheless, in Yuma he was apprehended before he could cross the border into Mexico. Richmond authorities requested Yuma to send his fingerprints."

Ed held his breath.

"Mucklestone relayed to me that Gus Mooreland's fingerprints matched those of Gunther Buford's."

Ed stared, stunned.

"You mean Buford," he stammered, "was captured?" Then he paused. "That's…uh…indeed great, but am I still going back to prison for my wife's murder?" A desolate expression settled on his face.

Huxley grinned. "I saved the best for last.

"Once Yuma received confirmation from Mucklestone that Mr. Moreland was indeed Buford, he was flown back to Richmond. There, they were able to break him into confessing that after he escaped he went to the *Clarion* intending to kill you due to your

487

article. We also checked with Mr. Casey. He gave a glowing recommendation of your character.

"So," he said, leaning back, tilting his chair on two legs, "you are not going back to prison. You're a free man."

Ed gawked at both men until his eyes burned. He could hardly believe the electrifying news. He let go of the toothbrush and had barely pulled his hand from his pocket to shake their hands when an unexpected trembling took over. Both hands began shaking. He stared at them. Then his whole body commenced to quiver.

Without warning, all the accumulated years of pent-up tension that lay twisted like a knotted-up rubber band inside him for so long, snapped loose—the trauma from losing Sarah...his prison experience...Jeb's tortures...his escape...grief over losing Maureen...trying to prove Gus was Buford...attempts on his life... Don refusing to help.

The whole gamut of it overpowered him, forcing a deep groan from his mouth that sounded like a woman in labor. With heaving chest, he buried his face in his hands and broke into uncontrollable sobs.

The two men looked at each other, smiled and waited...and waited.

Mr. Jenkins finally stood and approached Ed. He gently laid his hand on his shoulder. Ed looked up with swollen eyes.

"Congratulations, Mr. Bowman," he said softly. "You might also be interested to know the Department of Corrections is doing their best to change conditions existing back in the days of your incarceration. We have," he paused, "a pretty good idea of what you went through—especially on the chain gang. Do you have any questions?"

"I...I do have one," Ed managed, trying to control the shaking. "What about the road boss at the chain gang I was on...Jeb? Don't know his last name. He was...really bad."

"Hmm. Not sure." Jenkins stroked his chin for a few seconds while he returned to his chair. "Ah, yes," he said raising a finger as he sat down, "I do believe I know who you're referring to.

"The man I'm thinking of accidentally killed a prisoner years earlier when he was a guard at the penitentiary. He was demoted to working road crews—one work camp in particular. I do believe it was the one you were at. Yes, now I think about it, I'm sure. His first name was Jebulon.

"Just two years ago at the camp he killed a prisoner and a riot ensued. The inmates, even though shackled, managed to overcome the guards and wreck the place pretty badly. It caused a serious stir and officials investigated. With the testimony of so many prisoners telling of inmates tortured and killed, Jeb stood trial and was convicted. He's now serving a life sentence."

"I...I can hardly believe my ears," Ed gasped. "That's good...he got what he deserved. I know of one man for sure he killed."

"Well," Jenkins said, changing the subject, "I'm also here for another reason."

What else? Ed wondered. He didn't know if he could handle any more good news.

"Upon examining your accounting record at the penitentiary, we find there is a modest sum of money coming to you from your work in the furniture factory and the prison farm. Also, from the chain gang. After the necessary paperwork, which should come through tomorrow morning, you'll be released. You can collect your money from the clerk. It should be enough to rent a room and see you through until you obtain employment." He and Huxley stood.

Ed leaped up, grabbed their hands and shook them repeatedly. Too overcome for words he could only stammer, "Thank you... thank you."

Both men smiled looking pleased, and then called the jailer. Before they exited the cell Ed grabbed their hands and shook them again, and then peered through the bars and watched them disappear down the corridor. After he heard the steel door slam shut, he kept his feverish, flushed face pressed against the cold of the steel bars until his skin cooled.

He pulled the toothbrush from his pocket and stared at it. Ambling over to the cot, he lifted the corner of the mattress and tossed it underneath. Letting out a deep breath, he collapsed onto the bed unable to believe what transpired.

Pardoned.

Thank goodness he didn't try to implement Plan B.

To think I nearly blew it.

That night, he tried to sleep but couldn't. He should have been completely at peace but instead was disturbed. While his pardon and Buford's capture were incredible and he joyfully concluded God came through for him after all, his life wasn't fixed yet. Far from it.

There was one more thing he needed to do.

One that would take all the courage he could muster.

CHAPTER 84

~~~

Ed cracked his eyelids open as the first hint of sun crept through the cell window. Outside in the streets he heard the early rush of traffic and impatient honking of horns. Soon, he'd be part of all that. No more looking over his shoulder, no more fear of Buford, and no more panic about going back to prison. He lay there giddy with joy. He was finally free... Then his thoughts skidded to a complete stop.

Free? Who was he kidding? Not yet.

He still had one unpleasant task to accomplish. Yes, he avenged Sarah's death, Gunther Buford was arrested, Jeb got what he deserved, and he had been exonerated. Nevertheless, he still had one formidable task facing him.

He remembered the day he pulled Benny's body from the sweatbox and helped him hobble with his heel-strung foot to the hitching post where he was whipped to death both by himself and Jeb. He should have refused and tried to save Benny. Of course, he would have ended up dead as well, but he should have made the gesture. Why didn't he?

Was his rationalization right—telling himself he needed to stay alive so he could escape and track down Buford? Valid enough. But if the truth were known, at the core was his own sense of self-preservation—he didn't want to die. There was also his fear to defy Jeb.

The truth was hard to face. It revealed he wasn't the perfect, moral man he always thought himself to be—a man who would jump to right a wrong regardless of personal consequences.

Benny's pathetic words still grabbed at his heart. *"I been prayin' all night to die. But then I think about Ma. I'm all she's got. Promise me, if something happens, you'll let her know?"*

Ed ground his teeth and watched a daddy-long-leg crawl up the wall. Now he had to face Benny's mama for sure. If only he had heard from the California outfit before he had to leave Wendover.

491

He could have written an anonymous letter and been done with it. Of course, he could still write, but being in Richmond and sending a letter didn't seem right. His insides pinched tight. It had to be in person, or it would haunt him the rest of his life.

He skipped a breath envisioning the encounter, and took a nervous inhale. Confessing everything to her would be like shouting to the whole world, "Take a look at Ed Bowman—he's not the man he claims to be!"

Could he dare hear himself verbalize aloud how he contributed to her son's murder...stood by while Jeb finished him off and did nothing? Could she cope with that? Even more distressing, could he handle her reaction?

He swung his legs over the side of the cot, got up and plodded about the cell with slow, heavy steps. While he could empathize with any feelings Benny's mama might exhibit, she might really let him have it.

There were three possible responses she might use—be grateful to find out what happened to her son...fall to pieces and cry...or scream and get angry and kick him out saying she never wanted to set eyes on him again. Any of those responses would emotionally unravel him.

If ever he needed courage, it was now.

He ambled over to the window, raised himself on tiptoes and looked through the bars at the streets he would soon be walking. He wondered what Madge Yates was doing at that moment. Was she still alive?

He rehearsed the numerous platitudes about doing the right thing, including the one his mother always told him: *Son, do what is right, and you'll never go wrong.*

Lowering himself, he turned and moseyed over to the cell door and looked down the corridor. His release would be after breakfast. He wished it would hurry.

He lay back down on the cot, folded his arms behind his head, and studied the morning light that slowly crept across the plaster ceiling.

After breakfast, the jailer unlocked his cell door.

C'mon," he motioned with one hand, picking up Ed's breakfast tray with the other. "I'll show you where the office is so you can pick up what ya got comin' to you. Pretty good turn of luck for you. By the way, your attorney called. He'll meet you out in front and drop you wherever you need to go."

"Wow." Ed sucked in a surprised breath. "That's nice of him."

"Yeah, he's a pretty decent fellow."

"Does he do that for all his prisoner-clients?"

"Only those he feels deserve it."

Ed followed him down the long hallway and through the steel door into the administrative part of the building, passing the pegboard where the keys to the police cars hung. He momentarily closed his eyes, recalling his plan to get to Rob Hill in Powhatan County using Huxley as hostage. Thankfully, he was saved from doing that. Everything had worked together for his good.

"There's the office down at the end. Last door on the left. When you get through, check out with him." He pointed to an officer who sat at a small table near the front door, then reentered lockup.

Ed set aside the subject of Madge Yates and proceeded down the corridor and pushed the brown-paneled door open. He was met with a frumpish-looking woman in her fifties standing behind the counter, her drab, yellow hair pulled up in a knot on top of her head. All business, she handed him a form to sign. Ed wrote his name at the bottom and handed it back to her. She slapped an envelope of money on the counter and then turned away to answer the telephone.

Ed nervously opened it and counted the bills. Nine hundred dollars! He spread a big grin across his face—certainly enough to give him a good start until he could send for his bank savings from Tooele. He also thought about Avery. He owed him. Carefully pocketing the bills, he exited the office and strode down the hall toward the front entrance where the officer sat at a small table. He stared as Ed approached.

"You Ed Bowman?" he asked.

"Sure am."

"Heard about your pardon. Congratulations." He penciled a checkmark on the register by Ed's name and looked back up.

"Wait outside on the front steps. Your attorney should be here soon."

Ed nodded, pushed the front door open and stepped out into his new world. He gazed up into the azure sky feeling a glorious sense of liberation.

The intensity of the blue reminded him of Blue Lake. He closed his eyes trying to recapture the feeling the day he stood in the sparkling water and had the amazing experience that something supernatural had wrapped its arms around him and had reassured him that all was well. He knew now it was God.

He opened his eyes, disappointed he couldn't duplicate the same feeling, but at least knew now it hadn't been his imagination. Through the whole time God had been with him and he never knew it.

He wondered if Wendover people had heard about his exoneration yet—or even would. He felt a momentary temptation to write a letter with a few caustic words to Don. *See, I was telling the truth after all.* No, he'd let Don hear it from Kevin, then let him stew in his own juice. He thought about his and Don's past conversations.

Admittedly, baptism had sounded good. Also temple work to get Maureen out of spirit prison, and the idea of being married for eternity. But that crazy story about angels and God telling Joseph Smith *all* churches were wrong? That would have to include the little country church his devout mama went to, and his sweet Maureen who loved her Bible so. He let out a deep sigh. Well, he'd give Don's religion more thought later. Right now, he had to focus on two other people he had to see before he tackled Madge Yates. He'd leave her till last.

His first visit would be Avery, not only to repay him the five hundred dollars but also ask if he could borrow a car. He'd look up his address in a telephone book.

Next, he'd drive to Hannigan and visit Mr. Casey. Besides seeing the town again, it would be so good to see him. Later, after he contacted Madge Yates, he would contact Bob Wilkinson for the exclusive he promised.

He watched the far end of the street for Huxley's car. In a few minutes a gray Lincoln appeared. Ed saw the red-haired attorney at the wheel. He moved down the steps to the curb.

"I sure do thank you," Ed said, opening the car door and climbing in.

Huxley smiled. "Well, considering everything you've been through, glad I can help. Any place in town you'd particularly like to go? Relatives?"

"Well, I'd like to get back across the river. Up around Capitol Square—East Grace Street to be exact. Not sure of the number so I'll have to find a telephone book."

Huxley nodded. "Yep, I know the neighborhood well."

In no time they entered Richmond's main hub near Capitol Square. A metaphor signal-arm brought the car to a stop. While the car idled, Ed took a look inside the grounds, first at the capital building with its impressive Greek columns and portico, and then at the equestrian statue of Washington and the six sculptures surrounding it. One of them was Patrick Henry. *Give me liberty,* he whispered, *or give me death.* The man knew what he was talking about. Freedom was priceless, not something to take for granted.

The signal changed. Huxley shifted gears and took off. Ed heard the loud, familiar bong coming from the old bell tower on the Square as they pulled away. It always sent squirrels scattering up trees and pigeons fluttering into the air. He pictured the octagonal cupola at the top that housed the bell. It always rang for special occasions like when the General Assembly was called into session. If the session was at noon, it rang twelve times. If it met at one, only once.

He also heard noon bells chiming from nearby St. Paul's Episcopal Church. The bell-ringer in Capitol Square's bell tower usually had to synchronize his bell to ring in-between theirs.

Yet, the bells had a different meaning for him. They were pealing out to signify his personal victory—also, to praise God without whom he never would have accomplished it all. He indeed worked everything together for his good. He couldn't say it enough times. His mama had to be ecstatic.

In the next block, Ed spied the white-pointed steeple of St. Paul's rising high above the other buildings. Its next few bongs brought another one of his mama's sayings to mind. *Bright is the ring of words when the right man rings them.*

Yes, he was the only person—the right person—to tell Madge Yates about her son. But whether doing the right thing would diminish any emotional outbursts she might hurl at him would remain to be seen. Whatever they turned out to be, he deserved them.

He listened to the rest of the bells. Later, when he had time, he'd stop by St. Paul's and see what information the pastor, bishop, or whatever they were called, could shed on the Mormon Church. Maybe he could be reassured that all the devastating pronouncements Don declared about his never qualifying for heaven and going to hell, were wrong. A stirring rose up. How could he be destined for hell when he now knew God had been with him all the time?

Huxley stepped on the gas, picked up speed and left the tolling bells behind. Another two blocks and he whipped the steering wheel to the right at the corner of Grace Street and pulled into a service station on the corner.

"Is this okay?" He pointed. "There's a telephone booth over there."

"Yeah, this is just fine." Ed opened the door and slid out. He leaned back through the open window. "Sure do thank you, Mr. Huxley. Really nice of you. I'm grateful for all your help. I don't know what I would have done if you hadn't been willing to listen to me and follow through with Mr. Muckle—"

He waved off Ed's last words. "No problem. Good luck." Giving Ed a thumbs-up, he pulled away.

Ed sprinted toward the phone booth and grabbed up the directory. It would be great seeing Avery again. He chuckled. He probably won't believe his eyes.

After they had a good visit, and Avery agreed to loan him one of his cars, he'd head for Hannigan to see Mr. Casey. Afterwards, Madge Yates…that is, if he didn't chicken out. He crimped his mouth. No, he wouldn't. Come heck or high water he'd follow through. He not only owed it to Benny and his mama but also to himself.

Running his finger down the list of names, he found it—412 E. Grace St. He left the booth and hurried down the sidewalk. What a story he had to tell. Avery would want every detail.

Ten minutes and five blocks later, he saw the red brick house surrounded by weeping willows. To the right of the porch stood a single peach tree with a ladder leaning against the trunk. An empty bushel basket sat on the ground. He hurried up to the door and knocked. It took forever before it opened.

Avery's six-foot frame filled the doorway. At first, his face registered blank. Then his mouth fell open and recognition spread across his face. He blinked incredulously.

"Ed…is it…you?"

"Yup, it's me."

"Old buddy…come on in!"

Chapter 85

~~~

The next morning, weary from sitting up all night talking, Ed slept in, after which Avery's wife fixed a typical southern breakfast. Ham and grits, hushpuppies, hot buttermilk biscuits with sorghum molasses, sawmill gravy, sausage, pork chops, eggs and flapjacks, a feast Ed never imagined he would eat again. Energized and full as a tick, he was eager to head for Hannigan.

How would he feel seeing the town and Mr. Casey again? Would everything look the same? Would he run into Josephine?

"C'mon outside, Ed." Avery crooked his finger. Ed followed him into the back yard to a long carport shaded by two giant oak trees. Avery pointed to four cars. One of them, Ed noticed, was the Model T he escaped in.

"Here's the key to my '28 Model A roadster."

Ed did a double take. Avery was giving him his best one—the one he told him at camp was his pride and joy which not even his wife was allowed to touch.

"Use it as long as you need," he said. "It's all gassed up."

"Thanks so much, Avery. I'll take real good care of it."

Ed slid into the fancy upholstered seat and started the engine. The well-kept car purred like a kitten.

"I'll return it tomorrow," he said.

"No rush at all, ol' buddy."

Ed took off down the street and maneuvered into the downtown noon traffic. He drove by the Old Dominion's red-bricked courthouse where he covered the biggest murder trial to hit Richmond in years. A lot of water under the bridge since then, he thought.

He slowed the car, staring pensively at the building as he passed. He had hung so much importance to it. Strangely, it looked smaller...different. Like it wasn't part of him anymore.

He played his mind-movie of the two days of trial. He thought it curious he couldn't relate anymore to the Ed Bowman of then.

It was like his role as reporter, the trial, and what occurred after, happened to someone else a long time ago.

He glanced in the rear view mirror and studied his reflection. Did he look the same? He did, but inside he felt different—like someone else.

Everything, his life and priorities had changed so much since then. No longer was he the young, cocky reporter obsessed with winning the Pulitzer and trying to impress others for the wrong reasons. He was now content to enjoy life as the new person he had evolved into, although he hadn't quite defined that yet.

Nevertheless, whatever lay in his future, his goal was to contribute something worthwhile for the right reasons. Also, trust God to work everything together for his good without becoming impatient or losing faith.

He turned right, at the sign pointing to Hannigan. The last time on this road was the day he sped the forty miles back to the *Clarion* to write the conversation he overheard between Buford's attorneys. Instead, today would be a leisurely drive. After the bleak, white salt flats of Utah, he wanted to drink in all the colorful sights he once took so for granted.

For the next forty minutes he drank in well-cultivated farmlands, corn stalks standing brown and tall in the fields, the distant skyline, and mountains holding fond recollections of campfires, squirrel hunting, and leaves crackling underfoot.

Leaving the agricultural fields behind, he now entered Hannigan and cruised along the familiar streets, thrilling at the maples now ablaze in brilliant orange and reds.

He drove to his mother's place, recognizing the gnarled-limbed trees along the way he used to climb when a boy, and the block where he and the neighbor kids played Kick the Can, shouting, "Olly Olly Oxen Free!" He pulled up and parked across the street from the house, letting the engine idle.

It was run-down now, but the distant memories were still there. He could hear his mama in the backyard, her apron full of corn for the morning feed. "Here chickie, chickie." He could almost smell the apple butter from inside the house cooking all day, the sound of pine knots crackling in the wood-burning stove in the evening, and at dinnertime the sizzle of hot bacon grease being poured over fresh lettuce leaves. Then, at bedtime, his mama sharing favorite scriptures, one of which was, "*Where much is given, much is expected.*" He nodded. He had definitely received much. All the more reason he had to see he righted everything by following through on his promise to Benny.

He shoved the gearshift forward and drove further down the street. He stopped where he and Sarah had lived but felt disappointment. The house was now painted a different color— blue and white. The hammock in the front yard under the ash trees was gone, a new car sat in the driveway, and a couple of children played in the sprinkler. Did the new owner keep up Sarah's flower garden in the backyard?

He remembered pulling the last weeds of fall while Sarah busied herself in the kitchen making Cocoa cookies. The chocolate fragrance wafted across the yard, teasingly drawing him back into the house where they made love in the middle of the afternoon. The memory made his throat ache.

"Well, hon," he whispered, "Wherever you are, I tried to make everything right."

He stared at the house and yard again. Seeing the changes and new look strangely brought a kind of closure, as if all association to it had vaporized into the ether. Perhaps that was good. Wiping his eyes with the back of his hand, he pulled away from the curb.

"Now, for Mr. Casey." He pulled away from the curb.

Four more blocks and he turned on the road to the *Clarion*, noticing it was now paved. Nice, he thought, but he missed the old dirt one.

He passed three blocks of whitewashed houses with their wrap-around verandas, some new stores, noticing Slim's Meat Market was still there, and then spied the *Clarion's* familiar brown-roofed building. His breath caught in astonishment. It wasn't so small anymore.

He eased the car alongside the curb, turned the engine off, and studied the structure from across the street.

Stretching across the roof was something new. An enormous sign read, "*Casey Clarion, Karl Casey, owner and proprietor.*" An addition had also been built on one end, lengthening the office out a good thirty feet. The wide picture window across the front of the office he so loved was still there. That pleased him.

He opened the car door, and then paused. *Sarah died in there.* How hard would it be, flooded with the horrible memory of that night? Well, he'd just have to bear it as best he could.

He slid out of the seat and sauntered across the street, wondering if Mr. Casey would recognize him. Prison had changed his looks. He was a lot thinner, although had regained some weight in Wendover. He also had a small, rope-like scar running from his eyebrow down the side of one cheek, albeit not as prominent as it once was.

All that was minor compared to his concern over what once took place in the building—his struggle with Gunther Buford, seeing the blood from Sarah, holding her body, Josephine sobbing hysterically and screaming to the police, "He killed my daughter!"

Bracing himself, he took a deep breath and shoved the door open.

CHAPTER 86

~~~

Ed stepped inside the *Clarion* and then abruptly stopped, unprepared for the shock. Nothing looked the same. A blonde receptionist sat at a front desk. Beyond her were six young men pounding away on typewriters and talking on telephones—a far cry from the two lone desks of his and Richard's. Above the voices and clacking of typewriter keys he heard the sound of presses churning in the back. That hadn't changed.

The blonde looked up. "May I help you?"

"Yes. I'd like to see Mr. Casey."

"Do you have an appointment? He's very busy—"

"Just tell him Ed Bowman is here. He'll see me." He smiled, saying it in a tone he knew she wouldn't question.

She immediately got up from the desk and walked across the wide expanse of floor toward the back hallway, her jersey dress swaying about her hips.

Gone only a few seconds, she returned with Mr. Casey who had a stunned look on his face, his mouth wide open.

Ed's heart leapt. He still looked the same except for more gray in his hair. His belly was just as large, covered with his usual ink-smudged bib apron, and he still had his goatee.

Mr. Casey rushed up to him, "Ed!" He gawked. "Wha...I can't believe this! Is it really you?"

Ed grinned and extended his hand. "Sure is. How are you, Mr. Casey?"

"Forget the formality!" he exclaimed. He threw his arms around Ed and gave him a big bear hug, nearly knocking him off balance. The sound of typewriters quit. All the employees stopped what they were doing and watched.

"C'mon in!" With one arm wrapped around Ed's shoulder, he hustled him down the hall and into his office. He pushed Ed into a straight-backed chair, walked behind his desk, and plopped into his swivel chair. He leaned forward.

"Tell me everything."

"I'm a free man now, Mr. Casey," Ed began hesitantly. "Gunther Buford has finally been brought to justice—"

"We all know about Buford," he cut in. "It's in all the newspapers, but there was no mention of you. I assumed you were off in parts unknown, still hiding and maybe not knowing about it."

"Well, I sure knew." Ed grinned. "I was the one who tipped them off where to find him."

"Well, that's certainly a story worth hearing, Ed. You have no idea how badly I felt that my testimony never carried any weight at your trial. To this day, I can't believe they convicted you.

"Just before the story broke about Buford's capture, the District Attorney's office called asking questions and wanting a character reference, all of which left me puzzled. They didn't offer any information at that point."

Ed smiled. "I do thank you for what you told them, Mr. Casey. By the way, I've wondered about something. Josephine? Do you think she's changed her mind about me, or—"

"She passed away," Mr. Casey cut in, "six months ago." He leaned back in his chair. "Unfortunately, Ed, she stuck to her story that you shot Sarah. But enough about her. Tell me everything that happened."

Ed took a deep breath and settled back. For the next hour and a half he recounted everything—the penitentiary, the chain gang, Jeb, his escape, tracking Buford to Wendover, the attempts on his life, Maureen, his encounter with the Mormon Church, his arrest and the bishop's devastating betrayal of their friendship.

Mesmerized throughout, Mr. Casey kept shaking his head in amazement. "How did you handle everything emotionally, Ed? Prison...being convicted for something you didn't do? It had to be terrible."

"I can't pretend it was easy, Mr. Casey. Losing Sarah, let alone blamed for her death, was traumatic. In prison, the injustice made me bitter about everything—even about God. Not proud of that."

He uncomfortably shifted in his chair. "I lost faith in what my mama taught me—about truth always winning out and God always working everything together for my good. But she was right." He tugged on his earlobe.

"Guess it's just some circumstances require more time to

right themselves than others. I'll have to remember that life is unpredictable, and if problems come up in the future I mustn't lose faith."

"Well, it's all over now, Ed."

"Yeah." Ed let out a labored sigh. "But I don't know if I can ever forget it—especially what incarceration did to me. Prison teaches you pretty fast that you have to do what you have to do in order to survive, and there was a side of me I never thought existed." He stared down at the floor. "I did things in prison," he said, "I'm not proud of..." He trailed off his words and minced his lips into a hard line.

"Say no more." Mr. Casey rose from his chair and walked around to the front of the desk. He planked both hands on Ed's shoulders.

"Ed, you've got to put those things behind you. You were in an impossible and unjust situation. While I do understand what you're saying, the value of a man is not what he's done in the past. It's what he becomes. I have no doubt you're a better person for what you've been through. You now see things through a different set of lenses. That gives you an edge in life others don't have." He leaned back against the edge of the desk.

Ed looked up into his face and rendered a half-smile at the comforting remark.

"Thanks, Mr. Casey. There's one thing for sure. Going through all that at least mellowed me out. I'm over the cocky attitude I had as an aspiring reporter." He gave a sheepish grin. "I was so caught up with myself and Buford's trial, I thought in no time I'd be working for the *Richmond Times-Dispatch*—even win the Pulitzer some day." He laughed. It strangely felt good.

"Oh yes. That reminds me, Ed. The *Dispatch* telephoned me after the story broke about Buford's capture...a Bob Wilkinson. He hoped I knew how to contact you. I told him I knew nothing about your whereabouts, so I'll leave it up to you to follow up with him. He left his number."

"Well, I do need to touch base with him. Long story, but I promised him an exclusive. He used to be with the *Virginian Pilot* in Norfolk. I met him at the trial. Could you do me a favor? Would you call him back and tell him I'll contact him in a couple of days?

505

I'm just not ready yet."

"Sure will. But for now, Ed…" Mr. Casey folded his arms across his belly. "…what are you going to do about a job?"

His question took Ed by surprise. "Well, sooner or later, guess I'll have to start looking." He instinctively held his breath.

"Why not consider the *Clarion*?"

Ed's heart rate climbed. "Wow, that'd be great!" He jumped to his feet and grabbed Mr. Casey's hand. "This is more than I could have hoped for—and I don't care if you only have me writing the obits. I'll do anything."

Mr. Casey winced, and a troubled expression slid across his face. Ed questioningly raised his eyebrows.

"Ed, I shouldn't have kept this from you." He straightened up and took a deep breath. "Bob Wilkinson told me the *Dispatch's* editor in chief also wants to talk to you. I gathered from the tone of his voice they may want to hire you."

Chills rippled down Ed's back. "That's always been my long-held dream—"

"But," Mr. Casey interjected, "I also want you." His face took on an imploring look.

Ed stared out the back window of the office. He pushed his bottom lip forward, processing his thoughts slowly and carefully. *A job with the Richmond Times-Dispatch—his dream.* Yet, he felt a loyalty to Mr. Casey. He gave him his first job, been like a father to him, and stood up for him at the trial. His mama's words pushed through. "*Where much is given, much is expected.*" He gnawed the corner of his lip for a moment.

"Mr. Casey, while delighted the *Dispatch* might want me, I'll cross that bridge a little later. Right now, you gave me my first job and always believed in me. It feels right I should spend time here."

Mr. Casey stretched his mouth into a jubilant grin. "Great! It'll also help you get back up to speed after being out of the swing of things for so long." He gave Ed a regretful look. "I probably can't pay you as much as the *Dispatch*. But even though you're going to give Bob Wilkinson a one-time exclusive, there's probably a lot more to your story he won't have room for, so you might want to consider this."

He circled back to his chair and sat down. Leaning forward, he placed his elbows on the desk and with steepled fingers tapped his lips.

"Readers crave stories like yours. We could do a series and include everything from beginning to end." He glanced at his watch. "Too bad Josephine isn't here to see it, but you'll certainly be a hero to the rest of the townspeople." The tone of his voice signaled the end of their conversation. He stood and walked back around to the front of the desk. Ed rose to his feet.

"Give that some thought," he said, placing an arm around Ed's shoulders. After you write the series we can sit down later and talk about the *Dispatch*. Rest assured, Ed, there's no way I'm going to stand in the way of your future. The editor in chief will understand if he has to wait a little while." They sauntered out of the office and down the hall.

At the front door, Mr. Casey's good-bye consisted of another bear hug. Everyone in the office watched again in curiosity.

Ed exited the building and strutted across the street to his car. "A job," he whispered. He didn't care if he ever won the Pulitzer— and to think the *Richmond Times-Dispatch* may be on the horizon.

He liked the idea of a series. He'd write about things the public needed to hear—prison conditions, cruelty to inmates. "What's the saying?" he mused aloud, "the power of the pen…" Again, his mama's words rushed in. "*Bright is the ring of words when the right man rings them.*"

Yes, he was the right man to ring that bell. Even if Mr. Jenkins said they were trying to fix conditions, it would be a long time coming. His reform articles could help guys like Moose and Duff. He hoped they were still alive. He'd see about visiting them.

Opening the car door, he slid in and sat for a few seconds, then took a long, deep breath.

One more thing to do.

He turned the ignition, drove down the street and turned on the road back to Richmond. It was still early in the day. He wanted to get to Madge Yates' house and be done with it before dark. Somehow, the idea of going while the sun was still shining made it feel easier. Would it be?

He'd soon find out.

CHAPTER 87

~~~

Five thirty-one S. Eighteenth Street was in the older residential area near the Open Air Market on Franklin. By the time Ed got to that area, traffic became horrendous. Construction work blocked streets off, and heavy equipment forced him to park blocks away from his intended route. Nevertheless, he welcomed the longer time to reach her house so he could settle his emotions. Like his mama often said, he needed to gird up his loins for this one.

He parallel-parked by a city park and climbed out. He made a panoramic eye-sweep across the wide expanse of green carpet, sucking in the aromatic aroma of wood smoke and barbecues. The whole place was abuzz with activity. Families sat around picnic tables eating and laughing. Children splashed with delight in a nearby wading pool, lovers nonchalantly strolled about holding hands, and white-haired oldsters in shorts and bony-white legs sat chatting in lawn chairs. It was a glorious sight. He hoped they appreciated it.

He strode four blocks down to Eighteenth veering around hobbyhorse barriers placed by construction workers, and stepping over broken chunks of concrete lying on the sidewalks. Soon, he was in the five-hundred-block and the butterflies in his stomach frantically began flapping their wings. He slowed his steps.

He shaded his eyes with one hand and peered at the house numbers.

...525...527...529... He stopped in front of 531.

Madge Yates lived in a weathered, wood-framed house with a screened-in front porch. Blanketing the yard was the last of summer's flowers—purple asters, yellow chrysanthemums, and blue hydrangeas. Magnolia petals, brown and wilted, lay on the ground.

Leading up to the front porch was a three-foot wide brick path bordered by orange and yellow rosebushes with withering blossoms. Also, weeds that needed to be pulled. The whole yard could stand a good raking.

He stepped onto the brick footway, hesitated and tightened his jaw. A cold finger of dread traced his spine. He didn't have to do this. He could still write a letter. He could walk away this minute and no one would be the wiser. But if he didn't do this, it would eat at him forever.

He bit his lower lip and continued on toward the enclosed porch, his chest so tight he could hardly breathe. He determined to bear whatever Benny's mama dished out at him. All he could hope was she wouldn't be too hard on him. Trepidation cut deep gullies in his insides and he said a quick prayer.

Reaching for the rickety screen door, he pulled it open. The bottom part swung loose from its broken hinge and hung at a crooked angle. Stepping inside the porch, he turned and examined it. Easy enough to fix, he thought.

Moving across the porch, he approached the front door, took a tremulous breath and knocked.

He heard the slow shuffle of feet. The door slowly opened. A small, tired-faced woman appeared.

"Yes?" She looked at him questioningly.

"Are…you...Madge Yates?" His mouth went bone dry.

She nodded. The kindly smile on her face sent a ripple of hope through him.

"May I come in?

"I…I knew your son."

About The Author

~~~

Janis Hutchinson is a national and international, award-winning author of both fiction and nonfiction and "Writer of the Year" recipient by the *American Christian Writers Association* (2008). In demand as a speaker on Christian radio and TV, her articles and short stories have been requested for reprint in Christian magazines, literature courses, translated into other languages, and her two nonfiction books on Mormonism have garnered outstanding reviews. *Unfinished Justice* is her debut novel.

Her knowledge of criminal law in the book comes from an interest in the court system, twenty-three years as Legal Assistant to an attorney, and research of early Virginia's prison system and chain gangs. The unique judicial stance and Mormon doctrines concerning salvation and felons is from research and her expertise on the subject.

Her activities have included teaching on the college and church levels, guest appearances on Christian radio and TV talk shows, lecturing in various states on the subject of Mormonism and describing her escape from a Mormon splinter group that held her prisoner for nine months, and which nearly took her life. Her story is on her blog.

She is retired, lives in Everett, Washington, and has raised three children alone after being widowed twice.

Find out more about Janis Hutchinson at:
www.JanisHutchinsonBooks.com